Kiss & Die

Lee Weeks

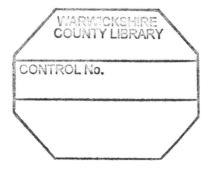

W F HOWES LTD

This large print edition published in 2010 by
W F Howes Ltd
Unit 4, Rearsby Business Park, Gaddesby Lane,
Rearsby, Leicester LE7 4YH

1 3 5 7 9 10 8 6 4 2

First published in the United Kingdom in 2010
by HarperCollins*Publishers*

A CIP catalogue record for this book is available
from the British Library

ISBN 978 1 40746 113 7

Typeset by Palimpsest Book Production Limited,
Falkirk, Stirlingshire
Printed and bound in Great Britain
by MPG Books Ltd, Bodmin, Cornwall

FSC
Mixed Sources
Product group from well-managed
forests, controlled sources and
recycled wood or fiber
SA-COC-1565
www.fsc.org
© 1996 Forest Stewardship Council

For my Aunt, Jean Rossiter.

FOURTEEN DAYS IN SUMMER

CHAPTER 1

August 2006

He would be beginning to feel the pain now, the dehydration. In a few seconds he would try to move his arms but he would not be able to – his tendons were cut. He would try to lift his legs but she had strapped them to the bed whilst she cut through his hamstrings. Now he would feel the panic. Now he would feel the true meaning of pain and pleasure. Now he would understand the price he had paid for it.

He would open his eyes and look around the room and then he would understand he was just waking to die.

'Hello, Mr Big Businessman.' Ruby pulled up his eyelid. 'Wakey, wakey. Feel that?' Ruby twisted the scalpel into his shoulder joint and scraped it against bone. His body was covered in lacerations. His flesh was sprayed across the walls and ceiling.

He groaned in pain behind the ball gag. His eyes rolled in his head. He tried to move. He wasn't going anywhere. 'You're as helpless as a baby, aren't you, big man?'

His eyes were locked on hers. He was fully awake and terrified. He stared at Ruby, wide eyed, not understanding how or why he had ended up in hell with this angel. His eyes pleaded with her. He looked back and forth from her to the door. They could hear noises outside in the corridor. There were people passing. They heard a man mutter and swear as he made his drunken way down to his room.

She followed his eyes as he looked desperately at the door, so near to help but so far. She swigged from the champagne bottle and then turned back to stare at him, a cynical smile on her face. 'What? You're not having a good time? You want to leave? You want your money back?'

She picked up his trousers from the floor and took the wallet out of the pocket. She came around to the side of the bed and leaned over him; her long black hair fell in his face as she tilted her head one way and then the other and tutted. 'But we're not finished yet.' She flipped open his wallet and took out his money. 'Now, how much am I worth? I'll tell you: more than the champagne.' She started taking out the notes. 'More than the cost of this room.' She took out more. Then she opened the wallet out fully and pulled out a photo. 'Nice family you have.' A pretty blond woman was kneeling between two pretty blond kids, a boy and a girl. A golden retriever sat in front of them. The little girl had a tooth missing at the front. The boy was lean, strong, with broad shoulders and freckles across his nose. She turned the photo over. *Love you Daddy from Belinda and Ben. P.S. Goldie says woof.* 'Very cute. Very sweet, your kids.'

Ruby removed the protective cup from his cock, lifted his limp member and injected into the shaft's base. 'We're still having fun, aren't we, big boy? You ready for more?'

He groaned.

She leaned closer and watched his cock grow hard. The process never ceased to amuse and delight her. She went over to the cloth she had laid out on top of the mock-leather writing desk. Her instruments were neatly lined up. There were two left that she had yet to use. One was a butcher's knife that she would need afterwards; the other was a long, thin spike. Ruby came back to him and tightened the length of thin wire she had tied around his testicles. She twisted it until they bulged purple. He whined in agony. She ran her fingers over his body, and poked her fingers into the deep cuts in his flesh. He rolled his eyes and snorted in pain. Ruby climbed on top of him, her sex already eager, wet. She talked to him as she slid herself over him. Her palms outstretched on his chest, they slid beneath her. Ruby rocked back and forth, her pelvis sliding on his blood.

He turned his head from side to side, aware of the pain, not aware of the pleasure. Each of his joints was cut to the bone, his tendons, his muscles sliced through. She took him inside her like a child sucks a thumb – for security, comfort, familiarity.

She was addicted to the sensation. It always made her feel special, wanted, loved. She closed her eyes and allowed herself to forget everything else and concentrate on the pleasure. For those few moments as she rocked back and forth on him and rolled her hips to take him deeper, she felt contented.

But it didn't last long. She reached behind her and picked up the end of the wire attached to his testicles and wrapped it around her hand and pulled so hard that his scrotum tore open. His body went into spasm with the shock and the pain. She picked up the scalpel from the bedside table and sang to him as she began to make deep cuts over his heart, 'Cross my heart and hope to die . . .'

She reached across him and picked up the photo, now bloody with her prints. 'Nice wife, nice kids. A dog even. You have everything.' She leaned forward and ran her fingers through his hair.

He groaned, his eyes rolled back.

She held the photo in front of his face. 'But it wasn't enough was it, Mr Big Man? You wanted Ruby didn't you? You wanted big fun.'

She twisted the point of her scalpel into the wounds on his chest, deep bloody slashes that now exposed his rib. She scraped it along the bone. He squealed with pain. Ruby giggled. She rocked until she lost herself in ecstasy. She sat for a few minutes to recover, head down, body spent. Then she tilted her head and looked at him as she smiled.

'I'm finished.' Ruby picked up the spike and positioned it above his open heart. 'You ready to die?'

He thrashed his head wildly back and forth and screamed into the gag.

She looked across at his family photo. 'Hello Belinda . . . Hello Ben . . . Hello Goldie . . .' She pushed the spike into his beating heart. 'Say goodbye to your daddy.'

CHAPTER 2

'Yap, yap.'
A toy puppy turned somersaults in the air. It was 10 p.m. and the night market was heaving. A tall man, athletic build, broad shoulders, wearing a black t-shirt and jeans was making his way through the market stalls. The height came from his mother's side. He was half English, half Chinese. He had a face that reflected his soul: scarred, but with a beauty beneath the sadness. His eyes were always searching. He was thirty-seven but looked older. He had seen a few hard winters. He pushed his ragged fringe back from his eyes, pulled his shades back down and kept walking, weaving his way through the stalls in Mong Kok's night market. He could have been mistaken for any other tourist except he wasn't sweating; he was used to it, this was his home. He wasn't shopping for knick-knacks either, Detective Inspector Johnny Mann of the Hong Kong Police Force was tracking the Triads that were moving through the market. Every few seconds he stopped to listen. Above the noisy bang and beat and Cantonese barking he was listening for one sound:

8

signature whistles. Triads were calling to one another with their high-pitched beeps that varied in length, in intensity. Each society had their secret signs. One society was moving as a pack tonight.

Mann signalled to his officers to fan out. He turned the corner onto Saigon Street where the night market spread into seafood restaurants and noodle bars and spilled out over the roads and pavements. It was August 2006. It was the twenty-fifth day of the Chinese month. It was the chosen day. Beneath the feet of the unsuspecting tourists, a Triad initiation ceremony was being held.

The young recruits stood nervously waiting to pass beneath the sacred archway of crossed swords. Amongst them were five young women and three boys, all of Indian descent, dressed in their plain sackcloth robes, ready for the ceremony. Their feet were bare and their faces smeared in dirt. They had come to give themselves as penniless urchins to the society and be reborn as brothers and sisters, committed forever to the family; *49s* in the Triad order. Amongst them was fourteen-year-old Rajini. She waited nervously with the others in the corridor outside. She looked at her hands, there was no ring but it was not a bad age to get committed to someone or something. She looked at her feet; she was barefoot. She didn't mind that. Her family had walked many miles barefoot on the way to Hong Kong. They had crossed through China and joined the thousands of others making their way to paradise.

But paradise was not the place she thought it would be. For twelve hours a day she sat at a machine and sewed. She dreamt of being a doctor, a teacher. But if Hong Kong had taught her anything it was that if you had money you could be anyone you wanted to be. She would become a *49*, the rank of a Triad foot soldier, and climb the ladder and earn good money doing whatever they asked her to; she knew there would be risks but she also knew there would be big rewards and then she could pay for herself to go to college and then she could be anyone she chose.

She followed the others under the archway of crossed swords and into the airless, dark room, filled with people, pressed in, hiding in the shadows. The heat in the room took her breath away. There was the sound of a chicken flapping its wings against the side of a crate. The incense smoke was thick in the dark room, which was lit only by the candles on the altar. In the gloom she could make out the Incense Master. He was old, tortoise-like, dressed in the robes of office, a long crimson silk stole over a cassock of white. He wore only one grass sandal, the other foot was bare. On his head was a three-pointed knotted scarf.

'Who is your sponsor?' asked the Incense Master. He stood with his index fingers curled into his palm to denote his rank.

'I am.' A young woman stepped forward from the shadows.

'Call forth your recruits.' The Incense Master lit

the joss sticks on the altar and began reciting the sacred poems that had been handed down since the beginning:

'"I passed a corner and then another corner. My family lives on the Five Fingers Mountain. I've come to look for the temple of the sisters-in-law . . ."'

'You are children of the Wo Shing Shing. You are a group born from its spirit. But now it is time for you to stand alone. You are the Outcasts.' He finished with a warning. 'Break the sacred oath you are about to take and you will die as this rooster now dies.'

The sound of the chicken panicking reached a crescendo, the noise of flapping wings and the gurgle of blood escaping from its cut throat rose above the squawking. Its twitching body was held above a brass bowl on the altar.

'You will die as he did. No mercy will be shown. We come together today to be reborn. You leave your last life behind you. You are *49s*. Four for the oceans that our ancestors believed surrounded the world. Nine for the sacred oaths. You belong to an ancient family dating back to the time of the Qing dynasty. You belong to one another. Never forget you are brothers and sisters, forever joined in blood.'

From the corner of her eye Rajini watched the officers close in around the door and secure it. She looked back to her sponsor. The Incense Master swung the smoking silver perfumed ball in the air and chanted the oaths. The body of the

11

chicken lay still on the floor and the bowl of blood was tipped into a cup from the altar. The Incense Master came to each recruit in turn. Rajini waited. He repeated the oaths to each one.

'With this blood we are united. With this blood we are one. Together we remain until death.'

Each recruit replied: 'I will never disclose the secrets of the Outcasts, not even to my parents, my brothers or sisters; I will be killed by the sword if I do so. I shall never disclose the secrets for money; I will be killed by the sword if I do so. I will never reveal the Outcasts' secret signs or oaths when speaking to others outside the Outcast society; I will be killed by the sword if I do so.'

The Incense Master passed the cup to each recruit in turn. 'You will be like no group before you. You will kill without mercy. You will belong only to your new family, cast away the old. You belong to the Outcasts.'

'Bound forever to serve one another.'

Rajini closed her eyes as the blood tasted thick, warm, it touched her upper lip and coated it. She sipped from the chalice.

The Incense Master looked deep into her eyes. 'No one leaves. No one ever betrays.' The blood sat in her mouth like the taste of a nosebleed. 'This is your new family. You will serve no other.'

Rajini bowed her head to him.

'Yes, Master,' all the recruits repeated together. The incense left a plume of smoke overhead as it passed along the line, each one tasting the blood of the killed chicken. At the end of the line the Incense Master placed the chalice back onto the altar. He stood and looked at his disciples.

'You are now *49s*, foot soldiers. But, one of you here has already transgressed. One of you has spoken of their coming here tonight. One of you gave information away. Now that one must be punished. They will be an example to you all. The Outcasts will not tolerate betrayal. When you leave this place you must do so quickly and disperse fast. Outside now there is one who is coming. He comes because we have a traitor amongst us.'

The Incense Master looked towards the sponsor. She nodded. 'All who are present here must witness the result of your transgression.'

He turned to Rajini. 'You share the fate of the rooster.'

As Mann turned the corner he saw the telltale sign: a red card taped above a doorway. Two girls came out, one Indian, one mixed race. Mann hung back and watched; an Indian lad was the next to emerge, he staggered out of the doorway and looked about to throw up. Mann hung back out of sight. He signalled to his officers to follow the lad, whilst he headed towards the entrance. It was the same as all the other buildings on the street and yet it wasn't. Above its door was a shirt maker's sign. The night shift should have been pounding away but the place was quiet. To the right a flight of stairs led up to a pink neon sign

13

advertising a woman's services and a massage parlour. To the left was a small Chinese medicine store selling loose herbs, dried fish and centipedes by the scoop. In between was a corridor. A metal grille, unlocked and half opened, gave way easily when Mann pulled it. Mann stepped into the corridor and listened. Further on, a solitary light bulb gave off a stark hue against the black walls.

Mann unclipped the gun holster that was strapped around his waist, but left the Smith and Wesson revolver where it was. Instead, he reached down and took out the knife from his boot. This was not a place to fire a gun. He needed silence, stealth. He needed caution. He held the knife tightly now as he walked on down the corridor and stopped at the door on the left. Above its arch were the symbolic crossed swords. He pushed the door open and stood in the doorway. The room was dark except for the light of one candle at the far right of the room. The air was thick with the smell of incense, smouldering paper and heat of the people, now gone. He heard the scratch of a rat's claws as it ran the perimeter of the room and stopped and the sound of another joining it. Cockroaches scurried over walls and ceiling to watch the rats. He looked down at his feet; he was walking on the red summoning cards of hundreds of Triads. He crossed the threshold, beneath the arch of swords, and propped the door open with a discarded wooden thread spool. There was little else to show that this had been a garment factory,

14

so far as he could tell the room was empty of equipment: the machines all gone. All that remained were tatters of material and empty crates. The candle on top of a stack of upturned crates: a makeshift altar. Mann walked across to it. Beside the altar were the discarded sackcloth robes of the Triad initiates, left to rot, no longer needed, and on top of them a shimmering Indian sari. From the corner of his eye he saw a rat jump into a box, two sticks protruded from its end. Mann got close. They were not sticks; they were arms. He looked down into the box. The rats were already feasting on the young girl's body, the cockroaches tumbling from the box's sides on top of her.

CHAPTER 3

Mann picked up the squealing rat from the box and flung it at the far wall. He stood in the solitude with the dead girl, listening to the police siren scream to a stop outside.

'Looks like the party's over.'

Mann turned to see a large frame in the doorway: Inspector Tom Sheng of the Serious Crime Division. 'The ambulance is on its way.'

'Too late. She was dead when I got here.'

Sheng and Mann had crossed paths more than either wanted. They weren't the best of friends. Tom was brash, arrogant. He played hard and worked even harder. He was a hard-hitting movie-type cop who forgot he wasn't an actor and life wasn't a set.

Sheng walked in and shone a light around and into the box with the dead girl. He squatted level with Rajini's arms, just visible at the rim of the box, held in front of her face as if she were offering them. 'Why did they cut her hands off? Why torture her first? Why not just execute her? We've never seen them mutilate like this before.'

'They must have wanted to show what they were capable of, put the fear into their new recruits,' said Mann, picking up the discarded initiation robes and Rajini's sari.

'Why strip her first?'

'Not worthy to wear the robes, more degradation. New rules, new society. Set the tone, scare the hell out of the new recruits. Kids are bound to be different.'

'Fucking kids are like that these days. Playing sick video games, watching sick movies. Their minds are warped . . . Plus . . .' Sheng stood, pulled at his tie. 'This fucking summer is driving everyone mad. This was supposed to be my first night off in a fucking month.'

Mann didn't answer. He knew that if Sheng had been somewhere important when the call came it wouldn't have been at home. He spent his few nights off playing poker and trying to stay out of his family's way. He loved his kids but he no longer loved his wife. He did things his way or not at all. But his way wasn't Mann's way. They could both be brutal. It was in Sheng's nature. It was nurtured in Mann.

Tom Sheng moved his torch to the ground. 'This place is littered with red slips. It must have been a big meeting. We're going to have to be quicker than this if we're ever going to catch the bastards.' He flicked light up at the ceilings to see the cockroaches scuttling into the corners. 'We'll let CSI get in here. I'll see you in the office at six.' He

17

dusted off his hands and walked back over the stone floor towards the door. He paused in the exit. 'I have a poker game waiting. Try not to fuck with anything before they have a chance to get in here.'

Mann didn't answer. He knelt, picked up the burnt oath papers and debris from the stone floor and crumpled it in his hand. Amongst the red dust on his finger tips was a tinge of yellow. He went back over to the box. Beside the young girl's body in the box was the rooster, headless, draped on paper over her hands. He reached in and eased the paper from beneath and held it up to the light of the candle. On it he saw a circle outline, inside was a lone wolf howling to the sky.

CHAPTER 4

Mann waited until the girl's body had been taken to the morgue before he headed home. He needed a change of clothes. He needed to shower away the smell of death.

Mann lived in a vertical village built around a shopping mall. It was devoid of character. The only trees were in pots. It housed thousands of middle earners. He lived on the fortieth floor in one of the older two-bedroomed flats. It had parquet floors, white walls and minimal furniture: a table and two armchairs and a large home cinema system. He had bought the flat eight years ago. It was a great location for work, just a few stops away on the MTR. But, it didn't matter how convenient it was, Mann was hardly ever in it. He lived there alone, but he hadn't always done.

A woman got out of the lift as he stepped in. He didn't recognize her. Even though he didn't know his neighbours well, he knew them well enough to nod to them when he saw them in the lift. This woman was a stranger. New tenant, visitor? He didn't know which. She wasn't keen to make eye contact. She hurried past him, her hair over her face, sunglasses on. Mann looked at her feet: pretty shoes. By the time he looked up she had gone.

He got to his floor, walked along the corridor and came to a halt outside his flat door. He put the key in the lock, turned the key and hesitated. Why did he always do that? He walked in, slammed the door shut behind him and threw his keys angrily down onto the coffee table. He knew that one day he'd break the glass top by doing it. It was a white cane table shaped like an elephant – ludicrous, feminine. He stepped over the piles of papers, documents his lounge was littered with and took off his t-shirt. Secured across his chest and beneath his arm he wore a pouch containing two sets of throwing stars, shuriken. Shuriken meant 'hidden in the hand'. They were the weapons of his enemy: concealed, versatile street weapons. Sometimes they were homemade or customized. Mann had designed his own. He had been fascinated ever since one cut a groove into his face when he was young. He still bore the scar high up on his left cheekbone, it was pale like a quarter moon.

He unstrapped the leather pouch from his arm. It contained six six-inch darts. They were feather tipped, needle pointed, weighted for direct, fast, hard impact. He took a slim dagger named Delilah from his boot and placed her on the table as well. She was his favourite; she had saved him many times.

20

He poured himself a vodka on the rocks and then stood looking out of his window. The block opposite was lit up sporadically: squares of life in the darkness.

He checked the messages on his home phone. His mother's voice came over clipped and awkward. It made him smile the way she talked to the answer phone machine as if she expected it to answer her at any moment. Pausing, giving it time to answer her back and then continuing in a fluster when it didn't. He would call her tomorrow. She didn't ask, but she needed him to. She wasn't one for showing or asking for affection. She was a great bottler of emotions but the past few months had left her needing reassurance. Mann was all she had. Her world had been rocked by secrets that refused to stay hidden. And, where there was one, there were a hundred.

He phoned his boss.

'I heard it was you who found her.' The voice of Chief Inspector Mia Chou. Always succinct. Straight to the point. They had known each for a long time. 'The ceremony was definitely an initiation one?'

'Not just . . . I found yellow papers.'

'So a new branch of a society has been created.'

'I found an emblem printed on paper: a lone wolf.'

'Anyone see anything?'

'No, the tourists never see anything; it's all strange to them. The locals see it all but they pretend not to. The building had been empty about twenty-four hours. It only took them a few hours to set it up. Tom Sheng's called a meeting for six.'

'Good.'

Mann could hear in her voice that she knew already. Whatever conversation she had had with Sheng it was probably face to face. Mann knew his thing with Mia wouldn't last. Sheng had been through most of the good-looking women at the station. It never bothered him to mix work and pleasure.

'We'll know more after the autopsy. Grab some rest,' said Mia. 'See you at the office in a few hours.'

He stripped off and went in for a shower. He bowed his head in the water and let the needle jets pummel his tired shoulders. He hadn't been back home for days. It wasn't home. It was a punishment, a reminder of mistakes made. He should sell the apartment but it would be admitting defeat.

He came back into the lounge in his boxers and dropped the louvre blinds. He sat down in one of the two armchairs, plonked his vodka on the elephant table then he sat back in the chair to close his eyes for a few minutes, try and get some rest. He rolled the vodka glass across his chest. The only noise in the flat was the sound of the ticking clock in the bedroom. He closed his eyes, they felt as if they had sand under the lids. His jet black hair fell across his forehead. The image of the dead girl flashed into his head. His eyes snapped open. There would be no sleep for him tonight. He went into his bedroom and pulled open the laundry pack his maid had left. He slipped on a fresh t-shirt and pulled on his jeans. He picked up his weapons and keys from the elephant table and slammed the door on the way out.

CHAPTER 5

It was 4 a.m. when Ruby slipped out of the hotel room, into the lift and out onto Nathan Road. She took a taxi to Stanley on the east side of Hong Kong Island, a place famous for its markets selling replica goods and for its beach. But Ruby wasn't interested in either. The hour was late. It was a winding road that took her there. Wrapped in plastic, the head rocked gently in her lap. She placed her hand on it to settle it.

She told the driver to drop her at the market, then she crossed the street and slipped out of view. The dark night gave her the cover she needed. She turned away from the brightly lit restaurants and bars and headed towards the water. She knew just the place. She walked quickly; her bag was heavy. The head knocked gently against the outside of her thigh as she walked. Inside her thighs were wet. His semen was inside her and his blood on her hands. She reached the place and, in the darkness, put the bag by her feet and leant over the wall, feeling for the line. She found it and pulled it up; she had strong arms, hard hands. After five minutes, the basket came to the surface. Ruby pulled away the strands of seaweed caught in the bamboo struts and rested it on the jut in the wall just below sea level. She reached down and took the head from the bag, unwrapped it, then she placed it just inside the basket and leant over the wall as far as she could whilst holding the head in her hands. She felt the cold water cover her wrists as she gripped the head and lowered the basket into the water. She held it there for a moment, waited until the water had made it too heavy for her to maintain her grip. She stared into the half-closed, glassy-looking eyes before she leant further over the parapet. The sea water was cold as it rose over her wrists. Her hands lost their grip as she gasped, 'Goodbye my faithless lover.'

The head stared back at her as it sank. Ruby turned away and left to go back home.

Back in the Mansions she turned the key in the door, slipped inside her flat and into her room, then she leant against the door, closed her eyes and sighed, relieved. She was safe but she had the feeling she always got afterwards: lost, empty. Her heartbeat was calming. She opened her eyes and looked around and smiled. Her dolls stared back at her, their bright eyes looked at her adoringly.

'I'm sorry, my babies, I couldn't bring your daddy back with me. He wouldn't come, I had to leave him in the hotel room. He wasn't a very nice daddy. He wasn't kind to Mummy. We didn't like him, did we?' She looked around the room at her dolls. They stared back. 'Mummy will find you a better one tonight. Mummy will find you one we can keep forever.' She clapped her hands in delight. From inside a cupboard a baby cried in answer. Ruby opened the cupboard door and took the baby doll from the shelf; it was still crying, 'Mummy, feed me, Mummy.'

'Shush,' she patted the baby's back, 'in a minute my love, Mummy will feed you in a minute.'

Ruby put the doll back and as her hand lingered in the cupboard it traced the outline of something lying there. It was small, no bigger than a mobile phone, it was dry and hard. Ruby touched its face and started to cry. 'Daddy wasn't nice to Mummy at all.'

CHAPTER 6

Kin Tak, the mortuary technician, looked at the clock on the wall: it was almost 5 a.m. 'Quick, quick,' he said out loud. 'No wasting time now. Finish the job. Finish it.'

Kin Tak had a form of Tourette's syndrome that had been allowed to grow in the dark environment of the mortuary. He tried to curb it. He tried to suppress it but he was on his own for most of the day and night and he talked to himself incessantly. He talked to the people in the drawers. He talked to the dead that roamed his icy rooms, looking for their heaven.

He had worked through the night to make the girl ready. He washed her young body. He worked methodically, meticulously, marvelled at her beauty as he passed a cloth over her young skin. He talked to her as he washed her hair to remove the blood. Now he dried it with a towel, it crinkled into black glossy waves. Kin Tak held it in his hand, 'Lovely, lovely.' It was as soft as cotton wool, as springy as air. He marvelled at her slender arms, her slim thighs. She had no imperfections. Her skin was smooth and flawless as the day she

27

slid from her mother's uterus, fighting for breath in the outside world.

Now he hummed to himself as he pierced the young girl's eye with the syringe and extracted fluid from the back of the eye. He was practising. Now that the pathologist had done his work it was Kin Tak's turn. The fluid, vitreous humour, was a vital source of information for determining time of death. But they knew when she had died. She had died a few moments before they had run away and a few moments after they had cut off her hands and slit her throat. Now Kin Tak was allowed to practise his forensic skills before he did what he liked doing best.

Kin Tak was a diener, a mortuary technician. His job was to assist the pathologist in a post mortem examination, take tissue samples, weigh organs, take samples for the lab and record the findings of the post mortem. But Kin Tak was more than that – he was a student of the art of beautifying the dead and he was a student of pathology. He was a devoted mortuary technician who lived and slept amongst the dead. His skin seldom felt the sun, wind or rain on it. It had become cheese-like in its appearance. He practised his stitching whenever he could. Choppings gave him plenty of practice. But this was not a chopping tonight; these were wounds he had not seen before. He picked up the severed right hand. It was not a clean cut. It was a broad, layered wound, some of the flesh was missing. He would have to improvise by stretching what skin he could to stitch neatly. But not yet, he wasn't ready yet. He moved down her body. Her small hips, not yet spread by childbirth. He combed her pubic hair.

The bell rang. Kin Tak felt the excitement turn his stomach but he was agitated. He hadn't finished with the young woman's body. It would have to stay where it was.

'Fuck. Fuck.' He snorted a giggle out of his nose and clamped his hand over his mouth to suppress it. 'Sex. Sex.'

He knew she would come tonight. She wouldn't mind the young woman's body being on view. She would be pleased. She was still learning and he had such a lot more to teach her. She would pay him the way she always did. She would give him her body. She would take off her clothes and lie on the autopsy table; he would gently part her naked thighs and stroke her warm wet sex; but she would never let him do any more. She said that if she did, she would have to kill him.

He rushed to answer it. He squinted at the bright security light at the entrance haloed in moths. He was ready for her, he opened the door and stepped back, startled as he saw Mann standing there. He craned his neck to look past him into the darkness to see if there was anyone else and then he shook his head, agitated, disappointed: 'Fuck.'

He stood back to allow Mann inside, then he scurried behind him almost tripping over in his haste to overtake him and get through the doors first. 'Fuck. Shit. Too late now.'

Inside the autopsy room he turned and stared at Mann. He couldn't take his eyes from Mann's face. He remembered all too well every bereaved, haunted person who ever stood in that place. He felt the sorrow as well as the beauty of death: he collected it like a library of loss. When he looked at Mann he remembered the dead person that Mann had loved. He remembered Helen. Kin Tak had developed his senses to a point where he could see the restless spirits as they followed the living around. Helen followed Mann. She hadn't always done. She had come back for a reason now. With a shiver, he unfroze his stare.

Mann followed him into the curtain of cold that lay behind the mortuary door. The place was always the same; even though it had recently had a facelift – new equipment, tables, the works – it still smelt the same: formaldehyde and meat.

'How's it going, KT? I hope you don't mind me dropping in. I knew you'd be here. Is the autopsy completed on the Indian girl brought in last night?' Mann looked over at the girl's body laid out on the autopsy table.

'Yes, very busy. Just finishing.'

'I want to know your opinion about the weapon that was used to cut off her hands. What can you tell me?'

'Ah. She was killed when her throat was cut. But . . .'

30

'Yes?'

'She would probably have bled to death just as quickly. The severing of her hands cut through the main artery. The blood must have been everywhere.' Kin Tak's eyes darted from Mann to the girl.

His eyes settled back on Mann and he waited. He wasn't prepared to go on until Mann had met his side of the deal. Give a little: get a little in exchange. Give and take. Mann understood. In Kin Tak's dead world his entire existence relied upon the knowledge of the whole story; he must know every detail about the death and how they came to have a date of birth on the outside of their mortuary drawer and a date of death ticket wrapped around their toe. But Mann could see that as much as Kin Tak wanted to know the details, he kept looking at the clock on the wall – he was nervous.

'There must have been two hundred people there. She was part of a Triad initiation ceremony. We don't know why she was killed. I found her in a dungeon. She was hog tied, her throat had been cut. I found her hands in the box.'

'Okay, thank you, Inspector.' He held up his hand, closed his eyes and breathed deeply through his nose. 'That's all I need to know.' He snapped his eyes back open and stood up straight, business-like. 'I can tell you, Inspector, that, after my examination, I conclude that her hands were severed by something other than a

31

chopper or a saw, or a knife. They were severed by something as sharp as a razor but with three blades to it. It bit into her wrists, it snagged there and it cut right through. Yes, each cut is clean but there are so many that her wrist was torn apart.'

'Have you ever seen that kind of damage before?'

'No. Now you must excuse me, Inspector. I have much to do and the morning is coming. It is good to see you, come again soon.' Kin Tak paused and turned and looked at Mann, as if he wanted to say something, then he shook his head and scurried on towards the door.

Mann walked back across the gravel car park to his car, his feet crunching on the surface. When he got to his car he paused and stood there for a few seconds. Whether it was the sound of his feet on the gravel or the smell of the shrubs around the edge of the car park that had done it, his memories would not allow him to get into his car or drive off. They demanded to be acknowledged. He stood for a few moments in the dark, listening to the first bird calling dawn, and he remembered that day when he had said his final farewell to Helen's body. When he had stood where he was standing now, but could not cry. All he could do was rage inside. Two years ago he had felt as near to the edge as he had ever been. That was, until now. Now, he felt he had built a platform over that edge and he was living, sleeping, existing on it and all around him was a sheer drop.

CHAPTER 7

It was 8 a.m. when Mann stood with ten other officers in the incident room. Next to him were the two men he shared an office with: Detective Sergeant Ng and Detective Constable Li – a.k.a Shrimp.

'Okay, this is how I see it.' Tom Sheng addressed the new team.

The incident room was on the twentieth floor of the police headquarters building. It was split into three sections. The first section at the entrance was where the Senior Investigating Officer set up base. The SIO was the person in charge of the enquiry and decided which line it would take. A screen separated that from the largest part of the room, the central section that had the bulk of the PCs, filing cabinets, and a large desk with four interfacing PCs. Along the back of the room was one long desk and a further five PCs and a phone between each. The third section was a staff room and a general 'spilling over' room for impromptu meetings. Each section was separated by screens. Each screen a multi-purpose white board.

'We work together on this. We need to move fast.'

Tom Sheng paused and looked around the room. 'Collaboration is the key word here. I want no fucking egos taking over on this one. Chief Inspector Mia Chou and I will be allocating jobs to those best qualified, not those in a certain department.'

Mann looked over at Mia. She was perched on the edge of the central table with her arms crossed over her chest. She was immaculate as ever, just a small strand of hair had worked its way loose from the knot at the back of her head. She flicked it away irritably. She never wore lipstick. She played her looks down, looks distracted from the seriousness of her career. She was a good cop, conscientious, steady. That's why she'd been promoted over him. There were very few other female officers of her rank. She'd worked hard for it. Mia did everything by the book. Mann did everything by his own rules. They were chalk and cheese but somewhere in the middle they both wanted the same things.

'There will be no favouritism,' Tom Sheng continued. 'First of all, let's be clear about events. What happened last night, Mann?'

Mann stepped up to the white board. He began pinning up photos. They were images of Rajini's body squashed into the box; her arms were sticks in front of her face, held up to the camera. Her hands and the rooster were thrown into the box with her. There were shots from the autopsy. Mann didn't need to look; he had it all stored in his brain whether he wanted it or not.

'We got an anonymous call through to the hotline

at 9 p.m. saying that there would be an initiation ceremony taking place that evening in Mong Kok.'

'Any trace on it? Any chance of voice recognition?' asked Sheng.

'No. I've played it back. It's someone being paid to read the details. It's been sent via a third party. I left with Officers Li and Ng and we split into three teams, each covering a different section of Mong Kok.' Mann put up a map of the area. 'There were thirty officers altogether.'

'So, you didn't have enough manpower?' Tom Sheng interrupted.

'It wouldn't have mattered if we'd had a fucking hundred times that amount,' Mann snapped back. 'It's the most densely populated area in Hong Kong. Every doorway leads to a dozen more. In the end, it was all bullshit. It was in Yau Ma Tei, not in Mong Kok. It was off the night market here . . .' Mann pointed to it on the map. 'We were set a false trail. We were never meant to arrive on time, just meant to arrive.'

'Why would someone want to run the risk of you finding it?' Tom Sheng asked.

'Because it was a special night. They knew we wouldn't find it but they wanted to make sure it was acknowledged. Not only was the girl sacrificed but a new society was born. It is a branch of the Wo Shing Shing. I found their emblem amongst the burnt oaths. And I found this . . .' Mann pinned up a photo of a lone wolf howling inside a circle. 'Someone wants their birth announced.'

'What's the purpose of these new societies? Why change the format? Why start recruiting girls and ethnic minorities? What is the need for it?' asked Sheng.

'The Triads have always targeted the teenage underdog. The young Indian population feel abandoned. They feel marginalized. They can no longer compete. The Indians and the other minorities used to be on a level playing ground, now someone's dug up the goal posts and moved them. School places are allocated by a points system and the higher up the social scale you are the more points you seem to have. Plus you have to read and write Mandarin.'

'What do we know about the victim?'

'We don't have a name for her yet. The autopsy showed she died due to asphyxiation when her throat was cut. We know she was of Indian descent, approximately fourteen years of age.'

'What's the latest on Operation Schoolyard?' asked Sheng.

Mia answered, 'We have one operative in the school. She's twenty but looks much younger. It's been hard to infiltrate; hard to get someone convincing enough. She joined a month ago as a student in the senior school. Her aim is to infiltrate into the new gangs. It's a tricky area, new to us, dealing with girls, and immigrants.'

'This initiation was brutal,' said Mann. 'She's young to handle this.'

'She's twenty,' said Mia. 'There are people in this

room who went undercover at that age. The difference is, she's a woman. But that isn't a problem. We need to play the same game and keep up.'

'All right.' Tom Sheng looked around the room. 'There's one thing we haven't covered. Operation Schoolyard is all about infiltrating the ranks of the new Triads. What we need now is someone to give us an insider's view on what is really going on at the top. We need to know who's making all the decisions that filter down to these kids. Who's pulling the strings? We need an insider.' Tom Sheng looked at Mann, He had a hard job keeping the smug look off his face. 'I think that's your job, Mann, don't you?'

CHAPTER 8

Mann was grateful to get out of the building. He left Headquarters and walked through the small lush garden that fronted it. The palms were being watered with a fine mist. It clung to his skin and cooled quickly as he took the steps up to the elevated walkways slung between Hong Kong's buildings like Tarzan ropes, allowing the city's seven million residents to escape the pavements and move from building to building all in the name of commerce. Money was king, queen and country.

Mann stood six foot two and weighed a hundred and eighty pounds. It was less than his usual weight. But he had been ill. He'd caught malaria in the jungles of Burma. He'd nearly died rescuing his eighteen-year-old half-brother who was supposed to be building a school for refugees and ended up getting kidnapped. Mann had had no choice but to go.

He checked his watch; he was early. He had time to phone. He stood on the walkway and took out his phone.

'Mum?'

She was pleased to hear his voice, he could tell. 'Are you better? I haven't seen you properly since you came back from Burma.' Her accent was old school English: loosened a little by modern times but still tight, taut.

'I'm all right, Mum. I've been busy.'

Mann allowed the pause that followed. He was used to pauses when he talked to his mother. They had so many things to say and yet they said very little. They loved one another but they were too alike. If one closed emotionally then so did the other.

'Have you time to come over soon?'

'I'll see. I have so many things to sort out at home.'

'Your father's affairs?' A frosty, hurt voice.

'Yes.'

Mann rubbed his face with his hand. He was irritable now. Talking to her agitated him at the moment, he couldn't help it. He took a deep breath.

'Look Mum, I have to go. I'll call you later.'

Mann closed the phone and slipped it back in his pocket. Now he really felt like shit. He knew what she'd be doing. She'd be staring out of the French windows, listening to the carriage clock tick. Her grey eyes would be filled with the colour of the sky. Her prim, upright figure would be stiff shouldered. She would be feeling like shit. Just like Mann.

Now his father's secrets were out, Pandora's Box was open. His father hadn't just had another family in Amsterdam; he had supplied most of Europe with heroin. His father wasn't just any Triad, he was a very good one. The chatter of the birds greeted him as he walked up into the botanical gardens off Albany Road at the top of Central district. Apart from that it was quiet; it was too early for the tourists. The place had the smell of the tropics, freshly washed, birds squawked. Fountains filled the air with their fresh cool sound. Across the square he saw a small figure sat on a bench, her head down, her feet scuffling at the seeds and fallen leaves that had yet to be brushed up by the park attendant. Mann thought how young she looked, a skinny little slip of a girl. She might be twenty but she looked twelve. That's why they'd been able to use her. He sat beside her but made sure they didn't look as though they were together. He turned his head from her. Neither acknowledged the other. He rested his arm on the back of the seat. The sparrows gathered around their feet.

'How's it going? Aren't you supposed to be in school?' Mann asked.

'Yeah, but I'm building up my rep as a wild child.' Tammy sipped her can of Coke. 'I'll go in a minute. I'm just missing maths.'

'Did you hear about last night?'

'I heard about it. I heard that someone got killed.'

'Yes. A young Indian girl. We are still waiting for formal identification. Do you have any idea who she is?'

'They say she was someone from the Mansions. Her family lives there, they have a tailors on the first floor.'

'Why was she killed, Tammy?'

'I don't know. There are a lot of rumours. They say she was an informer from another society, that she had told someone outside about the ceremony, that she had accepted money in exchange for information. I don't know. I think maybe she was just picked as a show of strength. Now everyone is really scared. A lot of the girls are really shaken up by it. I have seen them huddled together, whispering, crying. It's finally hit home that it's not a game.'

'Maybe now they will want out.'

Tammy didn't answer at first. 'I don't think so, Boss. They are tough kids, scary tough. They don't care about anything but money, MP3 players, watches. If anything, I think this death will bond them, strengthen their loyalty. These are just kids but kids see the cruelty of the world differently than we do. They frighten me. I think they will increase their members by this. It becomes more real, more exciting. They have no concept of death, of dying or being killed. They have no concept of the rest of their lives either. They feel no hope.'

'Who's doing most of the recruiting?'

'Older girls. Sometimes from outside school. They wait for the kids when they come out. The one who is recruiting me is called Lilly Mendoza. She is in my year. She's mixed race. Her mother is a singer in the hotels. They live in the Mansions.'

41

'I know her mother – Michelle. I've known her since before Lilly was born. Try and find out more about who's further up the ladder. We know they're a breakaway branch of the Wo Shing Shing, we need to know a lot more. We need to know what their specific aims are, who their high-ranking officers are. Keep pushing, Tammy. The faster we find out what's going on, the faster we can get you out.'

'Yes, Boss.' Tammy paused. 'Boss . . . how much longer do you think I will have to stay undercover? I miss the real world. I miss seeing my boyfriend, seeing my parents.'

'I hope it won't be for much longer, Tammy. This was only meant as a short operation. I know it's a hard one. You're doing a good job. Not many officers would have had a hope in hell of infiltrating this group. You'll be guaranteed a place in the Bureau after this. It will be great to work with you when you get out of this operation.'

'If I get a place in the OCTB it will be worth it, sir.' Tammy stood and picked up her bag. 'I gotta go, Boss. Got my school uniform to change into. See you later.'

'And Boss, I have a name for you for the new society: the Outcasts.'

CHAPTER 9

It was early evening when Ruby slipped in with the crowds and walked out onto Nathan Road. It was heaving. A new dump of rain had brought a sparkle to the air. The bamboo scaffolding was still dripping from the summer downpour. Ruby stepped out of the way of the drips and wove in and out of the crowds. She had heels on; she didn't want to get her feet wet. She headed towards the harbour. She took a right and walked up the steep narrow road to the first of her destinations: the Walkabout, the Australian theme pub. Sometimes it was full of youngsters: young and rowdy with no wedding rings on their fingers. But at this time of the evening it offered a good deal for lonely businessmen who didn't want to eat alone. They could watch the sport and eat a steak. The perfect place for her to start hunting.

Ruby walked in. She kept her head down as she walked to the far end of the bar and ordered a Coke from the young blond surfer type, his head a mass of springy curls. She took her drink and went to sit at a table in the corner. A cricket match was on. She made eye contact with a few of the older men. They were distracted by the match. Ruby drank her Coke and left. She didn't have time to waste. Ruby was always in a hurry.

She walked back up the road and took a detour to check out The Western, a saloon-themed pub. Ruby peered through the window; Annie the patron was swinging her gun-toting hips down the empty bar. She moved on. She knew what she was looking for. Hong Kong had lonely businessmen arriving by the hundreds every few minutes. Ruby could afford to be fussy. Plenty of fish in the sea.

Ruby continued on Nathan Road to a four-star hotel right in the heart of Tsim Tsat Tsui. Vacation Villas was in a great location, right next to the metro in the heart of the business hub, Kowloon side, and it was always busy. Businessmen stayed from all over the world. It had seventeen floors, a business centre on top, a rooftop pool and a good gym. But the main reason the businessmen liked it was because it had a twenty-four-hour cocktail bar.

Ruby came into the hotel by the Nathan Road entrance, past the few shops there and walked straight to the lifts. It was just one floor to the cocktail bar. The bar itself was not one of the stark new types, it was dark enough so that you could be lost in the shadows, just part of the wood panelling and the heavy brocade curtains. It was a bar to be anonymous in. It was noisy, busy enough so there was never silence, with singers to stare at to occupy a frazzled mind. It suited lonely businessmen and cops.

Ruby looked around the bar. Here there were lots of opportunities for her. It was early but the place was already full of lonely businessmen sitting by themselves. Ruby didn't risk going to the bar. The light was sharp at the bar, clear. It left her open to being recognized. She chose one of the tables at the edge of the bar. They were raised, two tall stools, perfect for showing off Ruby's legs in her short skirt.

Her eyes focused on a sweet-looking man. She liked his blond curls. He had wire-rimmed glasses, an open-necked shirt. His broad forearms rested on the bar as he turned his phone over in his hands. He looked restless. Ruby turned in her seat so she could be sure he'd get a good look at her legs.

She stared hard. It took him a few minutes. Others looked at her but she ignored them. Her focus was on him. The thought of it sent a thrill through her stomach. It sent a pulse to her sex. It had a heartbeat of its own. It tightened in anticipation and felt warm and wet and plump with desire.

Fifteen minutes in she had done enough. He stood and walked over.

'May I?' He gestured to the stool next to her.

'Please do.'

'The name's Steven.'

'Hello Mr Steven.'

He laughed. 'Steven's my first name. Littlewood's my family name. Friends call me Steve.'

Ruby lowered her eyes and smiled up through batting lashes. She glanced over his body. He was tall but not strong looking. She guessed he wasn't a gym user. That was good. She guessed he weighed about one hundred-eighty pounds.

'Hello Steve. We can be friends. My name is Ruby.' Ruby turned to face him and looked up into his eyes, cocked her head to one side and said, 'You have beautiful eyes – blue like the sea.'

He grinned stupidly as he leant forward and peered at her through his glasses. 'They like what they see.' He was slurring, embarrassed like a schoolboy at a village dance. He coughed to clear his throat and his head.

Ruby giggled as she smiled and slipped off the stool. 'You hungry? I take you for something to eat and then we have fun. I have all night.'

He shrugged and nodded. He was starving. He hated eating on his own. 'Yeah, sure.'

His phone vibrated in his pocket. He took it out to see who had messaged him. It was his wife. He switched it off.

'You ready?' She smiled beguilingly at him.

'Oh yes.' He grinned inanely back at her.

'Do you like Indian food?' she asked as she led him through the lounge, down in the lift and out into Nathan Road.

'Love it.'

'I know the best Indian restaurant in Hong Kong. Very cheap too.'

He closed his eyes and put his hand on his heart. 'I'd die for a good Indian right now.'

Ruby giggled. She put her hand over her mouth to try and hide it. He saw her and laughed with her.

She led him through the side entrance of the Mansions. She hurried him past the Indian supermarkets, porn sellers, Visa shops. She took his hand and led him up the stairs.

'Christ, where are we going?' He stopped and looked around him as they walked along a landing on the third floor that faced into the middle of the five tower blocks. 'It looks like a prison.' The opposite landing was so near you could almost have reached over and touched it.

'This is the centre of the Mansions. This is the most famous place for Indian food. You will see.'

Wafting up from the vents was the smell of curry. They walked up a further two sets of stairs.

'Christ, how many more? It better be worth it.'

'Nearly there, big man.'

He wasn't unduly worried. He was used to Asia. He was used to strange smells and dirty alleyways and heat and grime and he was used to places not feeling quite right. The small buzz of fear that he had felt when he first found himself alone as a foreigner on a faraway street had long since left him. Once every few months he made the same trip to Asia. He had lost his wonderment, his adrenalin rush at the fear of the unknown. He didn't care for Chinese food any more. Now he longed for curry and a cold pint of beer. Now he just sat in cocktail lounges that could have been anywhere in the world. Ruby understood it. She knew he was used to being out of his comfort zone and he would not back out now. He had come this far. He would have it all now.

They reached her apartment door.

'This isn't a restaurant.' He looked around, still smiling, a little less relaxed, a little less tipsy.

'This is where I live, big man. Come in and I will ring the restaurant and get us the best table. While we wait I will get you a drink, make you happy . . .' She smiled teasingly and brushed her hand over his crotch, softly, lingeringly. 'I like you a lot. I am going to give you a real good time.'

'Sounds good to me.' He pulled her to him, held her by the bottom and thrust his hips at hers. She quickly opened the door and led him inside.

He stood just inside. 'Are you boiling gammon? I haven't smelt that since I was young. My grand-mother always boiled gammon.'

Ruby didn't answer; she led him past the kitchen where steam rose from boiling bones, now stripped of their flesh and rattling in the scummy water. The bones belonged to a man named Matt Simpson. His glasses were still on the side of the sink. His head was feeding the lobsters. His photo was sitting in the arms of a boy doll dressed in a blue bonnet and blue booties.

Ruby took his hand and steered him into her room, she closed the door behind him.

Five men had entered her room, stepped into her secret world. Five men had entered, none had left. He was the sixth.

CHAPTER 10

Mann took the MTR over to Central, Hong Kong Island. He walked up towards Soho (short for 'south of Hollywood road', an area of chic and not so chic wine bars, open fronted, pavement style, in cobbled streets and steep alleyways. Mann stepped outside of the noise and took out his phone.

'Sorry, I didn't mean to be sharp.'

He heard her sigh. 'You have every right, son.'

'No, I don't. You did the right thing in keeping the truth from me for most of my life. It was great while it lasted.'

'It would have lasted longer if *she* hadn't got in touch.'

'It wouldn't have gone on much longer, I would have always found out in the end. His assets existed whether you wanted them to or not. Anyway . . . I'm glad *she*, Magda, did get in touch. I liked her, Mum, whatever Dad was or wasn't he loved her and I was proud to know her in the end. It was difficult, it was uncomfortable but I found a brother I never knew I had. I hope you will agree to meet him one day.'

'Perhaps, son.'

'I'll see you soon, Mum.'

The Cantina Bar was decorated with a mix of sci-fi memorabilia. It was a place he felt comfortable, cherished even, amongst the chirrups of R2D2 and the hyperdrive floor that seemed to collapse as you walked on it before it spun you off into a black hole. But, most of all, what attracted Mann to the Cantina was Miriam. She looked like an Italian sex siren from the fifties, with her cinched-in waist and ample chest and the outline of her voluptuous body beneath her tight dress. She was older, an English woman, a Japanese Yakuza widow: her husband had been a Yakuza member – the Japanese mafia. He had taken the fall for others. There was honour amongst those left behind. Now the Yakuza looked after her. They made sure the local Triads didn't overstep their mark. The Japanese Yakuza were brothers to the Chinese Triad; big players in the Asian Triad market. When necessary, when business crossed borders then the two could be bed mates. In Miriam's case the Triads left her alone to run her bar knowing that if they didn't they would answer to the Yakuza. Miriam had large dark and sultry hooded eyes that oozed sexual promise. A Roman nose, broad mouth and glossy black hair tumbled down her back in waves; her lips were red to match her dress. Mann and Miriam had a thing going which went back a few years. They understood one another, or so he thought.

'Where you been, Johnny?' she said as she turned on her stool and watched him approach. He leant down to kiss her. She turned her face and he kissed her cheek. It was then that he realized he was in trouble. 'You look wrecked.'

'I've been to hell and back, Miriam. I could do with some intensive nursing.'

'I left you a few messages.' She tried not to smile.

'I'm sorry, Miriam.'

The barman glanced over and batted his eyelashes. Mann smiled back. What was it with gays? They always fancied him. He brought him over a vodka on the rocks. Mann thanked him and took a large swig.

'I was worried. I heard you got ill.'

'I got malaria. I'm fine now. I just can't sleep. I need a bedtime story and a glass of milk. Let me buy you dinner, I'll tell you all about it.' Mann realized he was getting drunker than he meant to. He needed to eat. But not in the Cantina – the food was a variation on tapas and Mann needed a proper meal. He kissed her hand and followed it as it went back to her lap. Beneath his palm he felt the slide of silk stocking. There was a smile creeping in, a curl of soft red lips. But it wasn't yet the smile that she gave him which meant he wouldn't be sleeping that night, not yet.

'I was really worried, Johnny.'

He smiled, looked into her eyes. 'I've missed you, Miriam. I've missed the way you laugh. I've missed the way you pretend to be angry at me.

I've so missed feeling you fall asleep in my arms. But, work has had me running around like a headless chicken and, to be honest, I haven't been good company.'

She stood and stepped closer to him. Mann could smell her perfume. He touched the curve of her waist, the smoothness of her dress as it rounded her hip. She was relenting. She was giving in. She brushed her breast against his arm and touched the side of his face with her soft hand. She smiled, her eyes full of mischief. 'Let me pick up my nurse's kit on the way.'

Back at his flat, Mann stood back to allow Miriam through. She was a few paces in the room when she turned.

'It's been a while since we did this.'

He pulled her close. 'Too long.' He kissed her neck. She drew back.

'But you haven't been lonely.'

He pulled back at looked in her eyes. They were searching his.

'You're the only woman who comes here, Miriam, honest.'

'Really? Since when have you been wearing perfume?'

Mann turned his head and smelt the air. Miriam was right; there was a smell of perfume and it was one that he knew very well. The smell of Miss Dior was in the air; the scent of Helen.

CHAPTER 11

'Gin and tonic, right, Steve?'

Ruby was working fast to put him at ease. She could see by his face as he looked around her room that he was wondering if he'd made the right decision. He was wondering why they hadn't just gone to his hotel room or straight to the restaurant. *You hungry, big man? You want some fun? Spend the evening with me?* Now he wasn't so sure.

'Yes, Ruby. I thought we were going for something to eat? Is this where you live?' He looked around the tiny apartment. 'Jesus, what a shithole. Sorry – no offence. Is this it? Everything in this room: kitchen, bathroom? What's in there?' He pointed to the curtain.

'That is my bedroom.'

He got up, pulled back the curtain and tried the handle. 'You keep it locked?'

Ruby giggled. 'Maybe I let you see my bedroom.'

He squinted at the shadows. 'Plastic flowers . . . roses . . . and what are they? Dolls? Fuck, they're everywhere.' He laughed but at the same time he spun round and peered into the dark corners.

Hundreds of pairs of eyes looked back. 'Fuck . . . what is this place?'

'Hey, big man,' Ruby tried to distract him, 'have a drink. Sit down. Make yourself comfortable.' She handed him the glass.

He took a big slug of it. 'Jesus, that's strong.' He wiped his burning mouth.

Ruby lifted her glass against his. She pressed him backwards. 'Cheers. Sit. Sit.'

He sat on the sofa. 'Drink. Drink . . .' She drank her water down and poured him another gin.

She began to strip for him; he drank as he watched. He undid his shirt. Stripped to the waist, he eased back on the sofa, propped up on an elbow. She whirled around the room like a spinning top, laughing as she went. He laughed and tried to grab her as she danced around him. Ruby was down to her knickers. She straddled his lap and grabbed his hair. She ran her hands down over his arms. She looked at the tattoo he had on his upper arm.

MUM

She made a pouting face. 'Ahhh. You a mummy's boy?'

'Of course.' He grinned. 'Safer than putting a girl's name. It's hard to rub off when it's over.'

She stood and pulled his mouth to her sex. He drew away.

'Hey, shouldn't we use something? Ouch . . . go easy. You're pulling my hair out.' He laughed. He stood. 'Come on then, you dirty girl, let's go into your bedroom.' He lurched sideways. 'Jesus – I feel pissed.'

She eased him towards the locked bedroom door. She had the key ready in her hand.

'You just need to relax. You need to lie down.'

'Good idea.' He grabbed her bottom and squeezed it hard. 'Fucking hell!' He lost his balance and crashed into the wall.

Ruby looped his arm around her shoulder as she unlocked the door and pushed it gently open. It was complete darkness inside. He stumbled forwards and hit his shoulder on the doorframe. 'Where are we going? Through the secret door?' He laughed.

'You'll see . . .' She giggled and guided him inside, half dragging him now as his legs had started to buckle. 'Time to lie down, big man.'

Ruby steered him forwards. 'Lie down now. You're okay, big man. Just lie back.'

He resisted for a second and then with a half laugh, half sigh, he gave in and lay back heavily on the mattress. Ruby ran her fingers through his hair, soothing him as he slipped further into unconsciousness and she moved around in the darkness tightening the restraints.

CHAPTER 12

In the morning Mann dropped Miriam back at the Cantina and he drove to Tammy's school to give his talk.

The hall was darkened for the slide show projecting onto a screen behind him. He stood to one side. Three hundred children sat in front of him, in rows. A sea of white shirts and blue ties. They were hushed as the first ten images flashed up one after the other. Each image stayed up for three seconds unless he clicked to halt it: a girl dying with a needle in her arm, a boy whose face was badly disfigured from a chopping.

'Triads deal in death,' Mann continued. 'In some form or another, it's all about death. Whether its drugs, people trafficking, robbery, kidnapping. They aren't fussy. They will make money any way they can. They don't care who gets killed along the way. They use their members to fight battles just because they can. They don't care how many get killed. Why should they?'

Mann stopped at the eleventh.

A young woman lay face down, a rope around her neck. Her hands were tied behind her back.

'This is Zheng,' Mann said. 'She was on her way to study in England. She was looking forward to it. She was going to come back here and take her university entrance. When she arrived in London she was met by her contact but he didn't take her to the school, as promised, he took her to this bedsit you see in the photo.' Mann waited as all eyes studied the image of the girl lying face down. The room was in complete silence. 'They cut off her little finger.' Mann pointed to her left hand in the photo. 'They sent that back to Hong Kong to her parents and they asked for ten million Hong Kong dollars.' The hall gave a collective intake of breath. 'Zheng's parents couldn't raise that kind of money so they raped and murdered her.' The next photo to flash up was of a boy lying in a pool of blood, his chopped body twisted in death.

'This is Zheng's brother. He was an addict. He sold the Triads the information about his sister: which flight she'd be on, how much he thought his family would be able to find. They tricked him of course. They asked for ten times the amount his parents could pay and so, when they couldn't pay, they killed him too. Nobody wins with the Triads. If you want to be somebody in Hong Kong society you have to stand out from the crowd, not just be another *49*, another number.' The lights went back on.

He looked along the rows. The front ten rows seemed to be solely occupied by girls, all looking up at him.

'Any questions?'

About ten hands went up from the front. Mann pointed to the first hand. It was a girl from the fifth row back. She was mixed race. Part Chinese, part Filipino. She had come off well with the mix. She was striking looking, fair skinned. She had a touch of Spanish about her from the Filipino side, fair skinned, black haired. Mann realized he knew her, but he couldn't place her.

'Sir, do you give this talk to all the schools?' she asked.

'Pretty much.'

'Even the schools where the parents have money and there aren't any immigrants like there are here?'

The headmaster stepped forward to the mike to intervene; Mann waved him back.

'What's your name?'

'Lilly.'

'Lilly what?'

Lilly was a pretty girl with bags of attitude. 'Mendoza.'

Her mother Michelle was a part-time hooker; Lilly must have slipped past the condom. The father looked like he must have been Chinese. Hong Kong was not a great ambassador for mixing the races. The Chinese liked to keep to their own kind. But something else was bugging him: he'd seen Lilly last night. She was one of the two girls who ran from the building just as he got there.

'Okay, I know what you're saying. You feel like

59

this is a problem for kids from poorer back-grounds. Yeah, well I agree. The Triad organizations are always looking for an angle. They have mostly, not always, recruited from the poorer side of society. They know the recent changes in the education system discriminate against people coming in from other countries, non natives. They know it makes it tough so they exploit that.'

Another hand went up from a young Indian girl. 'Are you mixed race, sir?'

'Yes. My mother is English, my dad was Chinese.'

'Is it easy to get into the police force when you're mixed race?'

'It isn't easy to get into the police force what-ever race you are. You need a good level of English. You need to be able to read and write Mandarin.'

There was a muttering all around the hall. Lilly spoke up again. 'You need to be able to read and write Mandarin to clean toilets now.'

The children laughed. The headmaster coughed loudly.

Mann waited until the laughter subsided before he spoke again. 'Yeah, it sucks. It sucks that there isn't a level playing field any more. It really sucks that a lot of what made Hong Kong great is being wasted. Talents that you all have to give are being handed over to the Triads because we are turning into a two-tier society. But . . .' There was a general whispering. The headmaster looked nervous. '. . . but all I can tell you is that you have to be smarter than

60

everyone else. You have to work harder than everyone else. You have to prove them wrong. You join a Triad organization and, in the short term, sure, you will get new trainers, you will get told how great you are. In the long term you will be pushed down alleyways, asked to repay favours, asked to fight, kill, you will be ordered to become part of a drug run, part of a human trafficking chain. You might be sold into prostitution yourself or sell other kids. And there will be no escape for you. You will be a number to be called whenever they choose. In the short term you may think it offers you hope. In the long term you will never be free to make it.'

'Sir?'

'Yes, Lilly?'

'If your father is a Triad do you have to be one?'

'No. Everyone has a choice.'

Lilly had a smug look on her face. She made sure she was heard. 'And sir, is it true your father was a Triad?'

Mann felt the headmaster's stare as his head swung round to look at Mann. Mann's focus on the room slipped. His hands went cold. His pulse slowed. He looked to the back of the room. Right at the back the exit door was open to allow the breeze through. He could see the rectangle of blue. He refocused on Lilly.

'Yes.'

'What happened to him, sir?'

'He was chopped to death because he disobeyed the society.'

'Did he make a lot of money, sir?'

'Yes, but . . .'

'Did you inherit it, sir?'

Mann nodded. He was losing control. The hall burst out in chat. The headmaster stepped forward. 'Thank you very much for coming, Inspector. We have taken up a lot of your time. We are very grateful—'

Mann stopped him mid-sentence. He took over the microphone and looked around the room, waited the two minutes it took to obtain absolute silence. 'My father was executed when I was just a bit older than you. I was made to watch. That day has stayed with me forever. I didn't know he was a Triad then. I do now. I have to deal with the legacy of my father's Triad involvement. I have to deal with his mess. I used to be proud of my father when I was young. He was someone I looked up to. He didn't have a lot of time for me, he was always working, but I loved him and respected him. Until I found out that he made his money by manufacturing and supplying heroin. My father was a drug baron. When I look back now my memories of him all seem like a lie. I question everything I ever had from him and ask myself did it come from drug money? Did someone have to die with a needle in their arm to buy me that?'

The room fell silent. All eyes were on Mann.

'But, when you become an adult you are judged on who you are, not who your parents were or

62

are. You stand alone. You have a choice. Yes, you may have it hard but that will make you harder. Yes, you may have it tough and that will make you tougher. And you need to be. Hong Kong can fulfil all of your dreams or it can be the cruellest place on earth. You can be anyone you want in Hong Kong. It doesn't matter who your father was. It only matters what you achieve in your life and what you do with it. Don't throw it away on being just a number. The girl who died yesterday evening was left to die alone in a cardboard box. She was left like a piece of rubbish. That's all you are to the Triad bosses. I saw her body. I found her. No one should die like that. That's what happens when you join the Triads. They make you feel like you matter but you don't. In the end they use you and control you and you are not free to make your own decisions. When I look around this hall I see a lot of familiar faces looking at me. I know some of you were involved in what happened last night. I have come here today to offer you help. I will leave my card on the notice board in the corridor. Anyone want to talk to me? I will listen. I will be able to help. As Lilly pointed out, I know first hand about the dangers of belonging to a Triad society. I know what it can do. You ring me. We'll fight it together.'

CHAPTER 13

Lilly stood up and slow clapped Mann's speech. She pushed the girl in front; the whole row collapsed amidst lots of giggling. Lilly looked across at Tammy and grinned. Tammy had felt the tension grow in the hall. Now Lilly's eyes lingered on Tammy as if she knew. Tammy grinned back. Mann got down from the stage and called Lilly over. They were left alone in the hall.

'Sit down.'

Lilly sat and looked around the room as if she were bored.

'Tell me, Lilly, what's a bright girl like you doing coming out of a Triad initiation ceremony?'

She turned and stared hard at him, tried to read his expression. Her eyes were the colour of caramel. She had freckles across her nose. Her skin was light. She was taller than most girls her age.

'I saw you coming out of the building where the girl got murdered last night.' Mann could see from the way her eyes had stopped seeing him that her thoughts were backtracking. For a second she looked worried and then she rolled her eyes and looked at her nails, chewed off a bit of loose skin, made her

64

finger bleed, and smiled as she looked at him as she sucked the blood from her finger.

'Not me, Officer. I was at home last night doing my homework. Now, if you don't mind I have a lesson to go to. You know what it's like for us mixed-race kids – we have to work hard. We don't all have our dad's money to fall back on.' She went to stand.

'Sit. You'll go when I say.'

She sat back down with a groan and looked at her watch.

'Let me explain something to you. You're in shit up to your neck. The girl who died last night was mutilated, her hands cut off before she had her throat severed.'

Lilly snapped her head as she looked at him. 'I wasn't there.'

'But you were in the area. What do you think happens when people play with Triads, Lilly?' Mann watched her. 'What do you think you are going to get from all this? They're playing with you, Lilly. It could be you next week lying in your own blood. They're just sitting back and waiting and watching and enjoying the spectacle of kids like you killing one another. You're disposable.'

A crack appeared in Lilly's bravado. She looked towards the hall entrance, agitated, fidgety. She went to stand again.

Mann pushed her back in her seat. 'We can continue this at the police station if you like or we can do it here. What's the big global message they're selling you, Lilly? Somehow I don't think a designer handbag is what you're in this for. Tell me, Lilly. You want to belong, don't you? You want to leave your mark on the world but this is not the way.'

She blew an 'I don't give a fuck' out of the corner of her mouth. But he could see her bravado starting to dissolve. She was just a scared little girl. From the corner of his eye, Mann saw the headmaster standing at the edge of the stage. He knew he'd gone far enough without taking her in. He knew there would be no point in doing that. She would say nothing; she'd be a lot more frightened of her Triad masters than she would be of the police.

'All right, Lilly, you can go, but it won't be the last we see of each other. I will be watching every move you make from now on.'

Lilly got up from her seat in her own time and she pushed the chair back noisily, it grated across the floor, and then as she walked past Mann she stopped in front of him. She smiled up at him. 'Go ahead. I like being watched.'

Lilly left the hall and caught up with Tammy on the stairs.

'Hey, what did you think of the talk?' she shouted as the din of the girls hurrying on to their next class filled the stairwell.

'Yeah . . . it was . . .'

'Exactly – bullshit.'

'Were you there?'

Lilly nodded.

'What was it like? Did you see the girl get killed?'

Lilly shook her head. Tammy wasn't sure whether she believed her or not.

'Doesn't it worry you, Lilly? Don't you wonder if they might do that to you?'

Lilly shrugged. They stepped out of the way as other kids passed them. 'It won't happen to me. She must have done something bad. We are told the rules. She must have broken them. It serves her right. There's a code. Anyway, it's worth it. You'll see. It will be your time soon.'

They were stood at the long window, overlooking the car park below. Tammy glanced down at Mann walking across to his old BMW. A part of her wished she could go with him, another knew she had a job to do and it would be worth it. Lilly followed her gaze.

'He's hot. It would be great to get him in bed.' Lilly laughed at her expression. 'Sure . . . I've had other policemen. In the evenings I see them in the bars. I can always spot them. They have this way of looking at everything. They don't relax. But him . . .' she watched Mann drive off, '. . . I see him out a lot, but never with a woman. He's a loner.'

'How did you know that about his father?'

Lilly was proud of herself. She had put Mann on the spot. 'Everyone in the Mansions knows about him. He's the bent gweilo cop. He takes bribes.'

Tammy had a hard job not showing what she felt. There was no way Mann took bribes. He was one of those cops that would cross the line when it meant bringing someone to justice but he would never cross it for his own gain.

Lilly laughed at the look on Tammy's face. 'What? What, does he mean something to you? Do you fancy him?'

Tammy shook her head in disgust.

'He pretends to be a big moral man; really he's as dirty as they come.'

They stared out at the last of Mann's tail lights as he drove out of the car park.

CHAPTER 14

M ann headed back to Headquarters. The Organized Crime and Triad Bureau was spread over two floors, he was on the upper level. He'd been in the bureau for four years on and off. The off was ten months banished to the hinterland of the New Territories because of his tendency to piss off anyone who mattered in the police hierarchy. But the truth was, they needed him. They didn't want to but they did. No one was as devoted as Mann to catching Triads. No one hated the cancer in the Chinese society more than him. But then, no one else had his reasons.

He fed his card into the slot, took the escalators that were surrounded by so much glass they seemed to be outside, fed his card into another slot and then took the lift up to the twenty-third floor.

He negotiated the last security check, an enclosed glass turnstile affair that provided bombproof screens between the stairs and the department, and then he walked along the usual police corridors, the same anywhere in the world: abandoned file cabinets, fluorescent strip lights overhead and thin, stained carpets underfoot. A no frills environment, not softened with decoration, only the odd plant managed to survive on the ledge along the corridor.

The floor was laid out with offices around the outside, interview rooms, identity parade suite in the centre.

Ng and Shrimp were out of the office. Mann needed to clear his head. He picked up yesterday's sandwich from his desk and took the elevator to the top floor, and then the fire escape up onto the roof. It's where he always came to think. He needed head space now more than ever.

From below the sound of traffic was building. His eyes searched the horizon and spotted what he was looking for. He took a deep breath of smog-free air and smiled as he watched an eagle ride the air currents and circle over the buildings nearby. It flew by his window sometimes. It looked at him. It pitied him. It was free, ruler of the skies. Mann would have given anything to be able to jump on its back and fly away. He saw its mate on the horizon. They paired for life. He did not envy them that. He never wanted to feel the heavy burden of being in love, of caring too much, ever again.

He walked across the roof, past the massive tanks and noisy air conditioners that kept Headquarters' heart beating and lungs breathing. He broke the sandwich in two and laid the pieces out on the parapet before turning his back to the sun and walking across to the dummy. He smiled when he saw it. Shrimp had obviously been using it. He had dressed it in a seventies Hawaiian shirt and Bermuda shorts. It made for a good target. Mann walked away from the dummy, took off his jacket and left it hanging over a pipe. Across his chest he had the sets of shuriken. His throwing stars. Each set contained ten. Each one of the ten was different from the others. Different in size and in design. They were weighted to wound, maim or kill. The smaller shuriken were perfect for disabling an opponent. They could be fired several at a time and do serious damage to several opponents at once. The bigger the set the more deadly until the ultimate – the death star. There was just the one. He carried it in its own pouch but he did not carry it routinely. He had designed it himself; it was a thing of beauty and of precision. But he could only fire it once. It had to find its target. It was silent, deadly and able to arc in the air so that it could curve around the side of a wall. It could cut a man's head off.

Mann picked out the spikes from the sleeve on his arm, turned and ran towards the dummy; finding his mark he let fly the throwing spikes as he picked up pace. Three spikes embedded in its face, the other three across its chest. Mann turned at the sound of giant wings. The eagle kept one eye on him as it walked across the parapet. It picked up one half of the sandwich in its beak whilst grasping the other in its talons and it gave one last look at Mann before it dropped off the edge and turned and glided effortlessly away, the sun on the tips of its wings.

'How big is that eagle's wingspan?' It was not a question. 'Can I join you?' Mia came to stand beside him. She knew where he'd be.

'Sure.' Mann picked up a discarded feather from the eagle's tail. 'It's a black-eared kite eagle. Huge wingspan, weak legs, that's why it spends most of the time soaring on the air currents. See the way it moves in the air? There's no other bird like it for manoeuvrability. It's all in the tail feathers, like a rudder but far more sophisticated. I could watch it for hours.' He glanced across at her. 'What is it, Mia? You didn't come up here to talk about eagles.'

'I know things are tough for you at the moment, Mann, but I have faith in you. I wanted to add something to what Sheng said. I know he's not the best at putting stuff into words.'

'That's because he's a twat.'

Mia shrugged and looked away for a minute. 'Yeah, you're probably right. But even so he has a point. You are the best one for the job. It was a terrible thing finding out about your father but you can turn it to good. You want to make a difference, Mann. You could play with fire. You could step over to the dark side for a while.'

Mann looked at her to see if she was serious. She was.

'You have the connections. Use them. Jump into the lions' den. This is your chance to put your connections to good use. Go and see CK.'

CHAPTER 15

CK Leung stood at the window, staring down at Hong Kong's harbour. He was a slim, upright figure, narrow shouldered in a traditional black Chinese suit. His hair was silvered at the temples, neat, short at the neck before it touched the edge of his mandarin collar. He was watching the afternoon sun as it ignited the dark blue waters and blazed against the skyscraper walls. From the top floor of the Leung Corporation building he had a first-class view. A view like that didn't come cheap but CK could afford it. He was one of the wealthiest men in a place where the term wealthy was pushed to new parameters. Hong Kong was long famed for having the most Bentleys per square mile and the most billionaires. Lots of it was Triad-connected money. Triads had been in Chinese society for centuries, originally they did some good and supported the people but after the Cultural Revolution they turned to crime. Now they were the Chinese mafia. They ran minibus companies, taxi firms and laundered their money through nightclubs and film companies. CK was the biggest Triad boss in Hong Kong, the Dragon Head of the Wo Shing Shing – the largest Triad society, not just in Hong Kong, but fast spreading to the rest of the world. CK was a great opportunist, always looking for new ways to make money, always ahead of the game. Right now the Wo Shing Shing was leading the world in pirate computer programs and child pornography.

The PA gave a flustered protest as he stood in the doorway and attempted to stop Mann from getting through. He hadn't a hope in hell of stopping him and he knew it. They had met on a few occasions and they weren't pleasant memories for the PA. Now CK allowed him to save face. 'Let him enter.'

He shrieked as Mann's shoulder caught him and knocked him back against the doorframe.

'Sorry,' Mann grinned, pulling him upright by his tie. 'Didn't see you there.'

Mann stood in the entrance and looked across the dimly lit office: plush, chrome, cool black and dark mahogany, a mix of carved Chinese furniture and elegant Western style. Lamps lit the enclaves: calculated chic. The cold in the room hit Mann full frontal; it was like a fridge.

Mann's Armani soles made no sound as he walked across the black wood floor. The room was silent except for the low growl of the oxygen machine as it sucked in air, re-oxygenated it, and blew it out in an exasperated 'Pah'.

CK turned from the window just long enough to gesture that Mann should sit.

Now, as he leant back in the cool folds of the black Italian chair and felt it cradle him like a baby, he was not sure he should have come. His jet black hair fell as a broken crow's wing across his espresso pool eyes. In this chair, in this place, he found some comfort. Here he had something real and alive to hate, not a ghost, not a memory, not a nightmare. He had CK. Mann sat back in the chair and rocked gently. He turned his head towards the oxygen machine. He breathed in deeply as it breathed out. *Pah.*

CK turned away from the window and came to sit opposite Mann. Like everything about the room, the polished black mahogany desk was uncluttered by personal touches: a writing block, a laptop, but no photos of family. CK began slowly nodding his head as if answering an unspoken question. His expression hardly ever changed, only his eyes betrayed his humour; they changed from bitter chocolate to churned-up riverbed green.

Mann looked across at his enemy.

'The Outcasts . . . ring a bell? The new branch of the Wo Shing Shing. You recruiting from the kindergarten now, CK? From the minorities? What's going on? You running short of people to recruit?'

CK gave a dismissive wave of the hand. 'I do not want to talk about such petty aspects of business. I know nothing of street matters. I do not handle recruitment. I leave that to others. But there will always be those marginalized in society, those who need the help of their brothers. Society must look to itself for the rise of the Triads.'

Mann sat back and surveyed CK. 'A leader must still know where his armies are at all times. It will always be his job to approve changes. You must have approved the birth of the Outcasts. Who is in charge? The rumours have it that your daughter Victoria Chan is heading it.'

'A man can only rise to be the head of an organization by delegating, by trusting those beneath him to do their jobs. The tiers beneath him must be made strong to take his weight. The Leung Corporation is changing, expanding. We are branching out into new worlds and my daughter is part of this new generation.'

Mann pushed the fringe away from his eyes and stared back at CK. They had been enemies for as long as he could remember.

CK looked at Mann, his face shaded as he sat back in his chair. 'What really brings you here, Inspector? If that is all you are here to ask me then our conversation will be a short one. I was hoping for more from you. I have been waiting for this time for many years. You have found out much that has changed in your life. You have found out about your father?'

'I found out that he had a double life. He had another family across the world in Amsterdam. His life was a lie. He was not the man I believed him to be. You could have told me that a long time ago.'

CK leaned forwards, rested his elbows on the chair arms, and he pressed the ends of his fingers together. They interlocked in the air like long, thin, bony chopsticks. Without the sun the room had become dark, heavy, brooding.

'I have watched and waited over the years, hoping that one day you would come to me with the knowledge of who you are and who you were destined to be. Yes. I could have told you but it is always better to allow a man to follow his own path.'

'Yeah.' Mann turned away and allowed his eyes the comfort of the darkened room. He spoke quietly. 'Well, let me tell you. It's not a path I ever wanted to travel. I was happier in ignorance. I wish I had never found out what kind of man he really was.'

'And what kind do you think he was?'

Mann shook his head and smiled ruefully. 'If I said he was a personal friend of Mother Teresa, a defender of human rights and a generous bene-factor of the poor, would that do?'

'I could say yes but we'd both be lying.'

Amusement came into CK's eyes. CK rarely smiled. He was not a man to give in to pointless or telling gestures. In the Triad world showing emotions was considered a weakness. Every move-ment he made was calculated to give away as little as possible to his enemy. Mann understood and he played the same game. But CK had practised it for longer and Mann's quick temper always let him down in the end. It was fast to flare. But at full flame, it turned ice cold, his body slowed, his pulse barely ticked over. It was then that he could kill calmly and methodically if he had to, and he had to sometimes. Justice came in many forms. Over the years he had come close to killing CK many times.

'What he was . . .' CK continued, '. . . was a clever man with a shrewd eye for business. But he was troubled. He was a man with his feet in two worlds. He was a man whose emotions overtook him sometimes and he made mistakes.'

'He was a Triad: greedy, self-serving and worst of all he was naive. He was a fool who played with fire and got cremated.'

'No, you are wrong. He was a genius. He was a clever entrepreneur. He saw the wisdom of belonging to a great organization.'

Mann looked away in disgust.

CK remained calm as he returned to nodding slowly, deliberately. 'You need to rethink your mindset, Inspector. Triads merely adjust to their environment. They are a reflection of society and cater to its needs. If handled correctly a Triad organization can do much good for the community it serves. There is no denying that it can also further an individual's career. Your father was proof of that. It is a pity his mind warped in the end and it went badly for him.'

Mann counted to three as he took in a breath, held it for three then expired slowly. His heart rate slowed. 'My father realized his mistake and was executed when he tried to leave the society.'

CK inclined his head. 'Of course. When one joins a society, one pledges allegiance to his brothers until death. It is an ancient oath that must be honoured.'

'There's nothing honourable in belonging to an organization whose main purpose is to launder money, peddle drugs and sell people.' Mann stared coldly across at CK.

CK leaned forward, over the desk. 'Tell me, Inspector Mann, your loyalty in the Hong Kong Police must be in question, is it not? Son of a Triad . . . who would trust him?'

Mann did not answer. His head was freezing, his hands hot.

'Your father's assets continue to grow after his death. The time has come for you to step into his shoes. You will be a better Triad than he ever was.' CK's eyes turned the colour of seaweed. 'There are those waiting who will grow tired of waiting . . .' He leaned forward. 'If you wait too long they will come looking for you.'

'Let them come.' Mann felt the cold calm take him over. He leaned forward in his chair, no longer cradled. 'I feel the mortal shame of having a father who was a Triad. I have nothing now to live for except my honour and serving those who need me. Warn those that would come looking for me: I fear life more than death and I will kill them.'

CK pressed his fingertips together. He sat back in his chair. In the dusky light his eyes glowed.

'All this talk of death in one so young. All this talk of fear and fighting. Is there not one piece of your soul that longs for happiness? Money can buy you a little joy in this difficult world. Everyone deserves that, don't they, even you, Inspector? Dine with me tomorrow and let us continue our talks. I needn't be your enemy. I could be the best friend you ever had.'

CHAPTER 16

Ruby closed the door behind her. She hummed to herself as she took off her disguise and unbuttoned the front of her uniform. She opened the cupboard and placed her wig back on its stand. She went into the bathroom and switched on the light. She removed her make-up meticulously. She stood looking at herself. She turned her head from side to side to examine her face from all angles. She saw a blank canvas. Ruby was lucky to have good bone structure. Her skin was light. Her features were regular, nondescript. Only her eyes gave away her roots but that too she could disguise with make-up if she wanted to. Her eyes filled with tears as she stared into the mirror at her reflection. She asked herself: who did Ruby want to be? She wanted to be the person she once was: the child full of hope, the girl with dreams still intact. She wanted to turn back the clock and decide her own destiny. There had been a time when she was happy. A long time ago when she had sat on her mother's lap and her mother had brushed her hair and sung to her. She had felt loved. But that was before it all went wrong. That was before it happened. Ruby had believed in love once. She had trusted a man. She had been betrayed.

She glanced towards the locked door. She loved the feeling of knowing he was waiting for her, of knowing he was all hers. She undid the last few buttons and slipped the dress from her shoulders, then glanced at the clock on the wall. She had time. She would use him one more time before the end. She heard a noise. She paused as she slid her knickers to the floor. She held her breath as she listened and then she grinned in the darkness of the room that never saw the light of day.

She picked up one of her dolls and tipped it upside down. It cried one long realistic cry like a baby. Ruby held it to her breast and cooed to it as she pressed her nipple into its plastic mouth. 'Come on, baby. Mummy wants to feed you.' Ruby's nipple grew hard as she brushed it against the doll's cheek. She stopped to listen; he was calling her. He was in a lot of pain. She felt her stomach tighten. She felt her pulse quicken as her imagination took her down that delicious dark road of torture and sex. This was Ruby's favourite place now. It was all she ever thought about, all she had left.

'Coming, my love.'

Ruby picked up a small handheld saw and pulled back the curtain and opened the door, saw in one hand, baby doll in the other. The room was pitch black, sweltering hot. She switched on the electric light – one bulb hung down from the ceiling. The white on the walls gave off an eerie sheen. There were hooks hanging down from the ceiling. In the centre of the room the man lay naked on a plastic mattress. His arms were tied to a chain above his head. His legs were tied together and chained to the floor. The room had a toilet in the corner, a wash basin, a hose for washing and a drain in the floor that had once been enclosed behind a small screen. Ruby had removed it. The room was tiled completely with white tiles. Most of the Mansions' guest rooms had white tiles. It made them easier to keep clean. It meant the bedbugs and cockroaches had fewer places to hide. For Ruby it meant that she could hose off the blood easily.

Steve was strapped into the bonds waiting for her. Naked, his body now stripped down to its bare functions. Ruby put down the saw and finished injecting the penis. He was sweating. Of course he was, the heat in the room was 40° C. His chest hair had turned black as it stuck in wet rivulets and waves across his skin. It was hot in the room because there was no air con. She only switched the air con unit on afterwards. He was breathing deeply. He was scared but his cock was raging. She had injected four doses into the shaft's base. It would keep it hard long after he was begging her to end his life.

Steve stared at her. His chest rose and fell. He tried to talk but the black rubber ball gag filled his mouth. Ruby set the doll down, propped up against the wall, level with the man's head.

'There, you can watch Daddy now.'

Ruby knelt beside him and covered his cock with the hard plastic sheath. She taped it down. Then she stood and went over to the sink, bent down and picked up a weapon, a metal whip. In the confined spaces of the room she had to be careful not to hurt herself when she wielded it. She stood in the corner of the room by the door and lifted it above her head and brought it down across his body. He squealed in pain and twisted his body, trying to get away from the strokes. The wounds opened up before her eyes. The razors were so sharp that at first they slid through his flesh invisibly and then the delay and they split open. Now his body was bleeding onto the plastic mattress, the blood making its way down onto the tiled floor. He was frantic now.

'You see, baby, Daddy didn't come back for us, did he? And so Daddy has to be punished.' She struck him again, three more times across his legs, his chest. His flesh flew out in slithers. The doll's face was dripping with his blood. 'Daddy said he was single. Daddy said he loved us but Daddy was a liar, wasn't he?'

Ruby picked up the saw and pressed the button to start the motor. Unearthly noises escaped from the man's gagged mouth as he shook his head and pleaded with his eyes. Ruby took off the plastic sheath from his cock, straddled him and eased herself on him. She rocked, forgetting the saw in her hand that bounced and sang. It came to rest on the ball gag and slid back and forth across his face. Ruby didn't see it – she was coming close to orgasm. Only when she had finished did she remember that she had the saw in her hand. She looked at him and laughed. It had taken off most of his face.

She looked at the doll, its bright blue eyes still sparkling, the blood dripping from its face. Its mouth open in a sweet chuckle. 'Now that's not very nice, is it, baby? You mustn't laugh at Daddy.'

CHAPTER 17

Ng took one look at Mann when he walked back into the office that evening. He'd come straight from CK's.

'Don't bother taking your jacket off, it's late. We're going. That's enough work for you. I'm taking you home.'

Mia appeared in the doorway. 'Any news on the girl's identity?'

'Not yet,' answered Ng.

'Mann . . . did you see CK?'

'Yes, I saw him and I arranged to see him again tomorrow night. He's going to show me the world he thinks I belong in.' Mann shook his head.

Mia looked at Ng. 'Ng's right. You need some time out. Let Ng take you home. Grab an hour's rest. I'll see you in three hours. Now go.'

Mann started to protest but gave in. He wasn't going to win an argument with Mia and he knew she was right. This was no time to be slack.

Mann sat beside Ng in the passenger seat of his brand new Mazda and laid his head back on the leather headrest. The car was Ng's pride and joy, but then Ng didn't have to spend his money on his family or a mortgage. He'd inherited a flat from his parents, in what was once a slummy part of town – now the chicest address in Wanchai.

Mann watched the neon whiz by. He didn't know if he was drunk or just so tired that his world was spinning. He caught Ng looking across at him as he rested his head on the back of the seat, his eyes half closed.

'A couple of hours' sleep, something to eat, a few coffees, you'll be sorted,' Ng said.

'Yeah.' Mann looked out of the window. 'Somehow I think it's going to take more than that, Ng.'

The two fell silent. Ng switched on the radio and then switched it off. He had something he wanted to say.

'I don't think you should be the one to talk with CK or Victoria Chan. You're vulnerable right now. I see it in you. All the years we have known one another I have watched you struggle with things but I have never seen you so withdrawn. It's as if you don't exist in this life sometimes. You are not listening. You are not hearing what is said. I see your eyes always on the horizon, Mann. But the way is in the heart, not in the sky. Be kind to yourself right now. Stop punishing yourself and accept some help. I will take over talking to CK.'

Mann looked across at his old friend and he smiled. 'Thanks, Ng. You're a good friend. But somehow I don't see that working. I have something they want.

I have my father's inheritance. I have to use it to bring them down if I can.'

They parked up in his space outside his tower block and walked to the entrance. 'Fuck it – they've just changed the code,' he said to Ng, who was patient as ever. 'I've forgotten what it is.' He waved at the security guard. The old man behind the desk grinned at Mann and nodded enthusiastically as he came over to let them in.

'Hello, sir. You forget your number? No problem,' he said, letting them through the gate. 'Your cleaner was here earlier, sir.'

'My cleaner?' Mann shook his head to try to clear it. 'Okay.' He hadn't asked her to come; maybe she was just bringing back his laundry.

They took the lift up to the fortieth floor.

'Jesus, what kind of cleaner is she?' Ng stood in the doorway. 'This place looks like a student's bedroom and it smells like a brewery.' He stood amidst the remnants of meals left untouched and copious amounts of empty bottles. The louvre blinds were closed, the air in the room was dark and rank. Ng stepped over the piles of papers and document folders mixed up with the mess. He stood in the middle of the small lounge and surveyed the carnage.

'What's going on, Genghis?' Ng had called Mann that ever since he had first seen him as a wild-eyed, wild-haired youth, joining the police force to change the world, full of anger and mistrust, his world shattered from the death of

89

his father. He was older now but he was just the same inside.

Mann shook his head, threw some things off the armchair and plonked himself in it. His face was blotchy and his eyes were darker than ever, hooded and haunted. He reached forwards, tapped a Marlboro out of its packet and lit it.

Ng went to snatch the packet away. 'You quit, remember?' But a look from Mann and he thought better of it. Instead he began tidying, picking up the scattered papers and piling them on top of one another.

Mann drew on the cigarette.

'What are these papers?'

'These are my father's life.'

Ng looked around at the mountains of paperwork. 'All this?'

Mann nodded. 'These files have been like reading a diary for me. They document his life in business. Over there, behind you . . .' Ng turned to see that the piles, seemingly indistinguishable from one another, were actually in messy groups on the lounge floor, '. . . that was when my father started out in business. It was a small business, he made some clever moves. By the time he was twenty-one he had bought his first property. He expanded, bought up a few rival companies, made a good profit but it obviously wasn't enough for him. To your left . . .' Ng turned; there was a large triple pile of papers stacked next to one another, '. . . that represents ten years when he made

90

money slowly, steadily, ticked along, some years were good, some bad, until . . . scan the pile just by your right foot, the biggest piles, this group stretched across the floor. That's when he decided to get some help. That's when he turned a corner and suddenly he expanded his business so fast his feet didn't touch the ground. He had money pouring in. That's was the year he became a Triad. I haven't sorted through all of these yet. There is still a load to collect from the solicitors.'

'What about that pile?' Ng turned and pointed to a pile left just behind the door of the flat.

Mann stopped, stared. 'I didn't make that pile.'

CHAPTER 18

Mann threaded his way through the thousands of people who had come to watch the first race of the season at Happy Valley race course. The noise of thousands of excited Chinese was deafening. He put a few hundred dollars on a horse called Last Chance. Horseracing was the only legitimate form of gambling allowed in Hong Kong. More money could be taken in one night in Happy Valley than a whole year at a fixture in the West.

Mann looked upwards towards the private members' boxes. People looked down from their balconies and watched the races like Roman dignitaries standing in their amphitheatre, giving their thumbs up or down to the contestants. The race course was an oasis of green surrounded by skyscrapers and tower blocks.

Mann headed upwards through the stands. He had an appointment. He watched the screen as he made his way up. The race began. His horse, Last Chance, was tenth out of the stalls.

He took the lift up to the top floor, the private landing. He showed his ID. He walked on past the bowing hostess, her cheongsam in CK's colours: black and gold. CK was well known at Happy Valley. He had invested big money in horses. It was a great way to launder money. The private viewing room was in the centre of the stadium, prime position to look down on the races below.

'Good evening, Inspector. Thank you for accepting my invitation to meet here. The first race of the season is always the most exciting.' CK stepped forward to greet him. 'People have contained their eagerness for two months, not a small feat in Hong Kong. I see you have already placed your bet.' He pointed to the slip in Mann's hand and then looked up at the large screen that ran along one whole wall of the room. Above it flashed a continuously updated message as to each horse's position in the race. Last Chance was now sixth. CK spoke to the elfin-faced waitress hovering with a tray of champagne and she bowed, walked backwards and left to fetch his order for Mann's drink.

'Yes. Have you got one running?' Mann looked around the room. Beside him were twenty or so guests, top Triads and their officers, all trying not to stare at Mann and CK as they talked. Mann realized he was being given a rare honour of favouritism that most of these men had probably never seen.

'Asian Gold.'

Mann looked at the screen. 'The favourite and in the lead. Foregone conclusion then?'

CK acknowledged Mann's compliment but made it clear he didn't take it seriously.

'And you, Inspector?' He looked at Mann's ticket. 'You have backed Last Hope? When will you stop backing the underdog?'

Mann smiled. 'I see it as an opportunity. I don't see the underdog. It's called Last Chance. There's a difference.'

'Walk with me.' CK led Mann out to the private balcony above the track where they stood alone to watch the race.

The track was lit up like day. The thunder of hooves echoed around the auditorium. The screams of the people became one massive roar. Last Chance was coming up on the outside. Asian Gold was hanging on to first place. The jockey's whip was flying around its head. A huge scream of dismay went up in unison, a gasp of disbelief. Asian Gold had fallen. Last Chance was in second place. He was gaining on the lead. His head nosed in front. He was ten metres away from the finishing line. He was a nose ahead when he seemed to slow just before he hit the line. He came second. The crowd's roar dropped to a rumbling silence as they stood and watched the team of vets and medics run across to where Asian Gold lay. The jockey was up and on his feet. There was a few minutes' wait and then the sound of a shot echoed through the auditorium.

'I'm sorry,' Mann said to CK.

'One more beautiful creature lost to this world.

But I must also apologize. The jockey on Last Chance is one that I bought some time ago. He held him back at the end.' He turned to Mann, the merest hint of agitation in the hard line of his mouth. 'We will dine.'

The balcony door opened. The jockey who had ridden Asian Gold stood before them, still looking shaky from his ordeal. He was holding his arm. He had hurt himself in the fall. From below came the strange sound of sadness as Asian Gold's carcass was winched up and onto the back of a transporter.

'But first I would ask you to excuse me for a few minutes.'

The slight Irish jockey stood with his head bowed. The elfin-faced hostess appeared to escort Mann to his table in the restaurant.

As he entered the last of the customers was being escorted out. The place was being cleared. Three of the customers were glued to the window, their hands over their mouths in horror. Mann saw why. The restaurant overlooked the race-track. The young Irish jockey in black and gold had fallen from CK's balcony. His body was being transported away at the same time as the horse.

'Sorry to keep you,' CK said as he entered the now empty restaurant and took up a seat opposite Mann at the window table. 'The death of a horse must be investigated. Everyone involved in the event must take some responsibility.'

'I see the jockey took it hard.'

'Ah, yes.' CK glanced out of the window and realized that Mann must have had a good view of the events. 'I tried to console him but he was very distraught. He was dedicated. He lived for that horse.'

CK waited as the waiter placed his napkin across his lap.

'This is not the best restaurant in Hong Kong of course. But I like the traditional decor, the views; I like its atmosphere. I like the silence.' Now there was just the sound of twenty waiters with nothing to do but cater to two men's needs as they walked softly over the stone floor and wound their way between the heavy rosewood furniture.

The waitress was a pretty girl from the mainland, traditional beauty: slight in figure, delicate, child-like, dressed in a chic coolie outfit. She spoke to them in Mandarin. CK kept his eyes on her as she waited to take their order. Mann ordered his usual – large Zubrowka vodka, ice, twist of lime. CK ordered a bourbon straight. The waitress didn't need to take a food order. The chef was ordered to prepare everything on the menu. They would never eat it all but in Hong Kong waste equalled wealth. Duck heads arrived for them to pick at. CK watched the waitress walk away before he turned back to Mann. Mann smiled. He was oddly amused by CK's lechery. It was the first time he had seen a weakness for the flesh in CK.

CK studied Mann. 'I am pleased that you re-considered your position and accepted my invitation, Inspector.'

'My father has left me no choice. There are some things that I will have to deal with. There are decisions that will have to be made whether I like it or not. I think there are some companies with which I can be involved and not harm my integrity.' As Mann said the words he had rehearsed in his head they sounded strangely true and he felt oddly calmer for having said them. Now he was really worried.

'I am glad that you have finally begun to see reason. There is no escaping one's destiny.'

CK paused and waited until the young waitress was out of earshot. He stopped picking at the duck eyes and replaced his chopsticks on their holder. 'I can help you. I will make you an offer that I believe will be perfect for us both. You get to keep your integrity, I get the rewards I feel I deserve. After all, I have been looking after a portion of your father's assets for years. This is a deal for your ears only.' CK paused.

They were interrupted by the owner of the restaurant who came over and whispered something in CK's ear. The waiter hastily laid another place beside CK. CK nodded his agreement and picked the napkin from his lap as he prepared to stand.

'We have a guest.'

Mann looked behind him to see a Chinese

woman walking towards them. She was taller than average, more athletic looking. She had curves. She was elegant, in her mid-thirties, perfectly groomed, sharp features, with her hair pinned high on her head, her fringe short, blunt. She was twinset and pearls, pencil skirt, box jacket, conservative. But then Mann took a look at her shoes, patent leather, black, five-inch heels. He heard the rustle beneath the skirt. Mann didn't need an introduction, he knew her. She was CK's daughter and the widow of his one-time best friend, Chan, now one more drifting set of bones in the South China Sea. She was CK's only legitimate child; his other was a younger daughter, borne by a concubine and still at school in England.

When Mann was tracking Chan he had made a study of Victoria. He knew what size dresses she wore, which perfume she liked, where she played tennis, which lunch venue she preferred when she was entertaining her friends. Mann also knew that Victoria Chan married beneath her. She was privately educated in England. She had gone to Oxford and studied English. This was a woman who had juggled Chinese and Western cultures, had tried to catch the balls and then realized she hadn't been passed any. This was the woman who had done what her father ordered, but along the way she had compromised herself. He stood as she approached. She looked from

CK to Mann, where her eyes stayed as she walked towards them.

Mann knew what she must be thinking: Let's get a good look at the man who killed my husband.

CHAPTER 19

Mann waited whilst Victoria was seated. She declined food but ordered tea. He looked across at her. She was difficult to read. Surely she could not want anything from Mann? They had every reason in the world to mistrust one another. Yet they had things in common. They were both educated in boarding school in England. They both had a Triad for a father. But Mann didn't intend to follow in his father's footsteps. She obviously did. He waited for her tea to be poured and for the waiter to step away from the table. Mann wondered what she was really like beneath the cool exterior.

'My daughter has a business proposal she wishes to put to you.'

Victoria studied Mann as if he were on the menu. After she seemed satisfied about which bit of him she would eat first, she gave a slight curl of her perfectly defined vampire-red mouth. When she spoke she had the merest hint of a lisp. The tiniest gap between her front teeth. 'Good evening, Inspector. I trust you have enjoyed the evening's events so far. Did you win?'

'No. My horse had a better offer right at the end.' Mann sat back, sipped his vodka and studied her in turn. 'Tell me, Victoria, what is it with you? I just don't get it. Well-educated, independent woman of the new order. You could be anything you want. Why choose the life of a Triad?' Mann's eyes flicked towards CK. He wouldn't interfere. He was studying them both as if he were the proud coach of two prize fighters indulging in pre-match banter.

'I am proud to be working for the Leung Corporation.' She smiled, her eyes lowered and she inclined her head in a deferential bow towards her father. CK inclined his head back to her. His eyes lit up with menace as he listened with pride to his daughter.

Mann put down his drink, leaned forwards and smiled at Victoria. The ice maiden had nerves of steel. Mann wondered how long it would be before CK had to watch his back; when the pupil became the master. 'You can use your money, pretty it up to make it look respectable but we all know where it comes from in the beginning. It never crosses your mind that it's made from selling children into brothels, killing teenagers with drugs. It never for one tiny second crosses that mind of yours to feel a sense of disgust at the way you make your money?'

'All money comes down to a dirty beginning. I merely accept it once it comes into my hands and I use it to the best of my ability. We have donated large sums of money to local children's projects in Hong Kong. We are happy to reinvest in Hong Kong's future.'

'Schools?'

'Yes, part of our investment is in schools.'

'You're happy to recruit from the kindergarten, you mean?' Victoria Chan went to answer. He didn't give her the chance. 'Which schools? Schools on the immigrant, no hope, wrong side of the track?'

'If you mean the disadvantaged, then, yes. We aim to provide a better level of education for those struggling in this present system. A voice for the ordinary man who won't get heard.'

'That sounds almost democratic. If I hadn't seen the result of your policies myself I might have gone part way to believing you. A young girl was murdered at one of your initiation ceremonies. I found her body dumped in a box and being eaten by rats. You didn't give her a voice, did you? You and your underprivileged school kids are murdering one another on Hong Kong's streets.'

Victoria Chan eyeballed Mann. She was as cool as a cucumber; he had to give her that.

'The young girl's death had nothing to do with me. As a goodwill gesture, as I believe the name of the Wo Shing Shing was somehow implicated, I intend to offer compensation to her family, when you establish her identity. Believe me, I was horrified. It is not my vision of the future, to take a young woman's life who had so much to offer Hong Kong.'

'Don't make me laugh. Admit it; you don't give a shit about girls like her, they're ten-a-penny, plenty more where she came from. You've created a monster that you don't have the experience or the knowledge to deal with, it's out of control.'

CK went to intervene. Victoria's flick of the eyes, the tiny lift of her perfectly manicured hand told him, *No, let me handle it.*

'You have no evidence against me, Inspector; otherwise you would have arrested me already. I sincerely hope that you get whoever killed that poor girl.' Victoria reached down and opened her brief-case and extracted a slim clear folder. 'I thought you might be interested in seeing how I intend to help people like that girl's family and many more. Since my father asked me to take over his business concerns, I have found many things. It seems that your family and mine are linked.'

She smiled politely but remained as cold as steel. Mann looked across at CK. He was enjoying every minute of it.

'It seems our allegiance goes back even before my father took over the running of the company.' She pulled out a paper from the file and handed it over to Mann using two hands and with a small bow of the head. It was quaint how they still managed to keep to Chinese etiquette whilst selling souls.

Mann picked it up and glanced at it. It was a photocopy of a handwritten document of the kind rarely seen nowadays. He recognized his father's signature at the bottom. He recognized the wax seal, red stamp of his father's Triad organization, the Golden Orchid. Mann had seen it many times in the last few months. His lounge floor was covered in papers with the same seal. But he hadn't seen this one. He placed it back on the table and pushed it across to Victoria.

'Let me summarize it for you.' She was unperturbed, perfectly controlled. 'It's a copy of a document that I believe you hold. It is an old legal document that states that your father and the Leung Corporation were two of the original owners of the Mansions and together we hold the majority share. As you are aware, there have been many moves in the past to knock down the Mansions and build a luxury development. It is the best site in Hong Kong for redevelopment, right on the peninsula, right in the heart of the business district.'

Mann shook his head in disbelief. 'You're mad.'

She cocked her head to one side and her eyes narrowed to a feline stare as her mouth froze into a mirthless smile. 'On the contrary, Inspector. For years no one knew who owned the majority share. That's why no development of it was possible. But I have the evidence here . . .' she glanced down at the old piece of paper, '. . . your father was the missing major shareholder.'

'It's full of immigrant workers and refugees with nowhere else to go. Where is your community spirit now? Don't you care?'

'Oh, I care, Inspector. It's a fire trap. It's only a

matter of time before it burns down.' Her eyes settled on Mann's face, they were shining in the candle light, their colour changing, churning up the riverbed, exposing the weeds. She picked up her tea and sipped it, hardly wetting her lips as she did so.

'Don't even think it.' The place fell silent with the atmosphere. The waiters slunk away to the other side of the restaurant.

'You misunderstand me, Inspector.' She smiled demurely, her red lips curling at their edges into a smile. 'I am only stating the obvious. I am not insinuating that it is in my control. What I propose is that we turn it into the luxury development it was always meant to be but maintain some guest-houses, a restaurant or two.'

'Keep a flavour, you mean?'

'Exactly.'

'And exactly how stupid do you think I am? Got any other propositions? That one stinks.' He pushed the paper back across the table. He looked at her. She had a smirk on her mouth that said she had picked the ace from the pack and her magic trick had hit its mark. It had shocked one, thrilled the other. Mann's heart began to slow; the blood in his veins started to freeze. He felt the anger rise inside him. Mann sat back in his chair and looked hard at Victoria. All those years married to Chan must have been her incubation period. Now she had hatched into a black widow spider and Mann was on the menu.

Victoria Chan didn't flinch. She had learnt to suppress her emotions. Outwardly serene, but like a beautiful snake with exquisite markings, she lured and then waited to strike. She picked up the deed and closed the file shut, then she looked across at her father and bowed. 'Excuse me, Father, I have many things to attend to.'

CK inclined his head slowly in a gesture of compliance.

'It was nice to finally meet you, Inspector. Thank you for sparing me your precious time.' She stood and bowed ceremoniously: low and slow. 'Don't discount future dealings between us. Some things have a habit of forcing themselves on you whether you like it or not. Now that you know about your father's businesses, they can no longer stay hidden. Think about it and let me know.' She handed him a business card two handed, she bowed, looked up at him from beneath her perfectly arched eyebrow. Her eyes emerald, her mouth smiling.

He took the card from her and studied it. It was elegant, embossed, sharp edged, a lot like her. He turned it over in his hands; it was written in five other languages. Maybe Tammy was right – she did intend to conquer the world.

'We are not allies, Victoria. If you have taken over from your husband then you and I will be enemies, make no mistake. I don't care how much stuff you dig up about my father's sordid dealings; I don't care if it ends up we are twins, you will never make a friend of me.' A knowing smile crept across her beautiful mouth. Victoria's eyes flicked towards her father then flicked back to Mann. CK was enjoying the spectacle. He was intrigued to watch it. Mann was beginning to feel caught in a web with two predatory spiders.

'I can wait.' Victoria kept her eyes fixed on Mann's. 'I have only *begun* to look into the ways our paths cross and I am making it my business to find out all about your father: his partners, his investments, his legacy, *your* legacy. Whether you like it or not our paths have joined, and . . .' she inclined her head in a respectful bow, '. . . I believe we have a bright future together. It's just that you don't see the light yet, but you will.'

CHAPTER 20

It was late by the time Mann got back to the office. Shrimp and Ng were out. That left just him, a massive file mountain that he was too wired to tackle and a few sickly looking spider plants on his windowsill. He sat at his desk and closed his eyes for a few seconds. The evening had given him a lot to think about. His personal life seemed to be meeting his professional one head on.

'Mann?'

A hint of rose banged on the bridge of his nose like smelling salts. Mann didn't need to turn around to know who it was. 'Hello, Boss.' He swivelled his chair around to face her; his head still resting on the backrest. Mia Chou stood in the doorway.

'How did it go?'

'Interesting. I met Victoria Chan.'

Mia raised an eyebrow. 'What was she like?'

'Ruthless, serpent-like, ice cold like her father, just like he was in the old days, greedy for power and wealth. She has taken over Chan's job of advisor – Paper Fan.'

'CK seems on board?'

'Yes. I'd say he's grooming her to take over one day. But this is her proving time. She has to get this right.'

'Why is she interfering with recruitment?'

'He's letting her make decisions on all levels. He is letting her prove herself. She doesn't have to work her way up the ranks. She's jumping straight in at the deep end.'

'It's a brave choice for both of them. CK must have a lot of faith in his daughter,' said Mia.

'Or maybe he's setting her up to fail?' said Mann. 'Either way, we'll see, but she's not to be under-estimated. It feels to me like she has waited, bided her time and now she is ready to strike. She has been using her time wisely over the years with Chan. I get the feeling she knows a lot about what her late husband was really up to, more than you'd expect a trophy wife to. I think she made it her business to know, and she's been playing a game. She's not even making pretence at playing the grieving widow – she's reborn.'

'All those years she's been planning this?'

'I think so. But there is something about her – she has many faces. She can be many things. She played the dutiful wife, she plays the dutiful daughter. I think she was just waiting for her time to come and now it has. Marriage to Chan must have been a living hell. He was a lowlife. I did her a favour when I made him swim for the shore.'

'You left him in the middle of the ocean knowing

109

he couldn't swim and had a phobia about the water, that's not quite the same.'

'I don't feel bad. The sharks would have finished him before he drowned. That was nothing to the agony and suffering he caused to countless others . . .' Mann's voice trailed off. Helen's face came into his head. But it wasn't the face he wanted to remember, it was the face of her dying, stretched plastic across it. He shook his head. 'I did the world a favour. She wouldn't disagree. I liberated her. But perhaps I swapped one enemy for a worse one. She has already done a good job of setting me up. It's going to get really tough convincing anyone I'm in it for the right reasons soon, Mia. I'm not sure I'm ready to offer myself as the sacrificial lamb to the slaughter. I am not sure there'll be enough of me left to go round.'

Mann smiled at Mia. He opened a drawer and pulled out a bottle of vodka. 'For emergencies.' He got out two glasses. 'It's been too long since we had a drink together.'

'Yeah, just make it a small one.' Mann poured her his idea of a small one and handed it to her. 'Jesus. I'm glad I didn't ask for a big one. Mann, how much of this stuff are you getting through?'

'Not enough. Work keeps getting in the way.' He grinned at her. She didn't smile back. When she frowned her forehead had one long crease in it, it made her look like a confused child.

'Don't ever get Botox for that.'

'What?'

'That frown that goes right across your forehead. It makes me smile every time I see it. It reminds me of the night you got drunk when we graduated from police academy. Do you remember that night?'

They'd been young together. They'd had fun once. They had seen one another go through a lot of things and come out alone. Now nearly eighteen years later neither had found themselves a family. Mia had been mixed up with one married man after the other. The worst was Daniel Lu, another policeman, the head of Crime Scene Investigations. He had been her biggest weakness and it had been a bad one. She had wasted twelve years on him before he called it a day and went back to his wife. With Helen, Mann had probably come as near to finding love as he was ever going to and lost it. But he didn't think he was ever capable of loving totally. He had given Helen all he could of himself but it hadn't been enough. She had wanted more. She had called his bluff and left. The taxi that picked her up had taken her to her death. All the time Mann had just thought that she had left she was actually being tortured. She was waiting for him to come after her. Now both of them felt their time had passed. Mann could see it in Mia and the world could see it in Mann.

'Bits of it.' Mia hid her face in her hands and chuckled. 'Other bits are very hazy. I had a rough idea what happened when I woke up with "I love cock" across my forehead.'

Mann laughed. 'You passed out on me.'

'I'm not surprised. We used to drink a lot in those days. I don't have any regrets. It was a great time. You were going to be the best police diver that ever was and stamp out all Triads along the way and I was going to be commissioner by the time I was thirty.'

'Yeah. We were young.'

'Christ, we're not exactly old now.' Mia tried not to frown.

'I know but I feel it sometimes. I feel like I have seen too much to have any hope left.' Mann drank his vodka and poured another.

Mia pushed her drink aside. Sometimes it made her melancholy. 'Yeah, maybe we should have stayed in that bed. I should have certainly never taken up with Daniel, that's for sure. Daniel made me think he was offering babies and eternity rings. When I got pregnant I found out he wasn't free to give them, not to me anyway. I lost it. Now I can't have kids.'

'I'm sorry, Mia. I never knew.'

'Yeah, I had complications. I had a premature baby – it didn't survive. Daniel said he was sorry but our relationship wasn't the same after. I think he was relieved.' She smiled at Mann. 'At least I had the sense to know all you wanted was a good laugh and a shag and a relationship wasn't on offer. You were always honest about it and you were a good friend to me, always have been. You mean a lot to me, Johnny. I hope you know that.' She reached over and touched his hand.

'You know, Mia, I never saw you as the senti-mental type,' Mann said, surprised. It had been a long time since they had been off duty together. 'But, you know, maybe it's not too late for us . . . we can go back to that single bed in my room in the academy halls. I can see it now . . .'

Mia laughed. 'Yeah, so can I. You'd love that, wouldn't you? Your woman on tap and she's your boss; you'd have me bent over every desk in the department. But . . .' Mia finished her drink and shook her head, '. . . in the end you'd do a better job of breaking my heart than Daniel ever did.'

'Forget men like Daniel and Sheng. You always pick the wrong ones - you attract them. You carry your emotional baggage with you like a third arm. It's visible everywhere you go, Mia – get rid of it, cut it off, move on. He wasn't worthy of you then and he isn't now. You settled for less than you should have. You let your guard down too early. You got caught. You need to find someone outside the force. You shouldn't bother with men like Sheng.'

'Sheng isn't that bad. He is going through a bad time at home. His daughter has got in trouble. He's a good father. But, anyway, I don't know why I'm listening to you. Your track record isn't any better than mine.' As soon as Mia said it she regretted it. 'I'm sorry, Johnny. I didn't mean it to come out like that.'

'No, you're right, Mia. My track record stinks. I treated Helen badly. I couldn't commit to her.

Something about the grass is greener. But you know what they say about greener grass, don't you, Mia?'

'Yeah. It still gets weeds and it still needs mowing.'

CHAPTER 21

The next morning Mann, Tom Sheng and Mia met at the far end of the incident room. In the background an Urdu translator could be heard on the phone. He had been brought in to phone the Indian groups and see if anyone could identify the dead girl.

'We are pretty sure she came from the Mansions,' said Mann.

'Then we flood the place with uniformed officers asking questions—' Sheng said.

'No,' interrupted Mann. 'The Mansions are a volatile, unpredictable place. There are an awful lot of people who will run when they see uniforms coming in. They will think it's immigration. Even if they have nothing to fear they will panic.'

'Christ, we have created another walled city,' muttered Sheng, 'and right in the middle of the business district. The sooner it's knocked down the better.'

Mann shook his head. 'You're wrong. It serves a good purpose. It's the cheapest place to stay in Hong Kong. One hundred and twenty nationalities live there at any one time. Where are they going to go?'

'They're mainly made up of illegal immigrants, overstayers and drug pedlars, every type of scammer and Triad. Fights are commonplace. Deaths are a daily occurrence. Now we have young Triads taking over in there.'

'You go in there like some fucking stormtrooper and they'll split, reform and make an even bigger problem somewhere else. It's not only them in the Mansions. We also have the impoverished back-packers, poor migrant workers. Four thousand people live there amongst the sweatshops and saunas.'

'I agree with Mann.' Mia looked tired. They were all fractious. 'Mann and Shrimp can achieve a lot more by being discreet in there. We want to try and find out why she was killed as well as who she was.'

'I'll get down there as soon as this meeting's over with,' said Mann. 'I have other business in there. One of the schoolgirls active in the recruit-ment is a girl named Lilly Mendoza. Her mother Michelle is a singer.'

'Have you had trouble with her before?' asked Mia.

'Now and again. Sometimes she had to double as a hooker just to make ends meet and feed her habit. I've ticked her off a few times. She used to have a bad habit of fleecing the johns she went upstairs with after her set. We haven't had any complaints for a while. Either she's stopped or found a new angle. When I'm in the Mansions I'll pay them a visit.'

116

'What about Victoria Chan?' Sheng was watching Mann very closely. 'You met with her?'

'Yes.' Mann put down his coffee cup and looked hard at Sheng. 'She wants to redevelop the Mansions. She says she wants to make it a community project. I think we can be pretty sure she is lying and intends to make a luxury development out of it. She hopes that if her new group, the Outcasts, cause enough trouble then the Mansions will have to be pulled down.'

'Why does she have to go to those lengths, why doesn't she just do it?'

'Because the Leung Corporation doesn't own the majority share. I have inherited the majority share of the Mansions.'

A silence spread through the incident room.

Sheng shook his head and grinned. 'This is all a very convenient home from home for you, isn't it, Mann? Doesn't it feel more than a little fucking ironic that we devote our lives to hunting down and eliminating Triads when we have one on our own doorstep?'

Mann looked at Sheng and then at Mia. She was willing him not to rise to the bait.

'The thing is, your father wasn't just a Triad; he was a damn good one. He made a lot of money selling heroin to the kids of Europe. I wonder how many lost lives he was personally responsible for taking. A lot more than we have ever saved, that's for sure.' Sheng looked at Mia. 'How can someone whose inheritance includes large chunks of

Triad dough, be considered a secure officer in the OCTB? We don't know where his loyalties lie. Do you trust him to watch your back? Because I fucking don't.'

Mann thought about it. 'You're right, Sheng. You are *so* right.' Mann stood; Sheng got to his feet. 'I am never going to watch your back. I don't give a shit who sticks a knife into it. And . . .' He picked Sheng up by his jacket lapels. '. . . If I do ever cross the line, Sheng, believe me I'm coming for you first.'

CHAPTER 22

'Tailor, sirs? Copy watches? Copy bags?' It was the middle of the day and the Indian touts were out in force. They swarmed around the pink-skinned tourists like flies on fresh meat.

The Mansions were at the harbour end of Nathan Road. Nathan Road was the place to get anything made or copied. It was nicknamed the Golden Mile: it glittered, it sparkled, even when it was real it looked fake. It was a great snapshot of Hong Kong. Twenty-foot-high neon signs flashed their adverts. Girls with thigh-high socks and mini skirts chased one another across the linear images. Music videos blared down next to ginseng sellers and noodle bars. The middle of the buildings bulged like saggy pot bellies over the road, weighted with fifty competing neon signs. The back streets were impassable by car.

Shrimp was waiting for him. Mann hadn't any trouble spotting him – he had slicked his hair back *Saturday Night Fever*-style and was wearing a vintage black suit, purple shiny shirt, thin black tie.

'Hello, Boss.'

Mann held him back as he went to walk up the steps. 'Did you dress especially for this?'

'Huh?'

'Never mind.' Mann smiled to himself.

Shrimp shook his head and followed Mann up the steps to the Mansions.

Within a few paces they were engulfed by the din and chaos of another world. They wound their way through making slow progress amongst the money changers and the touts for guesthouses. The place was like every type of bazaar or busy market, a snapshot of Africa, India, Asia. Together they set up their food stalls side by side blaring out their brand of music. The Mansions belonged to no country. It was its own world under the canopy of fluorescent lighting and overhead pipes. It had corridors like narrow hospital wards. By day the ground floor was crammed with shoppers and stalls selling goods from around the world, food stalls that offered goat and Halal food, all castes, all colours catered for and fed. But there was a tense, precarious harmony.

Mann steered Shrimp through and towards the second set of lifts on the left. 'We'll start on the third floor. I have a friend who might be able to help us narrow down the search.'

The lift coming back down was taking its time. They stared at the TV screen above the lift doors. The lift was stopping frequently; people were getting in but then getting out again and sending it on its way. Mann called the security guard over and pointed at the screen. The guard nodded, stepped forward and waited for the lift to arrive.

'Out of the way, move.' The security guard pushed the queue back.

The lift stopped; the door opened. A young black woman was unconscious in the corner. The guard stopped people getting in whilst he held the door open for Mann and Shrimp. They knelt beside her. Mann pressed his fore and index finger to the side of her neck.

'She has a pulse, just.'

Shrimp felt inside his jacket pocket and pulled out a slim plastic pouch. He unclipped the top and opened it out. It had two syringes inside. He tore the plastic off one, pulled off its protective needle cover and pulled up her sleeve.

The queue started grumbling. There were now so many people waiting that single file had become treble. The security guard held his hand up for patience. In this city time meant money, whether you were dying or not. Shrimp injected into the muscle in her upper arm, her bicep. A few minutes later the colour began coming back to her face. She breathed deeply. She opened her eyes and looked at them. She knew instantly what had happened. She tried to stand.

'You want to wait for an ambulance?' Mann helped her up.

She shook her head. She staggered forward, leant on the side of the lift wall for just a few seconds and then lurched off towards the mall and was swallowed up by a thousand anonymous people.

'What did you give her, an opiate blocker?' asked Mann. They were joined in the lift by twenty others. Mann didn't bother whispering; out of the nationalities in the lift probably just he and Shrimp spoke Cantonese. With them were three Africans, four Indians and some giggling Filipinas.

'Yes. Naloxone. I got it when I was in the States. The other is epinephrine – adrenalin. If they're still breathing you use one. If not, the other.'

They were crammed inside the lift with Africans, Indians and giggling Filipinas. Mann turned to see Shrimp staring at the Africans. They spoke English to one another because they came from different parts of Africa. They were stereotypical in their appearance, striking in their presence; they had ebony skin and bald heads and big muscular bodies. They brought a menacing presence to the area; they were mistrusted because of their colour, their size. Shrimp was still staring at them. Mann smiled to himself as he caught Shrimp looking at their feet. The Africans stopped talking. One of them followed Shrimp's gaze to his feet and then waited till Shrimp's eyes came back up to meet his.

Shrimp grinned, embarrassed. 'Cool trainers.'

The African laughed, deep, guttural, but his eyes showed a menace, a mistrust.

The lift stopped at level three. A strip light flickered above their heads. A cockroach scuttled across the floor. The muted noise of the dishes clanging came from the direction of a kitchen to their right. The Indians got out and disappeared that way. The Africans and giggling Filipinas stayed put. Mann and Shrimp got out with the Indians. The smell of curry greeted them. The landing had three doors. Two were unmarked; the third had a glass panel and above it was a sign: *The Delhi Grill* golden on a red background.

'Have you eaten here before, Boss?' asked Shrimp.

'Many times. I'm half British remember; we don't go a week without a curry. But I haven't been here for a couple of years . . .' Mann didn't finish that sentence. It should have ended: '. . . since Helen died.'

The restaurant door opened and a tall, robust-looking Indian with a turban on his head and a handlebar moustache stood waiting to greet customers as they alighted from the lift.

'Hello PJ.' The two men had known one another for seventeen years since Mann joined the police force and PJ took over the restaurant on the third floor of the Mansions.

PJ came forward to shake Mann's hand. 'Welcome back, Inspector. It's good to see you again.'

'This is Detective Li,' Mann introduced Shrimp.

'Pleased to meet you. Please come inside. Try our speciality of the house – seafood tandoori – freshly made.'

He opened the door onto a chaotic scene. The

small space, once intended to be an apartment, was now converted and filled with long, bench-style tables crammed with diners.

Mann held up his hand to thank him. 'We don't have time to eat unfortunately, PJ.'

They looked around sharply as the restaurant door opened and a lad, who Mann recognized as PJ's son, appeared. 'Go back to work. Go back to work, lad, there's no trouble here,' PJ addressed him affectionately.

'This is one of your sons, isn't it? Mahmud? He has grown up. Last time I saw him he was a boy.'

PJ summoned him forward. Mann shook his hand. The lad had not inherited his father's stature; he was slight like his mother had been. His face had an intensity: large brown eyes, eyebrows that met in the middle, a serious face but handsome in a way.

PJ nodded and beamed with pride. 'Yes. I have high hopes for Mahmud.' Mahmud looked embarrassed, shy, bright. 'He will be a doctor some day, an accountant maybe. Who knows? He is such a clever lad. Now go, my son, back to work; otherwise we will have no money to pay for university.' He laughed, happy and proud, as he ushered Mahmud back into the busy restaurant.

'I hear you've had some trouble here, PJ,' Mann said. 'A young girl was murdered the night before last at a Triad initiation ceremony. She was Indian, possibly from the Mansions. We think her father is a tailor here. Have you heard anything?'

PJ looked nervous as he stepped out into the corridor and allowed the restaurant door to close behind him. The din died down and they were left with the heat and silence of the corridor. He wiped his face with his apron. He shook his head and gave a small nervous laugh as his eyes swept the vicinity. 'It is better if you mind your own business in the Mansions.' He leaned towards Mann and kept the smile on his face but he looked nervous. 'It will fetch worse problems down on my head if I don't. We have problems with the Dalits – the untouchables. We are not used to so many coming into Hong Kong. Now with them crossing over from India to China every day, hundreds more arrive and the Mansions is where they come. They bring with them conflict and it's not just them, now we have the Africans too. I worry about the way things are here. The Mansions have become a place of fear. The Triads are taking our children from us. The new Indians are causing trouble. The Africans are killing one another and raping our women and no one is stopping them. They are time bombs waiting to go off. They are attracting unwelcome elements into the Mansions. Some people are using it to their advantage. I am afraid for our future here. There's talk about us leaving – being forced out.'

'Who is saying it?'

PJ shook his head and glanced nervously back into the restaurant. The youngest of his sons, Hafiz, walked past in view of the door. He was dark eyed, pale faced; he had the look of Asian skin that never sees the sun. He had the look of a user.

'There have been names mentioned. I do not want to repeat them. It will only go badly for me but I want you to know, Inspector . . .' he stared hard at Mann, '. . . that I will pay whatever it takes to stay here. I am sorry for the family of the young woman. If I can help I will.'

Shrimp stepped forward. 'Mind if I take a look inside? I have never eaten in here. It's got a great reputation.'

'Please . . . please. Take a look.' PJ opened the door wide for Shrimp to see inside. Hafiz turned and looked at Shrimp before he quickly disappeared to the kitchen.

'Such a fab place. Love the décor. I'll definitely be back.'

PJ bowed his head. 'Thank you. You will get a good discount.'

As PJ disappeared back into the furore of the Delhi Grill, Mann caught a glimpse of Mahmud waiting for news from his father. He watched PJ shake his head, touch his shoulder affectionately and the boy glance Mann's way. PJ pushed past Hafiz and dismissed him with a wave of the hand.

Mann and Shrimp waited for the lift down. 'We need to keep pressure on. PJ's is the best restaurant in the Mansions. If a deal has been made it will be with him.' The lift didn't look like coming. 'Let's take the stairs,' said Mann. 'See if we can

126

help in the search for the girl's family. The tailors are all on the first floor.'

The echo of voices filtered up from the floor below, the sound of an Indian woman singing and sitar music. They overtook a young woman on the stairs; she had stopped to check her phone for messages.

It was Ruby.

CHAPTER 23

Ruby knew they weren't Africans as soon as she heard their footsteps on the stairs; they weren't wearing trainers. She turned and looked at their feet as they approached. Expensive shoes. Ruby knew then that they didn't belong in the Mansions. They were strangers. She kept her eyes down until they had passed. She was wearing a curly brunette wig and the same simple big-belted black mac that could be bought in any shop in Hong Kong: fashionable, chic but nondescript. In her oversized handbag she carried another wig and a change of shoes. They were the two things that would transform her. Also in the bag was the tool kit hidden inside the rolled cloth bundle.

As the two men turned to go down the next flight of stairs she glanced over the railings. She recognized Mann but not the other officer. She smiled to herself when she looked at Shrimp in his suit – there was something about a man in a suit. Ruby hung back until she could no longer hear their leather soles on the concrete stairwell. She knew once they got to the first floor they would be swallowed by the sari sellers, the samosa stalls and thousands of people and they would never notice her following them.

She walked past the lift and took the stairs. She didn't go in the lift on her own. Even though now they had cameras; cameras could be hidden, covered, cameras could have their recordings wiped if you paid the right person. It was all about knowing what someone wanted in exchange. Some people wanted sex. Some people wanted money but they all wanted something.

She kept her head down as she slipped quickly past the Africans who hung about the stairwells and doorways. They sat on the steps and watched the world. They sat in groups and talked of home. They walked up to the mosque and talked of Allah. But they were warm-blooded men. They watched the women walk by. They watched Ruby.

Ruby came out onto the first floor. The place was chaotic. She looked around for Mann and the other officer. She eased her way through the crowds of people noisily negotiating the prices of a new shipment of clothes just arrived from the mainland. She headed towards the end where the tailors had their shops. There the touts took over. Fluorescent lights flickered above the heads as they assaulted unwary people with fake Louis Vuitton bags or copy Rolexes, promises of made to measure everything. They didn't bother Ruby. She had her eyes on Mann and the one in a suit. She watched them making their way down the corridor asking about anyone who knew a young Indian girl who hadn't been seen for forty-eight hours. In Mann's hand he held a piece of the sari he had picked up next to the box with the girl's body in it.

'Getting warmer,' Ruby said to herself as she watched them working their way. 'Getting *very* warm . . . Boiling!' she said after half an hour when they had stopped outside a tailors shop. Ruby stopped opposite, out of view, she was tucked behind the shelves in a small Indian supermarket. She smiled to herself, her heart beating fast. Her hands sweating as she pretended to browse through the DVDs. They were all porn. The old Indian who owned the supermarket stared at her, his eyes feasting. Ruby let him. She didn't know him and he didn't know her but they might one day have something each other wanted.

Ruby watched the Indian man sitting on the floor and sewing leather belts. It was Rajini's father. Mann would be coming to him any minute. Rajini's father looked up at Ruby and his eyes momentarily questioned. He wondered what she wanted and then Mann blocked her view of him. Ruby was watching Mann's back. She wanted to hear the words being spoken but she couldn't. She wanted to hear Mann ask him if he had a daughter, if she was missing. All Ruby heard were the gasps of panic in the belt maker's voice. Ruby was content. She had done her job and a little more. She had been promoted to a *Red Pole* in the Triad ranks; the rank of an officer. She had shown her strength and proved she was worthy. It would be some time before any of the girls would show disrespect to her again. Rajini had been nothing to her, she meant nothing. Only the chosen could make it up the ladder. Ruby was one of the chosen. Rajini wasn't, it was simple.

Ruby moved on further down the corridor and waited there, out of sight. She watched Mann call on his radio. A female officer came, they left. Ruby followed them as they made their way down the stairs to the ground floor and back out through the crowds. She stopped short of the entrance and engaged a money changer in some conversation. She watched them talking on the steps and then saw them go their separate ways. The sun had set outside. But Ruby's day was just beginning. She walked past Shrimp as he stood on the steps and she followed Mann.

CHAPTER 24

As soon as he was sure the policemen had gone, PJ pulled Hafiz into a quiet corner of the restaurant.

'You bring nothing but trouble on our heads. What is it the detective knows that you're not telling me? Why was he here talking about a young woman's death? Who was it?'

'I don't know, Dad.' He pulled his arm back from PJ's grip. 'It has nothing to do with me.'

'I've seen you hanging out with those kids. They're a bad bunch. You're just like them. You don't care about working hard and making it, you only care about designer shoes and phones and you aren't prepared to work for them. Nothing comes for free, my lad. If you have signed up to some Triad society the price will be big. These Mansions will be running with blood soon: Indian against Indian, child against child. You have no idea about what you're involved in. If you had something to do with that poor girl getting killed I'll have nothing more to do with you.'

Hafiz looked at his father, stony faced. 'You're always blaming me. It's not always my fault, you know.' He took off the serving napkin from over his arm and threw it down. 'You know what? I'm not interested any more. I'm sick of working here for nothing. I don't want this to be my life. I want more. I hope the Triads do take over. I hope this place does burn down.'

PJ went to strike him. His eldest son Ali appeared beside them and stepped between his father and Hafiz. 'Don't, Dad. I'll see to it.'

PJ shook his head sadly. 'I am glad your mother cannot listen to you talk. She would have put a stop to it better than me. She would have seen it coming the way she saw everything coming.' PJ wiped his face with his serving cloth and looked close to tears. 'If she were alive, she'd have put a stop to it all.'

From the kitchen a bell sounded for the third time. A meal was waiting to be taken out. Mahmud hurried past the door, laden with plates. 'Thank goodness for the fact I have one son who believes in working hard.'

'I'm going out,' Hafiz said and he threw down his serving cloth as he left.

Ali looked at his father accusingly. 'You should go easy on him. These days are difficult for Hafiz. He's always chasing Mahmud's tail.'

'Yes and he's never going to catch it or add up to him.'

'We are all different, Dad, you should remember that. Nobody's perfect, not even Mahmud.'

'I know. I'm sorry but I'm worried for our future.

You find out who that young girl who died was and if Hafiz had anything to do with it. You do the right thing, Ali. I want her family compensated.'

'No, she's not our caste.'

PJ looked at him, shocked. 'You know the girl?'

'Only the rumours. The kids talk, I listen. Her father is a leather worker, her mother cleans toilets. She sews in a tailors on the first floor. We must keep our heads down. That's why it is important to get the right friends, Dad. We have to protect ourselves. Don't talk to Inspector Mann. Let me do it. Don't let Hafiz or Mahmud or anyone talk unless I am there. Victoria Chan warned us when she came to see us. She said things would start to go wrong here. Things would get so bad that they would push for the Mansions to be demolished. She told us to keep our heads down and we would be guaranteed a new restaurant after the refurb.'

'But how do we know she's telling the truth?'

'We don't. But we have no choice. She's been good to us this last year. She's proved herself to be a friend since Mother died. Say nothing, Dad. Do nothing to stop it.'

PJ looked at his son incredulously and he nodded, stern faced. It was that exact moment when the roles were reversed. When his son had grown old enough, wise enough, strong enough and knew more than his father.

CHAPTER 25

Mann and Shrimp stood talking on the steps of the Mansions.

'Shrimp, take the girl's parents to see her body and then come back here for me. Start asking some questions; loosen up some tongues. PJ was obviously nervous. We know Victoria Chan is stirring things up in there. Let's try and tweak a few consciences and see if anyone wants to share some information about the Outcasts. Someone must know something.'

'Yes, Boss.'

'I'm meeting Tammy. I'll see you back at the station.'

Mann passed the old Indian prostitute leaning against the railings on the corner of Mody Road, her foot up on the fire hydrant, folds of yellow chiffon tucked as trousers between her legs. When it came to sex, Hong Kong had something to cater for everyone's taste. She'd been there for as long as Mann could remember. She played with the end of her thick black hair, woven into one plait that she wore on the side, gold bangles up her arms and rings through her earlobes. She shimmered in the sharp evening light after the deluge of rain.

He headed down into the subway to get away from the heat; the approaching storm had sent temperatures through the roof and humidity to 90 per cent. He walked in the cool of the long, straight, airy tunnels that took the echo of his shoes and bounced it around the clean walls, took voices and amplified them. The subway was an artery carrying the workers to all the vital organs of Hong Kong. It made him feel like running along the endless tunnels: white, stark, cooling on his head, tolerable on his tired eyes. But something jarred on his ears; from behind him came the click of a woman's heels and the rustle of a mac. The heels grew louder. He turned to see a woman passing, her head down, her blond hair hanging down her back, thick, neat. She didn't walk like a tourist: she wasn't frantically looking at the exit signs in a panicked fashion. Mann watched her walk by. She had a good figure beneath her mac, small waist, long, slim calves. She walked quickly in her heels, black snakeskin with a matching handbag. It was a big bag, the new trend for women. Mann looked back to her hair. Nobody in Hong Kong had hair that colour; that amount of bleach would have destroyed it. If she wasn't a foreigner then it was a wig. She passed him and disappeared into the crowds.

Mann exited at the harbour and joined a thousand others standing around watching the light display. Every evening at eight o'clock the biggest laser show in the world kicked off. It involved forty-four buildings, cost forty-four million Hong Kong dollars to create and lasted fourteen minutes at a time. Especially composed symphonic music exploded in time to pyrotechnics and laser beams from the rooftops of buildings around the harbour.

As Mann rounded the corner the breeze felt cool, it dried the sweat on his brow, the shirt on his back. He needed that sea air. He needed to clear his tired head. Now the swirling light beams were dancing across the harbour to the clashing of cymbals. He took a right past the statue of Bruce Lee and saw Tammy sitting on a bench, away from the crowd. People were standing nearby, having their photo taken with Bruce Lee. Colour and light exploded into the stormy evening sky.

'Is everything all right, Tammy?' Mann sat next to her.

'Yes thanks, Boss. Good talk yesterday.'

'Yeah, right,' Mann sighed, looking away as he spoke. 'That Lilly is a real troublemaker.'

'I am getting very close to fixing up a date for my initiation, Boss.'

Mann rested his elbows on his knees as he listened; he stared at the ground and waited. Tammy was hesitating.

'You all right about that, Tammy?'

'But, Boss, there's something else.' Tammy hesitated. 'Lilly says it's common knowledge you're on the take.'

Mann went silent. Colours shot up the side of buildings, searchlights filled the night sky. 'Okay. I'll deal with it.'

'I asked if she'd seen the Indian girl die. She said she didn't actually see it, that she was outside when it happened. She said they were told that they were all guilty of it. That if one was to be named they would all be named.'

'It was all about binding them together then. The girl died to unite the others. It had to be graphic to convince the kids. Just saying it wasn't enough.

'You better try and stall the initiation, Tammy. We need to do more ground work. I've met Victoria Chan. She's got a lot at stake. She's going to be looking out for an informer. We need to make doubly sure before we go in. If I am being set up then we need to be one step ahead. Nothing is worth your life. These people won't hesitate to take it. We'll get the headmaster to say you're ill. We'll call it off temporarily until we are sure that you're safe.'

'All right, Boss.'

Mann watched her walk away, her head bowed, her skinny legs shuffling along in her sparkly cheap jeans and her new trainers. She was disappointed, he knew. To have put in so much work and come out with nothing.

He walked to the railings and gripped them as he stared out at the water. He thought about what Tammy had said. If the rumours were running rife about him being on the take it wasn't going to help to be seen in company with CK or his daughter. He was leaving himself exposed. There was only his word that his intentions were good. His word didn't seem to be counting for much at the moment. But it was too late to go back. He had been pushed across that line now and he had to use it or lose it. For a while he had to exist on the dark side.

Ahead of him was a party boat, bedecked with a string of coloured lights. The avenue of stars was still buzzing. The kids had been put to bed now, the couples were out. They perched on the railings like lines of seagulls in a seaside town. The girls sat on the top, the boys took their photos. *They look so young*, thought Mann. He didn't think he was ever that young. He knew you had to be young to really fall in love, unconditionally. You had to be full of compromise, still finding who you are, still trying to change into someone better. If Mann could turn back the clock he would have chosen a different route for Helen but not for himself. He couldn't give Helen what she wanted no matter how much she loved him. He had scar tissue over his heart that never healed; he wished that she'd never fallen in love with him. But the one thing he had promised himself was that he would keep hunting down the men who had met her along the road to death. He would never stop pursuing them. Mann had killed the one who finished her life but he had yet to find the others who tortured her, who did nothing to help her.

Now something nagged at him day and night. The memory of Helen had come back screaming at him. It wouldn't give him peace.

Mann headed away from the river and called Mia en route.

'Where is Tammy now?' Mia sounded tense.

'I have just told her to stall things, sit tight. I'm suspending Operation Schoolyard. She's at risk.'

There was a pause on the other end of the phone. He knew what Mia would be doing. He could hear her sigh. She would have closed her eyes. She would have frowned. She would be disappointed but she would respect his judgement.

'If you think so, Mann, then okay. But it means starting all over again, it took us so long to find Tammy and get her into the school.'

'I know. But this is uncharted territory. We've never put a female officer in this kind of risk before. I'd rather back out now. She's disappointed too.'

'Of course, she will be: big risks, big rewards. Talking of big rewards, on your way back come via the car park and look in your space. Your new car got delivered.'

'What new car?'

'Well, judging by the keys I have in my hand I would say it's a brand new Maserati in your space in the car park. Someone's given you an expensive present.'

Mann turned the corner to see the woman with the blond hair walking quickly away.

CHAPTER 26

Ruby left Mann at the Bruce Lee statue and texted as fast as she walked. She had done what she was asked to do. Her work was finished for the evening. She walked via the subway, through to Nathan Road and then back up the steps to the Mansions. The Africans were sat on the steps, watching. Ruby kept her head down as she passed them. She was sick of the way they sat around on the steps, talking, laughing. She was sick of the way their eyes followed her. They would regret it. They had had their day. The Outcasts would see to that. One by one they would be chased out of the Mansions or they would be picked off and slaughtered.

She passed Hafiz at the entrance to the Mansions. She hardly noticed him step in behind her but she knew he would be there. The Africans were watching him nervously too. Ruby felt Hafiz's hand brush her arm. She turned and looked at him and smiled. He stared hard at her and then grinned. She nodded. He pulled a whistle from his pocket and let out three small beeps and one long blast and repeated it three times. Ruby walked quickly away from him. She took the stairs up to her floor. She cocked her head, pausing to listen at each landing. She heard the whistles being answered. The Mansions were coming alive with the sound of running feet.

'He's on the next landing,' Hafiz shouted. This was Block C, floor twelve. Doors banged shut as the familiar whistles went up and down the landing. It was replica bag land, knock-off watches and fake designer goods, full of small factories, guesthouses, apartments.

'Corner him,' came a reply.

They chased their victim down the corridor. Their voices bounced off the concrete walls, their feet thundered and echoed up the piss-ridden stairwell and down the dark landings. The sickly hue of strip lighting threw their shadows up the graffiti on the walls.

'Don't let him get away,' a girl shouted back.

The African ran till his heart was bursting. He ran blindly, not able to stop and listen; he heard the cries from every direction. He knew they were coming for him. Their feet thundered, their voices ripped the walls apart. He saw them at the other side of the stairwell door. He had nowhere left to run. Beside him was the shaft that dropped all the way to the bottom of the Mansions. He went to climb in, it was dark, filthy. Cables and sewage pipes clung to its walls but there was nothing for him to hang on to. He turned to face them. They were kids, wild eyed, panting from their chase.

They held knives in their hands. He held his hands up for peace, surrender, compassion. One of them lunged forward and cut his forearm down to the bone. He cried out in pain as he withdrew his arm, cradled it, looked frantically around for an escape route. They closed in a circle around him. They were behind him now, all around.

'Come on kids . . . please. That's enough now. Let me go. I am sorry for whatever . . . please.' Blood poured from his wounds; it dripped onto the stone floor.

He didn't get to finish his sentence. They attacked him from all sides, slashing with a frenzy. Hafiz stamped on his dying body. The African's eyes popped from his skull and his teeth clattered on the concrete floor.

CHAPTER 27

Shrimp brought Rajini's parents back from the morgue and left them at the entrance to the Mansions. He went to the middle of the ground floor where there was a plan of the Mansions' layout. He took the stairs up to the next landing. The Africans stopped what they were doing to watch him pass. They followed him down corridors overcrowded with people, constantly moving. The smoke bit into his eyes. There was no ventilation in the narrow corridors. There was no natural light whatsoever. The wailing of an Indian woman singing was reaching a crescendo. There was not one part of China there.

He looked back to see if he was still being followed. Ahead of him the corridor had turned into a mini Lagos. The black men leant on walls, sat on the floor on rugs smoking. They filled the air with the boom of their deep voices. The air was thick, pungent with cigarette smoke and cooking. Shrimp was approaching the end of the corridor, now he was the only non-African on that side of the landing. He stopped, turned and started back down the way he'd come. Five of the men blocked his way. Shrimp recognized the man from the lift. He looked at his feet. He was the one with the cool trainers. Shrimp smiled. He grinned back. He was brutally handsome: his features were hardened by scars. His eyes had a light of some inner mischief. The others weren't smiling.

'Excuse me. Do you know where I can buy some trainers like that?'

'Come with us.'

Shrimp felt a large hand on his shoulder. He was steered inside one of the shops selling all sorts of goods: sweatshirts wrapped in cellophane hung down from every part of the ceiling, boxes of shoes were stacked to the roof. A crate was presented for Shrimp to sit on.

'Your name?'

'Li. My name is Li. They call me Shrimp. And yours?'

'David. You want trainers? Here.' David pulled down box after box and lifted the lids. He left them stacked beside Shrimp. He stood and watched Shrimp pretend to choose. Then he knelt down next to him, so close that Shrimp could make out every open pore, every scar on his face. 'I saw you with your friend in the lift. You helped the Kenyan girl, she's in trouble bad with smack. You a doctor?'

Shrimp shook his head.

'A policeman?'

Shrimp looked at the others. They stood around

the doorway. The corridor outside was full of dark faces watching him, not speaking, not moving. Gone was the laughter; they were listening intently. Shrimp kept his eyes glued on David. He reckoned anything that would happen would happen with him. The rest would take orders. If Shrimp was aiming to get out alive he had to be very fast on his feet. He had the advantage of being slight, slippery as well as athletic, but when he looked at the size of David's bicep, snagged on the t-shirt, he was having doubts about his chances. He nodded.

'So, what you doing here?' asked David.

'We had some reports of trouble. I wanted to take a look for myself.'

David wiped the sweat from his upper lip. Shrimp had never smelt the smell of stale sweat so pungent as it was in the small room. 'We are used to the heat,' said David, as if reading Shrimp's mind, 'but we are not used to the humidity. You guys don't sweat much, do you?'

'I'm sweating now,' Shrimp smiled.

CHAPTER 28

Mann looked at the card Victoria Chan had given him. The address was a building he knew on Peking Road, just a stone's throw from the Leung Corporation. He looked at his watch. It was close to ten. He knew where she'd be right now, where all the smart set went. She'd be in the Oceans bar having post-dinner drinks. On Peking Road, top floor. He stepped out of the lift and into the arms of the hostesses waiting to meet and greet at the entrance. This bar was uber chic, always a little too dark. He turned right and up the small flight of steps into the main bar. It had 360° views and floor-to-ceiling sloped windows that gave the impression the diner was floating in the Hong Kong sky.

The bar was crowded with Chinese entertaining clients and wealthy lonely locals looking for company. A round of drinks had a minimum charge which would have bought a dinner for a family of four elsewhere. But that was the very reason people came. Hong Kong was all about showing you could afford it and this was the bar of the moment. Mann got a seat at one of the tables that overlooked the eating area on the mezzanine below. He ordered his usual – vodka on the rocks. The pretty young waitress brought it along with a selection of nuts.

He'd taken his first sip when he spied Victoria Chan in the private booths to his left. He'd guessed right. There she was, tucked in the VIP area: private booths with sofa-type seating and endless skyline. He only just recognized her – no twinset and pearls today – a Roland Mouret Galaxy dress and a pair of killer heels. Her loose hair curled like a fifties film star. He knew it was her because she knew it was him. She was looking for him too.

Mann got the uneasy feeling he was on a film set and being directed and she knew he would show up when he did. She was sitting with CK's PA and what looked like five visiting businessmen: one Caucasian, two Asians, a Korean and a Japanese, obviously getting the special treatment and being taken out by the boss's daughter.

An interesting mix, thought Mann. She obviously had international aspirations and had her beautifully manicured fingers in lots of international pies, and she wasn't afraid of anything. A couple of Wo Shing Shing bodyguards sat with them. Mann recognized them from his visits to Leung Corporation: their bodyguards were as square as they were tall. The bodyguards zeroed in on Mann as he approached. They were on their feet before Mann had reached the table.

'Sorry to interrupt. Urgent message for Ms Chan,' Mann smiled at the businessmen. 'You'll have to excuse Ms Chan. I'll bring her back.' Mann eyeballed the bodyguard and smiled at Victoria. 'Just a quick word.'

Victoria waved the bodyguards back with a slight glance and bowed to her guests. 'Please excuse me, gentlemen. Order more drinks for our guests,' she hissed through a smile at the PA who looked flushed and flustered. She slid elegantly out from behind the table. 'Please try not to miss me too much . . . I have something that you are going to want to hear when I come back – something we have all been waiting for.'

The men nodded and smiled and made appreciative, reassured noises as they watched their host walk away with the tall stranger. The PA got to his feet and clicked his fingers at a passing waitress.

Mann walked Victoria towards the lift. Two hostesses in ornate cheongsams and a male waiter in a chic version of a coolie suit were meeting and greeting the guests as they arrived. Mann waved them away with a smile as he got into the lift and pressed the button to close the doors. He pushed for the ground floor thirty floors below and then opened the operations panel of the lift and pressed the emergency stop button. The lift slowed quickly and gave a small judder as it stopped.

'Kidnapping is an offence, Inspector,' she said, smiling. He could see that she was not in the least scared. She was not frightened of anything. 'But it is heart-warming that you had to go to such lengths to be alone with me. You could have just made an appointment like everyone else.' She stepped closer towards him. 'I like a man who takes what he wants and doesn't ask.'

Victoria smiled, her eyes a dark, sinister green pool of unsettling menace. She put her hands on her hips. The sleeveless dress showed her strong shoulders, the perfect line of her collarbones, her cinched-in waist. Nothing was left to chance. The look was calculated. The body was a tool for her, like everything else. It had to work for its affection. Mann thought how she would punish it into shape. She would hate to lose at tennis or anything else. She would demand results. Mann could understand part of that. He needed the gym to free his head. He needed his body to stay strong, agile, to be able to perform and to save his life. He didn't need it to look perfect. But she did. She was staring at him, a smug expression on her flawless face. She knew he was looking her over. She knew because it was what she had planned. Mann thought how different she was when her leash was taken off. This flirtatious display took him by surprise.

'Attempting to bribe a police officer is also an offence. Have the car removed or I'll have it scrapped.'

'I don't know what you're talking about.'

'I think you do. You might think you are being

clever, Victoria, but you fail to understand the thing that makes us so different and that will always separate us.'

'There is no difference that cannot be compromised. No deal that cannot be struck.'

'But I don't want anything. You cannot sell me something I don't want. If you have taken over the role of your husband then you will be my enemy, just as he was.'

'Do not tar me with the same brush as him. I hated my husband. He never added up to one good thing in all of his life.' A different light came into her eyes. It was a look that took her somewhere else for a few seconds, somewhere unpleasant. At least Mann knew she was honest in her hatred of her husband, honest about one thing at least.

'And you? What do you want to add up to? Don't think for one minute that I am taken in by your Little Miss Victim act. You have played your way into the top seat at the Wo Shing Shing. If I was your father, I'd watch my back.'

'My father has made mistakes. He has had his time. Together, you and I can turn the face of the Triads around. It can go back to serving the people, the way it once did. Together we can make a difference.'

'I don't need you in my life. Why would I?' She was inching towards him.

'I can create a need in you.' She breathed her perfumed breath into Mann's face and her eyes melted on his as she reached out and ran her hand up his shirt. 'A need so strong that you cannot ignore it. I know you are searching, I see it in you. You have needs. I recognize the same ones in myself. We are special, you and I; we will not find happiness easy to come by. We do not feel it the same way as others do. I can be everything you're looking for.'

The nearness of the lift was getting to him; Mann felt her creep forwards as she dug her heels into the floor, her hips brushed his, her head tilted to one side as she smiled provocatively. But her eyes betrayed her, they were focused inside herself not on anything else. Her body was a thing she gave easily. Her soul belonged to no man.

Mann wasn't playing; he looked down at her hand and lifted his eyes to look at her, dispassionate and cold. She withdrew her hand immediately and stepped back. The smile disappeared. The eyes narrowed.

'Or . . .' she held up her manicured index finger and made small circles in the air, '. . . I can pick up your world and the people in it and spin it around my finger till everything you care about is falling off it. I have the power.'

Mann took a step towards her and she stepped backwards until she was pressed against the lift wall. She didn't panic. She stared up into his eyes and seemed to expect, welcome, the anger. Mann watched as her eyes turned deep river green and she came so close to his face that he felt her breath on his face, tasted it, that adrenalin, that blood sugar.

Outside the noise of engineers clanking away at the mechanism to get it restarted echoed and then the lift started moving and Victoria pitched forwards. Mann held on to her, instinctively. He felt the curves beneath her dress. He pressed her to him. She looked up at him and closed her eyes. He leant forwards and stopped. He slid his hand up over her breast and caught her around the throat. Her eyes snapped open.

'Don't cross me, Victoria. You are a small girl playing with the big boys. Don't fuck with me. You will regret it. Every day I see my life slipping away. I am beyond fear. Beyond happiness. I just might take you with me.'

CHAPTER 29

'I mmigration police?' David asked.

Shrimp shook his head, slowly, cautiously, not sure what would be the best reply.

David reached out and slapped him on the shoulder. 'Good,' he said in a deep strong voice, still maintaining the grin but this time accompanied by a laugh. David turned and nodded to his friends at the door. 'He's okay. Bring him a drink.'

David turned back to Shrimp. 'You will have a drink with us, Shrimp?'

'Sure.'

David took the top off a bottle of Coke and handed it to him. Shrimp looked him over. The heat in the room was unbearable. The heady smell of the plastic clothes wrap was overpowering. Shrimp looked back to the corridor. More Africans were staring in at him. Shrimp drank his Coke.

David slapped him again and boomed laughter. 'I like you. Come.' He stood and picked Shrimp up by the arm. 'We will talk of the Mansions with you.'

He led Shrimp to the bar next door. They sat on stools in the small space, just two tables and

154

a dozen stools. David angled a tabletop fan onto them.

'I'll help you if you help me. What trouble are you here about? This place is nonstop trouble.'

'Have you heard of a new young group of Triads called the Outcasts?'

David nodded. He began rolling a cigarette; he licked the edge of the paper with his pink tongue.

'Of course. They are running wild in here. They take a block at a time. They were running this evening. Every night they pick on someone else. They pick on us a lot. That's why we stick together on this landing. They don't dare take us on together. Like little rats they watch all the time. They wait. They whistle up and down the corridors, calling to each other. It wasn't always this bad.' He shook his head sadly, looked down at his glass and then out at the corridor. Outside life had returned to normal. The sound of laughter and music returned. David's face clouded with thought, his eyes filled with a faraway sorrow. 'This place has been my home for six months. I came here looking for my brother. He's been missing for a year now. I ask everyone here. I show them this photo.' He took out a photo from his shirt pocket and slid it across the table to Shrimp. 'This is my younger brother, Ishmael.' It was a sunny photo of David with his arm around the younger man's shoulders, he was taller than David by a few inches. He was less bulky, his young face was full of laughter. He had a baseball cap on his head. On the right side of his face he had a scar that sliced his face from his ear to his mouth.

'Somewhere in the Mansions there is the answer to where Ishmael has gone. If I cannot find him alive, I will find his body and have something to take home to our mother. Ishmael was a peaceful man. He liked his women, but he didn't like to get into fights. I want to know what happened to him. Do you understand?'

'Yes. Can you get me a copy of this photo?'

'Yes. Take it. I have many.'

'Do you think it has anything to do with the kids in the Mansions?'

'Yes. I do. Someone here knows something. One of these kids knows what happened to him. Now I have watched them grow these last few months. They have lost their minds. They are out of control. They have become their own masters. They run around the roof like rats. They are always watching. They kill whoever they want to. They show no mercy. They care for no one or nothing. They are Satan's children. I will show you something.'

They stood and David led Shrimp through to the kitchen. The smell of rotting meat was intense. Sections of a skinned goat's carcass were hanging from the ceiling and crawling with flies. David led Shrimp into a room off the kitchen. In the corner a mattress had been laid out on the floor. A black man lay on it, on his side. His breathing noisy, his body very still. He had large wounds, pink in his dark flesh.

'What happened to him?'

'He was drunk. He laughed at them. They came after him with knives. The attacked him for no reason. They cut him to pieces.'

'He needs a hospital.'

'No. He is an overstayer, an illegal immigrant, and he is dying. He will be dead before dawn. It is better that you go.'

They left the dying man where he was and went back out to the corridor.

'Here's my card, David. You find out everything you can about who's controlling these kids, who's at the heart of it and I will do everything I can to find out what happened to your brother.'

Shrimp looked at the black men and he saw their faces. Each one homesick, sad and scared of dying.

David gave Shrimp his card in exchange and he held on to it with two hands and looked Shrimp in the eyes. 'We will meet again, Shrimp. Remember my face and I will remember yours.'

CHAPTER 30

Mann left Victoria in the Oceans bar and headed back to Nathan Road. He needed a drink. He walked through the lobby of Vacation Villas.

In an overcrowded town where there often wasn't room to walk on the pavements it was strange to feel lonely. Mann didn't recognize the concept of loneliness. He just didn't like going home. Home was where he had things to face. Out on Hong Kong's streets is where he belonged. He walked through the lobby and up the sweeping staircase into the large lounge area. It was all deep, cushioned sofas and leather armchairs, low wooden, glass-topped coffee tables. At the far end was a massive TV screen relaying the latest sport coverage from around the world. He said hello to the hovering waitresses in their unattractive cheongsams that looked like they had been made by the same tailor who made the sofa covers and curtains, and walked straight through to the bar: a twenty-foot rectangle. People sat around it like bored guests at a dinner party, trying not to make eye contact with one another.

As he walked in, Mann gave a discreet nod to one of the three Filipinas singing on a stage at the end of the room. They wore matching dresses and had the same hair extensions. But only one had a good voice – that was Michelle, the oldest on the far right. She clocked him and gave a nervous nod of the head back as she kept up her pretty good rendition of Dolly Parton's 'Nine to Five' whilst the other two, Cindy and Sandy, practised their synchronized hip movements. A Filipino named Trex banged out the tune on the drums and a Chinese named Tim played the keyboard. They worked right through the night every night, as long as the bar was open so were they. Michelle looked tired, thought Mann. Her face was rubbery, her features barely registering the changes of emotion from one line of the song to the next. Her eyes kept flicking back to him.

Mann made space at the bar, ordered a large vodka on the rocks and checked out his other inmates around the rectangle. They were the usual suspects – forty-somethings, lonely men staring into their drinks, flicking the odd peanut into their mouth. Next to him three men in their late forties were huddled around a young Chinese hooker in her early twenties. They were transformed from boardroom ball breakers into beaming schoolboys. What was it about Western men and Asian hookers? Unlike Asian men, who were the biggest users of prostitutes in their own countries, the foreign man liked to believe he was getting a girlfriend for his money. He took her on holiday, walked hand in hand along moonlit beaches.

Mann didn't have any moral high ground to even teeter on. He had paid for sex himself, but only the once. It had been as sexy as taking a crap. Mann liked to please his women. He liked to feel they were both in the same sexed-up space. For him any sex was definitely not better than no sex. He liked to take his time, it gave him pleasure. He didn't feel like it when there was a meter running. He looked across at Michelle, she was getting more nervous. She looked about to leg it. If Michelle was looking shifty, she had a reason.

He took his drink from the barman and was about to take his first sip when it was almost knocked out of his hands.

'I do apologize,' a man next to him spoke. He was English, in his mid-forties, with black curly hair, large light-grey eyes. 'Let me get you another.'

'No need.'

The barman handed Mann a napkin to wipe his arm.

'Please, I insist.' He signalled to the barman who replaced Mann's glass with a fresh one. 'Cheers.' He raised his glass. 'My name's Peter Thorne.'

Mann raised his. 'Johnny Mann. Thanks for the drink. You passing through?'

'Yes. Here for three nights then on to the mainland. What about you? You live here?'

Mann nodded. Two girls walked past and gave them the eye. He grinned at Mann. 'Temptation everywhere you look here. How does a married man cope with it?'

Mann shook his head. The alcohol had reached the spot, he began to feel mellow.

'I'm not married; I can get tempted all I like.'

'Clever man. Stay single. I try to be good but it's a lonely world on the road. I'm away from my family for eight months of the year altogether. I sometimes wonder what I'm doing it for. Like tonight – I ring home,' he picked up his phone, looked at the screen and then dropped the phone back on the mat, 'no reply. My wife texts me. She's out, of course, having fun.' He shook his head. 'Don't get me wrong, she's entitled to a life. It's not her fault I have to work so hard.'

'Yeah, this looks like hard work.' Mann glanced around the busy bar at the businessmen on expense accounts.

Peter Thorne grinned sheepishly. 'I suppose you're right. What do you do?'

'This and that. Import export. Excuse me.' Mann looked back at the stage – Michelle was gone. 'I'll be back.' He put his drink on the bar and went after Michelle.

CHAPTER 31

He caught up with Michelle in the ladies and jammed his foot in the toilet door just as she was shutting it. 'A word?'

'Christ, don't I get any privacy?' Michelle said, quickly stuffing something back in her bag.

'Is it my imagination or are you avoiding me? Give me your bag.'

A woman came in to use the bathroom. 'Sorry love, we're closed.' Mann leaned against the door to stop her from entering.

Michelle closed her eyes, took a deep breath and handed him her bag. He tipped the contents out in the sink, took out his pen and started turning over the contents. He flicked out a man's wallet. He opened it up. There was a driving licence on one side, a space on the other where a photo should have been. Michelle sighed heavily. 'I never saw that before, I promise, Inspector.'

'What were you going to do? Wait for him to be busy at the bar and then take a quick trip up to see if he'd left anything interesting in his room?'

'I don't know what that's doing in there, Inspector, I swear.'

Mann put the wallet in his pocket. He picked up a box of Viagra.

'It's for the old guys . . . it helps.'

'Very thoughtful, Michelle. And this?' He picked up a bag of meth amphetamine. Underneath were three foil strips of small white pills. He turned it over in his hand. 'That's a lot of GHD. You having to knock people out first these days are you, Michelle?'

She rolled her eyes and shook her head. 'Give me a break, Inspector. Some people get a bit nasty. It calms them down. It doesn't do them any harm. They think they had a good time.'

Mann shook his head and gave her a scathing look.

'I have kids to feed.'

'Your eldest is Lilly, right? I went to her school today. Did you know she was a budding young Triad? If she hasn't already, it won't be long before she takes the oath and then there's no going back. A young girl was murdered. Is that what you want for Lilly?'

She slumped back to rest her bottom on the basin and sighed heavily, closing her eyes for a few seconds. 'I don't know what she gets up to any more. I tried my best. I honestly did, but she is nothing but trouble. I wash my hands of her. Night after night she's out, I don't know where. Rizal says he can't keep an eye on her. He's busy with the other children and the business and Rizal and Lilly don't get on – they

163

fight all the time. If you can teach her some manners, go ahead.'

'How's the stall going? You making money?'

In the harsh make-up mirror Mann could see how spent she looked. Her eyes were dark and puffy.

'It's okay, I make the food before I come to work. Rizal sells it—'

'Or he gets a girl to sell it whilst he plays dice with his friends and then takes all the money, right?'

Michelle nodded but rolled her eyes and shrugged.

'You're a mug, Michelle. He's more of a pimp than a partner. I thought you would have learnt your lesson by now. You don't make it easy on yourself.'

'I know. I know.' She shook her head and turned back to check her make-up in the mirror. 'Ah well. It's my fate, huh? It's the way of the world. I must have been something very bad in my last life, huh?' She shook her head. 'Have a heart, Inspector. I know you've helped me out now and again and I appreciate it.' She tilted her head to one side and smiled at Mann.

'I'll tell you what I'll do. I'll make a deal with you, Michelle. I'll keep an eye on Lilly and do what I can, if you start being a proper mother to her and look after her, keep her off the streets. If you don't, I'll charge you with stealing from the hotel guests and you'll be back to singing in the slums of Manila.'

Michelle began shovelling her belongings back into her handbag.

'You are very kind to me, Inspector.' She stopped, mid-lipstick application. 'You are a good man. Are you married yet?'

Mann took that as his cue to leave. 'Sorry. I'd love to talk about my private life but I have to go. Remember, I'll be keeping an eye on Lilly for you, Michelle, but get a grip on your life before it's too late. You have a lot to offer the right person, don't put up with shit and get clean so you can think straight.'

Michelle had switched off. Her eyes were on the bag of ice. He knew she was just waiting for him to leave before having a quick snort – enough to see her through the next hour or two.

On the way out, Mann passed Peter Thorne. 'Remember,' Mann picked up his drink and downed it, 'regret's a bastard to live with.' Peter Thorne blinked rapidly, his eyes magnified by his glasses. 'Take care.'

CHAPTER 32

'What can you tell me about this guest?' Mann showed the receptionist his badge and the ID card he'd found in the wallet he'd taken from Michelle.

She tapped away on the PC. 'Mr Max Kosmos. American engineer. He has been with us for three nights and is due to check out tomorrow. He is a regular customer of ours.'

'Do you know where he is right now?'

'I rang his room an hour ago but got no reply. He missed a reservation he made for dinner in the restaurant here.'

'What's the room number?'

'One sixteen, on the sixteenth floor.'

'Is this key going to work?' Mann took out the key from Max Kosmos's wallet and handed it to her. She fed it into the key holder.

'Yes, sir. That's the one he has been using. He has two keys issued to him.'

Mann took the elevator to the sixteenth floor. He looked down the corridor: turquoise carpet, dried flowers in brass bowls on three-legged tables. He looked back to the door. The 'Do not disturb'

166

sign was still hanging from the doorknob. A news-paper was propped up against the wall. The trolley of fresh linen was halted where it had been waiting to change the sheets in the nearby rooms.

Mann knocked. 'Mr Kosmos. Security. I need a word.'

No reply.

Mann knocked harder. He waited. Still no reply. He slipped the card key in and out and the lock light turned from red to green. He turned the handle and pushed the heavy door open just enough to see that another room key was already in the power slot just inside the door. Someone was home. He slid Delilah from his boot and pushed the door open further. The room was lit by a sidelight. To the left of the door the bath-room light was on. The room was silent except for the air con. It was cold.

Mann held the door open with his foot whilst he stood for a few minutes in the doorway. Even though Mann couldn't see it, he smelt it. The first rule of a crime scene: take in everything, let your senses register it all. Now he smelt it the way connoisseurs smell wine, the overtones of blood, the undertones of butchery and death. This was a big room – plush. He couldn't see the bed. The television was on low in the back-ground, it was an English channel, BBC World News. Mann stepped further inside the room. The door sprang closed with a click behind him. To his right was a wardrobe, desk and minibar.

There were a couple of used glasses, whisky miniatures and small can of Coke. A half-drunk bottle of champagne was further along the desk. Just where Ruby had left it.

'Oooh, champagne.' Ruby picked up the bottle in the top of the fridge. 'For me?' she pouted.

'You must be joking. It cost more than you. Put it back.' Max Kosmos laughed hard at his own joke.

Ruby pretended to laugh with him. She squeezed his arm. 'You got great physique. What you weigh, two hundred twenty pounds?'

'Two hundred and twenty-five pounds of pure beef, baby.' He laughed.

Ruby smiled as she turned her back to him. She stuck her bottom in the air and hitched up her dress a little to distract him as she reached inside the small fridge to get his drink out. She turned to look at him over her shoulder, made sure his eyes were glued to her rising skirt whilst she stirred the sedative into his drink. She would start with a small amount; she only wanted to make him tired enough so that she could tie him up. She didn't want to knock him out so that he wouldn't feel the pain. She poured herself a small shot of gin and a lot of orange.

'Here, big man.' She handed him the drink and clanked her glass against his. 'Down in one, yes?' She needed to make him drink it fast. She watched him drink it down and she swallowed hers in one gulp and then she poured him another.

'Cheers.'

She clashed her glass against his. She could see his lips were wet, she smelt his sweat beneath his after-shave. She knew what he'd be thinking: he could handle his drink, and that it wouldn't be him who was drunk. He would think he was being clever and that he knew these Asian women. They took some loosening up. A few drinks and she'd be legless with her arse in the air. He could be in for a good night. Cheap too: he could probably get away without paying her. After all, who was she going to complain to? She was nobody and he was Mr International Businessman.

Mann pushed the bathroom door open just enough. This was a plush room, marble finish. Toiletries lined up on the back of the basin, once neatly rolled facecloths now soaked with blood. Someone had cleaned up in there and not cared about the mess. Blood ran down the sides of the sink. Bloody pools washed over the marble top. Blood stained the fluffy white towels. He looked at the mirror. In the centre were smudges: kisses in pink.

Ruby breathed onto the mirror and drew a heart in the mist and put an arrow through it. On one side she wrote Ruby and on the other she wrote a man's name, then she leant forward and kissed the cold mirror. She drew back sharply as her lip caught on a minute crack in the glass. A round drop of blood quickly bulged on her top lip and then dribbled down, she tasted it with her tongue, she touched it and watched it spread across her fingertips, a pretty colour: ruby red. She told herself that was why she had called herself Ruby. Rubies were precious, rare, the colour of a fresh cut just made, fresh blood spilt. But, someone else had named her it, the man who never came back, the man who left her to carry her baby alone and it had all been too much for her to bear. He had named her Ruby but it wasn't because she was precious.

She stopped to listen to him calling her from the bedroom. He sounded different, tired. She checked her watch. It had been ten minutes. The drug would be working by now. 'Clever girl, Ruby,' she said to herself in perfect English. 'You're a clever girl, Ruby. Now you get your reward.' She opened her handbag and gently slid her hand inside. She felt the cold metal of the scalpel and of the saw's handle. She felt the handcuffs. She patted them. 'Soon . . . very soon . . .'

Mann left the bathroom and took two steps further into the room. Mann's feet trod silently on the hotel carpet: browns, golds, mottled blood, soft and sticky underfoot. The room was cold and still, and had the smell of a morgue. The air con hummed like a waterfall. From the television came a newsreader's droning voice. The colours from the screen seeped into the room's atmosphere. Mann listened hard. There was no sound of breathing or sleep. To his right the wardrobe door was open. The safe door was locked. The bed was just around to his left now, past the bathroom wall. The corner was coming into view.

★ ★ ★

Ruby emerged from the bathroom and walked around the corner. He was sat in the chair by the bed.

'Why aren't you naked?' She went over to him and he tried to pull her onto his lap. His speech was slurred, his eyes rolling. She giggled and wriggled away. He tried to stand but he lurched and stumbled down again. He fell against the chair and tried to pull himself upright. He shook his head to try to clear it. His body swayed as he tried to stay standing. Ruby steered him towards the bed. His hands were grabbing her. She pushed him down on the bed. She stood over him and waited. She heard his breathing deepen and felt his body slump.

'Cheers.' She saluted his unconscious frame and poured champagne over his face to see if he would stir. His chest rose and fell. She placed the ball gag into his mouth and dragged him a little further up the bed. She lifted his arms above his head, handcuffed them and then tied them around the headboard; she took off his trousers, slowly, carefully, then his boxers. She opened his legs wide, took her tape and secured each leg to the bed. She took out her scalpel and cut around the shoulder joint, watching him all the time to make sure she had got the dosage right. His brow wrinkled and he groaned in pain. Ruby cut deeper. Yes, she was a clever girl. She knew how much to give him so that he could not move but he would still feel every cut she made.

Mann stepped over clothes scattered on the floor: a man's shoes, a pair of men's jeans: one leg inside out. He looked up. There were arcs of blood across the ceiling. The edge of the bed came into view. He saw a man's feet. He came around the corner. The bed was turned dark brown with blood.

'Jesus Christ,' he uttered aloud as he looked at the headless, pulped body of a man lying on the bed. He walked around to the side of the bed. On the bedside table lay a family photo covered in blood.

CHAPTER 33

Mann stepped back from the doorway and allowed Daniel Lu through. He had already got the hotel to erect a barrier on that side of the landing and to stop allowing guests back up to the floor. As the first officer on scene it was his job to secure it, stop it getting contaminated. Daniel handed him a protective forensic suit. 'Put this on. You can help me till the rest of the team arrive. This is the only point of entry, in and out. Perp must have touched it. Dust the door for me.'

Daniel Lu was the best CSI investigator there was. He was tireless, he was meticulous. He had been the one to first examine Helen's body when it had been found dumped in a bin bag at a reservoir in the New Territories. He'd never lost that look of sympathy and awkwardness whenever they met. It had been a hell of a day, a hell of a time.

Tom Sheng arrived straight after Daniel. 'Who found the body?' He didn't bother with pleasantries. There was little love lost between Daniel and Sheng. It wasn't just that they had Mia between them, they were opposite types.

'I did,' answered Mann.

'You had a tip-off?' He signalled to the two detectives with him to stay where they were outside the tape.

'No. I was coming up to give him his wallet. I took it off one of the girls. He didn't answer the door so I let myself in and found him.'

'Who is the woman who gave you the wallet?'

'Michelle. She's a singer in the lounge bar.'

Sheng shouted out to one of the officers outside. 'Go and pull in one of the singers, Michelle, have her taken to the station.'

Daniel had stopped in the centre of the room. His head turned methodically, taking in the whole scene. He stood over the corpse and looked up to the ceiling at the arcs of blood. He moved his position, looked up again. He started drawing a plan of the scene in a notebook. Daniel's mind worked on many planes, he was clever on so many levels. He was sharp and cynical and driven but the one thing that Mann recognized in Daniel was that he was unhappy.

'Do you know him?' asked Sheng, in the process of putting on a forensic suit.

'No. I've never seen him before. A man named Max Kosmos is registered to the room, I'm guessing this must be him.'

Daniel Lu walked around to the far side of the bed; he lifted the corpse's shoulder and checked beneath. 'The blood's settled. He's been dead

174

approximately fifteen to eighteen hours. He was killed here.'

'That would make it in the early hours of yesterday morning.' Tom Sheng looked around at the room. 'Nothing knocked over, no obvious signs of a fight. Motive?'

'Not robbery,' Mann answered. 'The safe is locked and he's still wearing his watch.'

He looked over the desk. 'His laptop's still here, and a briefcase.'

Daniel moved around the body and dictated into a machine as he went.

'Deep lacerations to his torso and legs, cut right through to the bone. The flesh has been scraped away. They cut his hamstrings, his knee ligaments, anterior and interior, his elbow joints, all severed to prevent movement. Whoever it was, they must have done this before. It's messy but it's accurate.'

'Cause of death?' Sheng was busy opening the safe with the hotel combination.

Daniel looked up from where he was busy measuring the depth of the wounds on the victim's chest. 'Leave that,' he said to Sheng. 'They might have tried to open it. It's an obvious place for prints.' Sheng stepped back, muttering under his breath. Daniel began photographing the injuries. 'The chest trauma is what killed him. The blood is pooled here . . . but not before the perp had their fun.'

Daniel Lu looked behind him at the brocade curtains, 'The splatter pattern around the room

175

means that all these injuries were inflicted whilst he was still alive. And this was a lengthy, prolonged torture. Perp took their time.' He took a gloved hand and hovered over Max Kosmos's chest. 'These are strange wounds, really deep. He was lying down when these were inflicted.' He traced the wounds with his finger. 'They extend all the way across. Something literally scooped his flesh out in long strokes.' He looked up at the ceiling where the three trails of blood and flesh had dried to brown sprays across the ceiling. 'I don't know what weapon made these. But someone definitely used our friend here for target practice.' He went back to his position at the end of the bed. 'They were standing here and used a downward action. They are about five foot three or four, I would guess. Right-handed.'

'If not robbery then some kind of revenge, retribution? This man wasn't just murdered, he was punished,' said Mann.

'It looks sexual,' Sheng said.

'Maybe,' answered Daniel. 'They cut off his penis but waited until after death to do it, unlike the amputation of his testicles which, judging by the amount of blood, was done when he was still breathing. Not a complete job though.' Daniel Lu lifted the scrotum. 'Sheng, make yourself useful, come over here and hold this up, I need to take a photo of the injury.'

For a second Sheng looked as if he was about to pass on the honour of helping Daniel but then thought better of it.

176

'Sure.' He lifted the scrotum to reveal that it was cut through by a wire which was still embedded in the wound.

'I've never seen anything like this done to a man,' said Sheng, wincing a little. 'I've seen girls left tied to the bedpost, serious injuries from sadistic role-playing. I've never seen torture on this scale and in such a public place. Perp took a hell of a risk.'

'It could have been accidental,' said Mann, busy dusting for prints around the safe deposit box and the minibar. 'Cock humiliation, servant-mistress stuff. Some people get off on pain, maybe Max Kosmos was one of them, maybe the game went too far.'

'It's not a game I can see me playing any time soon,' said Daniel.

'He bought her a rose, whoever she was,' said Sheng, looking at a single red rose lying on its side by the champagne bottle. 'Where do people get those on an evening? A restaurant, a bar?'

Mann picked it up. 'Nobody buys his girlfriend fake flowers.'

'Perp left it?'

'Yeah, I don't think it belongs here.' Mann took the camera from Daniel and photographed the rose before bagging and labelling it.

Daniel Lu placed the family photo flat between two pieces of absorbent paper and inside a plastic sleeve. 'Whoever did this was sat on him whilst they delivered the final wound. My guess is they used a butcher's knife to cut off his head. It must have taken a while. Judging by the saturation of blood here on the pillow I would say they tipped his head forward and cut from behind first. Then I think this print here,' Daniel examined an oval blood stain on the sheet, 'is from the perp's knee. I think the killer knelt on his chest and used their weight to put pressure onto the knife and sever the spine between vertebrae three and four.' Daniel pointed to the handprints in blood on either side of Max Kosmos's chest 'We should get some good results from these.'

'There are more prints in the bathroom,' said Mann. 'Perp cleaned up before they left.'

'Take what you need from the box and make a start,' said Daniel, tying bags around the victim's hands to preserve any evidence trapped beneath the nails.

Mann went into the bathroom. He lifted the bloodied towels from behind the sink and hung them over the wire across the bath – if they got put into an airtight bag they would be ruined. He looked at the lipstick stain on the mirror. A perfect pink pout. He took out some of Daniel's fingerprint tape and pressed it over then peeled it off in one sharp, exact move. When he was sure it was as good a print as he was going to get, he wrote on the edge and then filed it in an envelope before leaning forwards and breathing on the glass to frost it. A heart appeared. Mann breathed again to see it clearly. He stood back from it, staring. The writing was smudged; all Mann could make out was

Roses are red . . . written underneath

Sheng appeared beside him and reached past him and sprayed the mirror with a fixative spray. 'If it was so much trouble to get the head off, why did the killer bother?'

Mann stared at the misty heart in the mirror.

'And where is it now?'

CHAPTER 34

In the blackness the basket swayed with the movement of the tide. The silt at the bottom of the ocean occasionally burst upwards in a flurry of disturbance as the head settled. Floating particles of food were dislodged; flesh, minute shreds chewed and expelled by creatures and left to float feather-edged until they settled in another layer of silt for the bottom feeders. Through the murk a man's head nodded with the sway of the water, open eyed and slack-jawed. He wasn't alone in the dark. A lobster moved tentatively closer, it swam through the trap and reached out its feelers and touched Max Kosmos's face.

CHAPTER 35

Lilly walked through the first-floor landing and looked at the Africans as she passed. She wasn't afraid to look them in the eye. The dead African lying at the bottom of the lift shaft was testament to that. The body would be eaten by the rats and the mangy cats. When it began to smell the caretaker would be called and someone would take it away like they always did. No one would investigate such a death in such a place amongst such a group of people.

Although it was day, it could have been night – the fluorescent strip lighting above their heads wasn't working, a dripping overhead pipe had blown it. There were some corners of the Mansions that never saw light. Their booming laughs filled the corridor with a little bit of Africa. They were listening to the jangly sound of Kenyan folk music. The smoke around them was so thick it stung Lilly's eyes. They always stopped what they were doing to watch her as she passed. She had the mix that appealed to them. Her skin was light, her eyes big and round. She had the makings of a shape beneath her skimpy clothes. She had the sass, she was a girl who knew how to tease.

Lilly caught David's eye. He watched her from his stool inside the bar. He was not smiling. He didn't fall for Lilly's games. He knew they were deadly. He had seen her with the Outcasts. He knew she had secrets.

Lilly caught up with Mahmud. He was out with his sister Nina running errands whilst the restaurant was quiet. Lilly handed Nina a list. 'Mum wanted me to ask if you can get these things for her, she'll pay you later. I don't know when she's going to cook it. They are questioning her down at the police station. I don't know why she doesn't just get me to get them.'

'It's okay. Give it to me. I know these traders; I can get her a good deal.' Nina took it from her.

Nina walked on. Lilly hung back with Mahmud. 'What's the matter?' she asked him. 'You've been avoiding me. We can still be friends, can't we? Even if I'm not your girlfriend any more?'

Mahmud walked along looking at his feet. He was a shy lad, thoughtful. 'Yeah, sure. Just been studying hard, that's all.'

'That's not really the reason, is it?'

Mahmud went to defend it but he shook his head instead. 'It's all the trouble here, Lilly. I don't want any part of it. I knew that girl who was killed.'

'So did I. I didn't like it any more than you.'

Lilly walked alongside him. Mahmud looked hard at her. He searched her face to see if she was telling

182

the truth. 'It's all going wrong, Lilly. I don't know what's happened to you. You never used to like the gangs either. You've changed. Hafiz has changed too. I'm not having any more to do with it.'

'Nobody asked you to. But remember, Mahmud, we're all in this together. We are doing this so that we can have a better life.' Lilly turned frosty. 'Where's Hafiz, anyway?'

'He's working. He's in enough trouble with Dad, he doesn't need any more.'

Lilly shook her head, shrugged. 'A lot's happened. Things that you don't know about. I have to look out for myself now, Mahmud. I can't rely on anyone else. That's why I need the Outcasts. Victoria Chan has promised I will do well with them. She said she'd personally look out for me. She says I have what it takes.'

'Yeah, but what does she want you to do for it, Lilly? You heard what the inspector said at school. Once you're in you can't get out. They will kill you if you try.'

'Yeah, but you know what? Most days I feel like I am dead anyway. I don't have anything to live for right now.'

They stopped outside Rajini's father's tailors. Inside they could see her father sewing on the machine. On the chair next to him her mother was sobbing as she sewed.

'You'd think they'd take a day off. They only care about the money they're not going to get from her.'

Mahmud looked at her, his eyes full of anger and sadness. 'They are making Rajini's shroud.' Lilly walked briskly on. She was cross. He caught her up. They waited in silence for the lift. 'Let's go and sit on the roof. We haven't done that in ages.'

Lilly looked at him and smiled. 'Okay.'

They sat on the ledge and dangled their feet over Nathan Road. The sun was going down. As they sat their hands inched towards one another and rested, barely touching.

'Tell me what you want to be, Lilly.'

Lilly took her hand away and kept her legs still as she stared down at the busy road below. She looked down at her lap as she replied. 'I want to be rich. I want to have a house on the Peak. I want to have all designer clothes.'

Mahmud stared at her profile. 'Is that all that matters to you?'

She looked towards the sunset. A slither of orange was beginning to stretch across the evening sky. She looked everywhere but at Mahmud. 'Pretty much. I want to get out of this place. I want to have nice things.'

'Is that why you joined the Outcasts?'

'Yes.' She looked down at her lap again. 'It's all right for you, Mahmud; your father will find the money to pay for you to go to college. You are smart. You can achieve anything you want to. You will be able to afford to escape from here.'

'But I'll never be rich enough to have a house on the Peak. I might become a doctor and travel.

I might have a good living, enough to support a wife, a family, but I will never be rich, Lilly. It's not important to me.'

Lilly turned and looked at him, her eyes catching the light from the sky, her face glowing. 'I will, Mahmud. It's everything to me.'

'What about love?'

She turned away. 'I don't care about love. My mother loves Rizal, what good is love?'

'The Outcasts are dangerous, Lilly; they could turn on you just as quick as anyone else. They don't answer to anyone any more, they're out of control. Victoria Chan is a terrible person. Ever since she came into our lives things have just got worse.'

Lilly was angry. 'Victoria Chan is smart and beautiful. She's everything I want to be.' But she couldn't stay cross at Mahmud. She knew he was only worried for her. She knew he had always loved her. 'Listen to me, Mahmud. I know what you're saying,' she smiled sadly and looked at him, 'but she can give me things, things I could never get on my own. She can get me out of this place. You are so clever. You will get where you want to go without people like Victoria Chan.'

'I thought we could make it, you and I. I was hoping, you know? I always thought we'd stay together.'

She turned and looked him in the face, her eyes searching his. She reached over and kissed his cheek. 'Save your hopes for someone else,

Mahmud. You are too good for me. I am not the girl you kissed when we were ten. I am not the girl I was.' Lilly slid her legs back around and stood to leave. 'Forget me, Mahmud. You and I could never be and I am in too deep now to get out.'

CHAPTER 36

Victoria moved to her bedroom to answer her phone; it was too noisy to talk in her lounge. She lived in a luxury penthouse apartment on the road to Stanley. She was giving seven of her top lieutenants a special treat – she had provided her men with the entertainment. They were simple creatures; easy to read, easy to please. Tonight was a victory celebration of sorts. It was to celebrate the beginning of the end. The beginning of a fight that would take her all the way. There was no stopping her now. She would court the best of the lieutenants in the Wo Shing Shing. As each of her pieces slotted into their roles she controlled them like a conductor played an orchestra. They were the new breed. They were loyal to her father, loyal to the organization but they would want a new Dragon Head when she showed them her power. Victoria sat on the chair in her bedroom in the semi-darkness. Her black leather cat suit traced her strong curves like a second skin, her diamond earrings caught the flash of lightning as she turned her head towards the window and watched the storm coming in.

'You have done well, my daughter. But we need him broken before he can be rebuilt. Push for the prize now. Use every weapon you have. The Mansions are proving a suitable testing ground for you. You have been courting the right people. You have turned them on one another.'

'They all want the same thing. They want money, power. They want bigger, better. They don't think of the consequences. They don't think of tomorrow. The Outcasts are unique, fearless. They are easy to please. There is one amongst them who is the most talented and most ruthless I have ever known; she will stop at nothing and yet she wants nothing in return except to be allowed to serve. I only have to suggest something and it's done. I only have to dislike someone and they are dead. She sees me as her saviour.' Victoria laughed at the notion.

'Be careful, my clever daughter. He who treads softly goes far.'

'Trust me, Father. I know what I am doing. But when I have done it, will you be ready to hand it all over to me?'

'Yes. When you have proved yourself.'

Victoria closed her phone and walked back through the lounge. There was an orgy going on in her apartment. Two naked Russian girls snorted cocaine from her expensive glass table. Another sat on a man's lap as he played cards, eyes rolling in his head. She was passed one to the other. A girl in her early teens danced naked in the centre of the room, so tired she lurched as she twirled. Her nose was clogged with methamphetamine; her head was buzzing but her body spent.

Victoria passed through and came out to stand on her balcony to look out to sea. Out on the balcony the air was charged with the electricity of the storm. The gales were picking up, caught on a typhoon's tail. She held tight to the railing as the gusts tossed her hair into the air. Victoria smiled to herself. The night had been a good one; it would be over soon. Victoria turned back to face the wind. It took her breath away as it picked up her hair and whipped it across her face. All those years arranging flowers, holding dinner parties, watching her husband lavish his concubines with expensive gifts. All those years she took the pill without him knowing. There was no way she was going to bear a child of his. There was no way she would allow the tyranny to continue. Lucky for her he had never managed to father a child elsewhere. Now she was free and now she stood and tossed her head in the wind and laughed with the exhilaration of it all. Yes, Mann had done her a huge favour when he took care of her husband and whether he liked it or not they were joined to each other. She and Mann would rule the Triad world together. One day he would have nothing left but her.

The balcony doors slid open. The young dancer stood there naked, trailing a blanket behind her. 'Come here, Lilly.' Victoria beckoned her closer to the railing. The wind began to subside. They looked out as the first signs of dawn began to change the light and bring a mauve tint to the stormy sky. 'You are a good girl, Lilly, beautiful and clever.' Victoria stroked her hair. 'I have a present for you.'

Lilly shivered. Victoria unclasped a gold bracelet from her wrist and clipped it on Lilly's.

'We have achieved much but there is still some left to do. We have to seal the deal. Then you will have so much jewellery, so many fine things and you will be by my side always.'

She wrapped the blanket around Lilly's shoulders.

'There's just one more thing I want you to do for me.'

CHAPTER 37

The autopsy was due to start at 7 a.m. Mann had driven straight there after writing up his report on the murder at the hotel. He had dozed for an hour in the car whilst he waited for the autopsy to begin. He sat in the car park outside and watched the coroner, Mr Saheed, arrive. Mr Saheed was a tall man of Indian descent, with a dry sense of humour and a bad memory for recalling other people's lives. Mann gave him ten minutes then he rang the bell. Kin Tak answered. He glanced over Mann's shoulder as if he saw someone else standing there and then quickly turned away.

'Stop coming here!' he shouted out as he turned to lead Mann into the autopsy room.

Mann turned to look behind him. He saw no one there. 'Who's there?' he asked Kin Tak.

Kin Tak shook his head, small nervous jerks like a twitch. 'No one. No one.' He went off muttering under his breath, a running commentary to no one in particular and too low for anyone to hear or understand.

Mann was used to Kin Tak's outbursts. He knew

he was harmless. His strangeness was part and parcel of his job. Mann slipped on a white overall.

'Good morning, Inspector. We were about to start without you. Kin Tak already has some observations that he is bursting to share with you.'

Max Kosmos's body was lying on the steel autopsy table, tilted to allow the fluids to flow into the holes at the bottom and into the drain beneath the table. His abdomen had a greenish hue. It was beginning to swell with the build-up of gases.

Saheed switched the Dictaphone on. He turned to see what was holding Kin Tak up. He was staring at Mann.

'Get a move on, Kin Tak. I am waiting. It's not often we get to practise our skills on a tourist, is it, Inspector?' He looked up at Mann over his bi-focals. Saheed didn't remember that particular autopsy or what it had meant to Mann. He only remembered that Mann been present the last time they had to perform an autopsy on a foreigner.

Saheed started the autopsy. 'We have a white male of Mediterranean origin, five foot eight inches tall, two hundred and ten pounds. His head would weigh a further fifteen to twenty pounds, if we had it, which we don't. Someone went to a great deal of trouble to make this man suffer before he died. It doesn't look like it was an easy job or a quick one.'

Kin Tak shook his head. 'Very messy, bad job indeed, not the right tools at all.'

Mann approached the table.

Saheed continued, 'He died from the wound to his heart. It was made by a blade not more than half an inch wide, thin, long. By the marks on the edges of the rib bone . . .' Saheed ran his finger inside the chest cavity, '. . . it took several attempts to saw through the last four ribs on the victim's right side. Looking at the scraping on the bone I would say a small, fine-bladed saw was used. I concur with the initial estimate that death occurred sometime in the early hours of yesterday morning. I would expect cause of death to be a sudden trauma to the heart. He did not bleed to death, although he would have done undoubtedly, given time. I can say he was tortured over a period of four or five hours. What can you tell me about the circumstances leading to this man's death, Inspector Mann?'

'I entered the hotel room and found him, his legs tied to the bed. You've seen the photos?'

'Yes. Daniel Lu e-mailed them to us. It was quite a bloodbath. What was the motivation, in your opinion?'

'Not your average robbery, if it was one. She took his wallet but that was to barter in exchange for drugs, we know she bought a good deal of sedative.'

'I will have the results from toxicology for you in a few days.'

'It can't have been *just* sexual, although there was an element attached to it. He was seen leaving the bar with a woman the night he died. He was a known user of sex workers, men and women. We might find it's a spurned lover, an angry mistress.'

'Perhaps we can help you with some part of the theory. We found something in his chest cavity.' Kin Tak picked up a specimen tray from the table behind him and tilted it for Mann to see.

'Penis.'

'Yes, it's his penis.' Saheed looked over his glasses at Mann. 'But, that's not all . . . Kin Tak has discovered something very important that links this murder with another. Haven't you, Kin Tak?'

Kin Tak was too excited to spit the words out so Saheed did it for him.

'What did you notice about the blood splatter patterns, Inspector?'

'Arcs of flesh and blood across the ceiling, sprayed around the room.'

Mann looked at Kin Tak.

'Yes, yes. And were there distinct arcs but following exactly the same line?' Kin Tak almost shrieked.

Mann thought back. The memory was implanted in his mind. There were three pronged arcs of flesh and blood crusted onto the hotel ceiling. 'Yes. That's what it was.'

'It is the same weapon that took off the Indian girl's hands.'

CHAPTER 38

Mann drove back to the office. It was eight thirty and the place was buzzing with the anticipation of a major murder investigation. Mia was waiting for Mann when he got back.

'We've had a confirmation, it's Max Kosmos. The gold ring on his finger is a matching wedding ring to his wife's. The wife seemed bitter, angry.'

'Is she on her way to Hong Kong?'

'No. She says she's staying with the children. You attended the autopsy?'

'Yep and it's thrown up something. The weapon used to torture Max Kosmos is the same one used to mutilate Rajini.'

'Tom Sheng's not going to like that. He'd love to tell us to fuck off. Well, professionally anyway. He's not the best at sharing cases. I'd rather you interview Michelle. You know her. Sheng's heavy handed.'

Mann nodded.

'You better go and do it now. He's busy getting the incident room set up so now's your chance. You have half an hour.'

★　　★　　★

Michelle was sat at the table when Mann punched in the door code and entered the interview room. Ng followed. Michelle looked up and kept her eyes on Mann's as he walked in. Ng went to stand at the far wall. The room was only twelve foot square. The centre was taken up by the Formica-topped table shaped as a right-angled triangle. It was chained to the floor, as were the four red plastic chairs around it: two on the long side, one each on the others.

Mann sat opposite her and pushed the photo of Max Kosmos across the table.

'How long have you known him?'

'About nine months.' Michelle hadn't had a chance to change and was still in her blue stage outfit. She had bags beneath her bloodshot eyes, blue eye shadow, smudged mascara. There was no natural light in the interview room although it was well lit for the two cameras that tracked events. The light bounced off the white polystyrene tiles on walls and ceiling. On the floor were grey carpet tiles.

'Please, Inspector, let me go, my babies are at home. Rizal will be expecting me by now. There are things to get ready for the stall. What am I doing here?' A couple of fat tears squeezed their way out. She wiped them hastily away. Her hands were shaking as she lit a cigarette that Mann passed over the table top. 'Plus, I need a fix. Just a small amount, please.'

'You'll be out of here as soon as we are satisfied

with the information you give us. We'll let you call Rizal after the interview.'

'What do you want to know?'

'Max Kosmos – how well did you know him?'

'He wasn't a friend, as such. We had a meal together sometimes. He was lonely.'

'What kind of meal? Afternoon tea or breakfast?'

'All right, all right . . . Yes, I went to his room, sometimes. We had sex. He paid.'

'When was the last time you had sex in his room?' He could see she was about to lie. 'Listen to me, Michelle. I found Max Kosmos, what was left of him, spread all around his hotel room. You want to tell me how he got like that?'

She stared at Mann, her eyes searching his face. She looked across at Ng. He stared back. 'He's dead?'

'Yeah. Cut to bits. His head hacked off, his skin stripped.'

Michelle shook her head slowly from side to side, her eyes open wide. Her face registering the shit she just realized she was in.

'Oh my God. I had nothing to do with it, Inspector, I swear.' She began to hyperventilate. 'Please believe me.'

'But you had his wallet.'

Michelle dragged on her cigarette and looked nervously from the table to Mann's face, as if weighing up just how much truth she could get away with not telling.

'When did you see him last?'

'Three nights ago. But I swear he was fine when I left him.'

'And night before last?'

'No. He knew I wasn't interested.'

'Why?'

She hesitated, looked guilty. 'He roughed me up last time. I couldn't work for a few days.' She looked at Mann. She looked spent. It had been a long night.

'Why did he do that?'

'All right, he accused me of stealing money from his wallet.'

'And did you?'

She shrugged. 'Sure. But only when he turned nasty. What happened to him?'

'You tell me. He got killed by someone he took to his room that he probably intended to have sex with. The barman says you left the same time as him last night. You will be taken in if your prints are in that room, or any part of your DNA is in there. Now I can't help you if you keep lying to me.'

'I promise you I didn't do it, Mann. Sure, I talked to him last night, in between sets, in my break. He wanted me to go upstairs with him but I was in the middle of a set. Anyway, I could see what mood he was in. He looked like he hadn't slept for a couple of days. I told him I wasn't well. He went out for a while and then he came back in with a girl. They sat at one of the tables, they had a drink. They left the bar about eleven. I left just after. I'd had enough. I knew Lilly was up to something; I thought I might find out what. I wanted to get home. There's a lot going on. Lilly and Rizal . . . things aren't good at the moment.'

'Who did he leave with? Did you know her?'

Michelle shook her head. 'No. I didn't get a good look at her. So many girls do a circuit of the hotel bars. I never saw her face. She could have been anyone.'

'Tell me more about him. What kind of sex did he like? Was he into S & M?'

She shrugged her shoulders. 'He liked what everyone likes. He liked to get a bit rough. He didn't like getting it back. I told you he got carried away sometimes, he got nasty.'

'Bondage?'

'Sometimes.'

'Did you use props, handcuffs, tape?'

She shook her head.

'What about threesomes? Was he bisexual? Did he like ladyboys, young men?' She hesitated. Mann waited. 'Okay, let me reword it. What kind of men did he like?'

Michelle looked flustered. Mann sat back in his chair and waited. Michelle looked around the room. She glanced over at Ng leaning on the wall. He stared back. Mann looked at the clock on the wall, it was 1 a.m. Michelle was jumpy.

'All right, okay. Once, twice, I don't know . . . I got him a boy.'

'What kind of boy did he like?'

Michelle rolled her eyes irritably. 'Regular boy. He didn't like ladyboys. He didn't like gays. He liked a normal-looking boy.'

'What did he like? Was he a giver or a receiver?'

Michelle couldn't look at Mann as she answered. 'A giver.'

'And you found one willing?'

'Sure. This is Hong Kong, remember. People will do anything for money.'

'Who was he? Someone you know well?'

Michelle shook her head. 'Just an Indian lad, lives in the Mansions. But you won't find him. He's a tout for a restaurant. He is just a lad, hungry for money. He means nothing.'

'Do you often work with a male partner?'

'Not often.'

'But you have done before?'

'Once or twice.'

Mann looked at her hard. 'How come you had Kosmos's wallet?'

Michelle stared at her hands resting on the table and then she took out a cigarette from her bag. The wardress stepped forward to light it for her.

'It was passed to me.'

'Who by?'

'Look, Mann. I'll tell you the truth. We have a little scam going here.'

'Now, why doesn't that surprise me?'

'Cindy, Sandy and me. We get stuff for the working girls; we sell them dope, Viagra, GHB, whatever they need. I got his wallet in exchange for some pills.'

'Who did you get it from?'

'Well, that's the thing . . . we don't see the person. We get left a message. The waiting staff pass it to us, or the barman; we get told what they want and we put it in an envelope. Sometimes we leave it in the ladies, we all know where to look, sometimes we put it in an envelope and pass it back to the waiters. But, this girl, I have never seen. Honest. I'd tell you if I had.'

'What did she want from you?'

'She isn't your average customer. All the other girls just want Rohypnol. She wants a type of GHB but not the usual. I had to source it. I found it from a supplier in Shenzhen. This time she bought a lot from me. The most she's ever done.'

CHAPTER 39

Mann finished up his interview with Michelle and got to the incident room just as everyone was cramming into the room, trying to find somewhere to sit or stand. Shrimp was busy pinning up photos of Max Kosmos's body lying in a halo of blood-soaked Egyptian white cotton sheets.

Daniel Lu came in late and stood in the corner by the door. Mann looked across at Sheng, he looked like he hadn't had any rest either. He pulled at his tie and took off his jacket. His clothes were expensive but too flash. Around his wrist he wore a heavy gold chain that matched a thick gold ring he wore on the right hand.

'As you all know a businessman named Max Kosmos was found murdered in his hotel room last night.' Sheng addressed the whole room. 'The reason we still have the members of the OCTB in here is because . . .' Sheng flicked his head in the direction of the right-hand white board on which were photos of Rajini, '. . . the death of the young woman murdered in a Triad initiation cere- mony and this man's death are linked. It's been confirmed that the same weapon was used in both murders. One to cut the girl's hands off and two to torture Max Kosmos. Ng, what can you tell us about him?'

'He was a forty-five-year-old American from Chicago. He's middle management in an engineering projects firm. He is a frequent visitor to Hong Kong and does the Asia circuit every few months. Always stays at the Vacation Villas. This time he checked into the hotel four days ago. He was due to stay another day and then fly on to Australia.'

'What was he working on here?'

'Checking equipment supplied for container cranes down at the docks.'

'Any Triad links?'

'From him or his company, no. From the companies at the docks? Plenty.'

'Mann, you were the first on the scene?' Sheng had the look of one who was a chronic over-indulger: red faced, puffy eyes. He carried a little too much weight around his middle. It had aged him.

'Yes. I went to Vacation Villas to speak to Michelle Mendoza after I saw her daughter Lilly near the scene of Rajini's murder. Lilly's been identified by our agent in Operation Schoolyard as a recruiter for the Outcasts at school. I wanted to find out what her mother knew. I've kept an eye on Michelle over the years. She is a heavy drug user, mostly ice. She has an abusive partner,

Rizal, and a couple of small kids as well as Lilly. When she gets desperate she has a habit of fleecing the customers. She looked nervous when she saw me so I followed her to the cloakroom and got her to empty her bag; that's where I found Max Kosmos's wallet.'

Sheng interrupted. 'I will interview Michelle myself as soon as we're done here.'

'I've just done it,' said Mann. He looked across at Mia. She wasn't looking at Sheng. He was glaring at her. He knew she must have given permission. 'She told me she knew Max Kosmos. She had had sex with him before on a few occasions. The last time was three nights ago. She said she saw him leave with a woman at about eleven on the evening he was murdered.'

Sheng folded his arms over his chest. He was furious with Mia and Mann but trying to hide it. He listened to Mann's account whilst looking at the floor, perched on the side of the table, tapping his foot, agitated. He looked up. 'Is she lying?'

'She's certainly not telling the whole truth. The barman confirmed that he saw Max Kosmos leave with a woman but also added that Michelle left just before.'

'Maybe she is part of a double act or maybe she got a call later and then went to his room.'

'Did Michelle say he was into anything weird?' asked Mia.

'He was into threesomes – boys and girls. They were sometimes joined by a young Indian lad from the Mansions. I'll press her on that. Get a name. We'll search her apartment and get a print from Rizal. I don't put anything past Rizal.'

'Had to be someone he accepted easily into the room,' said Mia.

'Not necessarily,' said Mann. 'People let their guard down in hotels. You never think twice about answering the door. You expect it to be a safe environment but the truth is anyone can get in a lift and come up to the floor and knock on the door.'

'If it was the woman he was seen leaving the bar with then she must be attractive – twenty to forty?'

'Maybe even younger,' said Mann. 'Lots of girls can make themselves up to look eighteen these days. That's all she needs to be to pass unhindered into clubs, bars, hotel lounges. It's not as if anyone ever checks ID.'

'A schoolgirl murderer – that would be the first in Hong Kong,' said Shrimp.

'What about the wallet?' said Sheng. 'How did she say she got that?'

'She told me about a system she has for giving dope in exchange for wallets, money, whatever the girls manage to get. She's dealt with this person before on a few occasions. This time the drop was much larger than usual.'

'So, the perp's planned this and it might not be a one-off. Fuck, that's all we need. Daniel . . . injuries?'

Daniel pinned up photos. 'Apart from sexual mutilation and decapitation, he was tortured. If you have a look at this photo . . .' he pointed to the close-up of the bedroom ceiling, '. . . you can see three arcs of blood which went across the ceiling. They were made at exactly the same time. That means the weapon we are looking for has three blades and is capable of lifting out the flesh and firing it at great speed and velocity in an arc several feet across the ceiling. It has stripped him of most of the flesh from his torso.'

'My guess is it's a customized street weapon but it is an unusual one,' said Mann.

'Each band of metal is at least an inch wide.'

'So it's the same person?' said Sheng.

'No, not necessarily. The weapon is the same, that's all,' answered Mann.

Daniel continued, 'Added to that, his chest was opened by several frenzied cuts and slashes with what looks like a small-bladed knife, there is scraped off flesh, and the bottom four ribs were removed, two of them by breaking. Victim was alive until this point.'

Daniel was filling the central board with the images of Max Kosmos's mutilated body. Mann didn't need to look closely at the photos, he still held a snapshot of the scene in his head. Later on, years from now, he knew it would feature somewhere in his dreams. The incident room was hushed, even though it was full of officers, and only the sound of a DC tapping on a keyboard came from the far end.

'Trace elements left behind at the scene, Daniel?'

'We found three types of hair in the room, apart

from the victim's.' Daniel continued. 'Pubic hair on the victim's body that's not his. We also found a long human hair, it's been analysed. It is hair that's been treated, dyed, bleached before that. The chemicals in it are linked to ions used for human hair that's made into wigs, or hair pieces.'

'Lots of women wear wigs or clip-on hair pieces made from real hair,' said Mia. 'We'll see where the hair came from. We might get lucky with a particular manufacturer.'

'Perp used a wire to wrap around his testicles, the type electricians use,' said Daniel. 'They used bondage tape to tie his legs. I think it's a common enough one; it's one that sticks to itself. We are still analysing it to see if we have anything of the perp on there, but the perp doesn't seem to care what we find: we have DNA and prints.' Daniel finished pinning up the last of the photos. 'This print,' he pointed to the knee print on the sheet by Max Kosmos's body, 'is a woman's knee: slightly different shape to a man's, narrower, trapezoid. Men's are rectangular, more prominent bone at the top.'

'We have a woman killer, alone or with an accomplice, but definitely a woman. What can we tell about her from the scene? Risk taker. Not interested in money. She's in it for the thrill, retribution, revenge. She doesn't care if she gets caught. She likes to take it to the edge – she gets off on it,' said Mann.

'She must have worked up to this,' said Sheng.

'Max Kosmos could easily have come round. Perp knows their stuff but they must have had practice along the way. Find out if any other businessmen are missing here in Hong Kong. Find out if there were any un-followed complaints, anything at all that would fit this. Can't have been the first time she harmed someone.'

Shrimp stepped up to the board and pinned up the photo of Ishmael. 'One of the Africans in the Mansions told us that his brother had a secret girlfriend in the Mansions and that he has now disappeared. He is pretty sure the Outcasts had something to do with it or that they know something.'

'How long ago was that?'

'A year. Should we alert the business community about the killer?' Shrimp asked.

Mia Chou shook her head. 'No, definitely not. We risk hitting the Hong Kong economy where it will do the most damage. Hong Kong only exists for business. We can't risk putting the businessmen off coming.'

Sheng looked around the packed room. 'Okay, let's be clear about who's handling what. Daniel Lu will handle all forensics for both murders so that we can see what's reoccurring. Michelle Mendoza stays in custody. I will handle all interviews from now on. My team will do all the background on Max Kosmos. We'll get a search started for all missing foreign businessmen that fit the perp's specs in case there are other victims we don't yet know about. Mia's team will deal with Rajini. Ng, you can liaise between the two departments. I want to know what is cross-referencing across both camps. Keep us on track. If there is a link to the Outcasts then it follows to the Mansions too. Rajini Singh was from there. Max Kosmos was staying just a few doors up from there. Shrimp, your English is Americanized, I want you to be the businessman decoy and go undercover in the bars, stay in Vacation Villas. It'll take a couple of days to set it up. We need to make you look good, give you a watertight cover. You'll be watched by a team from my department. You'll be wired all the time. We need to get behind the Outcasts, our murderer could be one of them. Operation Schoolyard continues.'

'No,' said Mann, 'it's too risky. I'm stalling it for now.'

Sheng didn't answer at first. He stared at Mann coldly then he turned to Mia. She nodded. Sheng threw up his hands exasperated. 'No fucking way . . .'

'Something's not right. Tammy's at risk. We need more information. I've told her to sit tight. It can't be rushed into. There's too much at stake. I want it to work. No way am I letting her walk into a trap.'

CHAPTER 40

Ruby picked up the black doll and held her at eye level.

'I'm sorry, baby. I should have never brought your daddy here but I was lonely. I never meant to hurt your daddy. I got frightened. He shouldn't have tried to touch me. I am sorry, baby. Your daddy was special to me; he was the first that I kept here; he was the first that I . . .' She couldn't bring herself to say it. 'I never meant to hurt him but then I couldn't stop.'

She grew angry, shaking the doll without realizing. Its eyes banged in the plastic sockets.

'I told him not to touch me. I told him. He didn't listen.' She stopped and breathed hard, calmed, she kissed the doll and placed it back down on the shelf. She put the photo of Ishmael in its lap. She turned back and smiled at all of the dolls. 'Who wants to get a last look at Daddy before Mummy has to let him go?' The dolls' perfect little ruddy plastic faces smiled back. 'Of course you all do,' she laughed. She scooped the dolls up in her arms and pulled back the curtain and opened the door to her bedroom. His breathing was laboured. Ruby had removed the ball gag. There was no need to keep it. No one would hear him now. She crept in the room in the dark.

'Shhhhh,' she whispered into the nylon doll's hair, 'Daddy's sleeping.'

He stirred as she came close. He let out a gasp of fright. It sounded strange. He had no nose, no lips, no side to his face.

Ruby put the light on, it bounced off the white tile still visible beneath the blood splatters. It threw deep shadows around the room. Steve's wounds were still oozing.

'Oh, Daddy's very naughty. He's just pretending to sleep. Shall we wake him with this?' She picked up the electric saw.

Steve thrashed around. He tried to speak. Ruby tiptoed around him, placing each doll around the room.

'What's that you say? See if he's ticklish under his arm? So sweet baby, so clever . . .' She switched the saw on and knelt beside him. His arms were stretched above his head.

She brought the saw down into his armpit. He screamed. Blood and bone sprayed around the room. Ruby carried on until she had sawn through the shoulder joint. 'There . . .' She stood with the dripping saw in her hand. Ruby picked up another doll and held its mouth to her ear again. 'What? See if Daddy is ticklish *there*? Ruby giggled. 'You're a very naughty baby. But okay . . .' Ruby fired up the saw again and ran it up the length of his leg towards his groin.

CHAPTER 41

Tom Sheng caught up with Mann on his way back to his office.

'Who gave you permission to interview the suspect?'

'My boss.' Mann walked away.

Sheng held Mann back by the arm. 'Let's get this straight. You run everything by me from now on. Something doesn't smell so good about you at the moment, Mann. I am getting the whiff of corruption. You're in the wrong place at the right time these days. I'll be watching your every move. I am going to sit in the monitoring room and run that tape back. If I find anything, I mean *anything*, I don't like, you're suspended.'

Mann felt his breathing slow. He held his breath deep inside his lungs, took it right inside his diaphragm. 'Do it, Sheng. I've got nothing to hide. Mia wanted me to interview Michelle. Your interview techniques have been known to start with a hand up the suspect's skirt. You're a dirty bastard.'

'If you don't like the colleagues you work with then why don't you fucking leave? You have your father's money. You have your Triad family – fuck off. From now on you work on solving Rajini's murder and following up on the Outcasts and only that, leave the rest to me. And, of course,' he smiled smugly, 'carry on doing what you seem to do best: ingratiate yourself with the top Triad brass. It's a home from home for you.' Sheng was inches from Mann's face. He was frothing at the mouth.

Ng came up beside Mann and steered him away down the corridor towards Mia's office.

'Leave him. He will never change. Rotten wood cannot be carved. We have work to be done.'

Mia looked at him as they walked into her office. He could see by her face she was expecting him to go ballistic. He'd already decided he wasn't going to. It didn't stop him imploding though. He began to feel like his feet were in quicksand. He had the feeling Sheng wasn't alone in his thoughts, he just didn't hesitate to voice them.

Shrimp was the last one in, he closed the door behind him. Mia looked at him.

'You okay with going undercover?'

Shrimp beamed. 'Yes Boss. I need to choose my outfits carefully, grey suit, striped shirts, fancy glasses, jazzy tie. No, forget the tie, keep it young conservative.'

'Don't get carried away,' said Ng. 'The only reason you're doing it and not me is that you sound like a Yank. Otherwise it would have been my operation. You know Mann can't do it because he's known in all the bars.'

'I want you and Mann to head back to the Mansions now,' Mia said. 'Get as much information as you can before Sheng goes marching in there and all hope of solving this case marches out. Don't let the rules stop you from asking questions about Max Kosmos. Ng will feed it back to the other team. Find that weapon.'

CHAPTER 42

Tom Sheng got back to his office and made a call to Mia. She was alone in her office.

'I'm overruling Mann on Operation Schoolyard. I'm taking it away from him. We can't trust his judgement any more. We can't be sure his motives are what they should be. I've seen the new car in the car park. That's a hell of a pay-off. He has obviously thrown himself into the task of infiltration wholeheartedly.'

Mia was fuming. 'That's utter bullshit and you know it. You don't like Mann, you never have. You asked him to do his best to get inside CK's head and that's what he's doing. You of all people should know you have to live it when you go undercover. You can't tell me there weren't moments in those two years you spent undercover when you didn't know which way you felt any more.'

There was a few seconds of silence on the other end. 'I earned my promotion, Mia. I did two years for the Wo Shing Shing. But I always knew why I was in there. I always knew what my objective was. I never got a brand new fucking Maserati.'

'Then you lucked out, didn't you, Tom? What do you want me to say? Poor fucking you? You're jealous of Mann. You need to seriously take a look at yourself, Tom. I am beginning to wonder what I see in you.' Mia heard the stony silence but he didn't hang up.

'All right, all right. I'm a bit jealous of Mann, I admit it. I know you had a thing with him once. I know you will always have a special friendship with him. It pisses me off, that's all. Plus, you know, if I had his dough, you wouldn't see me for fucking dust. Of course, that's after I'd picked you up in my new Porsche and we'd driven off into the sunset.'

Mia couldn't stay cross. 'Just get a divorce – that will be better than a Porsche for me.'

CHAPTER 43

'Thanks for your time.' Mann and Shrimp were back in the Mansions. 'I just want to ask some more questions about the death of the young girl. We know her identity now. She lived here in the Mansions. Her name was Rajini Singh. Her father works on the first floor.'

'Sure. Let's go somewhere to talk.' PJ's eldest son, Ali, led them up two floors. They came out onto the landing and turned sharp left, past the open maintenance shaft. At the bottom of it the African's body was just beginning to smell. Ali called out to an old blind Indian woman sat just behind a metal grid and beneath a sign that read *Delhi Guesthouse*. She was turning beads in her hand and sanding them with fine emery board.

'Hello, Grandma. I've got two men with me. Nothing to worry about.'

The old woman rested her work in her lap and held up her hand in greeting. Her hand was covered in white dust. She cocked her head to one side to listen to the strangers pass.

Mann stopped by her. 'How are you, Flo?' He squeezed her hand.

She searched her memory to find the voice. Slowly a smile cracked across her face. Her eyes were milky with cataracts. She had no teeth, just wizened gums. 'Well, I never. Inspector Mann?'

Mann knelt down and kissed her cheek. 'Clever as ever and still as beautiful, Flo. Are you well?'

She laughed and held on to his hand. 'I can't complain. I sleep nearly all the time. My granddaughter Nina looks after me. Who is that with you?' She tilted her face towards Shrimp. 'He smells very nice. I like a man who looks after himself.'

'My name is Li. Nice to meet you, Flo.' Shrimp stepped forward and took her hand. She held on to his as she seemed to savour his voice for a minute and then she turned her head back towards Mann. 'Where is Helen?'

Shrimp glanced Mann's way. He hadn't meant to. He had been there when they found her body in a bin bag. He had been there at the autopsy. He had been there all through the investigation but he hadn't seen what Mann had seen. He hadn't seen the tape of Helen being raped and murdered.

'She's not here right now, Flo.' Mann had no intention of telling her the truth. She was dead and so was the man who killed her. There were lots of secrets that Mann carried alone.

She lowered her head and shook it as she took a moment to assimilate the knowledge. 'Here . . .' She felt in the pile of beads, carved chopsticks and hairpins and she pressed a small, round object into his hand. He opened his palm and looked at it. It was a hairpin with real hair woven into a plait within the clasp. 'I made it myself. It's my own hair. Give it to Helen when you see her next.'

'Thank you, Flo, I will.' He put it in his pocket.

She went back to her work whilst they walked on down the passage. There were no lights on. The old woman needed none. There was no natural light in the closed-in corridor. Everywhere was white-tiled, linoleum floor. The fizzing smell of rotting food in the heat and humidity permeated everything. Ali wiped his brow with his handkerchief.

A young Indian woman in her early twenties stepped out from one of the rooms. She had beautiful, turned-up, brown eyes, long lashes, light skin with smooth jet black hair hanging in a thick plait to her waist. Mann knew her.

'My sister, Nina,' said Ali. The young woman's eyes fixed on Mann and she nodded in recognition. Her eyes lingered on Mann before they moved to Shrimp and he got a smile from her.

Ali caught her smile. 'Go to the market now,' he said, sharply. 'The cook is waiting to start marinating for the tandoori. And take Grandma back up to rest now. She spends too long sat in the doorway.'

'No she doesn't,' Nina snapped back. 'She needs to be out of the room when she is not sleeping. She needs to interact with people. She needs to be useful, to be still a part of the world.' Nina scowled at her brother as she turned and slipped away, covering her hair in a beautiful shimmering veil of purple as she went.

Mann smiled to himself. She was the real boss of the family; like so many other Indian families, they were matriarchal. He watched her turn and look back at them as she waited for the lift, her headdress pulled further over her face as she held it over her nose and mouth. Mann could see her eyes were still smiling in Shrimp's direction.

They turned and followed Ali along the corridor until he stopped and opened one of the doors. It was a bedroom with a tiny en-suite. The room was turned into an office: laptop, filing cabinet, table and chair, the bed pushed up against the left-hand side, white tiles on the wall the same as they were in all the guesthouse rooms. Ali shut the door behind him. He motioned for them to sit on the one chair and stool, whilst he sat on the bed. Ali switched on the air con, a noisy box cut into the window. A thin piece of old sheeting was cut around the air con box for a curtain.

'Do you live here?' asked Shrimp.

Ali flicked his head towards the right. 'Next door. I was born in these Mansions. This is my home; rough on the outside but it has a big heart. Or it used to be. We have nothing but trouble here now.'

'Did you know the dead girl?'

Ali shook his head. 'There are so many here now. It's the newcomers causing the trouble.'

221

'Have you heard of the Outcasts?'

'Sure. That's all we hear about at the moment. Their graffiti is all up the walls. They call themselves the lone wolves, draw it on the walls. They look like kids, but when they get in a group they are more like animals.'

'Have they threatened you?'

Ali thought for a moment before he replied. 'Not me, but my family. First we started getting offers to protect the restaurant for a cut of the takings. We paid them off like we always do. It's part of life here. But last week a new group came in demanding money and making threats. "Give us the money or else we will torch the place." That kind of thing.' He looked at Mann. 'It's the one thing we all dread in the Mansions – fire. It's not exactly the place you want to be if that happens. The restaurant is on the third floor. They start a fire there, the seventeen floors above have no chance.'

'Did they speak to you?'

'I wish. No, they waited until I wasn't there. They spoke to my uncle. He works on the till. He's an old man.'

'What did he tell them?'

'He told them to fuck off. Then they kicked the shit out of him. Indians in Hong Kong don't get the fucking respect they deserve. When it was a colony it was different. We were all under the same British umbrella, so to speak. Indians had respect. But not now. The kids can't get jobs. They go for interviews but they never get the work. It's the same all over. You have to be able to speak and write Mandarin. Who the fuck can do that? We are pushed further from the mainstream Hong Kong business world. Now the young ones are coming up with no prospects. The Indian community is big on education, these are smart kids. They don't want to work in the restaurants, become tailors, sell fake goods. They want to be lawyers, top businessmen. They are not getting the chance.' Ali looked at Mann and realized he'd missed out a vital piece of information: 'These were not your usual Chinese bullyboys – Triads. We get enough of them and we pay up when we have to. These were different.' Mann waited. Ali lowered his voice. 'These were just kids. Well, not just any kids; these were Indian kids turning on their own kind; newcomers, they are to blame for all the trouble.'

'What about your brothers? What do they think?'

Ali fidgeted. 'My brothers? Mahmud is a bright lad – he will go far.'

'And Hafiz?' asked Mann.

Ali hesitated. 'Look, Hafiz is a bit wild. He is a good boy at heart. He gets a lot of flack from the old man. I hope he will be all right in the end. I hope, if things turn out well for the Mansions, if we get someone to invest in it, I hope that we will all be okay.'

Ali was looking at Mann when he spoke. Mann didn't answer. He was feeling claustrophobic in the tiny room. It was impossible to tell where ceiling began and wall ended. Large white tiles were everywhere. He'd seen a place like this in one of his nightmares.

'Do you know a girl named Lilly Mendoza?' asked Shrimp.

'Yes, I know Lilly. We all do. She's a little tramp but she has it hard. Her stepdad Rizal is a nasty piece of work. He will try it on with any of the women. He doesn't care who they are. He has a bad streak a mile wide.'

'Does he try it on with your sister?' asked Shrimp.

Ali looked shocked at the suggestion. 'If he did I would kill him. And look, I'd like to help about the girl Rajini but I don't know most of the Indians living here. We tend to stick to our own kind.'

'The caste system?'

Ali shrugged. 'In a small way. No one wants to admit it but there's no way I would marry someone from a lower class than my own. It just isn't an option.'

Mann and Shrimp left Ali in his office and waited for the lift.

'What do you make of him, Shrimp?'

'Fly boy. Likes his wealth on display. He's a nice enough guy but he's streetwise rather than clever. He thinks he's being clever, telling us stuff he hopes will steer us away from his brothers. He's protecting his family.'

'Exactly.' Mann gave Shrimp a sideways glance and a grin. 'His sister Nina likes you, Shrimp. I think you should come back tomorrow, follow up some leads.'

'Her family won't like that.' Shrimp gave an embarrassed smile. 'Did you hear the way her brother talks? I reckon a Chinese guy would rank among the untouchables, don't you?'

Mann slapped him on the back. 'Yeah, but your mission is to boldly go where no man has gone before.'

Mann took out the hair ornament that Flo had given him. Her pewter and white hair was woven into a tight clasp. Helen's image flashed into his head. It took his breath away. Mann saw her twisting at the end of a rope, a black hood over her head.

'You all right, Boss?' Shrimp was staring at Mann.

Her body covered in blood. He saw the hand raised to whip her.

Mann rubbed his face with his hands as if trying to erase the images in his head. 'Yes. I'm all right, Shrimp. I just want to focus on work. Let's go and find Rizal.'

CHAPTER 44

Mann and Shrimp walked back down to the ground floor where the Mansions' arcades fanned out and ran parallel to the main hub. Around them was a dilapidated row of backpacker suppliers. They found Rizal playing dice amongst the knocked-off North Face backpacks. A young Filipina with bad skin and heavy features was sat on Rizal's lap, her arm around his neck; she had on shorts and a top that pushed her small breasts into a cleavage. They stopped playing dice and looked up as Mann and Shrimp approached. The girl kept her eyes on Mann whilst nuzzling at Rizal's ear.

Rizal was playing dice with two other Filipinos, one slick, expensive-looking glasses perched on his head, black trousers, shirt open to his waist, he looked like a musician from one of the many Filipino bands in Hong Kong. The other one was slobby with a badly stained, shiny red shirt, a manual worker, tough, strong.

Rizal looked them up and down. He recognized what they were straight away. 'The food is finished, sold out. Come back tomorrow.' Then he turned to the others and grinned as he spoke under his breath in Filipino. The other two men laughed.

Mann grinned back. 'That's okay. We'll wait.' Mann indicated that Shrimp should pull up a spare stool. There was only one. Shrimp dragged it over and sat next to Slick.

'Wait for what?' Rizal rolled his eyes at his friends and raised his voice an octave. 'Huh? Wait for what? The Food Is Finished,' he said as if they might not understand English.

Mann pulled a stool out from under Slick. Slick fell on the floor, jumped to his feet and went to retaliate. Shrimp reached out to stop him.

'You were ready to leave, weren't you? We mean no harm, we come in peace.' He nodded gravely and then grinned. 'Now fuck off.'

Mann resisted the urge to smile. He had seen Shrimp change over the years, grow to be a man. He had seen him come off the worse in some fights, and seen him pull it out of the bag. Now he was seeing him act as a hard man when inside he was still a little boy learning about life, boundaries, the universe. The older guy in the red shirt was still watching the scene unfold. Mann saw the knife in his belt. The girl got off Rizal's lap and disappeared to pastures greener.

Rizal leaned back to look Mann over. He wiped his hand on his dirty vest, a cigarette hanging from the side of his mouth. 'I told you, the food is finished. We are all out of pork. Come back tomorrow.'

227

Slick, still seething, was obviously weighing Shrimp up to see if he could take him. He probably could, muscle for muscle – but then it wasn't about how much muscle, just how you used it. Shrimp had yet to flesh out. Slick laughed at Rizal's retort. Mann caught him mid-throat with the side of his hand. Slick clutched his throat and tried to breathe and then Mann slammed the flat of his hand between his shoulder blades. 'Sorry – thought you got something stuck in your throat.'

Slick fell onto his knees, choking.

'Just trying to help. Shrimp here is an expert on all things. What do you say, Shrimp?'

'He needs to go away somewhere quiet for a few hours and contemplate his life.'

'Okay, I don't want any trouble.' Rizal told his friends to go. 'What do you want?' Rizal put his cigarette on the edge of the card table whilst he packed up his dice.

'To tell you something for a start. Michelle's in custody.'

Rizal didn't blink. He picked up his dice and put them in his pocket. 'Whatever she did, ain't got nothing to do with me. What was it this time? Stealing from a john?'

'She's on a possible murder charge.'

'Huh?' Rizal looked at Mann, his jaw dropped and then he burst out laughing. 'Michelle? You have to be kidding. If she had it in her she'd have killed me a long time ago.'

'Yeah, that's what I said, but then someone

pointed out you might have put her up to it which is why I'm here. We need some blood from you. We need to take your prints. I can take you in now or you can save us a job and go there yourself.'

Rizal shook his head, rolled his eyes, irritated. 'You ain't got nuttin' on me. If Michelle is banged up it has nothing to do with me. You wanna find Lilly, her daughter. I won't have any curry to sell. How am I going to feed my kids? You should let her go. We have real live problems round this place. People die every fucking day here and no one cares. Just coz it's some rich foreigner there's fucking trouble.'

'This new group of kids, the Outcasts, have you heard of them?'

'I know them. Outcasts, lone wolves.' Rizal snorted with derision. 'Just a pack of mangy dogs. Just a bunch of ugly kids. That little bitch Lilly's one of them. She's always looking for trouble. Don't worry. I'm going to teach her a lesson she won't forget.'

'Do you know who's doing the recruiting?'

Rizal locked his eyes on to Mann's and then he looked away and shrugged. 'I think it's Chinese. I have seen some new faces in the Mansions, expensive suits, and expensive-looking women.'

Mann heard footsteps coming along the corridor. He looked over at Shrimp. Shrimp had moved to the far side and was watching someone approach. Slick and a new man appeared; he was as broad as he was tall. A strong-looking fighter. They had the Filipino's choice of weapon – the street knife: solid, long bladed. It was the art of Eskrima, the Filipino martial art. Its masters trained in street alleys, barefoot on broken glass, where space was limited and you had to kill quick and get away fast. Hands were used as weapons, blocking, breaking bones.

Rizal looked pleased with himself. He jumped up and scurried to the back of the newcomers. One of them stepped forward, bare-chested, his scarred torso showing years of fighting. He was the oldest, around forty, strong and stocky.

The fighter spoke. 'The Mansions has its own set of rules. You come into our world, you play by them.'

Mann looked across at Shrimp. He knew he was more than capable of beating them in a clean fight but this was anything but that. Shrimp had studied Muay Thai which was nothing like as dirty as this type of combat.

Mann looked at the fighter and said, 'Chain of the hand. Kadena de mano. No weapons.'

The fighter nodded. He put his knife down.

Mann looked at Shrimp, who was placing his beloved suit jacket carefully on a chair well out of the way of the action. He looked every bit the hero in his purple shirt and suit trousers. Mann was glad he'd worn his jeans and t-shirt. He undid his shuriken belt and placed it under his leather jacket, on the floor of the corridor, and then he beckoned the fighter forwards.

The guy was agile. He was a short man but he had the traditional Filipino broad powerful shoulders, strong lean body. His hands were his weapon; they were lightning fast. He dealt Mann the first punch and followed up with three more before Mann got the message. He could already taste the blood in his mouth from two punches that had threatened to take out his teeth. Now he gauged not just the fighter's range but also his preferred lead arm, his speed on his feet, and he gauged something even more vital. The fighter had a weapon concealed in his belt.

From the corner of his eye Mann was aware of Shrimp. Shrimp was going in fast and furious. Mann knew why that would be – he wanted to inflict the most damage on his opponent and the least damage on his suit. Slick had not expected it. He did not have Shrimp's athleticism. Shrimp was hitting Slick with moves that Mann hadn't seen him use before. He turned in the air and dealt a jump sidekick that landed in the centre of Slick's chest and sent him crashing back against the wall just as another hit him to the side of the head. His head was brought down onto Shrimp's knee and Slick didn't recover. Mann could hear him moaning as he dragged his body away and out of Shrimp's reach.

The fighter was flying around Mann with his arms in every direction like flick knives, looking for gaps in Mann's defence. He rocked back and forth on his agile feet. Mann had seen enough.

He let down his guard on his left side and waited for the punch. His opponent obliged with a left cross. When the fighter's arm was full stretched, Mann caught his wrist and bent it back. He smashed the palm of his hand into the fighter's knuckles and heard them crack. He dealt three fast blows, bent the wrist back, one, snapped it then he twisted the arm and smashed down, two, popping the elbow, then three, he punched down hard on the forearm to break it. Mann flipped him over, his broken arm behind his back, and locked his head. A knife dropped to the floor out of the fighter's waistband. Mann picked it up and pressed it against the fighter's throat.

'Yeah . . . not now, old man. I'm too busy to play.' He looked up – Rizal had legged it. Shrimp went to go after him. 'Leave him, Shrimp, we'll find him when we want him. He has nowhere else to go.'

CHAPTER 45

Ruby was satisfied. She opened the vent above the cooker to let out the steam. She had an urge to clean. She had washed the white tiles, scrubbed the bed, she had cut up Steven Littlewood's body, stripped the flesh from his bones and now they were sawn into manageable pieces and boiling on top of the stove.

Ruby pushed her hair back from her face, she was sweating. She was naked. She had such a lot of work to do. Why were men always so messy? Did he have to get his blood everywhere? Ruby had worked for hours, cutting up his body. When she was finished she placed her dolls back on the shelves in the lounge. Some of them still had bits of flesh stuck in their hair. They had drops of blood on their faces but Ruby had decided she had better things to do than keep cleaning. Some things just didn't matter any more. She mustn't waste her precious time now.

She was going down to the government hospital that morning. She had been there many times. Ruby walked along the corridors and no one noticed her. Sometimes she wore a nurse's outfit.

233

Sometimes she wore a white coat. Now she could give a decent injection. She could keep someone alive long after they wanted to die. Today she wanted to see if any of the babies there needed her.

The government hospital. There weren't enough beds. There wasn't enough staff. They always needed another pair of hands.

Ruby smiled at the good-looking young doctor as she made her way along the corridor. It was late afternoon. It was a good time for her to visit, between the doctor's rounds. There were people asleep on the floor in the corridor. There weren't enough beds. People lay on mattresses. Their relatives cared for them. Ruby stopped by a family: an old woman was being fed by her daughter. It was hospital congee; a watery rice soup. Ruby knelt down beside them.

'You must be very tired,' she said to the daughter. 'Go home now and rest. I will look after your mother. Don't worry.' Ruby smiled.

The daughter hesitated but accepted gratefully. 'Thank you, nurse.'

Ruby smiled reassuringly at her. 'That's what I'm here for.'

Ruby watched the daughter leave. She tied a tourniquet around the old woman's arm and tapped the inside of her elbow to raise a vein. She slipped the needle beneath the woman's papery skin and into the vein and then she depressed the plunger and emptied the syringe. She repeated the procedure again. Then she moved to the other arm and delivered two more ten ml doses of air.

She leaned in and whispered, 'Thanks for letting me practise on you.' Then she stood and went on down the corridor to the maternity unit.

As she was walking out she heard the old woman scream in agony.

CHAPTER 46

It was 2 p.m. when Nina knocked on Lilly's door. Rizal answered. He looked at her, intrigue in his eyes.

'Yes?'

'Is Lilly in?'

He shook his head, pulled up his vest and scratched his stomach.

'Do you know when Michelle will be back?'

He shook his head, his eyes glued to the flesh showing around her slim midriff.

'Who's going to make the curry for the stall? I have brought the meat, the spices.' She lifted up her arm with the carrier bag in her hand.

Rizal shrugged and walked back into the flat. He sat down on the sofa and opened a beer, put his feet on the table and kicked off the news-papers. Rizal looked at her. She was still waiting in the doorway.

Nina looked at her watch. 'Do you want me to do it? You will lose customers otherwise and Michelle will lose money. Plus I can't get rid of this pork anywhere round here.'

Rizal waved the beer bottle at her. 'Sure. That

would be very nice. You're a good girl, Nina. Come in, close the door.'

Nina glanced nervously backwards. She didn't like being alone with any man, let alone Rizal, but Michelle was a good friend to her. If Ali caught her coming out, she would be punished. She was going to be married next month to a man old enough to be her father, but it wasn't for her to choose. The one thing she had to be was pure. Any scandal and the man might call it off. She was already at the age when she should be married with three children. She had delayed whilst she was needed to run the restaurant but now she must bend to her father's will. She must marry a man she didn't love. She looked back at the landing. It wouldn't take her long. She could have it done in half an hour and then it would slow cook for the next eight and that would be all she had to do. It was worth it to help Michelle. They relied on one another in the Mansions.

Nina placed the groceries on the kitchen surface. The kitchen and the lounge were all one room. Rizal rested his arm on the back of the sofa, turned to watch her over his shoulder. She worked with one eye on him and one eye on what she was doing. She chopped the meat and fried the spices and onions. The room filled with the familiar smell that the whole landing had come to know. She worked quickly, her hands flew around as she tried to finish the job and get out. She was so busy stirring she didn't notice Rizal standing behind her until she turned. He was watching her bottom moving beneath the silk sari as she stirred vigorously. She turned and nearly fell into him as she went to put a pan in the sink. She jumped back.

He laughed. She stepped to the side and placed the pan in the sink.

'It's a joy to watch you work. You have really quick hands. You love to keep busy, don't you? I see your whole body moving when you're working like that. You have a nice figure. I hope you have someone to show it to, do you, Nina?'

Nina ignored him and began to tidy away the things she had used. She had finished. She could leave it now. He stepped forwards and pulled her to him from behind. His hands around her waist . . .

'Please . . . no . . .' She pushed down on his hands, she struggled to get away. He held her tighter. His rough hands slid up under her top. Nina screamed, struggled.

'You're strong.'

Nina *was* strong. She lifted her grandmother in and out of bed every day. She carried heavy groceries all day long. She pushed him off and lurched forward out of his grip, knocking the spoon out of the pot, showering Rizal in scalding curry.

He screamed in pain. 'All right. All right.' He lifted both his palms in the air as if he hadn't meant to touch her and it was all a mistake.

There was a knock at the door. After much cursing Rizal answered it, still wiping the curry from his face. It was Shrimp and two other detectives.

'Please . . .' Nina stepped past Rizal. She kept her eyes locked on Shrimp's, willing him to help her.

'Are you all right, miss?'

She nodded and hurried past, disappearing down the stairs.

A dirty-faced, naked child came to cling to Rizal's leg and there was the sound of another one crying somewhere in the flat.

'What?' He looked nervously at Shrimp. 'What do you want?' He shook the child away from his leg, irritably.

'We just want a word. Can we come in?'

Rizal muttered under his beery breath as he turned and walked back into the flat and Shrimp and the detectives followed. Shrimp could see that it hadn't taken long for the place to fall apart without Michelle.

'When is she coming home? I can't cook. My business is going down the pan. I'm lucky Nina helps.' Rizal handed the crying child a piece of bread and pushed it protesting into another room. He threw off the papers from the couch and half fell, half lurched as he sat heavily down. He broke the top off a beer and drank it. He offered one to Shrimp. Shrimp declined.

'Michelle's still helping us with our enquiries. These gentlemen have come to tidy your flat for you and collect the samples that you forgot to give us downstairs. Is Lilly about?'

Rizal wiped his mouth with a disgusted growl. 'She doesn't come near here unless she wants money. She should be here to help me with all this.' He swept a drunken arm around as the noise of the crying child in the next room began to rise again. 'She should be cooking for the food stall. She should be doing something to help her family, right?'

'Where do you think I would find her right now?'

Rizal leant the rim of his beer bottle against his cheek as he thought. 'Right now? How the fuck should I know? Out with her boyfriend probably. The girl's got no morals. If you know what I mean. She gives it away to a lot of boys.' He looked at Shrimp questioningly. He got a blank face back. 'Not just boys. She likes her men does Lilly. Way older than she looks. Likes to hang around the bars at night-time, if you know what I mean. All dressed up. Skirt up to here.' Rizal ran a hand across his lap. Then he wiped his hand on his filthy trousers before finishing his beer and slamming the bottle down on the table.

'I will leave these officers here to do their job. Do what they ask; otherwise you'll be taken down the station.'

Rizal sat back on the sofa and put his feet on the table. He lit a cigarette. 'Tell Michelle I miss her. Tell her her loving boyfriend is thinking of her and misses her,' he said to Shrimp's back as he left.

Shrimp looked around for Nina, she was gone. He took the stairs down to the Delhi Grill. He went to find her.

CHAPTER 47

It was 4 p.m. when Mann got back for the meeting. Forensics had come back with some answers.

'Have you heard from Tammy?' Mia asked. She looked straight ahead as she walked purposefully. Mia had a spring in her stride. She walked like a dancer, shoulders back, chin up.

'Not since I told her to lay low. I've been caught up in the murder.' Mann took out his phone and sent her a text telling her to phone him.

The incident room was full. Mann walked in with Mia. Ng and Daniel Lu were already there. Sheng joined them as Daniel picked up an e-mail he'd just printed off.

'Saheed sent over some results. They identified a drug called Haloperidol in Max Kosmos's body. It's an anti-psychotic drug and a major tranquillizer. It blocks a number of receptors in the brain. It's given to elderly patients to keep them calm. It's given to schizophrenics to stop delusions. It was given to prisoners in Russian prisons to break them, as a sedative. It numbs the brain.'

'Why would our perp use that?' asked Mia.

242

'My guess is because it would allow them to torture more effectively. It sedates the victim but it doesn't affect the short-term memory. The victim will feel the pain but not be able to react to it.'

'The perp is one sadistic son of a bitch.' Sheng swigged at a bottle of water.

'Yes. But crucially also a sexually active and a female one,' Daniel continued. 'His penis was found in his chest cavity and it has traces of glycogen-containing epithelial cells on it – that's vaginal fluid. It had injection marks around its base. There are traces of a drug called Papaverine used by paraplegics.'

'Did Michelle mention it, Mann?'

'No.'

'It makes the penis hard,' continued Daniel. 'A thirty milligram dose injected into the base of the penis should keep it hard for six hours. The more you inject the longer it lasts – days if given enough.'

'What a way to go,' someone muttered from the back of the room.

'Not if she bites the head off after she mates. No sex, no matter how good, is worth that,' answered Mann. 'This isn't about sex. Just like rape isn't about sex, it's about humiliation, dominance. Was he anally raped, Daniel?'

'No.'

'Can they tell us if he had sex with another man?'

'No, they can't.'

'So, we still don't know whether she works alone

or in a team. Could be two women. Or it could be just one very determined one.'

'She must have sedated him well. He would have been in an immense amount of pain,' said Mia.

Daniel continued, 'We have identified Michelle's and another set found in several sites. We have blood that is not the victim's. It's a tiny amount in the bathroom. It was found on the mirror. We will be able to extract DNA from it and we have a saliva swab that matches it from the champagne bottle. There is no shortage of the perp's DNA.'

'And Michelle's DNA?'

'No. We have just prints so far.'

'If it's a double act then maybe Michelle's the torturing side and not the sex side,' said Ng.

'But then, if Michelle was there, why didn't she steal his watch, his laptop?' asked Mia. 'That doesn't fit her profile. We know she steals from guests. Why would she leave things in the room?'

'Perhaps she was told to, maybe? To throw us off? But she didn't mention the Papaverine either did she?' said Sheng.

'We can't be sure she supplies that,' answered Mann. 'Plus, I don't think she's a murderer. Michelle's an addict. She will try and leave out more than she says.'

'Everyone's capable of murder if they have to.'

CHAPTER 48

Rizal took the back stairs up to the apartment. The flat was on the fourteenth floor, a landing where several families lived long term. Rizal texted Lilly on the way. He knew she couldn't be far away. She would come if he worded it right. Rizal smelt the familiar aroma of pork curry along the landing. Nina had done a good job but she had left Rizal feeling frustrated; his mind was still on her body. He turned his key in the lock and stepped inside. The babysitter, a young woman who lived nearby, was watching TV, the twins were in bed. He dismissed her and she scurried off. She'd had trouble with him before. He opened a beer and sat on the sofa and waited.

'I got your text. You said she needed me?' Lilly stood in the doorway, leaning on the doorframe, a defiant look on her face. She was out of uniform she had on a micro mini and a tight top. She eyed the collection of empty beer bottles around Rizal's chair and her expression changed to one of disgust. 'What do you want? I thought my mother was back. I smelt the curry. Where is she?'

'Still at the station.' Rizal swigged from the beer

bottle. 'I want to talk to you. I don't want to worry your mother. I thought we could sort it out between the two of us. You're in trouble with the law?'

Lilly shrugged, with a cocky smile. 'They got nothing on me.'

'I knew you'd get in trouble hanging about with those Indian kids. You think you're smart running with those mangy kids, the Outcasts? You think it makes you into someone big?' Rizal swigged his beer. 'Is he your boyfriend? That Mahmud?'

'No. It's nothing to do with the Outcasts.'

Rizal wasn't listening. His mind had moved on to other thoughts. His eyes slipped down her body as he swigged his beer.

'I'll be out of here soon. I have plans. I am going to make it big: live in my own penthouse, drink the best wines from France. I won't have to live in this pit and smell your sweat and listen to you fart all night.'

Rizal stood, swayed on his feet a little. 'You can't do it alone. I can help you. You're a little princess. I know what you like. You like it here. I've seen you watching us at night. I've seen your eyes open. I've seen you looking at me when I'm giving it to your mother. You listen to her moan. She loves it.'

'She makes money whilst you sit on your drunken arse.' Lilly made a dash for the bedroom.

Rizal knocked over the table in his speed as he lurched out of the chair and made it the couple of metres to the bedroom door and pinned Lilly to the wall.

She shrieked. 'Don't do it, Rizal. Dad, don't hurt me. Please.'

He held her pressed against the wall and slammed the door shut as her siblings started to cry; his beer breath was in her face. 'Don't call me Dad. My name is Rizal. Your father was some Chinese john that your mother dropped her knickers for. Just another john and she was just another whore, still is. She'll never change. She has no ambition, not like you, my little princess.' He released his grip a little and stroked her face. 'You're prettier than your mother. You're a pretty girl and smart. You know what it takes for a girl to survive around here. She has to have something to give. You got money to give me, Lilly? You're living here in my house. You got money, huh?'

Lilly shook her head.

'Then you got to give me something else.'

She squirmed beneath his probing hands.

'You like it. I know you do. Why else do you come back here? You're a little whore like your mother. I will teach you a few lessons. Now . . .' He took her hand and pressed it hard against his crotch. She squeezed her eyes tightly shut and turned away in disgust. 'It needs working, no?' He held her face in his hands as he locked the door and made her look into his eyes. He looked at her mouth. 'It needs something to bring it to life.'

Lilly left Rizal snoring. She felt sick to her stomach. She stood in the hallway outside the flat and took out her phone and called Victoria Chan. 'I have thought about it. I want to do it,' she said. 'I am ready.'

'Take ten officers with you. Teach her a lesson.'

CHAPTER 49

Tammy had been staring at the text from Mann for most of the day. It was 9 p.m. She had four missed calls from him. She was following new orders. Tammy understood but it didn't feel right. She had no choice. It was just after 9 p.m. She was on the way to meet Lilly. In preparation for her initiation, Lilly was going to introduce her to someone further up the Triad ladder, a *Red Pole* in the Outcasts. She hoped it would lead her to Victoria Chan. That would be the ultimate prize for Tammy. It's what Mann had wanted. If she could find evidence against Victoria then she would be doing him a massive favour. Her loyalties lay with him. Tammy hoped he'd understand that in the end. She hoped he'd know she didn't want to disobey his orders, she had no choice.

Lilly was waiting for her outside the MTR station.

'Where are we going?' Tammy stepped in beside her as they walked away from the station.

They walked along the backstreets of Yau Ma Tei for ten minutes, dodging in and out of the stallholders setting up along the way, wheeling their stalls along the street. They moved in and out of the crowds of tourists making their way through the night market: two skinny Chinese girls with attitude.

'I told you, the boss wants to meet you,' answered Lilly. Tammy knew something was wrong; Lilly wasn't able to look her in the eyes. 'You do want to meet her, right?' Lilly was texting, looking around. She seemed nervous.

'Yeah, sure. But . . . does she live around here?' Tammy knew the area well. It was not a prestigious address. It was a sprawling low rise of old tenement blocks and a place where jade was sold, where old men bartered their bright canaries in the bird market.

'No, but we just have to meet the others first.'

Tammy followed Lilly as they slipped past the tourists and onto Saigon Street, a side road that led to the night market. It was ten thirty and the market was in full swing. Bubbling tanks of fish and crustaceans blocked the pavement as they stepped into the road and Lilly led Tammy into the side entrance of the Seafood Grill.

They passed the owner who scowled at them, looked like he was about to object but was in too much of a flap, his once-white apron covered in fish entrails, his face bright red from working in the heat of the kitchen.

'Come on,' said Lilly as she led Tammy through to a basement stacked high with boxes of defrosting prawns.

Tammy looked around her as they left the road behind. One way out, one way in. If Lilly planned to kill her then this was the ideal place to trap her. She looked at Lilly's demeanour, the tension in her upper back, the way she walked purposefully as if she only had to get somewhere as fast as possible. Lilly sensed her hesitation, caught her glances over her shoulder at the diminishing exit and she moved quicker down the corridor. Lilly looked at the kitchen porter as he stood back to let them pass, his pale face pocked with volcanic acne. He glanced first at Lilly and then at Tammy. She slowed, levelled with him and looked into his eyes. They flicked towards Lilly's back as she carried on down the corridor and then he gave a small, almost twitch-like shake of the head as he looked back to Tammy.

Tammy turned and ran. Lilly was a second behind. Tammy pulled the boxes of prawns over behind her as she bolted past. The waiting staff, their arms laden with dishes, yelled at her to stop, but she didn't. She ran through to the street outside. She knew it would take Lilly just a minute to catch her. She heard the telltale whistles calling for back-up. She knew it wouldn't take long before they found her. She ducked into an alleyway and phoned Mann.

'I need you, Boss.' She hadn't hesitated. Mann was the one she trusted to help her now.

'Where are you, Tammy?' Mann was stood in Mia's office.

'I'm in the night market, Boss. They're coming after me, the Outcasts. I need help. I thought I was meeting Victoria Chan. I'm sorry, Boss.'

'Stay out of sight. I'm coming.'

CHAPTER 50

Tammy slipped back out of the alley and took a roundabout route that led her back to the middle of the night market. It was only just getting going, stalls were still being set up. She picked up a black peak cap from a stall with Iron Maiden written on the front and threw the stallholder some money. He looked at her, looked at the note, shrugged and put it into his money pouch as he turned away without a word of thanks. Pulling the cap down over her eyes, she headed towards the busiest part of the market, between the road junctions. The plastic canopies that met above the busy street trapped the heat and the din of toys and music and shouted Cantonese.

She pulled on the cap, kept her head down and attached herself to other groups of people. Tourists were out early with their kids. The market was full of foreign voices. But, above it all, Tammy heard the whistles. She lifted her eyes enough to look either side, to the back of the stalls where they met the pavement, and sensed movement along- side her. They were looking for her. She was being closed in on. She stopped, ducked down beneath a stall and crawled on her hands and knees over the boxes of merchandise, the discarded food cartons and the scavenging rats. She only had to wait a few more minutes. It wouldn't take Mann longer than that to get a unit here. She just needed the noise of a police siren to scare them off. She could hear her breath as she squeezed through the minute spaces. She doubled back on herself slowly, crouching low, and waited. Above her head a stallholder was arguing with an irate mother whose child had bought a duff toy an hour ago.

Above their arguing she heard sirens and her heart leapt. She shook her head in relief. It was then that the stallholder saw her and reached in and dragged her out. 'Thief! Stealing my toys whilst I am being distracted. What are you? A team of thieves?'

Tammy tried to shut him up. 'I'm a police officer. Do as I say. Shut up for Christ's sake. Please . . . shut the fuck up.'

The stallholder lifted his voice again. 'Thief!' He had heard her well enough but he wanted a distraction away from the argument with the irate mother.

She had no choice but to run. She looked up to see what appeared to be the whole market closing in on her. Either side of her the tourists stared as the gang members wove between them. Tammy saw the first knife flash bright amongst the tack and plastic. She ran.

CHAPTER 51

'Police officer down,' Detective Inspector Johnny Mann shouted into the radio.

The noise all around him was deafening.

'I said police officer down. For fuck's sake get an ambulance here.'

The woman clutched her little girl to her as she stood staring down at Mann and Tammy who was convulsing on the pavement amidst the nodding puppies, replica toys, t-shirts and sunglasses.

'At the junction of Saigon Street. There could be other casualties . . . I don't know . . . Just move it.'

Mann knelt over Tammy's unconscious body and pushed his fingers over the wound in her chest to try to stop the bleeding. 'Give me that. Quick . . .' he shouted to the woman who was still holding the white silk shawl she had been haggling over. 'Another one . . . more. Quick! Quick!'

She looked around, flustered, threw it to him. He pressed the fabric into the wound. Above the screams of frightened tourists, Mann heard Ng shouting for him.

'Over here, Ng. It's Tammy, she's hurt.'

Ng crouched beside them for a second. Shrimp

ran past. Ng called out to him: 'Check if there's any sign of them, Shrimp.'

'I'm on it,' Shrimp answered, leaping over the smashed stalls, dodging the screaming tourists who were caught in the middle of it, frantic to get away. He caught sight of the backs of running gang members and increased his pace. As he exited out from the tunnel of stalls he heard voices. He came face to face with an Indian boy holding the bloody knife in his shaking hand.

Shrimp pinned him to the ground and read him his rights.

The ambulance screamed down Saigon Street and came to a halt as its lights filled the night sky above the bright stalls.

Mann felt Tammy's pulse . . . nothing. He knelt over her, locked out his arms, placed one hand above the other over her chest. Tammy's body bounced under Mann's pressure as he pressed hard and fast rapid presses onto her chest. Blood seeped through his fingers turning the white silk shawl crimson.

CHAPTER 52

Mann watched one of PJ's customers dip naan bread into the bright red tandoori sauce and wipe it around the metal bowl. His stomach knotted. Tammy's blood was ingrained in his fingertips. It had been a terrible night and it showed. Mann was ashen faced and his eyes were smudged and dark with tiredness. Mann had helped the paramedics for forty minutes. They had stabilized Tammy before leaving the market but she was barely alive. He waited for PJ to finish wiping his hands on the white starched napkin that hung over his arm, traditional waiter style, then he called him over.

'Is everything all right, Inspector?' PJ smiled, but his eyes showed concern as he looked at Mann's face. Mann gave a small nod and half a smile by way of answer and thanks for the concern. He took a sip of water and wiped his mouth on the cloth napkin – a nice touch, cloth napkins in a place where all you could eat came for less than a coffee in a plush hotel.

'Please sit down at a table, eat.'

Mann kept one eye on Hafiz as he talked. He kept

glancing over. He worked hard to serve all of the tables; the place had a hundred customers all crammed into what was only ever meant to be someone's front room.

Mann raised his hand and shook his head. 'No time, thanks, PJ.'

He looked across at Hafiz who was waiting on the tables. Mann watched him work the tables. Hafiz passed them on the way to the kitchen. Mann grabbed his arm, held on to it tightly. 'You all right?'

Hafiz was sweating heavily. He looked at Mann's hand on his arm and then he turned to answer the shouts for service that went up from a table behind them. He nodded. Mann released his arm.

'Walk me to the hall, PJ. I have some questions.' Mann got up to leave.

PJ did as he was told and they stood in the airless landing outside the restaurant. PJ stood eye to eye with Mann. The two men: tall, broad-shouldered Mann, PJ with the weight of fifteen more years around his girth and too many poppadoms.

'Tonight there was trouble in Yau Ma Tei. The Outcasts were involved. Several were wounded. Many were arrested. A young police officer was badly hurt.' Behind them, through the glass door, Mann could see Hafiz watching them.

'I am so sorry, Inspector. It is a terrible thing. When people risk their lives in public service.'

'The thing is, PJ, some Indian youths were

258

amongst those arrested.' A look of confusion crossed PJ's face. Mann continued. 'And your son Mahmud was one of them.'

PJ gasped as he clutched his apron. 'No, he can't be.' PJ shook his head and then instinctively swung round to look through the glass door at Hafiz who was staring back at his father. 'I do not understand how this has happened. My cleverest son. He will be a doctor, a lawyer. He is the one who has gone bad?' PJ turned back to Mann. 'It must be a misunderstanding. It cannot be true . . .'

'It's serious, PJ. We're still holding him. He's not talking to us. He won't tell us why he joined up and he won't tell us who recruited him. I can't help him unless he helps me. He was caught with a knife in his hand.'

The colour drained from PJ's face.

'Is this the first you've heard of Mahmud running with the Outcasts?'

'Yes. It's the first I've heard of that.' He shook his head, dazed, in shock. 'If Mahmud got caught there then it was an accident. You couldn't get a smarter boy than him. There's no way it was what it looks like. Mahmud is too smart for that. What is the charge?' His voice came out loud but shaky.

'Attempted murder of a police officer.'

CHAPTER 53

Mann went to the hospital and sat in the chair by Tammy's bed. He watched the nurses come and go, checking on their patient. The machines breathed for her. The drips fed into her system. Pouches of blood hung from hooks. Mann looked at her and wondered what she was dreaming of. Mann's dreams scared him. He was too frightened to fall asleep any more. He was frightened to be alone. He felt he belonged to the life of shadows more than ever. Nothing made him happy. Everything brought him a heavy burden. He hadn't smiled in a long time. He hadn't had a good sleep for weeks. Mann had so many snapshots of hell locked into his brain that he could barely contain them. When he slept, someone let them out. He longed to run on the top of a mountain range, to lift his head and feel the icy wind cut into his lungs. He longed to be free of the burden of knowing too much, feeling too much. He closed his eyes briefly. He listened to the comforting sound of the machines. He didn't want to go home. Home was where his heart had been broken. Home was where he didn't belong.

His body felt heavy. He listened to the sounds of voices in the corridor outside and was comforted by the noise, the odd shout, laugh, whispered concerns and the swish of a uniform, the rolling of trolley wheels. Now, in the quiet of the room, listening to the comforting electronic beep of Tammy's heart, he felt safe enough to close his eyes and try to sleep. He tried to find that mental paradise – once it had been a white sand beach, listening to the gentle lapping of the waves, feeling the sun on his face and the breeze over his skin. He and Helen dreamed of escaping to a beach hut somewhere. That was in the early days of their relationship. That was when Mann had let his guard down and Helen had found the cracks in his armour. But it hadn't lasted and over the five years they were together by the end, they were almost strangers again, come full circle. Helen knew it was over, that's why she had pushed so hard to go to the next stage in their relationship: marriage, kids. The more she pushed, albeit gently, the more Mann realized it was never going to be for him. The more she loved him the more trapped he felt. It was then that he realized he wasn't someone who would find happiness through loving another. He was irrevocably damaged.

He was just a scrawny eighteen-year-old, when the men held him back and forced him to watch his father's execution. His father had taken twenty minutes to die as each man aimed his cleaver and felled his father like a tree. The last blow split his skull. Mann had been as helpless as a baby to stop it happening. The men had left him weeping. He had crawled on his hands and knees to his father, and cradled his bloody body. Mann had scars in his heart and soul that would never heal, no matter how much Helen tried. So Mann had let her go when she called his bluff. He had let her leave when she said it was now or never. He hadn't realized the taxi would take her to hell.

He sat back in the chair and willed sleep to come. He felt his body become heavy, his muscles released their tension. Mann's dreams were often in English. But his dreams were nightmares in any language. The background noise of the corridor outside filtered in as dull lullaby, comforting, droning and then it stopped resisting and let the muscles go and Mann drifted into an uneasy sleep. He found himself back with Helen. She was laughing, smiling. For a few seconds he was so happy to see her face and then her expression changed. Mann couldn't wake up. He was caught in hell with her. He was twisting with pain. His head was inside the hood. He was with Helen. Her voice was his. Her screams coming out of his own mouth. From outside the darkness he heard two men talking. Mann had always believed he killed the man who took the last breath from Helen until now.

'Sir?'

He was awakened, startled by a nurse staring into his face. He could smell her starchy uniform, hear it crackle. It was light in the room.

'Any change?'

The nurse turned away and went back over to check on Tammy. She changed her drip and set up a new bag of blood and saline. She moved around the bed with a hypnotic calmness, a precision that Mann could have watched for hours. Her tasks were executed in sequence, in silence. Her hands moved, her starchy uniform touched the bed and creased. Her eyes watched and her ears listened. She shook her head as she finished taking Tammy's obs.

'She's holding on,' she said with that look of sympathy that Mann knew well. It said, you should go; there are worse times to come, go and get some rest. Mann knew she was right but he also knew that he had scores to settle first.

CHAPTER 54

Mann stormed past CK's shrieking PA. He grabbed Victoria by the arm as she sprang out of her chair and tried to get away. He pushed her across the room.

'Is this what you're all about? Is this what you want me to be a part of? You pleased with yourself? A young woman lies seriously wounded in the hospital. Do you want another death on your hands?'

Victoria backed away. 'I did not order the attack on your officer.' But her eyes were shining triumphant; they told him that she had known he would come. He was still a piece on her chess board.

'You sick bitch . . .'

She backed up until she could go no further. 'You want someone to blame, look in the mirror. I warned you.' She flinched as he pushed her again and she knocked into an Andy Warhol original. It juddered against the wall.

'She is worth a million of you – you power hungry, mercenary, twisted . . .'

He watched her eyes flick to something behind

him. He turned to face the two same bodyguards from the Oceans bar. Mann reached inside his jacket and took out a set of six two-inch-diameter stars. He sent them out in an arc and they spun through the air and cut into the face and arms of the two square-set guards. One of them pulled his gun. Mann unleashed Delilah, her cord attached. She struck the bodyguard's hand before he had time to aim. The gun fell to the floor, his forefinger still attached. He shrieked in pain and clutched his bleeding hand. Delilah recoiled back into Mann's hand and he held it to Victoria's throat.

'It's all right, leave us,' she hissed.

The bodyguard reached down to pick up his gun and retrieve his finger.

'Leave it.' Mann glared at him. The bodyguards shuffled out. The PA hovered. 'Get out,' shouted Mann, 'before I cut your fucking head off.'

'Leave,' Victoria rasped.

She turned to him when they were alone and he released his hold, took Delilah away from her throat. 'You ought to learn some manners if we are going to work together.'

'The only thing I am interested in doing is watching you die. Slowly. You disgust me.'

'It is your fault the young policewoman got injured. If she dies, it will be blood on your hands. I merely passed on the information that she was an officer in the Hong Kong police. The Outcasts have their own rules.'

Mann relaxed his grip on her and threw her down into her chair. She landed awkwardly with a muffled scream; her tight dress rose up over her thighs.

She smiled up at him as she turned her chair to face him. 'I told you I would play dirty. I warned you when we met. You did not listen. This is my time to get what I want. I didn't suffer all those years of living with a bully like Chan for nothing and I will stop at nothing to get what I want. And there is so much more to come. The wheels are set in motion. But you can change everything. You can stand in the road and stop it from happening. Only you have the power. I want you to take it.'

She reached down to the hem of her dress and eased it slowly back down over her legs. 'You have a bad temper, Inspector. You should learn to step back from your feelings. I could teach you.' She brushed her hair back from her face. 'I could share many things with you.'

'You did all this to set me up? You knew all about Operation Schoolyard?'

'Knew? Not exactly. Let me just say, I knew enough. This is Hong Kong. I have the power and the wealth to buy most things. I have friends in high places. Don't think you have any secrets from me, Inspector.'

Mann shook his head, nothing made sense; all he knew was that he had let Tammy down.

Victoria smiled at him, malice in her eyes. She could see his pain, his doubt. 'You think your world is safe. You think you can trust those nearest to you? Think again. You have a traitor for a friend. I knew just enough to use the information. It is not my fault she got injured, it is yours. I told you to listen to me. I told you I had the power to pick up your world and smash it down over your head and all those you care about. I can destroy you, Mann, never doubt it. But I don't want to. I want us to be friends. How long do you think you'll be allowed to stay on in the police force when you are clearly such a risk to your fellow officers?'

'You low life. I find you repulsive. You are an evil bitch. If you were the last woman on earth I wouldn't have you.'

Mann saw her face tighten, her mouth twitch. He saw her weakness. She didn't like to be turned down. He grinned. 'Be assured: I'll be watching every step you take from now on. You want a war. You got it.' Mann walked out, picking up the body-guard's finger as he went.

CHAPTER 55

'Yes sir, I do understand but I am following up on the arrest of your son.' Shrimp was standing his ground with PJ. He'd left Rizal to it and come in search of Nina. 'I need to speak to the other members of your family.'

From the corner of his eye Shrimp saw Nina pass them on the way into the kitchen, head down. She had her sari pulled up over her head and had wrapped the fabric around to cover her face.

'She knows nothing. She is busy. Let her go. Please, I assure you, Nina is a good girl. She works very hard. She doesn't have time to talk . . .' PJ looked ready to burst into tears as he wrung his hands and shook his head.

'I just need a few words. I won't keep her long. I am only trying to help Mahmud.'

Nina had just returned from her encounter with Rizal. She was upset. She hadn't seen Shrimp. She was hurrying through the restaurant laden with groceries.

'Excuse me, miss?' Shrimp said. Nina hesitated but did not turn to look at him. 'Can I have a word?' Shrimp stepped around PJ.

268

PJ flushed with panic and exasperation. 'Okay, okay. Nina, come!'

Nina walked over and, recognizing him, smiled at Shrimp. PJ signalled to Hafiz to fetch Ali. 'Sit at the table over there. We will get busy soon but it will be all right for a few moments.' The place had just a few stragglers in.

'Sorry miss, I just need a quick word.' Shrimp wished he didn't feel so nervous.

'You don't have to answer anything,' PJ snapped at his daughter but he smiled at Shrimp, obviously flustered but still remembering to be polite.

Nina's eyes flicked back and forth across Shrimp's face. 'The detective won't keep me long. I am happy to speak.' She set down her packs of shopping and gestured to Shrimp to follow her as they went to sit where PJ had said.

Shrimp could see the sorrow in her pretty face. Her eyes searched his, she looked away, shy. Shrimp's heart was beating fast. He knew he was blushing. He had an overwhelming desire to kiss her. He shook it off and his voice came out a little cracked. 'Thank you,' he coughed to clear it. 'Thank you for talking to me. I just wanted to ask some general questions about the circumstances leading up to the stabbing of the officer in Mong Kok. Did you know your brother was involved with the Outcasts?'

Nina shook her head. 'There is no way Mahmud is guilty of hurting the police officer. Mahmud wouldn't hurt another human being. He is the

most gentle of boys. He hated the gangs. He did
not belong to the Outcasts or any of them. He
didn't need to – he was set to become someone
all on his own.'

'What do you think he was doing there?'

'I don't know. Maybe he was tricked. Maybe he
was lured there. Maybe he thought he was going
to do some good. I just don't know. But you can't
keep him in prison if he didn't do it, can you?'

'I caught him with the knife in his hand, Nina.
I made the arrest myself. What can I say to you?
He is denying it but won't tell us who did it. His
silence will be seen as guilt. I can see him going
to prison for it if he doesn't tell us who was
responsible.'

Nina turned away from Shrimp and her eyes
filled with tears.

'I'm truly sorry.' Shrimp wanted so much to
reach over and touch her hands. They were rough
from work but they were still beautiful hands. 'If
Mahmud didn't do it then we have to find out
who did and why he is shielding them. Are you a
friend of Lilly's?'

She looked back at him, her eyes panicking. They
flicked up as her father passed. She willed Shrimp
to wait before he spoke more. PJ had passed when
she nodded.

'I wondered why you were in the flat just now.
It looked like there was a problem with Rizal. Is
everything okay?'

'Oh, thank you. Yes. I was cooking the curry for

Michelle for her stall. She will lose business otherwise. The Filipinos in the Mansions rely on her to feed them. We don't eat pork you see but she cooks it for them. But Rizal isn't nice. I won't go in there again unless Michelle is there. He isn't a good man.' She looked away, embarrassed.

'And Lilly? She's a friend?'

'She's younger than me. We don't have so much to talk about. She is more a friend to Mahmud and Hafiz. She's their age.'

'Do you think she is the cause of a lot of trouble here at the Mansions?' Shrimp asked.

Nina shook her head. 'I think she has been led astray by the older ones. The Outcasts have taken a hold here. Nothing is the same as it was.'

'A young girl was murdered. She was from here. She was an Indian girl.'

Nina nodded, she looked to see if her father was listening. He was pretending to be busy as he marched past them carrying things that didn't need to be carried, wiping down already clean surfaces. Nina waited until he had passed. She whispered, 'We all know about the troubles. We see it every day here. My father hardly leaves this restaurant so he doesn't see it but we do. I knew Rajini. I liked her. She was quiet. She just wanted to go to school. She wanted to succeed.' Nina shook her head sadly. 'Maybe she wanted too much. I feel very sad. I hear she had a horrible death.'

'They cut off her hands.'

271

'So I heard. They brag about it – their new weapon, they call it, but it's not new it's very old.'

Shrimp looked at her. She realized he didn't know. She stood and reached one of the Indian artefacts down from the wall. She handed him a coiled whip. 'Be very careful. It is very sharp. It is called a urumi. It's an ancient Indian martial arts weapon. This is the weapon talked about by the Outcasts. I see them practising on the roof here.'

Shrimp took it from her and allowed it to unravel towards the floor: three razor-sharp strips of metal, a flexible whip.

CHAPTER 56

'Hey.' Ali caught up with Shrimp when he came out of the Delhi Grill. He was walking down the stairs. 'Leave my sister alone. She doesn't go on dates, not with you or anyone.'

'I didn't ask her for a date. I am trying to solve the stabbing of a policewoman. I'm trying to find out as much as I can to help save your brother from going to prison. Isn't that what you want?'

'We told you what we know.'

'Don't you want to help your brother?'

'It's not a case of that; we don't know any more than you. Why don't you ask him?'

'He's not talking. He fears something else more than us, more than life in prison. What would that be, do you think?'

'The gangs.'

'How long do you think he's been a Triad?'

Ali looked away in disgust. 'Don't be stupid. Mahmud is no Triad. Whatever he was doing there, it wasn't Triad business.'

'What's his relationship with his father like?'

'He is his pride and joy. You know we all do

what we can. Things haven't been easy. Our mum died five years ago. Since then we all have to help in the restaurant.'

'Even you?'

He grinned. 'It's not my thing. I help in other ways. I buy the extras we can't afford. I paid for Mahmud to get a better education. I paid for the extra lessons to learn to read and write Mandarin. I can't do it. Mahmud is clever. He takes his studies seriously. He isn't out chasing girls or taking ice. He has his heart set on being a doctor.'

'So what the hell has gone wrong?'

Ali shook his head. 'We are in crisis at the moment. The Mansions has gone fucking mad. People being chopped, killed. We are all scared of the future but now terrified of the present. We have nowhere else to go. We told you what we know.'

'Did you? I think you left out more than you said.'

'Where are you going with that?' He pointed to the urumi, wrapped in plastic, in Shrimp's hand. 'That's private property.'

'You'll get it back. Listen, Ali, no one wants to cause more trouble here. If you just let it run the Triads will take over this entire place and you'll have gang wars every night. Is that what you want for your family?'

Ali took a deep breath and shook his head. 'I'm sorry. I heard the rumours. I had an idea that it was Rajini, I should have been more helpful. I have to keep my family safe. I have to put them

274

first. I know Mahmud was not involved in the attack on the officer. My father is about to have a breakdown thanks to all of this. I have to go. There's nothing more I can tell you.'

As he walked away, he stopped and looked at Shrimp earnestly. 'But please keep trying for us. I am sorry to be strict about my sister but stay away from Nina, she's been through enough. She marries next month.'

Shrimp tried not to look like the news had impacted but inside a small jolt of pain had shot through his heart.

As he was about to step back onto Nathan Road, Nina caught up with him.

'I am sorry. I shouldn't have said those things.' She looked behind her, breathless. She didn't want to be seen talking to him. She stayed within the threshold of the Mansions.

'No, you should. It's no good hiding anything, Nina, it will just come out in the end and make even more trouble. Look, if I can help you in any way, if you need me, you call.'

She smiled gratefully as Shrimp handed her his card. It occurred to him he'd never seen anyone so lovely.

'Can you read Mandarin?'

She nodded. 'I am learning.'

He handed her his card. 'My mobile number is on the back.'

He watched her go. She turned back to smile as she disappeared back into the crowds.

CHAPTER 57

Mann headed back to Headquarters. He went straight to find Sheng. He caught him in the locker room; he smashed him back against a locker, held him by the throat.

'Did you order Tammy to carry on with Operation Schoolyard?? Did you countermand my order?'

Sheng breathed in his face. He waited until Mann loosened his grip and then he shook himself free.

'No. I didn't. You don't need help fucking things up, you can manage it all by yourself.'

Mann let him go. He took the lift up to the top floor and the stairwell up to the roof. He needed to breathe. He felt his lungs collapsing. The only calm for him was on the roof. He pushed open the fire escape door and immediately the heat hit him. The sun was directly overhead. The sun was in his eyes. The dazzling light bounced off buildings and windows. He put on his sunglasses and stood, breathing deeply. The air was clean. The smell of the ocean. The sea was vast and beautiful on the horizon.

He walked across to the parapet. The eagle had been there and left its droppings, full of tiny bones. Mann picked up three black tail feathers, beautiful, flawless. He knelt down out of the wind, wrapped them in cloth and placed them inside his shuriken pouch.

'I thought I'd find you up here.' Mia walked across the roof and stood beside Mann looking at the harbour and the sea beyond. 'What's the latest on Tammy?'

'Still critical.'

'I heard you paid a visit to Victoria Chan's office.'

'News travels fast.'

'Only some news – only when it's to certain people's advantage. You better stay away from them now, Mann. I've been told by the top brass to warn you off. You can't go in there and threaten her. This was supposed to be stealth not aggression.'

'I'm playing the game, Mia. I'm doing what they expect. Any less and they'd know it wasn't for real.' He shook his head and took a deep breath in. 'It's beginning to feel like whichever way I play it I can't win. Victoria Chan knew about Operation Schoolyard. She knew about Tammy.'

'How?'

'She made it her business. She paid someone here at the department.'

Mia wasn't having it: 'It's not possible. She's lying. Only a handful of us knew the details about Operation Schoolyard. It's gone wrong before,

Mann, it doesn't mean that someone's corrupt in this department.'

'It's not the first time we've had corrupt police officers either though, is it? Why the hell didn't Tammy do as I ordered?' Mann shook his head, slow, heavy. 'Tom Sheng denies he had anything to do with it. I don't believe him.' He stared hard at Mia. 'Is there something you're not telling me, Mia?'

'Like what? I know as much as you do.' She turned back to stare out at the rooftops.

Mann shook his head, exasperated. 'Some people have waited a long time to see me in this kind of a mess. My judgement's all to hell. I am not thinking straight.'

Mia reached out and rested her hand on Mann's arm. 'I know you have too much in your head right now with your father's mess but don't be such a hard man. You're not always in this alone. You want to talk, I'm here.'

'Thanks, Mia, but it's probably best for me to work it out alone.'

'What about your mother? Is she helping with it?'

'No. She is doing what she does best, ignoring it and hoping it will go away. I don't blame her. I've done my best to do the same but it's not working so well for me.' He smiled ruefully. 'It seems like a massive task. I thought I could walk away from my father's past. But I can't. Now it's up to me to finish the job. The thing is, all the years my mother chose to ignore it and leave it untouched, his wealth has been growing, the investments are now huge. I own a large part of a company that mines diamonds in Sierra Leone; I own several cocoa plantations on the Ivory Coast. Each project could take me a year to unravel in order to try and do something positive with it. I wish I could give it all away and forget it existed.'

'What about the family in Amsterdam? Do they have a say?'

'My brother Jake is named in some of the documents. I will try and guide him through it all when I've negotiated my own way first. His stepdad Alfie is a nice guy. He'll want me to do what I think best. He's a cop. He's not going to want Jake inheriting Triad money. I'll talk to him. I keep meaning to call. I just don't know what to say. I wish my dad's business could wait until the murder investigation was over but with Victoria pushing me and causing chaos I think I have run out of time. I feel like she's out to break me. I feel like she knows every move I make. Sometimes I think I'm losing my mind. I can't stop thinking about Helen. I even feel her presence in the flat, smell her perfume. I feel like someone's been in there, someone's been looking through my drawers, looking through the papers.' He shook his head. 'Maybe I'm just getting paranoid. But now, with Tammy going against my orders I'm wondering if I ever gave her them. Did I not make it clear?'

'Let's see if the Indian boy can tell us any more. He's waiting to be interviewed now.'

'Okay but . . .' Mann sighed. 'I don't think it's him, he's covering for someone he cares about.'

Mann left the bodyguard's finger on the parapet for the eagle and followed Mia off the roof.

CHAPTER 58

Shrimp stood opposite Kin Tak in the autopsy room. 'Could this be the weapon?' He took out the urumi and allowed it to slowly unwind to the floor.

Kin Tak coughed as a gasp turned to a phlegm rattle in his throat. He took the urumi from Shrimp with outstretched arms as if it were a baby. He laid it flat out on the counter and reached for his tape measure. He measured the strands of the urumi and wrote down his findings. He examined it under a magnifier. 'I can say, without doubt, that this is the weapon. This is it.'

'I have downloaded a demonstration from the Internet. It's awesome,' Shrimp said when he got back to the office. 'This little baby has three one-inch bands of razor-sharp steel. It's basically a flexible sword.' Shrimp let it unravel slowly towards the floor.

'It looks tricky to use.' Mann watched, fascinated. He appreciated the centuries-old skill that had first dreamt up the weapon.

Shrimp went back to his desk and turned his monitor so that Mann and Ng could see. 'It's not easy. It was only given to the most gifted apprentices in Indian martial arts schools.' Shrimp pressed the play button on the video link and two combating Indian men, practising urumi combat, came to life on the screen. They were sparring with the urumi and using a two-bladed knife to defend themselves. 'You need some strength but it's mainly down to agility and technique. This is the ideal weapon for a woman. You can tuck it into your belt or pop it into your handbag, and you can take out several opponents at once with this little baby. Someone knew what they were doing to be able to use it accurately. The damage it causes is easy to identify when you've seen it once. The speed with which it comes through the air, the razor-sharp edge of the three blades makes an unmistakable wound. It took Rajini's hands off like a hot knife through butter. And it made a mess out of Max Kosmos.'

'It's a horrible-looking thing.' Ng shook his head as he picked a Danish pastry apart; he didn't share the others' enthusiasm for weaponry.

'You see how the metal coils are whipped in circular movements in the air and then cracked down on the opponent, blocked here by a sword?'

Mann peered in at the video. 'Blow it up for me, Shrimp.'

'It will lose definition but I'll try.'

He clicked to enlarge the picture and Mann leaned across and pressed the pause button. The picture was a little blurred but still clear enough to see what Mann wanted. 'Look what they have in their hands. It's not a sword. It's the same knife we found on Mahmud, the one used to stab Tammy. It's the double-bladed one.'

'Right, are you all ready?' Mia appeared at the door.

Shrimp was busy typing in the knife's details into a search engine. 'Bundi knife. That's its name.'

Mann picked it up from his desk. 'let's see if Mahmud knows what it's called.'

CHAPTER 59

Mahmud looked every inch a frightened little boy – he also looked like he'd been passed over a cheese grater, his face and arms cut from when he was thrown headfirst into the police van the night before. Mann sat across from Mahmud in the interview room and stared at him. Shrimp leant on the wall and watched. Mia was watching from the monitoring room.

'Mahmud Khan, you are under arrest for the attempted murder of a police officer.' Mahmud stared at his lap. He was shaking. 'Do you want to tell me what happened?'

Mahmud shook his head.

'Let me tell you then. You were caught by one of my officers in the act of escaping. You were found in possession of the assault weapon used to attack police officer Tammy Wang. Is that correct?'

Mahmud nodded.

'Is this yours?' Mann picked up the knife; a two-bladed traditional martial arts knife now wrapped in polythene. He turned it over in his hands.

Mahmud nodded again.

Mann turned to Ng. 'What do you think of this,

284

Sergeant Ng?' Mann and Ng were doing the 'hard cop, soft cop' routine. Mann rested his hands on the table and leaned over Mahmud. 'Sergeant Ng is an expert in weapons and in martial arts,' Mann lied. 'He says this is a hard weapon to use, difficult. Don't you, Sergeant?'

'It takes some skill: double-bladed, serrated edges; it needs a strong arm to wield it. It needs a vicious mind. He doesn't look the kind to me. He looks like a peaceful type.'

Mahmud didn't speak. He stared at the table. Mann slammed the knife down in front of Mahmud. He jumped. It rocked on the table. Mann leaned across and punched his fist, his fingers extended, into Mahmud's lower abdomen and held it there and pressed into him. Mahmud doubled as the wind was knocked out of him. He tried to stand but Mann held him down.

'Two entry points right here. Her stomach was punctured and her liver is perforated.' Mann pushed Mahmud's shoulders back into the chair and lifted his head by his hair. He held him there and looked into his eyes. 'If she survives, she'll be on a machine; she'll need a liver transplant. That's no life for a twenty-year-old, is it?'

Mahmud didn't answer. Mann let him go. 'But neither is belonging to a Triad organization. They use people like you. Use them to do their dirty work and then they throw them away and get another one – as easy as that.'

Mahmud sat staring at the knife in front of him

as if it terrified him. Mann sat back down opposite him again.

'Why didn't you run with the rest of them?' Mahmud didn't answer. 'You don't have to worry, you know.' Mahmud looked up. He shook his head and shrugged his shoulders as if he didn't understand what Mann was getting at. 'About your gang, the Outcasts. You don't have to worry about the other members of your gang or the Wo Shing Shing. You don't have to worry about them or the Sun Yee On either. Shall I tell you why?' Mahmud's eyes flicked up towards Mann's. 'Because you are never going to see any of them again. You're not going to see your family either. That wasn't just a Triad you knifed. That was one of my officers.'

Mann got up and paced about the room, then came to stand behind Mahmud, just out of his range of vision. 'Your dad is really proud of you. He says you can read and write Mandarin. He says you will be a doctor someday. What do think of that, Sergeant?' Mann addressed Ng.

'I think he's going to break his old man's heart,' Ng answered.

'Yes, that's true. You know why?' Mahmud didn't answer but his eyes darted around the room. 'Because the only medical career you'll be pursuing is stitching up your own arse when it gets split from having too many hard cocks up it. But don't worry, you'll get used to taking it – you're going to be in there for the rest of your life.'

Mahmud shifted uneasily in his chair.

'So what made you take the oath? Why become a Triad? Or is your brother Hafiz the one I should be talking to? He was with you that night, wasn't he?'

Mahmud shook his head but he looked down at the table.

'What about your girlfriend, Lilly Mendoza? Did she tell you to target the girl? Are you protecting Lilly?'

Mahmud looked up at Mann, hopelessness in his eyes. 'I don't know anything. Lilly's a friend, that's all. She's not my girlfriend. Hafiz wasn't there. I don't know how I came to have the knife in my hand. Someone handed it to me, that's all.' Mahmud looked close to tears. 'I hope she's okay, the young woman, the officer. I'm sorry.'

Mann turned as Mia stood in the doorway. Her face said it all. Tammy was dead.

CHAPTER 60

Shrimp sat on the mosque steps. Amongst the neon and brashness of Nathan Road whose buildings bulged and leant like collapsing card houses, it was white and beautifully uniform: an oasis on the eye. It was a perfect square, a white dome in the centre, towers at each corner, it had arched windows running along each face.

Shrimp had got a text from Nina asking him to meet her at lunchtime. He had arranged to meet with David first. David came down the steps from prayer and sat beside Shrimp. He shook Shrimp's hand.

'Have you brought me any news of my brother?'

Shrimp shook his head. 'Not yet, I'm sorry. How are things at the Mansions?'

David didn't answer for a few minutes. They sat on the steps and watched the people hurry by. He shook his head. 'Things are bad. Very bad. My friends and I will have to take action soon. We have no choice now. They are children but they are killers. They meet on the rooftop at night. They wear their weapons openly in the day. No one stops them. They rule the Mansions now. But, they forget, where we come from, we are used to fighting, street battles. We are used to death. We will arm ourselves and fight to live.'

'When they have the meetings on the roof, do you go there?'

David shook his head. 'To go there would mean death, my friend. They would eat you like hungry piranhas. But, since we talked I have watched the people very closely. I see a woman come and go, beautiful, in disguise. She keeps her head down so that I cannot look into her eyes but I know she belongs with them, even though she is older. I think that is the woman you talk about. She is the leader.'

'Is she Chinese?'

'I don't know. She hides her face but her skin is paler than most. She wears nice shoes. I notice things like shoes, it's what I trade in.'

Shrimp looked at his watch. 'I have to go now. Keep watching for me, David, and I will keep looking for your brother.'

Shrimp left David, crossed the road and made his way up the stairs in block B, fifth floor.

He stood as he saw her approach. He almost didn't recognize her. She was wearing jeans. 'Nina?' She came down the stairs as he was coming up.

She smiled nervously. 'Hello. Thank you for coming. I'm sorry if it's been inconvenient.' Her long hair was loose. It fell around her shoulders.

'Of course not; it's no trouble.' Shrimp felt his

heart hammer inside his checked shirt. He had chosen to wear his vintage American cowboy boots beneath his Levi's. 'I didn't recognize you, sorry. I was really glad to get your text.' Shrimp felt his face turning red. 'You look lovely.'

'I can wear jeans sometimes.'

'You look lovely whatever you wear.'

'I can't go outside the Mansions like this. But I can wear it for you, here,' she smiled.

In the ill-lit stairwell Shrimp couldn't get over her beauty.

'We can sit here, if that's okay.' She led him to the stairs. They sat on the concrete stairwell in the shadows.

'Anywhere will be fine. Is everything all right? Your text sounded urgent.'

'My brother, Mahmud? I worry about him constantly. The whole family is distraught. My grandmother cries all the time. My father cannot work without stopping every few minutes to say prayers. We are still hoping that Mahmud will come home any day. How is he? Have you seen him?'

'He's been moved. I wasn't there when he was interviewed but he didn't say a lot. He needs to help himself. But . . .' he looked at her face, '. . . I will go and see him for you.'

'We are all stuck in our own way here, but Mahmud – he has everything. He will be someone. He is innocent. He doesn't need help from Victoria Chan or anyone.'

'Has she promised you things?'

'Yes. She has . . . she promised us a lot.'

'What?'

'My father dreams of a beautiful new restaurant. Ali thinks he will be a billionaire before he is thirty.'

'And Hafiz?'

She shook her head. 'I know what you're thinking about Hafiz. But he doesn't listen to me. Now he talks about these people as his new family. He has a new phone. He has money in his pocket. I can't blame him wanting more.'

'What about you, Nina, what do you want?'

They heard doors banging on another floor, music drifting up from below. They heard muted conversations in other languages. Her eyes glued onto his. In the dark stairwell he wanted to reach for her but he didn't dare.

'I want to find happiness. I want to feel happy.' She had a package of food for him. 'I brought you something to eat. Here . . .' She unfolded a napkin with two samosas inside; the smell of cumin burst out into the rank air. They sat with arms touching on the cramped stairwell. Shrimp ate the samosas.

'Thanks for the food. You're a fantastic cook.'

'Thank you. I love cooking.'

'Have you been back to cook curries for Rizal?'

Nina looked anxious at the mention of it. 'No. Lilly will have to do it. Is Michelle coming home soon?'

'I don't know. She's in a lot of trouble. She's suspected of having murdered someone.'

'I don't know what's happening to the Mansions. They're falling apart. All the nice people are being put in prison, all the bad ones left out. It's not right.'

Nina fiddled with her hair; Shrimp rested his elbows on his knees and struggled to think of what to say. He felt more nervous than he had felt for a long time.

They turned at the sound of a door banging on the next landing. Nina smiled at his concerned expression. 'Don't worry. No one will see me. I know the Mansions well. I was born here. I know the stairwells and the landings; I can get away if I need to.'

They looked at one another and exchanged an awkward smile.

'Do you live with your brothers?'

'No. I live with my grandmother in a flat on the fifth floor. Do you have a girlfriend, Li?' She looked away as she asked.

'Call me Shrimp, please, everyone does. No,' he looked at her and looked away, 'I don't, right now; my work kind of takes over most of the time. I like going out though, like a boogie. What about you? Do you get out? Your brother said you were going to be married next month.'

Nina became agitated. 'Anything could happen between now and then. The arrangements are being made. I have to go along with it but I don't intend to go through with it.'

'What are you going to do?'

She gave a small shrug of her shoulders. 'Run away? I don't know yet. It's not fair. I am being given to an old friend of my father's. He's an old man.'

'Don't you have a say?'

'No. I should be married by now but when my mother died everything changed. I took over the running of the restaurant. The last few years have been difficult for all of us. I am old to be unmarried.' She was getting increasingly more uncomfortable. 'Sorry, I have to go now.'

Shrimp jumped up beside her. Before he had time to think of something to say, Nina reached up, kissed him on his cheek.

'Meet me here tomorrow, same time?'

'Nina?' Shrimp called to her as she disappeared.

She stopped and ran back to him. 'Yes?'

'I am sorry if I caused offence or said anything wrong. I like you.'

She giggled. 'I know.'

CHAPTER 61

Mahmud sat in his cell. He'd come back from the hospital. He was shaking from the shock of having his left arm broken in two places. Not even the Mansions could prepare him for the remand centre. He was inside with so many young Triads who were used to the streets. The gang warfare continued inside the prison walls. He'd been beaten in a race attack, because he was an Indian who had killed a Chinese.

He sat on his bed, clutching the edge, and stared at the door, listening to the clanging of closing doors and the taunts of the prisoners. He listened to the horrible screams of the abused. He felt terrified to close his eyes in case he was attacked again. He was too distressed to eat. He hadn't eaten since he'd arrived.

The prison guard appeared at his door and ordered him to stand. 'Someone wants to see you.'

Mahmud cowered. He shrunk back into the corner of the bed. He feared the worst, a trap, a set-up. He feared this time they would kill him. The guard ordered him to march out. Mahmud kept his eyes on the ground as he walked past the people who had beaten him. They taunted him as he went. They told him he would die next time.

Mahmud sat opposite Shrimp. A guard stood in the room.

'How long will I have to stay here?' Mahmud was dressed in the prison-issue tracksuit that had seen many inmates before him – one size fits all and it swamped Mahmud. He looked like he'd lost weight. He hadn't brushed his hair or his teeth. His eyes had taken on the hollow look of one who has lost hope. But he leaned towards Shrimp, eager for any news of help, from any quarter, no matter how unlikely.

'A long time; unless you tell us what happened.' Shrimp felt sorry for him. He could see how terrified he was. His face was swollen. 'You took a beating?' Mahmud nodded. 'I'm sorry.'

Mahmud looked through his tears. The last thing he wanted to do was cry. He was terrified. He wanted to open the window and jump out. 'They broke my wrist. They stamped on my arm. I can't write now.' Mahmud talked as if in a dream. He talked as if it didn't matter. He shook his head. His shoulders slumped over.

'Yeah, the sooner we get you out of here the better, Mahmud. But you have to work with me. As long as you're not telling us what happened then we can't help you. You're not telling us anything new. You were caught at the scene. I caught you myself, you didn't even run. What were

295

you doing there? Did you give time for someone else to get away? You were with the Outcasts that night, and yet you say you are not one of them. Your dad says you said you were going to study. What took you across town that night?'

'I don't belong here. I am not a Triad. I hate the Outcasts for what they've done to our family. I hate the way they've ruined everything in the Mansions. It was always tough but we all looked after each other. We were all a family. It didn't matter what colour you were. Now it's like living in hell. Now they are turning on each other.' He paused. 'Have you seen my family?'

'I've seen your sister. She asked me to come.'

Mahmud's eyes glued onto Shrimp's. The mention of home, of his family was enough to make him well up. 'How is she? And Hafiz, how is he? My father and Ali? What about Grandmother? How are they all?'

'They are all right. They are worried about you. They want you to come home. They don't understand why you're here. Your father wants you to co-operate. Nina wants you back.'

Mahmud nodded, blinked away a tear. 'Is she still to be married?'

'I don't know. I hope not.'

Mahmud searched Shrimp's face. 'Do you know my sister well? Shrimp nodded. 'Then you have to stop her. You have to help her. Her life will be ruined. Tell her it is not too late. Tell her to run away. I will be okay here, tell her not to worry.'

'Mahmud, listen to me, it is an honourable thing to cover for your younger brother but we will uncover the truth in the end. Hafiz was involved in the fighting that night, wasn't he? He had a wound on his arm. He ran from the scene, didn't he? You saved him.' Mahmud stared down at his hands. 'Or was it Lilly?'

Mahmud looked at Shrimp and shook his head. 'Lilly and I were good friends once, but not so much now. She has changed. She is getting into more trouble every day.'

'You've known Lilly a long time?'

'All my life. Her mum has been so kind to us all since my mum died. Nothing was the same after that. Nina had to look after things. Grandma became an invalid. We all had to help in the restaurant. Michelle and Lilly have been like family, until now.'

'Michelle is a hard-working woman. Do you ever help her out?'

'Sometimes, when she needs things doing and Rizal is busy. I don't mind helping.'

'She's an attractive woman. Does she ever ask you to join her in the hotel sometimes? Sometimes she entertains guests, alone. They need a bit of something extra? It's nothing to be ashamed of.'

Mahmud shook his head and blinked at Shrimp. He didn't understand.

'What about Rizal? Do you get on well with him?' Shrimp continued.

Mahmud flushed with anger. 'Rizal is a scumbag.

He has something going on in every part of the Mansions. He thinks he owns the Mansions the way he struts around, and he abuses Lilly. She's told me. She hates him. She would kill him if she could.' Mahmud stopped, controlled his anger and remembered he wasn't talking to a friend.

'The head of the Outcasts is Victoria Chan, right? What contact have you had with her? Does she come to the Mansions?'

Mahmud stared down at his hands whilst he considered what to say. He looked at the guard. He was shaking again.

'Sometimes she comes. She came to our restaurant first a year ago. She sat down with all of us. She told us that the time would come when the Mansions would be knocked down. We didn't believe her. It has been the same for so long. She said we could sign a document that would mean we would definitely have a place in the new Mansions, better, bigger. She made it seem like we were special. She said as we had been there so many years we could expect extra-special treatment. And what she wanted was to help us have a place in the new Mansions. We only had to let things happen: let the Outcasts do what they wanted, let people be murdered every day, let decent people live in fear. She said our family would be okay. But they're not.'

'What happened that night? If you tell us who organized the fight then we can help you. Was it Rizal? Why should you be banged up in here while he is free to do what he wants on the outside? Mahmud, listen to me . . . you want me to get you out, I will do my best. Tammy was a friend as well as a police officer. She was young, sweet, so sure she could make it. She had a boyfriend, she had parents. Their lives are ruined now. She was their only child. I want to get the person who did this.'

Mahmud shook his head. 'She says different things to different people. She hooked in the Outcasts to do her dirty work. I don't know if there were orders to kill the officer. I was just in the wrong place and was passed the knife, nothing more. I can tell you nothing else.'

'I need something more to work with if I'm going to get you out of here. I need a name. Was it your brother? Was he ordered to target the officer?'

Mahmud lifted his eyes slowly and looked at Shrimp incredulously as he shook his head and then stood to leave. 'You do not understand anything. Soon it will all be too late to help any of us. I have nothing more to say. If you love Nina then save her.'

CHAPTER 62

'It's not your fault, Genghis.' The office was subdued. The news of Tammy's death sat heavily on the whole of Headquarters. Questions were on everyone's lips as to why she was put at such risk. Mann was staring into space and seeing nothing but his thoughts when Ng came back into the office and found him.

Mann shook his head angrily. 'I should never have put her into a mission like that. I pitched her against the skills of Victoria Chan. Why didn't Tammy get out when I told her?'

'It was always just going to be a matter of time before we put a female agent in there and before it went wrong. It just means she was unlucky – it happens. There's nothing you could have done; it wasn't just your decision. We're a team, remember?'

Mann shook his head. 'No, Ng. I was her operator. The buck stops with me. No matter what you say, it doesn't help. Maybe others have lost agents, maybe it happens, but it hasn't happened to me before and it was my duty to protect her.'

'She knew the risks. Every undercover cop knows them. It's a dangerous world to go into but, even with the rewards and promotion, it isn't always worth it. I was eighteen months undercover in the end. I got so used to it, I hardly knew where I belonged any more. Every undercover cop crosses the line. Otherwise it wouldn't work. When you come out it's really hard to go back to your ordinary life. I was used to leading the life of a highly paid Triad. I drove fast cars, snorted cocaine, slept with beautiful hookers. I had so much money. You're told to use it, to exploit your talents, to gain trust. You are told it will be worth it for your career. But you are never the same again. I had looked deep inside myself and seen something that could be harnessed and used for evil. I have spent the rest of my life telling myself I did a good job but knowing that it came easy. It takes a stronger man than me to come out untarnished with your soul intact.'

'You never took the promotion,' Mann reminded him.

'No.'

'Tom Sheng did.'

'Tom Sheng liked what he saw when he walked on the dark side. I turned into someone I didn't like; he respected the man he saw in the mirror, I hated him. Sometimes our paths crossed, Tom and me. We were both undercover at the same time. Both as members of the Wo Shing Shing. We were in different branches, responsible for different things. I was part of the team in charge of getting the drugs into Hong Kong. He was part of the one responsible for getting it distributed. We liaised as Triads, never as policemen.' Ng paused. 'I didn't take the promotion because I wasn't sure what I did was right. I wasn't sure it made me a better cop. I want to save lives not help distribute the drugs that end them, even if the overall goal was a good one. I have been a Buddhist ever since. Your father was a Buddhist; he tried to do good in the end. He just ran out of time.'

'My father still has a hold on this world. His legacy lives on and now I have to wonder whether even Tammy has paid the price for it. Was I too distracted with my father's business that I wasn't thinking straight? Did I fuck up?'

Mann read Ng's eyes. There was a sadness in them that he understood. The sky above was faultless, the sun bounced off the rooftops. Mann looked for the eagles. He saw one watching him as it hovered by the window. Mann turned back to Ng.

'I wish I had the one answer to it all, Ng.'

'You do have, in your heart. Your eyes are on the horizon again, Genghis. Remember the way is in your heart, not in the sky.'

There were no stars that evening, just cloud. Mann had been to see Tammy's mother. Ng had offered but Mann wanted to. He wanted to feel the full weight of it. She thanked Mann, comforted by his concern. It was all Tammy had ever wanted – to be a police officer. She died doing something she loved. She died making a difference.

It was bullshit. Mann had to look away when she said it. He felt like he had personally sent Tammy to her death. He felt like his was the hand that held the knife. His mood was beyond just getting drunk. It was still steeped in anger. Five hours later Mann had bypassed any comfort he might have hoped to get from the alcohol he consumed that evening. It didn't seem to matter how much he drank; he just got more sober. He headed for a side of town he hadn't been to in a while – old Wanchai; a small remnant from the Suzie Wong era. In his pocket he had the piece of bondage tape used to tie Max Kosmos's legs.

Halfway through the evening he headed down the steps to one of his old haunts, the Bond bar in Wanchai. He hadn't been in the Bond bar for a while. It used to have a Bond Girl theme, not anymore. He'd heard it had been revamped. A big muscled doorman stood at the entrance. He was dressed like a gladiator. He looked Mann over as if trying to find a reason not to let him in. He grunted something and stood back to allow Mann to pass. As Mann walked through to the bar he could see that the place still specialized in sleaze; the bar was darker than ever. Each girl was sat in the middle of a raised podium bar, her body very close, and at eye level with her customers who sat around.

Mann went to sit at one of the far podiums. Four other men were sat around on black leather stools. The Bond bar had changed into the

Bondage bar. The main attraction hadn't changed: it was still half-naked girls, mainly foreign.

The blond girl in front of him was wearing a collar around her neck, a tight black PVC bodice around her middle that ended just below her large bare breasts, and a strap with a big buckle that went between her legs.

'Hello, Johnny.' She spun around on her revolving podium and picked up a glass to mix him a drink.

'Hello, Lola. How's business?'

Lola was a British woman in her early forties but looked younger with the help of a bit of Botox.

'Ouch – this fucking thing pinches.' Lola adjusted the strap that went beneath her crotch. She handed Mann his drink. 'Business is booming, thanks, Johnny.'

Around the podium were four businessmen. Lola leaned forward in a pretend whisper, hoping that the other punters around her station would feel obliged to eavesdrop. 'I pick up some really good clients in here. I've invested in some new equipment.' She winked at Mann. 'Medical, ethereal, you insert a wire down the man's urethra and this machine gives off sound waves – boy does it produce some great results. You should try it. You might even like it.' Her eyes settled on his face. 'Actually, forget it; you look like you need bed rest for a month. You're looking dead beat, Johnny.' She turned away briefly as one of the men opposite needed a refill. She turned back and adjusted her strap again.

Mann shook his head. 'I'm all right, Lola. I'm not getting much sleep, that's all. There's a lot on at work.' Mann looked around at the other seven girls, who were wearing various dominatrix outfits. 'All these girls work as mistresses in their spare time like you?'

'Some. But none of them compare with me, hon.'

She passed Mann a card. It was a photo of Lola dressed in a PVC cat-suit-type outfit, a mask on her face, a whip in her hand.

'Thanks.' He took it from her and studied it. 'Nice card. I'll let you know; meanwhile . . . do you know anyone who might specialize in a double act in a hotel room? Two girls, boy-girl even, bondage, rough stuff?'

'Plenty, why?'

Mann produced the piece of bondage tape from his pocket. 'Is this stuff standard issue, Lola?' He handed it to her.

She took it from him and rubbed it between her fingers. 'Yes and no. It's definitely bondage tape but it's thicker than usual.'

'Where would I be able to buy this?'

Lola shrugged. 'Web sites.'

'What about from you? I heard that you had supplied this place with all the outfits. You must have a good source for anything you need.'

Lola looked taken aback for a second and then she turned to top up the other customers' drinks. She made small talk. She turned back after a few minutes.

'I have some, it's true. I bought up some old stock but it's just for emergencies. It's difficult to tear with your teeth. It needs a knife to cut it.'

'Did you sell any on?' She shook her head. 'Where did you buy the stock from?'

'It was a stall in the Mansions. It was only there for a few weeks. A woman was selling off her stuff.'

'What kind of woman?'

'Might have been Indian. I can't remember. She wasn't Chinese, anyway.' She looked at the piece in her hand again. 'Where did you get this piece from?'

'It was wrapped around a dead man's foot. Whoever did it tied him up with this before they tortured him. Have any of your businessmen clients been talking about an experience that wasn't pleasant?'

It was hard to know what she was thinking. Lola only had one expression left that wasn't Botoxed out or filled in. 'You got to remember, Johnny, some men really like it mean. Some of them really *want* to be hurt. All the other women I know who make a living from being mistresses are as sweet natured as they come, just like me.'

She batted her eyelashes at Mann.

'Yeah, right,' he smiled.

'We do it because it's an easy way to make money without fucking. But, I will ask around for you.'

'This wasn't just hurt; his flesh was stripped. His balls virtually cut off.'

She looked momentarily shocked which was

registered on her face by her eyes opening up wide. 'Shit, that's seriously nasty.' She shook her head. 'That doesn't sound like an S & M game to me.'

'Yeah, I agree.' Mann finished his drink. 'She went to a lot of trouble to make sure he felt the pain. He took a long time to die. You give me a ring if you remember anything else, Lola.'

Mann left Lola. He walked back out onto the street. He got a call from CK.

'I wanted to express my sympathy at the death of your officer and to ask you to join me this evening.'

'Tonight's not the night.'

'Tonight is exactly the night, Inspector.'

CHAPTER 63

On the roof red papers twirled in the air and were sucked up and spun in the wind. The sound of whistles filled the air – three beeps and one long tone. The roof of the Mansions was bathed in the black of late night. A storm was coming. The belly of the cloud was lit with neon from the city below. Gusts of wind whipped up the waves in the harbour.

Hafiz caught Lilly by the arm and turned her sharply round. 'My brother is in prison because of you.'

'Let go.' She wrenched her arm free. 'That's bullshit. You know it is. I never asked him to be there. He messed it all up. It was all under control. She wasn't supposed to get killed. She was only supposed to be taught a lesson. 'Just rough her up a bit, I was told. You want someone to blame, you look to your own family. Mahmud should have kept well away.' Lilly shook her head sadly. 'Look I'm sorry about Mahmud, believe me. But think about it, Hafiz. They can't charge him if he didn't do it. They will have to let him go in the end.'

They turned to see the roof around them filling with members of the Outcasts, skinny kids with light jeans, big shoes and gelled hair. They were just like millions of others – nondescript, except that in their hands they carried weapons and the red invitations that had summoned them to a meeting. 'If you see him tell him I'm sorry.'

More members of the Outcasts began to appear. They came from all over the city to the Mansions. Nathan Road down below was crawling with teenage feet answering the call of their mistress. Thirty minutes passed and the assembled children cheered as the announcement went up that 'she' had arrived. They waited nervously for her to address them. She moved amongst them as she made her way across the rooftop. The wind was blowing. The distant sound of a storm charged the air with an eerie light.

Victoria stood in front of the gathered crowd. Her hair was loose, it whipped around her face. Her leather cat suit was sleek, moulded to her figure.

Hafiz and Lilly gathered round her with the others. The roof was moving with black figures, small shadows.

From the distance a rumble of thunder grew louder.

Victoria lifted up her arms as if to embrace them all. She stood on the top of an air conditioning vent. 'You are all my children, my Outcasts, and I love you just like a mother would. I promise each one of you that I will change your life. I promise you money, power. You can be whoever you want to. You stick with me and I can take you right up to the sky.'

Above her the lightning lit up the belly of the cloud. The children gasped.

Victoria tossed her head on the air triumphant. 'All I need from you is everything. I want everything now. Go into those Mansions and cause trouble. Run wild. Run free. You can be whatever you want. As long as you're prepared to fight for it. Are you?'

The children held their knives in the air as the night sky was filled with their howling.

CHAPTER 64

The Piccadilly Club was a private members' club. It was British gentry style: polished brass, cracked leather chairs, Dunhill fixtures. It only accepted the wealthiest of clients but that didn't stop there being a waiting list to join.

Mann was frisked at the entrance by two of CK's bodyguards, then he was escorted up to the top floor. Eighty floors in the speed elevator later he was met by a portly English butler dressed in a plaid waistcoat and black trousers.

'Follow me please, sir. You are expected.'

He led the way to the Red Salon. It was a lounge and private dining area. Its theme was deep, rich, cherry-red wood and brilliant gold. Around its walls was a library of classics shelved on a mahogany bookcase and there was a mahogany writing desk.

CK was sitting in the centre of a rectangular seating area. He was surrounded by his lieutenants, *Red Poles*. On their laps were Eastern Bloc hostesses: tall and sharp featured. They were young, beautiful; or they had been, once, when they had first been trafficked over. Long-sleeved dresses barely hid the needle marks in their arms.

CK watched him approach and so did the *Red Poles*.

'Good evening, Inspector. Join us. Let me introduce you to my officers.'

Sitting next to CK was the pretty waitress from the restaurant at the race course, dressed in a straight-backed cheongsam. She sat bolt upright. She had a black collar around her neck and a chain attached. CK held the end. She had been transformed from an elfin-faced young beauty into a rouged doll. Her face was as white as a sheet and her eyes were as dead as a fish lying on ice in the fishmongers. Mann could see that she had sold her soul to the devil sat next to her. Two monkeys were being handed around and being fed rice wine. They were trying to perform acrobatic tricks but they kept losing their balance and crash landing onto the floor and the table. The fruit bowl turned and flew off the side of the table. The monkeys rolled on their backs, screeching.

Mann looked around at the assembled officers. 'Don't bother. I know as much as I need to know about them. I haven't met the monkeys before, I take it these are the brains behind this outfit?'

CK lifted his hand to prevent any thoughts of retaliation and then he waved his lieutenants away.

One by one they got up and filed past Mann, the hostesses, half carried, half dragged as they tottered on their heels. Each *Red Pole* stopped to eyeball Mann as they passed him. Mann was used to the game. They didn't go far. The dining area was around the corner to the right. Mann could still hear them talking, low, the girls were giggling, screeching.

The waiter arrived with Mann's drink. He took it and felt the strong liquor burn his lips, the ice cool his throat and stomach. The Chinese girl did not leave. She stared ahead of her as if she saw her dreams. She was caught in the world of heroin. She existed only in her own mind. One of the monkeys had run off with the Russian hostesses. The other now stared at the Chinese girl, watching her face. It mimicked her expression. It jumped onto her lap and reached its baby-like hand up to touch her cheek. It grinned, worried, frightened. Her eyes turned slowly towards it. It screeched and jumped down onto the floor where it gobbled the spilled fruit and chattered away to itself.

'What do you know about the death of my officer?'

CK smiled. He looked across at the Chinese girl as he addressed Mann. 'Beautiful, isn't she? She is my new pet. She is not permitted to talk. She is not permitted to move unless I tell her she may. If she pleases me she gets her reward. It is important to understand one another's weaknesses as well as their strengths, isn't it, Inspector?'

'Was her weakness always for heroin?'

A waiter appeared, bowed low and took the monkey away.

'No, her weakness was for wealth. I merely pushed her to see what she would do for it. It was her own flawed character that let her down, not my cunning. Before you let people in close to you, you must know their Achilles heel. Everyone has one. Your officer died because someone you know well has such a weakness. You have an enemy within. It is someone you have known many years. But, I have known him for even longer. I have something he wants.' CK looked across at the girl. She looked as if she were crying. 'Come, we will eat. Then we will talk more.'

As they approached the dining area the noise of screeching grew louder. They rounded the corner and saw the *Red Poles* and the hostesses sat around a traditional Chinese table. But there were no dishes on top of the table; the centre was bare except for a monkey's head held in place by a metal clamp. The monkey was screaming in panic. One of the *Red Poles* was smashing its skull.

CHAPTER 65

The next morning Mann opened his eyes but he could see nothing. He had no idea where he was. He lay on a strange surface. His head was banging. He opened his eyes wide but it was too dark in the room to see far, he could only make out the things nearest him. He looked across to see chains beside him on the bed, leather cuffs. He looked up to the ceiling above his head. A chain hung down from a hook. His heart hammered in his chest. From another room he heard the sound of a man in pain. He turned his head and watched a woman approach the bed. At first he could not make out who it was and then he recognized her.

'Lola?'

Lola walked towards Mann carrying a tray with a cup of tea, a biscuit and two Paracetamol. 'Be with you in a minute, hon,' she shouted out to the man in the other room.

Mann collapsed back on the bed. 'How did I get here?'

Lola stood at the end of the bed, her hands on her PVC hips. 'You came in a taxi. When I opened the door at four this morning you were standing in my doorway, my card in your hand and a friend on your arm.'

Mann was already shaking his head, sitting up, swallowing the pills and groaning as the head rush hit him. 'Sorry, Lola. I appreciate you letting me in.'

Mann slugged at the tea. He looked at his phone; it was eight o'clock. 'I'm in a bit of a hurry now, Lola.' He stood, in his boxers. Lola looked south and smiled.

'Do you want to stay a while, hon?'

He laughed. 'I really wish I could, Lola.'

They heard a bedraggled plea for help from the next room.

'Be quiet, slave!' shouted Lola. 'Your mistress will come when she's ready. Unless you want me to punish you harder than I've ever done before. Do you?'

'No please, mistress, no, don't hurt me again.'

Lola rolled her eyes. 'Why do men always say "no" when they mean yes?'

Mann checked his phone; he had a missed call and a message from Victoria Chan: *Spend the day with me. I have something to share with you. Will pick you up from yours at ten.*

He stood and gave Lola a kiss on the cheek. 'Got to go, Lola. Thanks for everything.'

'You're welcome, hon.' She went back into the other room. She stuck her head back round the door as Mann was leaving. 'Don't forget your friend. She's fast asleep in the corner. She was up most of the night drinking my sake.'

Mann looked over in the corner and couldn't make out the small sleeping figure until he reached it. It was the monkey from the Piccadilly Club. He picked it up. It dangled drunkenly off his arms. Mann's eyes felt like someone had stuck hot pokers into them as he opened Lola's front door and stood on her step waiting for his lift. He heard the roar of the car's engine long before it cruised to a halt and purred noisily. Shrimp got out of the Maserati and looked momentarily lost for words as he saw Mann standing with a monkey outside Lola's dungeons.

'Don't ask.'

Mann handed Shrimp the monkey. 'Take this for me. Ask Ng to keep it. I need to go home and get showered. I will be in in a couple of hours.'

'You all right, Boss?'

Mann didn't know if he was or not. As Shrimp dropped him off near his flat, he phoned Mia.

'Where are you now?'

'On my way home. I need to change, I feel rough. I'm sorry, Mia. I don't know what the fuck is going on any more. I don't know if I can trust myself to make the right decisions. I don't know if I can trust anyone else either. Victoria Chan has left me a message about spending the day with her.'

'Do it, Mann.'

CHAPTER 66

'Get off!' Shrimp lost the phone briefly. 'What is it, Shrimp?' Ng was eating and talking at the same time. 'I'm just about to leave for work.'

'Stay where you are. I need to see you.'

'What's wrong and what's that noise? You have a party going on in the car? Jesus. Who's that? She's drunk, whoever she is. You shouldn't pick up drunk women, believe me, I have done it. It's a big mistake.'

'It's a monkey, it needs drying out, Ng. Can it stay with you for a bit? Just for a few hours till it sobers up. You'll like it, it's cute. Please, Ng, it will be like a pet. I promise to get it tomorrow.'

'Okay. Okay. I don't know why but yes . . . bring it round.'

Shrimp pushed the monkey back in the seat. 'Now behave and don't be sick.'

Shrimp left the monkey at Ng's. He would take it to the New Territories and release it in a day or so, when it got over its hangover.

★   ★   ★

Mia was waiting for Shrimp when he arrived back at Headquarters. 'You're undercover from tomorrow. It's all ready to go. Chief Inspector Sheng wants to see you in his office to go through the brief. Any final business you have, tie it up today. Mann's not going to be around. He's spending the day with Victoria Chan. Did you see Mann this morning?'

'Yes, I saw him.'

'How did he seem?'

Shrimp hesitated. 'He seemed okay.'

Mia waited until his eyes had stopped darting around the room and come back to hers.

'I'll repeat it for you. How did he seem?'

'He seemed tired, Boss. He seemed like he'd had enough. He seemed like he didn't know who he was any more. He seemed so sad.'

'Okay. I get the picture.' Mia sat at her desk, and buried her face in her hands for a few seconds before looking up. Shrimp was standing waiting. 'He's not the easiest person in the world to give help to but we can do it anyway. He needs us now more than ever even if he doesn't realize it. We can help him in lots of ways. Take the pressure off him. We catch this killer as fast as we can and that leaves him to sort out the rest of the mess.'

'Should he be spending time with Victoria Chan, Boss? There's so much talk around this building. It's a lot for him to deal with at the moment.'

Mia didn't answer straight away. She held her head in her hands whilst she thought and then she looked up.

'Yes, Shrimp. Don't underestimate him. It's when his back is against the wall he works the best. I suggest you make this the last day of being seen around the Mansions. Do what you have to today.'

When Shrimp arrived at the Mansions, Nina was waiting for him on the landing. She was in the shadows of the stairwell. She was back in her sari today. She shimmered with sequins around her face.

'You look very handsome.' She smiled coyly, her eyes shone in the darkness. She came towards him. They sat together in the usual place on the stairwell, from far above them was the echo of a door, from below, the sound of music. 'Did you see Mahmud for me? Is he all right?'

'I won't lie, Nina. He's not doing too well. He has a broken arm. He said he can't write to you, he's sorry. He will phone when they let him.'

Nina's eyes fixed in a panic onto Shrimp's.

'He is still not telling us what happened. He will be put on trial and convicted if he doesn't tell us soon. All the evidence points to him. I'm sorry, Nina. I will keep trying to help him but he's not helping himself.'

Nina bowed her head and started to cry. She buried her face in her hands and turned away from Shrimp so that he wouldn't see. He couldn't help reaching out for her. He put his arm around her shoulder and she shifted closer and rested her head on his shoulder. He felt the soft fabric of her sari fold in his hands. He felt the nearness of her body beneath. He kissed her forehead. He hadn't meant to. He hadn't even known he was going to do it. He drew back instantly.

'I'm sorry. I didn't mean to be disrespectful.'

'Don't be sorry, Shrimp. I have felt it since the first time I saw you. You and I have met before in some other life. We are soul mates. We are meant to be together.'

Shrimp was startled for a moment and then he looked into her eyes, still wet from tears, and saw that she was right. In some wonderful weird way she was right. He kissed her softly on the lips for so long that he lost track of time. By the time he left her he knew he couldn't live without her.

CHAPTER 67

David called a meeting with the other Africans. More than thirty of them crowded into the bar next to his shop. The place was in sombre mood. David sat at the back of the room and addressed the men.

'We have to act for ourselves. The Mansions has its own rules, its own government. Each race has its own country in here. Africa is a big country. We should have a say in here. We should have respect. We are allowing these stairwells to run with African blood. We are allowing a bunch of kids to hunt us down. We can't allow it any more. We know who some of them are in here. We take out a few of the ringleaders and the rest will back off.'

'What if they don't?'

'We have nothing to lose. They will pick us off one by one.'

David stood. 'I know where to start.'

Three of the men followed him down to wait at the ground-floor entrance. They sat on the steps as they always did, but not just to pass the time, they were looking for one boy, Hafiz.

★   ★   ★

322

Hafiz looked across at David as he passed them and moved through the ground-floor money changers and guesthouse touts. He had a smile on his face and a swagger in his walk. He had money in his pocket, a gold necklace and an expensive watch. Since Victoria Chan had befriended him he earned more money from servicing the needs of her wealthy friends than he ever did with Michelle. He looked disdainfully at the Africans. He would have liked to have bent over for David. He wouldn't charge. But he knew that it wasn't allowed. The Africans were out of bounds. Hafiz had a new respect amongst the Outcasts. He had stamped on the African's head. He had shown that even though he might be gay he could be as nasty as the rest of them, nastier even. Hafiz only had to whistle and the whole of the Mansions came alive. He was someone now, in his own right. He didn't need to work in the restaurant if he didn't feel like it. He didn't need to go to school. He had all he needed. Rich men showered him with gifts; he was going to be somebody.

He stood for a second and stared back at David. Hafiz felt triumphant. David could look all he wanted. Hafiz just had to get his whistle out and that would be another African dead down the maintenance shaft. But today was different. Today David stared back at Hafiz with a look that frightened Hafiz. It seemed to look right inside him. It seemed to know all his secrets. Had David seen Hafiz stamp on the African's head when he was lying on the ground? Had the African lived long enough to tell him? Hafiz doubted it, anyway what did he care? He was the prince of the Mansions.

Hafiz walked on and glanced back over his shoulder. David had stood and was walking his way. He walked quickly through the crammed corridor, on his way to the stairs. He turned to see not only David but three others following. Hafiz broke into a fast walk and then a run. He had a choice now, as the Mansions thinned out he could run to the back, along the back wall and try and escape that way, but there were fewer stalls that way and more Africans. Instead he chose the stairs and took them two at a time. His hand was shaking as he tried to squeeze it into his jeans pocket and bring out the whistle. There wasn't time to stop; he could hear them coming. Their deep voices boomed up the stairwell. Hafiz was making small whimpering noises, talking to himself, trying to reassure himself. He was running scared. He dodged along and onto the inside landing of the seventh floor and he ducked down into a doorway and took out his whistle. He was shaking so much, so breathless he fumbled, got it to his mouth, tried to blow and screamed as David's big foot stamped on his chest, trapping his arm where it was. David took the whistle from him and threw it over the balcony. He dragged Hafiz up by his arm.

'Please . . .' Hafiz was crying like a baby. 'I'll do anything. Don't hurt me please.'

'I know you'll do anything. You killed a decent man. My brothers here are going to teach you a lesson. You like cock, Hafiz? You like black cock? You like expensive things, watches, jewellery? We have a necklace that will fit you.' David grinned at him as he threw him towards the others. 'This is your lucky day.'

CHAPTER 68

Peter Thorne had had enough of the cock-tail bar in Vacation Villas. He was in the Western instead. He had had a long day. The jet lag was getting to him, it was early evening. He was sat at one of the tables for two on the lower level of the bar, which was long and straight and had more than its share of dead animals and antique spurs on the wall. It was a sawdust and spit sort of place that played country music with a touch of hard rock.

He closed his phone and left it by the beer mat. His wife had hung up on him. He had been curt, cruel maybe and he hadn't said the words he should have. He hadn't said he loved her, he missed her. Instead he had berated her about the fact he was working and she was at home. Her life went on as always: the kids got taken to karate, to ballet, she went to the gym, and she met her friends for lunch. Her life was encapsulated into a tiny box world whilst he was working on the other side of the world. Tonight she had tried to talk to him about money. They needed this, that, the other. She saw him as a cash cow. She saw

326

him as someone who was happy to be on his own for six months of the year. It was true, he had been once. He had thought he was someone then. He had been the bright boy in the company. He had been promoted over those who had served many more years than him but it had meant more travelling. Now, seven years later. His family enjoyed the house with the pool. His kids went to private school. His wife didn't need to work. But he had lost himself. His pleasures came down to anything money could buy.

He had started having the affairs to bring back some excitement into his life. Buying a woman for the night was like buying dinner. In the beginning he thought it enriched his marriage. He went home feeling like it wasn't all work, work, work. He could have a few secrets; a life of his own. He could hang on to the single status whilst still enjoying the married one. He thought his wife would never find out. Why should she? He was on the other side of the world paying for sex with a stranger in a hotel room. But now, he looked into his wife's eyes and he recognized that he had ruined something precious. He realized that they were slipping irrevocably apart.

So here he was listening to 'The Gambler' by Kenny Rogers and staring into his glass.

Ruby passed the window and stopped to glance in. She saw Peter Thorne. She'd seen him before at the bar in the Vacation Villas. Tonight he wasn't looking so happy. It was early evening. He sat at a table, rather than the bar. Ruby watched Annie saunter up, her holsters squeezed over her ample hips. Her laugh good and loud as she threw her head back and tried too hard. Even Annie didn't stop long. Ruby got that gut feeling she always got when she knew he was perfect.

CHAPTER 69

'So nice to see you again, Inspector.' Victoria Chan was waiting outside Mann's block of flats when he came out. 'I would love to think that it was my charm that you could not resist.'

Mann climbed into the back of Victoria's Bentley. 'I decided to accept your explanation of my officer's death, although I don't like it. I have to take some of the blame on my own shoulders. I have also realized that my father's estate will not wait forever. It needs me to deal with it.'

Victoria looked more stunning every time he saw her. It was as if she wanted to show him that she could be every woman rolled into one. Today she wore jeans and a boxy white denim vintage jacket. Her hair was in a pony tail. She looked young and fresh faced.

'I wanted to show you it doesn't have to be all about money. It can be about holding on to something precious. We all have regrets, Mann. I have them like everyone else. But I don't want any more. I want to look forwards from now on.'

They drove out to the New Territories then

exchanged the Bentley for a helicopter. They flew over the reservoirs and nature reserves, hugging the coastline.

'I wanted to bring you here to this coast. Do you know it?'

'Of course I know it, every keen surfer knows it. It's the only beach you can surf in Hong Kong. It's beautiful.' They looked down on the fine white gold sand and rolling coastline where the forest came right up to the beach. 'I've been coming here since I was young. It's a trek but worth it. I've never come by helicopter before, of course.'

They set the helicopter down on a stretch of level beach and Mann and Victoria alighted. The pilot switched off the engines. Victoria stripped off, tugging at her jeans and giggling as she nearly fell over. She had on a simple black bikini that drew all the attention to her perfectly toned body. She laughed at him.

He stripped down to his Calvins. The thought of getting into the water was all that mattered to him right now. He longed to feel the sand beneath his feet, the cool water creep over his body. He ran after her as she tried to beat him to the water. He floated on his back, felt the cold water creep over his scalp; he closed his eyes and listened to the dull sound of water filling his ears. He thought of Helen. This would be her idea of heaven. They had come to the beach together many times. Mann dived beneath the water and tried to forget everything just for a while, he wanted to feel his body tired, his mind empty. They stayed in the water for an hour. Victoria talked anything but business. She talked about the scenery, the fish, the shells. She asked him about the things he loved.

'This is my idea of heaven. In the sea, sun on my face.'

'Is that what you'd like to be, a Robinson Crusoe? On a desert island, a beach hut?'

'Yes, absolutely.'

After their swim, they lay on the hot sand. Mann turned on his side and ran a fistful of sand through his fingers. He hadn't felt so relaxed in ages. But he had to give himself a reality check. He looked across at Victoria. She was sunbathing. Mann could see her freckles coming out. Her strong features softened as she relaxed. Her face looked pretty as it turned pink in the sun. Her hair was wet and loose and splayed out on the towel. She was showing him that she wasn't Miss Immaculate; she could take the make-up off and get sand in her hair. She was his type of woman.

'Why is it you look like an angel but you behave like a devil?' he asked.

She opened one eye, put up her hand to shade her eyes and looked at him. 'Haven't you realized yet?' She lay back down and closed her eyes whilst she talked. 'I am everything you ever wanted in a woman, a partner, lover. We are the same, you and I. We were caught between two worlds when we were young. We were lied to by our fathers. We have a legacy whether we like it or not. Okay – I might be a little more self-serving than you. We can't all devote our lives to public service, but I need someone like you in my life to balance me. Of course,' she sat up and rested on her elbows, 'it helps that the someone is just as rich as me. I could never settle for anything less.'

'You play a deadly game, Victoria. Your Outcasts are killing people, not just other gang members. They are running through the Mansions in vigilante groups. They are killing anyone they don't like the look of. Is that what you had in mind?'

She closed her eyes again. 'They are the product of society, not me.'

'Oh, I think they're your babies. Whether you can control your offspring, the monsters that you have created, I don't know.'

'I have been honest with you, Mann. I want to redevelop the Mansions. I told you that. I promised them a place in that redevelopment.' She sighed and smiled. 'I can see you'll take some persuading to trust me.'

'Yeah. Don't hold your breath. The more I see the less I trust.' Mann got up and got dressed. 'Let's go. I need to get back to the office.'

Victoria looked momentarily disgruntled but she recovered. 'Okay, of course, Inspector. Your wish is my command.'

They got back into the helicopter. The pilot circled around the beach area one last time.

'It's so beautiful, isn't it?'

'Yes,' Mann answered. 'Beautiful, remote, unspoilt, and hard to get to.'

'Yes. The perfect place to build the most expensive beach resort in Asia.'

Mann looked at her incredulously. 'You'll never get permission. This is owned by the Park.'

'It was. I bought it. Well, to put it precisely, *we* bought it. You and I. If you want, we will keep it as it is. Then you can build yourself a shack on the beach and have your own private slice of the sea. We don't have to develop it. We can keep it just for ourselves. We can come out here every weekend and lie naked on the beach and swim in waters that no one else swims in.' The helicopter circled in the air, its shadow like a dark flying dragonfly buzzing over the surface of the water. 'Or, you can see the place you love turned into an all-inclusive spa resort. You see, you have the choice. You can join me and influence the decisions I make. You can haggle with me for the amount of government housing I erect alongside plush residential developments or you can refuse and let me do it my way. But then, we all know what my way is, don't we?'

She smiled at him and Mann could see that the sun had already brought a golden glow to her face.

'So what's it to be?'

Mann looked down as the sea turned turquoise in the shallow waters and folded along the shore.

'Your beach to leave alone, unspoilt, untouched for whatever reason you choose or you can leave me to build my beach resort. It's up to you. You have the power in your hands to build a better Hong Kong, a better world.' She laughed. 'But only with me, of course.'

CHAPTER 70

It was late by the time Mann got dropped off back at Headquarters. Mia was waiting for him.

'What is it?' he asked.

'A man's head has been dredged up by some fishermen. It has been in the water a few months. They've pulled it up at Aberdeen. I need you back on the job now.'

'Caucasian?'

'We don't know – there's not much of it left.'

Mann was already out of the door.

'Do the fishermen have the exact co-ordinates where they found it?' Mann and Mia were speeding along the road on their way to the scene.

'No, only a rough position.'

'Are we positive it's not Max Kosmos?'

'Yes. It's in an advanced state of decay. There's very little of it left. We'll get divers down at first light to see if we can find any more of it.'

'I'm going with them.'

'You're no longer part of the police dive team, Mann.'

'The more divers we have on this the better.' He

changed the subject. 'Where did Ng get to with checking out missing businessmen?'

'We have a long list. Ng decided on cross-referencing in two areas; reported missing by family or close friends, not just work, and last seen in Hong Kong, still missing.'

'Is Sheng here?' Mann asked. He looked across at Mia and realized it was the first time he'd seen Mia with make-up on in a long time. She couldn't have been at the office either when the call came.

'No, just Daniel Lu. Sheng's unavailable, we couldn't find him.' Mia didn't look at Mann.

'How far did you get with Victoria Chan?'

'She offered me my own private surfing beach.'

'She certainly knows the way to a boy's heart.'

'To mine, anyway. I am waiting for the killer strike. She's laying the world at my feet, all I have to do is kiss her hand and sign a pact with the devil.'

'What did she say about the Outcasts?'

'She says they have a life and a direction of their own. She says she is just the figurehead, her intentions are good, that they were bound to exist even without her help; all that bullshit. I don't believe her but some things she says ring true. She is offering me a lot to come onto her side. She wants us to work together, find a balance between her way and mine.'

'Ouch, that's good. She's clever. She has made a study of you, Mann. She knows all of your buttons and she's going to keep pushing them until they add up to a jackpot.' Mia looked across at him. He had a look on his face that seemed to be wondering if everyone knew him better than he knew himself. 'Use it then, Mann. We need to reverse the fishing reel and hook her in with whatever it takes. You are our bait, I'm afraid.'

Mann looked out as they drove. He tried not to look at the road. He felt sick. 'Make no mistake, CK feels nothing for anyone. CK is as coldhearted as they come. Maybe he's just setting his daughter up to fail. Victoria is a chip off the old block. But, you're right, I do need to use it.' He looked across at her and grinned. He was a little surprised. 'Never had you for the mercenary type, Mia. You're making me walk the plank with a tank full of piranhas beneath me.'

'You don't have to do it, Mann. It's a big ask, I know. You can just say no, take some time off.'

'The last thing I need is time off, Mia. I can't bear my own company at the moment. I need to work. I need to be useful. I will take it all the way and hope I can deliver.'

'Then stay focused. I don't need one of my officers off his face 24/7.' He glanced across at her. 'Yeah, maybe that was a little harsh of me. But it's tough love. I know you, Johnny. I want you to put it all behind you, move on.'

Mann looked out of the window, at the harbour just ahead he could see the flashing blue lights of several squad cars. 'It's easier said than done,' he said.

Mia didn't answer, she just drove.

They parked up by the cordon of flashing police cars around the water's edge and walked over to join Shrimp and Ng.

They'd reached the water's edge and Mann's attention was diverted. 'Jesus, is it in a *lobster pot*? Are these the fishermen who found it?'

'Yes, Boss.'

Mann knelt down over the pot. A large lobster scuttled around the basket and settled on the skull. 'There's still a small amount of flesh, the pot must have protected it to a certain extent, apart from providing the lobster with a permanent meal.'

'The lobster's young,' said Shrimp. 'It's probably not the first lobster to feed here.'

Mann took Delilah out of his pocket, poked her through the slats and dislodged the lobster. 'Where did you find it?'

The fishermen pointed out to sea.

'Can you be more specific?'

They looked at one another and then collectively shook their heads.

'They say they were fishing in the permitted zone when they trawled it up in their net. It must have come loose with the bad weather.' Ng leant down to whisper to Mann. 'I think they're bullshitting. They were somewhere they ought not to be or up to some kind of illegal bomb fishing. Whatever it was they caught themselves a net full of trouble.'

'Were you out in the storm?'

The captain nodded.

'Maybe this pot was dislodged from its home. Come to police headquarters in the morning. I want you to show me on a map exactly where you were fishing.'

The captain started to grumble.

'You're not going anywhere with this boat till we've had a chance to take a good look at it. Co-operate and we'll speed things along. Piss me off and I'll impound it for good.'

Daniel Lu came to join Mann and Shrimp and took a closer look at the head. 'It's not Max Kosmos then?'

Mann felt sick. He stood and took a few deep breaths. 'Somebody get that fucking lobster out.'

CHAPTER 71

'According to the fishermen's co-ordinates they were just west of here when they dragged up the head in their net.' The six-man team of divers included Mann. Daniel Lu was along as part of the forensic recovery team. 'Allowing for the movement from the storm, it could have come off the coast around Stanley. There are places along the wall where people fish, deep areas that you access quite easily. We've tried north and now we'll try south. We'll take the boat in south of the beach, where the sea defence is deepest.'

'This has to be the last dive for today, Mann. I have to get back to the office. We've been out here since seven o'clock this morning. It's four now.'

Mann was stood looking towards the beach. It was dotted with families. Either side of it were the tall sea walls, sloped with boulders in places to accommodate the storm swells.

'If the perp doesn't have a boat, this place would not be deep enough to throw in a body, even if you rolled it down the stone boulders and into the water.'

'I understand that, Mann, but Hong Kong is completely surrounded by water. We can't check every part. People are allowed to fish off any wall, any beach. If someone wanted to weight a body and throw it in they could throw it off countless places.'

'Sure. I know what you're saying. It's a difficult thing to work out but Ng and I looked at drift patterns, storm surge. It hit this defence pretty hard. It could have shifted anything that was underneath. We'll drop one at a time, at five-metre intervals. We'll sweep the defence. Further along . . . there.' Mann pointed to a place where the wall met an overhang. He shielded his hand from the bright sun. 'By those small buoys tucked in beneath the overhang.'

The boat came to a stop and bobbed in the water. The first diver dropped into the water at the start of the sea defence. Mann strapped his oxygen tank on. He pulled on his mask and slipped over the side. As he dropped into the murky water, he sucked in air through his mouthpiece and listened to the sound of his own lungs working. He felt the cold water close over his body and scalp. Hong Kong's harbour wasn't the cleanest. It was dark. It was full of debris, cloudy and thick. Discarded fishing nets were a major problem; lethal to fish and dive.

He felt the pressure around his ears as he dropped down into the cold darkness. His weight belt took him slowly down. He reached out his hand and touched the stone wall of the defence. He shone his torch towards the wall, to the lines leading down from the buoys, and he shone his torch downwards. The wall had been constructed more than thirty years ago. It looked neat from above the waterline but below it descended into jutting crevices. An eel stared at him, its massive head amplified by the water. Mann hated snakes. This was enough like one to make him jump as it came out towards him and then made a dart into one of the cracks.

He held on to the wall as he worked his way downwards. His hands touched the top of a lobster pot. A creature disturbed the bottom and a flurry of silt clouded up into Mann's face. Mann recoiled instinctively; he dropped his torch, fumbled and reached out to find for it in the dark waters. He shone it into the pot and a green face stared back at him, an eel had made its home in the mouth. Mann shone his torch to either side. It was not alone.

CHAPTER 72

Ruby lay on the beach, shielding her eyes as she looked out to sea. The sand was warm beneath her and she ran her feet through it, feeling the sensation of the grit between her toes. She was watching the police boat bob in the water. She watched the divers like black seals as they plopped into the water and she played a game with them. 'Getting warmer, getting warmer, no cold again, hot very hot.' She watched Mann turn backwards and flip off the boat's side and into the still water and she knew he would find what he had searched for all day.

Ruby lay back and closed her eyes in the warm sunshine. The night had been a long one for her. Peter Thorne had pleaded and cried like a baby in the end. He had cried for his wife. He had cried for his children. The more he cried, the longer she took to kill him.

She spread her hands out and clutched the sand in handfuls. She had a strange feeling inside her. She knew now it was all coming to an end. She knew that she must plan for it. She would not let them simply track her down. She would choose her moment. With her babies, in her room. With a man worthy of them, that would be her moment. A strange sound escaped from her throat: anguish, despair. Ruby gripped the sand hard, her arms outstretched she stared up at the sky and watched the Earth turn. She knew it was time for her to leave this life. She must go home and plan. She had Peter Thorne's body waiting for her. She had work to do. She picked up her bag and walked back along the beach to catch the bus home.

CHAPTER 73

As Mann walked into the incident room that evening Mia's expression told him she had something she wanted to say. He'd missed two calls from her but he'd had a rush to get back from the morgue after the autopsies. Mann raised his eyebrows and nodded towards the door. She shook her head. Whatever it was would have to wait.

'We have identified four so far. All of the heads are less than a year in the water. The two newest, less than a week. We haven't identified those two. It's likely that they haven't been reported missing yet.' Ng turned to the white board and the photos of the dead men. 'The four we know about are: Max Kosmos, a man named Louis le Poul, went missing five months ago on a stopover from Singapore, worked for an oil refinery, selling parts to rigs. A man from the UK, a Welshman called Colin Humphreys, bit of a playboy, worked for a luxury cruise company out here to take on staff. He'd been in the water about eight months. The other is a Korean engineer called Sam Lee, doing a tour of Asia, overseeing projects for Hyundai, his wife reported him missing three weeks ago.'

'Do these men have any connection to each other?' Mann asked.

'No. All frequent visitors to Hong Kong, all travelling married businessmen.'

'Where were they staying?'

'All in hotels around the Mansions. All off Nathan Road, big hotels with twenty-four-hour cocktail bars. They were all married, all well known for playing away. Their disappearance was never traced directly to Hong Kong because they moved all over Asia. Some airline records were accurate about who bought tickets but some weren't.'

'This is her serial killer ID: she kills foreign businessmen who play away,' Sheng said, fiddling with his watch strap, a sports Rolex. He looked as rough as ever. His face was blotchy, sweaty. His shirt button strained across his stomach.

'They have to be married,' added Mia, 'but they don't have to be Caucasian. We have a Korean amongst the dead. Saheed estimated the other heads had been in the water anything from two days to a year. The head that the fishermen found seems to be the longest in the water of the seven. Saheed said it was in the water about a year. It's hard to tell because the lobsters do a pretty good job of stripping the flesh and eating the bone as it breaks down. We only have a partial skull left. But Saheed said he is pretty sure it's not Caucasian. He thinks it's African.'

'Have them check the rubbish dumps, building sites, alert all fishermen. She must be disposing

of the bodies somehow,' said Sheng. 'Post surveillance in Stanley.'

'Perp won't use that site again,' said Mann,
sipping his coffee. 'They'll have seen us, I'm sure.'

Sheng flashed him an irritated look. He looked
like he was about to add a comment but decided
not to. Mann was beginning to feel like he'd been
the subject of some conversation and it wasn't
friendly.

'We have thirty million visitors a year; most of
them come here for business,' said Ng. 'The
average stay is three days. We are a major stop-off
point for other countries. Every few seconds men
pass through on business trips and every few weeks
some men go missing in Asia.'

'It's easy to see why: burnout. They've had enough
of being mortgage slaves and opt out,' said Sheng.
'They get so used to being on the road. Their wives
don't even care whether they come home or not in
the end as long as the bills get paid. You go and set
up home in the Philippines or Thailand, it costs
pence to live there. Find a few girls to double as bed
mates and cleaners, no one need ever be found again.'

'Seems like you've thought this through . . .'
smiled Mann.

'I've been working, if that's what you mean.
Doing my job. We can't all be lying on a fucking
beach getting a sun tan.' Sheng was tapping his
foot, fiddling with his coffee cup.

Mann was beginning to get the gist of what must
have been said between Sheng and Mia. He knew

he would be hearing all of it by the end of the meeting. Sheng had a lot of pent-up aggression that wouldn't stay behind bars.

'Okay, we get two hundred plain clothes officers out there sitting in bars, listening to talk,' said Sheng. 'I want every sex worker who is seen working the plush hotels pulled over and discreetly interviewed. At the risk of pissing the guests off we have to step up security. Anyone not seen by hotel staff when they are expected? Anyone not answering their door for cleaning for more than twelve hours, security in that hotel go in. Shrimp, we have your ID ready. Your team is ready to go. You are the Manhattan VD in a book distribution company. You will be staying at Vacation Villas. We need to move this along now. You ready?'

Shrimp nodded but he thought of Nina. He would not be able to see her. For the first time he felt a conflict in his heart. He had never believed in love at first sight until now. Now he couldn't imagine loving anyone else.

'I don't see that working. She's smart and cocky. She's not going to get caught in a bar by us. I think we should wait to go in heavy.' Mia stood, arms crossed. 'She's on a roll now. She's speeding up. The first head was a year ago, the rest have all been in the last six months. Three of the heads are within the last month. She's bound to trip up sooner or later. If she gets freaked now and goes underground she might just emerge worse in six months' time.'

'I agree,' said Mann. 'Get Shrimp in Vacation Villas undercover. Let's try and coax her out of her web.'

Sheng stopped fidgeting and eyeballed Mann. 'Your role in this investigation is being re-considered, Mann. Until that time you won't be required to attend meetings. If we want to find you we'll contact the Leung Corporation. You concentrate on what you're good at, sucking up to Triad bosses.'

There was a stunned silence around the room.

Mann looked across at Sheng and smiled as he shook his head. 'It'll take a lot more than you to get rid of me, Sheng. You've tried so many times over the years and yet I'm still here.'

'Yeah, well I've suspected there's been a mole in the OCTB for some time. Busts that don't come off, tip-offs that look set up. Now Tammy's dead. My money's on you, banana boy.'

Mann shook his head and almost smiled ruefully. It had been a long time since anyone called him that to his face. The room went silent. They waited for Mann's retaliation. Sheng's racist views were well known. It amused Mann more than made him mad. He kept his cool.

'I have access to CK's world and I intend to use it. But I'm not the only one. CK has prior know-ledge about a lot of things. Things that only someone in this department could know. You were undercover, Sheng, you reaped the rewards. Maybe you kept in contact with your old buddies?

Tammy died because someone countermanded my order. It had to be someone high ranking: that's you or Mia. You know what I think?' Mann's eyes turned black as he glared at Sheng. 'I think it's you who can't be fucking trusted.'

'That's not the way it looks on paper, son of a Triad. Who are people going to trust – you or me?' Sheng rocked on his feet as he grinned at Mann. His eyes lit with triumph. 'Fuck off, Mann. You don't belong here any more.'

CHAPTER 74

Shrimp came to find Mann on the roof. 'What would we do if we couldn't stand on top of the world like this?' he said, looking out over the evening sky. The eight o'clock night-time display was starting.

The bowlights of giant tankers were blinking on the horizon.

'Thought you might like to let off steam.' He handed Mann the urumi. 'I caught the boss practising with it.'

Mann smiled. 'Knowing how competitive she is she's bound to have mastered it by now.' Mann took it from Shrimp. It was light. Its handle was the same as a sword. 'Yeah, it's a beautiful weapon, hard to defend against.' Its three blades uncurled, shimmering in the laser lights that lit the sky around them, vibrating like a metal snake as it clacked against the roof tiles. Mann lifted it, felt its weight and balance in his hand. He whirled it overhead and brought it down, wrapped around the dummy. Bits of Hawaiian shirt and stuffing flew out.

'It's a hell of a weapon.' Shrimp looked at him.

He waited. Mann knew he had come to the roof to say something. He was rubbish at hiding anything. 'What is it, Shrimp?'

'You all right, Boss?'

He turned to look at Shrimp and smiled. 'Sure. I will be okay. Just do your job and do it well, Shrimp, I'm counting on you. We're still the same team we always were. Isn't that right, Mia?'

Mann knew she was standing watching. She came towards them,

'Yes. It's true. We've always been a unit.' Shrimp left. 'You can take a lot worse than that, hey, banana boy?' When he looked up Mia was smiling and frowning at the same time. 'I used to call you that – for slightly different reasons. Do you remember?'

Mann smiled. 'I remember. Shall I tell Sheng or will you?'

'Yeah. I'll save it for the right moment, I think.' They stood in silence for a moment.

'You're my boss, Mia. What do you want me to do?'

'I want you to do what you're good at. Use your instincts and keep pushing, Mann. Nothing else matters at the moment but getting to this killer. I can't force Sheng to do anything. He's the SIO in this. But we have our own investigations and I need you on that. But . . .' She smiled, concerned. 'Do one thing for me first; go home, get some rest for a few hours. Take a day looking over your father's affairs, make a start on it. This might be the calm between the storm.'

'Before.'

'Before what?'

Mann smiled across at Mia. 'If you're going to talk to me in your perfect schoolgirl English get the idiom right – it's *before* the storm.'

'All right, smart arse.' She smiled back but her eyes still penetrated, searched for the answer inside him. 'You afraid to go home, Johnny? I've seen you sleeping in the office a few times recently.'

He screwed up his face, shook his head, but hesitated too long.

'Bullshit. Yes you are. You prefer to sleep here. You prefer to sleep sat up in your chair, don't you? What is it? Ready to run at a second's notice?'

He shrugged.

'Where you going to run to, Johnny?'

'Shit . . .' Mann smiled ruefully as he shook his head exasperated. 'I hate it when that happens. Why are women always right?'

'It's just a con.' She smiled back at him. 'Fortunately for us women it usually works.' She held his gaze and her eyes were full of sympathy.

'Okay, you're right, Mia. I feel like shit. I haven't slept properly for weeks and I don't want to go home. I really am thinking of taking some time off. In fact I might take the rest of my life off. I'm thinking of handing in my badge. Sheng is only saying what others are thinking.'

'That's crap. I trust you more than any officer in this department. You will always be the best man for the job, Johnny.'

'Why? Because it takes one to know one? Haven't you heard all the shit going round this building? The whole station is talking about it.'

'Since when did you care what people say? I have known you all my police career. I have never wanted anyone else on my team. You're the best the OCTB has to offer, Mann. Don't fall apart over this; you've weathered bigger storms. You know what you have to do, don't you? You have to prove them wrong.' Mia shook her head as she gave an exasperated sigh. 'Anyway, this is your life.' Her eyes searched his; they were full of sympathy. 'What else would you do?'

'I don't know, lie on a beach somewhere, be a professional surfing bum, find myself one of the six thousand islands in the Philippines and disappear for a few years?' He shrugged. 'Try and feel human. Maybe try and start again. I seem to have made a mess of the last thirty-seven years and now it's catching up with me. I can't close my eyes without seeing people that I haven't managed to save. I am afraid to go home because I wait at the apartment door for Helen to shout hello. I wait for her to come out of the bathroom with a towel round her, I wait to hold her in my arms and smell her hair, feel her soft skin. Instead when I close my eyes I see her being tortured.'

Mann knew what she was going to do, she was going to say she knew how he felt and that time would heal as it always did. But time didn't heal; it just papered over the cracks. Now Mann felt that there were only cracks left. And he felt his life was falling between them, seeping away. Mann shook his head and closed his eyes for a few seconds.

'Maybe it's all for a reason, Mann. Maybe this is your time to put all your ghosts to rest.'

CHAPTER 75

The next morning Hafiz's body was discovered on a stairwell.

Sheng knelt beside Hafiz. 'They say it can take twenty minutes.' Daniel Lu didn't answer him, he was busy drawing a plan of the scene. 'Twenty minutes to die.' The smell of burning tyre was still an acrid taste in the air. The smell of roasted flesh.

'He wouldn't have taken that long. He hasn't much fat on him.'

Daniel was knelt beside the body, examining the blackened corpse. Hafiz's charred body was lying on its side, hands tied behind his back. His knees up around his chest, where the body had shrivelled as it burned.

'They'll save a bit on the cremation anyway. They could ask for half price, half the job's already done for them,' joked Sheng. Daniel didn't comment. Sheng left him to it. 'I'm going to talk to the family. I'll catch you back at the station.'

Sheng made his way back down the stairwell. The Delhi Grill was the site of mourning. It had Indians queuing to pay their respects to PJ and the family. He walked past the mourners and found PJ sat at one of his tables, Flo next to him. Ali was standing, talking to people as they approached the table. Nina was busy laying out plates of food and drinks for the mourners. She kept her head down, she moved silently around as she worked.

PJ looked up as Sheng approached.

'Mr Kahn, a word please.'

Ali gently eased the mourners out. Nina got a chair for Sheng. He thanked her. She smiled at him. His eyes lingered on her as she went about her work again, refilling the plates of food ready for new mourners.

He turned back to PJ and Flo. 'My sympathies for your loss.'

'Where is his body now?' asked PJ. He had aged twenty years. His face hung in sorrow.

'He will be moved shortly.'

PJ groaned and hid his eyes as he wiped them. 'Still on that stairwell?' Sheng nodded.

Ali placed his hand on his father's shoulder. 'It's all right, Dad.'

PJ rounded on him. 'It's not all right,' he said angrily, shrugging off Ali's hand. 'You said it would be but it's not. Two of my children lost. One dead, the other in prison. How is that all right?'

Ali looked nervously at Sheng and back at his father and spoke to him in Urdu.

'English please.' Sheng spoke. 'I can get a translator here if you need.'

'No we don't need that.' Flo spoke. Her eyes burned with sorrow and anger. 'We can all speak English. Hafiz was murdered by the Africans.'

'Did anyone see it?'

'Of course not. We smelt it though. The Mansions was full of smoke. People said you could hear him begging for mercy as he burned to death.'

'Did anyone try and help him?'

Flo shook her head. 'No one helps in these Mansions, not unless you want to be killed next.'

Sheng stood. 'I will leave you for now, I'll get someone in to take your statements. Hafiz's body will be taken to the morgue for the autopsy. It will be released to you as soon as we have finished with it.'

PJ nodded his head, his eyes on the table. 'Nina, show the officer out,' PJ said, always polite, always respectful.

Nina stopped her work and walked Sheng to the door. He stopped to speak with her.

'What do you think about it, miss?'

Nina looked up at him. Sheng wasn't usually partial to Indians. He had never dated an Indian woman but this one had something about her that appealed to him. She had a full chest beneath the silk and the sari; she had a beautiful face and light skin.

'My brother had got in with the wrong people.'

Sheng raised an eyebrow, he nodded. He smiled. 'Do you live here with your family? You're not married?'

Nina shook her head. 'I live with my grand-mother.' She looked away shyly and down at her feet. 'I am engaged to be married.'

'Not yet though, hey? I tell you what – it would be really helpful to catch your brother's killers if we could meet for a private chat about it all. I would like to help you and the Indian commu-nity. I am sure, with the right information, I could change things in here. Does that sound good?'

'Of course. Thank you. You're very kind.' Nina smiled nervously. She was anxious to get away.

'Fine then. We'll have a private meeting, you and I, somewhere quiet where we can talk and I'm sure we can achieve a lot.' Sheng grinned. 'I'll ring you here and arrange something. Don't go anywhere.'

CHAPTER 76

Shrimp looked closely at the computer image of the skull found by the fishermen. It was worn smooth, its right side was missing. The teeth were all there except for the molars on the right at the back. Shrimp clicked on the program until he had produced a projected image of the whole skull.

He took the photo of David's brother, Ishmael, and enlarged it. He studied it closely: Ishmael had only one significant scar on his face, the one extending from his mouth to his ear on the right side. The skull was missing on the side.

He enlarged and cropped the photo till he was left with an A4 photo of his face. He scanned it into the computer and superimposed it over the skull found by the fishermen. He took it straight to Daniel Lu's department.

'I'm impressed. It's a good match. Can you get his brother in here for a DNA match?'

'Possibly,' said Shrimp. 'They're a bit wary of police stations.'

'Okay, I'll give you a swab kit. Have you time to go back in there? You're undercover from tonight.'

'Yes. I'll ring him. Get him to meet me. I'm not worried about being recognized undercover. I'm not moving from the bar. It's all travelling businessmen in there. Plus, I have a great disguise.'

Shrimp phoned David. 'Can you meet me at the park at the back of the mosque?'

Shrimp could see by David's face that he was expecting bad news. They walked away from the park aviary and past the old men playing chess. They found a shaded bench and Shrimp told him what he believed. David listened, his head down.

'The scar on Ishmael's face, how did he get it?'

'He was hit with a metal bar. It cut all the way from here to here.' David ran his finger down the side of his face. 'It knocked out four of his back teeth.'

'He was doing the same sort of business as you here, wasn't he?'

David nodded and then shook his head perplexed. 'I don't understand. He was doing well here in Hong Kong, he even had a girlfriend.'

'Did you meet her?'

'She was someone from the Mansions. He said it had to be kept secret. He said her name was Pearl, or Rose, I can't remember. He liked her a lot.'

'Did he tell you anything about her, age, height, second name, anything you can think of?'

'He said she wasn't Chinese. He didn't say if she was tall or not. He said she had a nice figure. She was young.' He shook his head. 'My mother will cry forever when she hears this news.'

'I am sorry, David. I need to ask you something else. Was he married?'

David shook his head. 'No.'

'You sure?'

'Yes.' David looked across at Shrimp. 'So, she has killed others?'

Shrimp nodded. 'We think so.'

'Why did she kill my brother?'

Shrimp shook his head. The words in his head: *there always has to be a first.*

CHAPTER 77

Ruby had seen Hafiz's burnt body on the stairs but it meant little to her now. They would all die at some time. The difference is that Ruby would choose when and how.

Humming to herself, she picked Peter Thorne's head out of the sink. She held it tightly to stop it slipping and slid it into a plastic bag, then another and two more. Then she tied them tightly and placed the head in her handbag, ready. She had a lot of things to do today. She went around the room and gave each of her dolls a kiss.

'Mummy has to go out now so be good, babies. If anybody knocks on the door, don't answer it. Mummy is taking Daddy somewhere special today.'

She stopped by a doll with a shock of curly blond hair. 'This was your daddy.' She placed the photo she had taken from Peter Thorne's wallet into the doll's lap, resting it on the stiff edge of her frilly skirt. 'I know, I know.' She looked around at her dolls. 'Everyone needs a daddy.' She scanned the room and her eyes stopped on a baby doll sucking its thumb, it had a blue cap on its head. On its tummy was a photo of a man, his family had been

363

cut out, only his head remained. 'Do you love your daddy, Steven Littlewood? Or you, little Louis?' She picked up a ruddy-faced chuckling doll with painted plastic hair coming down its forehead in a kiss curl. 'Of course you do.'

Ruby began dancing. She twirled around the room spinning and laughing. She clapped her hands in the air. From the cupboard came the noise of a baby crying. Ruby stopped, walked slowly to the cupboard and opened the doors. She stood at eye level with the baby on the shelf. Its mummified remains wrapped in muslin. Next to it the crying doll was smiling again. 'Look after your sister. Don't let her be lonely.' Ruby talked to the blue-eyed doll. 'Mummy has a special treat coming for you. For all of you.' She turned and held her arms open addressing all of her dolls. 'We are going to have the one daddy I have been searching for all this time. He is going to be the one and we will keep him. We will keep him forever.'

Ruby felt a pang of sadness. Her eyes became blurred. A tear fell. She hid it from her dolls and wiped her face, annoyed. For the first time she realized she was afraid of dying. Her world spun at that thought and she let out a small cry from deep in her chest. Maybe it wasn't too late for her to run away, start again? She looked around at her dolls and shook her head. They needed her. They relied on her. She was their mummy. They belonged together in this room. Every day she heard the news that the police were searching the Mansions, coming nearer to her. They were closing in. One day they would find her. But . . . Ruby took a deep breath and stood tall, she was the mistress of her own destiny. She would let them find her but, by then, it would be too late and she would not die alone.

CHAPTER 78

Shrimp set his bag down at the reception desk in Vacation Villas. 'My name is Ian Townsend. I have a reservation for three nights.'

The receptionist scanned down her computer screen. 'Yes, Mr Townsend, we have you here. You're in room sixty-one on the sixteenth floor.'

Shrimp knew he would be – they had requested it. It was the same floor they had found Max Kosmos's body on. This was the floor for businessmen on large company expense accounts.

'It's our executive suite. Morning paper, wake-up call?' She passed over a form for Shrimp to fill in. He gave it back along with a credit card, false documentation that had been rushed through.

'Neither, thanks.'

'Do you need help with your luggage?'

'No. I'm good, thanks.'

Shrimp took the lift up to his floor. The piped music was playing a mix of classical and what sounded like Bavarian folk music. He came out of the lift and followed the room number signs, took a right at the end and found his room. He put his card key in the slot, opened the door and stepped into the suite. It was the opposite layout to Max Kosmos's room, this room had the bathroom to his left and the wardrobe to his right, the lounge area was straight ahead, and the bed to his right. Shrimp laid his case on the space provided. He walked around, inspecting every part of the room, behind the curtains and under the bed. He checked the minibar. What was it about minibars and the fascination for stale Mars Bars and expensive packets of nuts? When he was satisfied he knew every inch of the suite he knocked on the adjoining door. After a delay of three seconds there came a knock back. It was faint, but it was there. The two undercover operatives were in place.

He phoned Mia. 'I'm in, Boss.'

'Okay. You know the brief. We don't think she will operate in the day so your work starts from five. The rest of the time you can carry on as usual but we'll keep you off the streets in the day. You can help Ng in the incident room; he's inundated with dealing with the crossover between the crimes. Did you get anywhere with Mahmud?'

'No, but he's very fragile. He's been beaten badly. I don't think he is guilty of Tammy's murder. Someone handed him the knife. I don't know why he went there to the market that night. Now with Hafiz dead I was hoping he might not feel the need to cover for him any more, but he still refuses to say any more about what happened.

I am hoping Daniel Lu might come up with something that might help us. Unless he talks no one else will.'

'Yeah, the facts are pretty plain. Tammy was stabbed with the bundi knife Mahmud was carrying. Chase it up tomorrow with Ng. Don't forget the wedding ring. Keep safe, Shrimp.'

'Okay, Boss. If nothing happens I'll see you back at the office in the morning. Has Mann checked in today?'

'No, not yet.'

Shrimp unpacked. He'd brought with him the usual striped blue and green shirt that the businessmen seemed to favour, even with jeans. He laid out his toiletries in the bathroom. He lined his hair products up. He had studied the businessmen abroad. A lot of them liked their hair. It seemed to be the one thing they spent money on – that and their glasses. They liked expensive specs. He checked his mike and got an affirmative from the men who were waiting for him downstairs and the ones in the room next door. Shrimp checked himself once more in the mirror and then prepared to leave.

At the same time, Ruby slipped into Vacation Villas with a group of tourists.

CHAPTER 79

She kept her glasses on, her head down. Her hair was tucked up into a blond wig. The hotel was busy – no one noticed her. They had people coming in off the street all the time, sometimes they headed down to the bakery, sometimes they came into the small shopping mall at the entrance, but no one thought twice about a woman walking through the doors of Vacation Villas, straight into the lifts to the upper floors. Her mouth was dry, her bag heavy. She had Peter Thorne's head in it. She got to the sixteenth floor. The lift doors opened. She stepped out to the Bavarian music and the floral spray that swamped every hotel floor.

Shrimp stepped into the lift opposite.

The landing was quiet. She came to the end, turned right and stopped outside Peter Thorne's room. She checked her phone. She had a message. Ruby read it then shook her head. Didn't Victoria realize it was too late now? She hovered for a moment outside the hotel room, unsure, and then she turned and walked back down the corridor. She smiled to herself as she patted her bag. She had thought of a much more fitting place to leave it. If Victoria was going to play a game then Ruby would up the stakes. Victoria would have to learn that the game had taken on a life of its own. When you start a fire you can't always predict which way the wind will blow it. Ruby was seeing things differently now. She no longer cared for the promises. She no longer held the dreams she once had. It was all gone now. Ruby must prepare for the end of the game. She would go hunting tonight and this time it would be for someone very special.

That night she headed to an Irish pub she knew. Ruby walked down the steps, past the Guinness posters, into a bar with dark alcoves and dark wood, shamrocks a plenty. The Pogues were playing. On the screen at the end of the bar Manchester United was playing Arsenal.

Ruby chose a different table to last time. It wouldn't do to form a pattern, a recognizable trait. She went to the left of the bar, beneath the TV screen. She could watch them as they watched the game. She tucked herself away with her glass of Coke. This place was good. The clientele was businessmen. There were several sat at the bar. Several more alone at tables, eating dinner; pub food that they found familiar, comforting when they were away from home. This was a good place to start the night's hunting. She slid from the stool and took off her mac and then sat back down and crossed her legs.

A group of three men were sat at the bar talking

business and football. Well, two of them were, the third looked bored. He was dark haired, red faced. He looked a little bit the worse for wear. His eyes wandered round the room and came to settle on Ruby. She stared back and allowed a small smile as she sucked her Coke through the straw. The man continued staring. Ruby watched him staring at her legs. *He was going to be easy,* she thought. *He had only one thought in his mind and it wasn't business and it wasn't football.* Ruby was looking for someone specific tonight, she could spot a policeman a mile away and he wasn't one. Ruby knew where she could find one.

CHAPTER 80

Mann didn't draw the blinds that evening. The sky was clear outside. A plane blinked at him as it passed high above. Mann wished he was on it, he wished he was anywhere but there. He poured himself another vodka and took a slug. The liquor burnt as it made its way down into his empty stomach. Mann gave a drunken sigh, placed his hands against the cold window and leant his forehead against it, closed his eyes. Never had he felt so vulnerable or alone. He rolled his forehead over the glass. The more he thought about things, the less he understood. He had done as Mia had said and he stayed at home sorting his father's papers. He stood alone in his apartment surrounded by the piles of communications from solicitors and accountants. On the table was the original deed to the Mansions. It had been amongst the last of the papers to be delivered to him. Victoria Chan was right, they had several shared interests whether Mann wanted it or not. He could see why she and CK wanted him on board so badly. His father had made some shrewd investments.

He picked up his phone and dialled a number.

'Hello stranger,' a deeply accented Dutch voice answered.

'Hello Alfie. Sorry, meant to keep in touch but you know how it is – work took over. How are things? How is Jake?' Alfie took his time answering. 'Is he there?'

'No. He is not here much now. I think he is not coping well. We all miss Magda more than I can say.' Mann bowed his head and listened. He knew Alfie was choked. He knew just how Jake felt. He felt it too.

'She was a brave woman, Alfie.'

'Yes.' Mann could hear Alfie dragging on a joint.

'What is going on with Jake?'

Alfie sighed. 'I don't know. He is drinking, taking drugs. He is getting out of my reach. He stays away for days. He doesn't want to go to university in October any more. I have tried to talk to him about Burma, about what happened but he will not.'

'You have to give him time, Alfie. He'll be all right.'

'I hope so, Johnny. I hope so. He needs his family.'

Mann showered and dressed. He couldn't think in the flat. He had to get out. He had already drunk enough to render most people unconscious but the alcohol had little effect. He walked across the shopping mall and down to the MTR station, getting on the first train that came.

CHAPTER 81

Ruby waited until she saw Mann leave. She smiled sweetly at the doorman who was sitting behind his front desk. He got up to let her in. It was a different man than last time. He wouldn't have remembered Ruby anyway, but they changed buildings on a rota and she hadn't seen this man before. 'Sorry, I've forgotten my key.' He looked at her and hesitated. She felt in her bag for her purse and discreetly handed him two hundred Hong Kong. 'Silly me. I'm so forgetful. I hope you don't mind?'

'No, no, of course, miss, please come in.' He was delighted with the generosity of her tip. She took the floor up to Mann's apartment and let herself in. She gently closed the door behind her. She opened her bag. She had a special surprise to leave Mann this time. This would really freak him out. She looked at her watch; she hadn't time to stop longer. She had much to achieve before the night was over.

CHAPTER 82

Mann stood in the stark light of the carriage holding on to the handrail. He felt as if every person in the carriage was staring at him. He felt that he was falling off the end of the world.

He walked into the Cantina. Miriam was talking to someone: a European, a businessman, by the look of him, he wasn't a local. He was Miriam's type; tall, fifty-ish, a hint of Cary Grant about him. Mann listened to her laughter, it filled the bar. He smelt her perfume. He watched the curve of her waist, the smoothness of her dress as it rounded her hip.

She came over. Mann looked over to see her friend putting on his jacket.

'Hello, Miriam. Thought we might pick up where we left off the other night.'

He saw the look in her eyes as she stared deep into his, then he realized the rules had changed.

'Not tonight, Johnny. I have a date.' The European was waiting for her.

'Okay. No problem but, if you change your mind,' he smiled, 'there's always a place for you on my pillow.'

She kissed his cheek. She turned back to smile at him at the door. He knew she was waiting for him to say something else. She wanted more from him. He understood, the way he always did, that their relationship had run its course. She was pushing him, even though she knew in her heart that pushing him just pushed him away. She knew but she couldn't help it.

He turned back to the bar and finished his drink then he took a taxi across town. He turned his phone off. Mia was trying to reach him. He didn't want to be found. He had a lot to think about.

He walked into the Blue Velvet lounge, just before midnight. It was a place he hadn't visited in a long time. It had once been a trendy night-club on the edge of town, now a hostess bar with pole dancers and dwarves serving drinks, dark corners, and private booths. Enigma was playing: haunting erotic music.

He sat watching the stripper. She wore a long blond wig and a shiny red bikini. She squatted in front of him and her thighs opened as she held on to the pole and leant back, crotch in his direction. He smelt the aroma of cheap perfume and stale sex and as he held his drink on his chest he felt the ice-cold glass penetrate into his heart. He looked across at the other punters in this lowlife club, a Triad hangout. It was a place that the bosses like CK kept a tab open for their officers' entertainment. Ice was laid out in white lines on one of the tables at the side of the room.

A noisy group of *49s* were out of control at the far end of the bar and grabbing at the dancers, drinking each other unconscious with shots.

Mann was aware that someone had come to stand next to him – too close to be anything but a friend or an enemy. He turned. It was Lilly.

'You buying drinks, Mr Rich Policeman?' The pole dancer left for pastures new.

'Finished your homework, Lilly?'

'I don't need to learn anything else, Mr Policeman. I could even teach you a few things. You look like you need a friend. You want to buy me a drink and I'll tell you all about it?'

CHAPTER 83

Shrimp came out of the lift and walked through the lounge bar. The place was rowdy and full. The evening was in full swing, the atmosphere loud as the drink took the voice levels up and the inhibitions down. He spotted at least one of his colleagues, sat on a lounge chair reading a guide book. The large television screen at the end of the lounge had changed from showing sports to catwalk models. Shrimp walked on through to the bar. The place had a liberal sprinkling of sex workers, small groups of guffawing businessmen and then the lone peanut eaters at the bar. He spotted another colleague looking suitably melancholy on a stool at the far end.

Shrimp found a space in the middle of the bar. He could see the girls in the band from there. No Michelle, she was still being held by the cops, just Cindy and Sandy, their repertoire severely cut down from not having Michelle. He looked about to see if there was anyone else he recognized. No, he was pretty sure no one would know him. He had chosen just the right look to blend in:

open-necked shirt, high-waisted jeans, wire-rimmed glasses. His hair was parted differently, roughed up a little but not quite stylish. His wedding ring was large and loud.

He looked at the few lone girls sat at the tables around the bar. He made eye contact with one of them. She got up and walked away. For a moment he thought it was Lilly with a caramel-coloured long wig and short skirt. She disappeared somewhere behind him. His eyes settled on another. They played the game: look up, look down. Shrimp fiddled with his fake wedding band. He made sure he kept up the staring. He had to look desperate. He pretended to check his phone and then placed it on the bar. He ordered a Coke from the barman with the gelled hair. He put Shrimp's drink on the beer mat and scribbled the amount on his tab.

'Thanks for your help, buddy. You're doin' a great job.'

Shrimp looked up to see a girl watching him from one of the side tables. She had thick black hair. In the subdued lighting it was hard to see her face. He smiled. She smiled back. He looked away and looked back to make sure the signals were loud and clear. She was still looking his way. She'd kept her eyes focused on him. She was pretty, thought Shrimp, she was keen. He slid from the stool and walked over to her at the same time as he whispered into his wire, 'Contact made, am on the move.'

Shrimp's heart hammered. 'Can I buy you a drink?'

'Okay,' the girl tilted her head to one side and giggled.

CHAPTER 84

They walked to the lifts. The girl obviously knew the layout to the hotel. She knew where the lifts to the rooms were. She kept her head down. She didn't make eye contact with him; instead she turned her back on him and read the adverts on the walls of the lift. Shrimp tried to engage her in conversation. She wasn't keen on doing anything but hiding her face and giggling. Even if they had cameras in hotel lifts, which would cause a riot if they tried, the amount of businessmen who played away, they still wouldn't have caught a proper look at this girl. He opened the door for her to walk in before him.

'Shall I make you a drink?' she asked, hovering by the minibar.

'A Coke will be great.'

Shrimp watched her closely. If she was going to try and drug him, this was her chance. He watched her open him up a mini Coke and pour it straight into a glass. If she had managed to get anything in his drink she would have had to be some magician. Still he didn't touch it.

She was looking ill at ease now. She sat on the

bed and stared at him, a sickly smile stuck to her face. Shrimp wasn't sure if she was nervous or smug.

'Do you want me to pay you now?' he asked.

She shook her head, embarrassed, and smiled shyly. 'That's okay. You can give me a present later.'

Shrimp needed to push her on a couple of vital points. He felt his face heat up. Now, alone in the room with her he was struggling not to show he was a novice and he was acutely embarrassed. 'Do you want me to use a condom?' She giggled behind her hand and nodded. 'Do you do any bondage, you know, S & M?'

The girl's eyes opened wide, she shook her head. She got up to go to the bathroom. He spoke into the microphone. 'I don't think she's the perp.'

'She may have changed her MO,' the reply came back from the undercover agent listening in the next room. 'Whatever happens you have to hold on to her for at least an hour. You can't be seen going back to the bar too early. You have to make it look like you are still on the prowl.'

'I'm a real sleaze bag.'

'Yep.'

The girl came back in her bra and pants and giggled coyly as she stood holding on to her clothes. Nope, no sign of a whip anywhere, thought Shrimp as he sat back down on the edge of the bed and handed her a game controller.

'It's your turn – Super Mario.'

CHAPTER 85

Mann's mouth tasted like a dog had shat in it. He had been dreaming of drinking a gallon of water. His head was so hot he was sweating hard. He pushed back the sheet that covered him and realized he was lying next to someone. He reached out a hand. His hand lingered as it touched a woman's body and then it moved up over her waist, along her ribcage, up over her arm and froze. He realized it wasn't the body he was expecting. He thought he would feel Miriam's familiar curves but he didn't, instead it was a skinny little body. He withdrew his hand sharply and opened his eyes. Lilly was lying on her side smiling at him. Mann jumped up. He had his boxers on. That was a tiny consolation. Lilly lay there, naked.

'Shit . . . what the hell? Lilly, get up. Put something on.' Mann backed away from the bed.

'That's not what you said to me last night.'

Mann shook his head. He tried to remember he couldn't. 'There's no way, Lilly. How the fuck did you get in here?'

Lilly laughed, she leant up on her elbows. Mann

felt sick. Her skinny ribs stuck out, her pierced navel, her tiny breasts. She was a child. Mann turned his head away, sick to his stomach. Lilly got out of bed and picked up her clothes as she went. She paused as she passed him. 'You couldn't get enough of it last night. Practically forced me to do stuff I didn't want to. I just wanted a place to stay. Come home with me, you said, you can sleep in the spare room, you said.'

Mann closed his eyes, his heart was racing, he felt the bile build in his throat.

'Lilly, do this. Lilly, do that.' Lilly stayed where she was and made sure Mann had no choice but to look at her. 'Tut, tut, tut, Inspector Johnny Mann. You should be ashamed.' Lilly grinned. 'Well, I can't hang around. I got school to go to. Thanks for a very nice evening though. I am sure we'll see each other again.'

Mann heard the door bang behind her and the sound of her laughter as she walked down the corridor. He stripped off and stepped into the shower. He closed his eyes as the water streamed over his face. He leant against the side of the cold cubicle. His head was banging; he rested it on the cold tiles. Could he really have had sex with Lilly? The only sound in the flat was the ticking of the clock coming from the bedroom. He needed to get dressed. He needed to sort his life out. He walked along the wooden floor, staring straight ahead at his open bedroom door. He nudged it with his foot. It glided open. The clock's ticking was so loud now it blocked out everything else. Mann stepped inside and looked to his left, his bed unmade; he pulled off the sheets and threw them in a heap on the floor. He swore out loud so many times it became part of his breathing. He picked up his socks from the floor, as he bent down he saw a bag under his bed. He pulled it out, opened it, peeling back layer after layer of plastic. He peeled back the last layer. A familiar face stared back at him.

CHAPTER 86

'Give me the clothes you were wearing earlier, before you showered.' Daniel Lu stood in Mann's bedroom and handed Mann a forensic suit. 'Touch nothing.'

Mia was hovering outside in the hallway. Ng was suited up and helping with the search of the bedroom. He'd been the first to arrive after Mann's call. Mann looked behind her – no Sheng.

'Don't be fucking ridiculous. This is my home. I've touched everything in here.' Mann took the suit all the same and slipped it on over his t-shirt and boxers. He hadn't got very far with dressing.

Ng emerged from the bedroom and stepped over the officer on his hands and knees searching for hairs on the carpet. 'They'll never find anything in this mess, except a dead mouse or something.'

'You know what I mean. Don't move anything.'

Flash bulbs went off around the room. Daniel's team were busy grid searching his lounge. The whole of his building was sealed off.

'Were you alone here last night?' Mia stood in the doorway, waiting for an answer.

'No.' He didn't look at her. He knew if there

386

was one person who would guess he was trying to hide something it would be Mia.

'Well, did you get her name by any chance?'

'No.' Mann didn't like lying to Mia but he had to give himself time to think. This was his problem and he had to think it through before he involved anyone else.

Mia sighed. 'You better start remembering, Johnny, because whoever she was she put a head under your bed.'

'It's not just any head. I know him. I met him the other night at the bar in Vacation Villas.'

'Still believe in coincidences?' Daniel Lu spoke whilst at the same time bagging up Mann's bed sheets. 'Someone's gone to a lot of trouble to set you up, Mann. They must want you bad.'

'What did she look like?' Mia was exasperated. Her frown line had gained extra depth. 'Mann, talk to me. This girl you had back here last night, what did she look like?'

Mann shook his head. 'I didn't get a good look at her. She'd left by morning.'

'That good, huh? Bloody hell, you're a liability at the moment. You're going out of your way to mess up. What the hell do you think you were doing getting blind drunk and picking up women when we are in the middle of a murder investigation and one, may I add, in which your operative, your officer, Tammy Wang, was killed? Does it mean shit to you, Mann?' Mia was too fuming now to stay any longer. 'Take the head down to Saheed. This is your baby, Mann. This is all yours. You messed up, you clean up and then I want you in my office with a full report on my desk. I want that girl found. I want her DNA off those sheets, Daniel. Mann, you are a walking disaster at the moment.'

The men said nothing after Mia left. Mann finished getting dressed. The whole of his flat seemed to be being taken for evidence. All he was left with was the piles of his father's life – the one thing he didn't want. Daniel came to find him in the kitchen. Mann was holding on to the edge of the sink, head bowed, trying not to throw up.

'You can get this down for Saheed to look at now. He's ready to do the autopsy. We'll be a while longer here. It's better that you leave us to get on with it.'

Mann nodded. 'Where's Sheng?'

Daniel Lu shook his head and shrugged. 'Your guess is as good as mine. He hasn't been seen since yesterday.' He picked up his key to leave. 'And you better get your locks changed, Mann. If it wasn't your mysterious woman then someone else went to a lot of trouble to leave this here.'

CHAPTER 87

Mann sat in the car park and rested his head on the steering wheel. The head was on ice in a box on the backseat. Kin Tak tapped on his window.

'Inspector?'

Mann nodded, pulled his keys from the ignition and opened the door. 'Sorry.' He clutched his bottle of mineral water as if it were his leash on the world. He'd sat outside in his car until he felt ready. He hadn't had the stomach for it ten minutes earlier. They crossed the gravel path carrying the box. 'Sorry I'm late.'

Mr Saheed was business as usual. 'Hello again, Inspector.'

Kin Tak unpacked the head and placed it in a stand on the autopsy table.

'His name is Peter Thorne. He's a forty-five-year-old businessman from the UK,' said Mann.

Saheed made an incision in the scalp from behind the ear, around the back of the head to the other ear. Then he peeled the scalp away from the top of the head and placed it over Peter Thorne's face. Saheed talked to Mann as he worked. 'We have already established that the head was removed after death.' He looked at Mann over his bifocals. 'Moved to your apartment, I hear. You should try not to take your work home with you, Inspector. A fine-bladed chopper was used to sever the spine between the third and fourth vertebrae.'

Kin Tak fetched a small electric saw and pressed the button to start it. It buzzed and whined like a dentist's drill but louder, much louder, as it cut through the bone. Mann clenched his teeth. The sound was like nails down a blackboard. The smell of burning bone filled his nose. He swallowed. He squeezed the plastic bottle of water without even realizing he had. It cracked as it popped in his hand as it expanded again. Kin Tak took a small hammer and chisel and dislodged the portion of skull that he had sawn through. There was a sound like a boot being freed from sticky mud. He laid the top half of the skull to one side and began stripping the membrane with a pair of pliers. Kin Tak reached inside and extracted the brain.

'We will leave that cooking for a few days,' Saheed said as he placed the brain in a bucket of formalin. 'I can't dissect till it toughens up. I will let you know what I find from the swabs in the mouth and the fluid tests. They will tell us whether there are drug traces. But I can confirm that the same blade has been used in this case as in the others. Inspector, are you listening? Are you all right?'

Mann shook his head, he took a swig of water. 'I have to go.'

CHAPTER 88

Mia was waiting for Mann when he got back from the autopsy.

'Saheed confirms, it's the same killer.' He looked at her face and looked away. She was pale: angry, upset, disappointed, the adjectives went on and on. Mann knew that he couldn't keep Lilly a secret, and he didn't intend to, but first he had to work out what had happened before it was too late.

'And the same killer that was in your bedroom. I am going to have a hard job from stopping Sheng breaking out the champagne. How do you think it reflects on the rest of us? We are supposed to be a team, Mann, have you forgotten that?'

Mann tried to focus on what she was saying but his mind kept coming back to the thing that felt more immediate, more gruesome than anything else right now. Was what Lilly had said true? Christ, could he have done it? Could he have had sex with Lilly? He shook his head. He didn't remember. How had they ended up back at his flat? He didn't remember anything.

'You listening, Mann?'

Mann nodded.

'Someone went to a lot of trouble to plant that head in your apartment, why did they do that?'

'The perp gets off on that. She loves the thrill. She doesn't care any more. For some reason she doesn't care about her own life. She doesn't use a condom. She doesn't care about leaving her DNA. She's left traces of herself everywhere.'

'It's all linked to you, Mann.'

Mann looked across at Shrimp and Ng. Mann could see by their faces that even they were beginning to wonder what was going on in his head.

'Who was Peter Thorne to you?'

'He was a man I met in a bar, the night I found Max Kosmos's body. There is nothing more for me to say, Boss.'

'Why you?' Mia crossed her arms over her chest and frowned. 'It has to be someone with a personal grudge against you for some reason. It could be a past girlfriend of yours, Mann.'

'I've dated my share of nutters but I don't remember one who had all the makings of a serial killer.'

'The head could have been brought in by someone posing as your cleaner, Genghis. When we went to your apartment the other day the doorman said the cleaner had just left but she hadn't cleaned, had she?'

Mann shook his head. 'I've already talked to the man on the desk. He doesn't know one cleaner from another and this isn't his usual block. They work a rota. The way he described her it could have been anyone. Anyway, I cancelled my cleaner and I left instructions at the desk telling them not to allow anyone in to my apartment, not my cleaner or anyone else.'

Mia shook her head and ran her hand back through her hair to scrape back the few strands that had fallen down from their clasp. 'I'm sorry, Johnny. I'm under pressure, that's all. We all are.' She turned to Ng. 'Did Thorne have any connection to the Leung Corporation?'

'No. He had never worked for them.'

'Or to Mann?'

'No.'

'We know Victoria Chan is out to get you. She has the power. She has the contacts.'

Mann shook his head. 'I certainly wouldn't rule her out of this. But murder? I can't see her getting her hands dirty.'

'Oh, I can. I can see her bathing in virgin's blood and using testicles for earrings,' said Mia. 'She's as ruthless as they come. And you still don't remember who she was you were with last night?'

Shrimp's eyes darted back and forth and always back towards Mann. He ran the pencil through his fingers like a cheerleader's baton, a nervous tic.

Shit . . . Mann wanted to throw up. Had he raped Lilly? Had he had underage sex with a child? Had he abandoned every moral fibre in his body? If he had, what else was he guilty of? Did he know himself any more? Did he trust himself?

Mann shrugged. He didn't know anything any more. Nothing seemed real. Nothing was fitting. 'Well, we do know now that Michelle has to be innocent. We have to let her go. Unless it was someone working for or with her?'

'She was in prison. She can't have snuck back and left the head. It has to be someone else.'

'I need to talk to her again,' said Mann. The eagle flew by the window. Mann wanted to reach out and jump on its back.

CHAPTER 89

'Inspector?' Michelle looked at Mann as he walked into the interview room. She twisted one hand around another. She bit her lip. She had on a plain blue t-shirt and prison trousers. Her eyes were swollen bloodshot bags. She was trembling from withdrawal. Mann felt sorry for her.

'Sit down, Michelle.' Mia and Ng were watching from the monitoring room outside.

'How are you doing?'

She shrugged. Mann passed her a cigarette.

'Michelle, another man has been murdered. His name is Peter Thorne. Ring a bell?'

She lit the cigarette and looked up at Mann. She shook her head. 'I don't know who you're talking about.'

'Can you give us any more information about the woman who you get the drugs for? The woman who gave you Max Kosmos's wallet in exchange?'

She shook her head and dragged heavily on the cigarette. 'I told you, Inspector, I never see her. She's very careful about that. Never gives the instructions with the same person. Sometimes she even sends a guest up and pretends it's a song request. She's clever.'

'You forgot to mention you also get her a drug called Papaverine. Any reason for that?'

'I forgot that's all.'

'Do you know what it does?'

'Yeah, I looked it up. It makes cocks hard.'

'Why didn't you tell me you supplied it?'

'I didn't think it was important.'

'Anything else you want to tell me that may or may not seem important to you?'

She shook her head. She was getting agitated. She scratched at the skin on the inside of her wrist. She drew heavily on her cigarette.

'You know Victoria Chan well?'

Michelle thought for a moment before answering. 'I know her as well as everyone does. She's been coming to the Mansions this last year. She's been offering us deals to sign up and become part of the refurb project. She's been a good friend. She wants to help us.' She blew the smoke out in a disgusted groan. 'She isn't like some people who you think are good but turn out to be bad.' She paused and looked at Mann. 'Just like you, huh, Inspector? I used to look up to you. Not any more.' Michelle looked around her. 'I want someone else in here as well.'

'There are cameras, Michelle. Everything is recorded.'

'Even so, I don't feel safe.' Michelle looked up at Mann. 'I talked to Lilly on the phone this morning. She didn't go home last night. She said she'd stayed with you.' Michelle stared hard at Mann, giving him the chance to deny it.

Mia's eyes opened wide. She stared at Mann on the small screen and shook her head, waiting for Mann to deny it.

'She says she stayed in your apartment last night and you had sex.'

Mann looked up at the camera. Mia stared back at him.

CHAPTER 90

Mia caught up with Mann and Ng in the locker room. 'I have to suspend you. You're now officially a suspect, Mann. Don't go anywhere until it's all cleared up.'

Mann looked at Mia's face. She was fuming but she was also devastated. He nodded. He knew she had no choice. He would have done the same thing.

'She has refused a rape test. She is not pressing charges. She is probably looking for some payout. Christ, Johnny, I don't know what the hell is going on. Either you have been stitched up better than Kin Tak can sew up a corpse or you are so out of your head you just don't know what the hell you are doing any more. Which is it? Either way your fucking judgement is seriously impaired. What the fuck were you thinking?'

Mann took a deep breath in through his nose and bowed his head against the locker door. He rocked his head from side to side against the cold metal. 'I don't know. I blacked out. I don't remember anything after leaving the bar. I woke up this morning and she was in my bed. I don't think we had sex but I don't know.'

'Jesus Christ! Yeah, well that doesn't inspire huge confidence in me. You have lost it, Mann. You have compromised your judgement. You've been crossing the line too often recently, Mann. At a time when Victoria Chan is after your blood and stopping at nothing to stitch you up, you seem to be doing everything to give her a helping hand.'

'You don't have to suspend me, Mia. I resign.'

'No. I don't accept your resignation. I don't want your badge. Just go home, Mann, stay out of trouble till we sort it out.'

Mann took out his weapons belts from his locker. Ng was watching him.

'You're not alone in this, Genghis. Shrimp and I will do everything we can to clear this up fast and then you'll be back.'

'I hope so, Ng, I feel like I've been nicely sewn up. Mostly by myself. I am no use to you or any one here any more. As Mia said, I'm a liability.'

Ng watched him leave.

Shrimp caught up with him as he took the lift down.

'Boss, I didn't get the chance to tell you something about Tammy's death. It couldn't have been Mahmud. I checked the autopsy report of the wound that killed her; the knife went in at an angle, right to left across her body. Mahmud is left-handed. He couldn't have done it. Shall I get him released?'

'You better check with someone else, Shrimp. I wouldn't trust my judgement at the moment.'

Mann walked through the turnstile to the exit. He stood in the garden outside Headquarters, his head bowed, he shook his head. He felt defeated.

CHAPTER 91

Michelle was released. Her body ached for ice. Her heart ached for her kids. Rizal looked up when she unlocked the door. She went to kiss him. He looked her up and down, turned away in disgust and threw the rubbish off the sofa so he could sit. Lilly emerged from the bedroom with just her t-shirt and pants on. Michelle's eyes flicked back and forth between the two. Lilly stared back, brazen. Rizal looked away sheepishly.

'Where are the twins?' Michelle started tidying up.

'The twins have gone to the old woman down the hall.'

Lilly stayed where she was, leant on the doorframe, her midriff showing, her skinny legs were bare.

'Get dressed.' Michelle stood, a pile of papers in her hands. 'And go and see that they're okay. Take them for an ice cream, Lilly. And while you're out, go to the Delhi Grill and ask Nina if she can help me out with some groceries. I need to get cooking straight away.'

Lilly screwed up her face and was about to argue

but one look at Michelle's expression told her she should do as she was told. She shrugged, turned and took her time about moving out of view. Michelle watched her. She saw her look over her shoulder at Rizal. He nodded that she should comply with her mother's request. He looked about for the remote. Michelle reached down the side of the sofa, found it. She held on to it. She searched his eyes for the truth; she found it as he turned to watch Lilly walk past.

'Don't hurry. I want a word with Rizal,' Michelle told Lilly as she left. After she'd gone, Michelle turned the volume of the television up high.

'What are you doing? You gone deaf in prison?'

'No. I just don't want the neighbours to hear what I have to say to you.'

Rizal swore and opened another beer as he turned his eyes to the television and ignored her.

Michelle threw the remote at him; it hit him on the side of his head. 'You will listen to me. I can see what you've been doing here. You've been having sex with Lilly. Don't think I haven't seen the evidence before. I do her washing. I knew when she'd had sex and I knew when she'd been at home that night. You know what is the worst part? I chose to ignore it. I thought it couldn't possibly be.'

'What the fuck is your problem? It's not as if she's my own daughter and you turn tricks at the hotel. Do I get jealous? Lilly is no fucking angel and she's no baby. She knows what she's doing.'

Michelle made a lunge at him. 'You're a filthy

pig. She doesn't stand a chance with you here. This is my flat. Get out.'

Rizal looked at her and snorted in disgust. 'You need me. You can't do it all on your own. Anyway, I am the father of the twins. If I go, I take them with me.'

Michelle's eyes turned dark. 'Don't touch my children. They're not yours. They never were. Now get out!' Her body was shaking from the anger.

Rizal got slowly out of his seat, a mock smile on his face. He came to stand next to Michelle. She stood her ground. Her chest rose and fell as her heart hammered.

'Don't worry. I'll go. But I can tell you a lot of things about your daughter. The things she likes, the things she asks me to do for her. You wanna ask her where she goes at night. She doesn't sleep here. She has a secret place where she goes. She stopped being your baby a long time ago.'

Michelle turned her eyes away from his. His beer breath was rank in her face.

He grabbed her face and turned her to look at him. 'I'm going out with the boys. I need to get out. You make me sick.' He squeezed her face until her neck was stretched and she began to feel the pain as his fingers dug. 'But when I feel like it, I'll come back. Do you hear me? I will come back when I am ready and you better have something good waiting for me and you better accept it.'

He pushed Michelle away and she landed painfully against the corner of the cabinet.

'Remember, you don't mean nothing to me. Lilly is getting somewhere. She's making connections, wealthy ones. She is going to be somebody. You don't have any moral high ground to stand on. You're just an old junkie hooker.'

After he'd gone, Michelle sat on the sofa and cried. She realized it had been a long time since she'd done that. The television blared as her shoulders shook and a pain shot through her heart at the realization of what she had become. She looked around the flat; it was a stinking mess, it smelt of sweat and beer and decay. She felt a huge feeling of shame but she also felt something else. She felt a seed of hope inside her. She hadn't had ice for the time she'd been in custody. She'd already weathered the worst of the withdrawal. She stopped crying. She got a bin bag and began throwing all Rizal's belongings inside.

CHAPTER 92

Rizal headed down to the bars. He was fuming. He took the stairs all the way until he saw Nina and Flo waiting for the lift on the fifth landing. They were making their way down to the Delhi Grill. The mourning was draining on them all. Hafiz's body was in the morgue. More people arrived daily to pay their respects. Flo had been for a rest and was now ready to face it again.

Rizal stared at Nina. He stared at the flesh beneath the folds of sari. He didn't bother to hide it. 'You're looking real pretty today, Nina.'

Flo's head turned at the sound of his voice. She leaned on Nina's arm. 'Is that Michelle's man?' she asked in Urdu.

'Yes, Grandmother.'

Flo smiled his way and nodded. 'He's a pig.'

Nina smiled to herself.

'What's so funny?' Rizal was weaving on his feet. He stank of sweat. His eyes had turned nasty. The lift was a long time coming. There was no way they could turn back. It took her grandmother a long time to go anywhere.

Nina shook her head. 'Nothing.' She was feeling

anxious now. Flo had a habit of speaking her mind.

'He smells like a pig.' Flo nodded her head. She grinned her toothless grin.

He shook his head angrily. 'What is it, old woman? What's so funny? I've had enough of people taking the piss. I will wipe that smile off your old mouth in a minute.' He was getting riled.

'She means no harm. She's old. Her brain's not right.' Rizal looked ready to flip.

'I said you are a pig,' Flo spoke in English. 'I said you smell like the meat you eat.' She gathered up some phlegm and spat it out. It landed at his feet.

Rizal froze. He looked down at the phlegm and lifted up his hand to strike her. The lift doors opened. Mahmud stepped out. His eyes were on the floor. When he lifted them he saw Rizal about to strike his grandmother. He charged at him, his arm still in plaster. Rizal wasn't expecting it. He fell back against the wall opposite and the open windows of the maintenance shaft. He grabbed on to them either side, and landed painfully against the edge as he stopped himself falling into the filthy shaft. Nina hurried Flo into the lift.

Mahmud stood his ground and glared at Rizal before stepping in to join Nina and Flo. 'Don't ever come near us again or I will kill you.'

★　　★　　★

Flo was back in her room when she heard the door open. Nina had brought her back for her nap. Nina was running errands.

'Nina? Is that you?' Flo called out. No one answered. She listened to the sound of soft feet walking towards her room. Her hearing was good. She could tell if it was a man or a woman, she could tell if they were tall or short. Something wasn't right.

'What do you want? Where is Nina?' Flo asked as her door opened and she felt the presence of someone standing in her doorway. 'What do you want?' she asked again, trying to put force behind her voice. 'I am tired, get out. Go away.' No one answered her. Flo's head turned as she followed the sound of the person entering her room and walking around to the side of her. 'Nina. Nina . . .' Strong arms held her tight. She clawed at the hands but she could not reach them. She was being strangled.

CHAPTER 93

'Tom?' Mia stood in her office calling Sheng's mobile. It went straight to answer phone again.

There was a knock at her door. Ng walked in with Shrimp behind.

'Has Michelle been released?' asked Mia. Ng nodded. She sighed and sat back down, exasperated. 'With Mahmud cleared as well, we're back to square one. I had them as our team. I thought they would turn out to be working it together. I keep coming back to Victoria Chan and CK.'

'Mann's going to try and take them on alone. He can't do it at the moment. It takes someone with all his wits about him to take on one member of the family, let alone two. I know CK too.' Ng was aware of Shrimp staring at him with a new respect. Ng glanced his way. 'Yes, you aren't the only person to have gone undercover, Shrimp. I was a rookie then. I spent a time in the Triad ranks as a *49* and then a *Red Pole*. It was the most difficult thing I ever did. You have to be able to separate your mind from what is going on around you. You have to immerse yourself completely and still be aware it's not really you. It's a very hard thing to do.'

Shrimp patted Ng on the back. 'Big respect, old man.'

'It was a long time ago but that kind of experience stays in the mind and CK hasn't changed at all. Mann is no match for him at the moment. Mann's father's estate is a curse. It is attracting trouble to him like an open wound in a shark-infested ocean.'

'I know, and the trouble is that conflict of interests is going to be a permanent problem unless Mann can resolve it,' said Mia.

'Given time, he will make the right decisions,' said Ng. 'He needs the pressure taken off him to do that. They are forcing him out of the job he was born to do and back into a world he was born into. It will break him. He will snap if he is forced to bend against his will.'

'So, we carry on without him and hope that we can clear his name,' said Mia, sounding as upbeat as she could but feeling anything but.

Shrimp and Ng agreed. It was the only thing they could do. They walked back to their office. Ng reached over to turn on his PC and hung his jacket over the back of his chair. He turned to look at Shrimp whose face was frozen in a puzzled expression. He was staring across at Mann's desk: papers, files, messages in his in-tray, memos stacking up on his desk.

'What do you think he's doing right now?'

'He's probably drinking himself into a stupor.'

'What's he going to do, Ng?'

'I don't know, Shrimp.'

Shrimp looked lost. Mann had been his mentor and his friend. He couldn't imagine him leaving the force. Mann lived for it more than any of them.

'I've seen him go through some bleak times. I've seen him be self-destructive but I've never seen him as bad as this. He's always had his work but it's not enough at the moment. I think it's almost like he feels he doesn't belong here any more.'

'What can we do?'

'We have to leave him alone, wait until he comes out of it one way or another and then we have to clear his name.'

'I'm on it.' Shrimp picked up his jacket.

'Where are you going?'

'I need to get them to leave Mann alone. I'm going to go and see CK. I'm going to face him and tell him we'll have him in for questioning about the murder charges. We'll bring his daughter in for inciting racial hatred, for being an accessory to the murder of a police officer.' Shrimp stood and picked up his vintage denim Gaultier jacket.

'No. You'll blow your cover. Anyway, we mustn't be hasty. We must think it through. He is not a man to be easily outsmarted.'

Shrimp wasn't happy about it but he shrugged and left, throwing his jacket over his shoulders.

Ng waited until Shrimp was out of the office and then he dialled CK's number.

'I need to see you.'

CHAPTER 94

Ruby stood over Sheng's naked body. The ball gag was in his mouth. His arms were tied together and chained to the wall behind his head. His legs were open and chained to the wall either side of the mattress. The lamp shone down onto him. Ruby was very pleased with herself. She might be young but she understood that sex was every woman's ultimate killing tool. A woman's body was her weapon. She had fooled three policemen in one night. Sheng was still recovering from the Rophypnol.

She went over to him and knelt beside him and whispered in his ear:

'You fell for the oldest trick in the book. Never judge by appearances.' She ran her hand down his body until it settled on his cock. She stroked it. 'You were ruled by this weren't you?' He didn't move. 'Tut tut tut. You should have kept your eyes open. You looked away once too often. I have very quick hands. I have very nimble fingers. I can put something in your drink faster than you can look down my cleavage.' He was still dopey, coming round slowly. 'You're still not listening to me. I know just how to wake you up.' Ruby picked up the autopsy pliers and she rested Sheng's little finger between their open pincers and then she shut them – *snap* – tight.

Sheng's eyes opened wide. He stared straight at Ruby and then at the finger she held in her hand and he screamed into the gag.

'One finger, two fingers, three and four.' Snap snap snap . . . she cut his fingers off and placed a finger on each of the dolls' laps and when she had run out she began cutting off Sheng's toes.

CHAPTER 95

Mann didn't answer the door straight away. He sat in his armchair in the lounge; Daniel Lu had let Mann keep the lounge furniture. The bedroom was empty; every item removed and now being scrutinized in the lab. The telly blaring. He thought it was Ng. He shouted, 'Fuck off,' and turned the volume on the telly up. The knock came again. Then Mann realized the knock was different; it wasn't Ng's. He paused the film and slipped out of the chair. He walked to the side of the door and called out.

'Who is it?'

A woman's voice answered. 'Victoria Chan. I need to speak with you. It's urgent.'

Mann looked through the spy hole. Victoria Chan looked back.

'What do you want?'

'To talk, as I said.'

She raised her hand, knuckles at the ready to knock again. She wasn't going to go away. He unlocked the door and walked back into the room, his back to her. She walked straight in and seemed oblivious to the mess. She was wearing a black pencil skirt, a checked jacket, red stilettos, matching red handbag, red lipstick. Her hair was tied up.

She strode over to the armchair and sat down. 'There were things I didn't want to discuss in public, things that are just between us.'

Mann looked at the TV. He threw the mess off the other chair and sat down. He cleared the glass-topped table and placed the bottle of vodka down on it. He studied her with a cold eye.

'You have nothing to say that will interest me.'

'I had nothing to do with the death of your officer. I cannot help the fact that I used the information given to me and told of her infiltration into our ranks.'

'Shut up. I don't want to listen to you. I know where the blame for it lies. I have been suspended, and when I look at you, I see you had a big hand in it. Congratulations. But, before you start gloating, it won't be for long. And just because I am suspended from the force doesn't mean I have switched sides.'

She sat with her legs to one side, her hands on her lap. She looked around the room. 'I can't see you getting reinstated in a hurry, can you? I see that you have been going through your father's papers.'

Mann studied her. She had balls. She was a woman who would never give up. She looked at the pile next to Mann's chair. He'd been going over Tammy's autopsy report. He picked it up and moved it out of her line of sight. 'Believe it or not, there's a system to this chaos. Now, can we get to the point? I'm a busy man.'

Victoria settled back into the chair. 'Take the afternoon off. Let me get some food in. You look like you could do with some time out. Take a shower, relax. I may not be a friend but I am a business associate whether you like it or not. We have things to talk about. I expect by now you have seen that what I said is true. Many of your late father's enterprises are linked with the Leung Corporation dealings.'

Mann rubbed his face. He pushed his hair away from his eyes. He suddenly felt completely drained. She was right, at least in that one small thing, he needed a break. 'Okay.' He stood up. 'There's a list of numbers in the kitchen. They all deliver. You choose.' Mann got up and began to pick up the piles of papers.

'I'm surprised you live alone here. No adoring girlfriend?' she called to him from the kitchen. 'Although it does look like a woman lived here once. There are things in here that no man would buy.'

'My private life is none of your business.'

'Of course it isn't, but you're a good-looking man. You are not short of women wanting to marry you, I'm sure. But you choose to stay single. Why is that?' She took off her jacket and draped it over the chair. Beneath it she had on an expensive white lace blouse sheer enough to see a broderie anglaise slip beneath.

'Why do you bother asking? You already know all about me.' Mann marched back and forth to his bedroom, armed with the piles of papers.

Victoria followed him. 'I knew about Helen, yes. I don't know all the details but I can guess. I know Chan was capable of terrible cruelty. You weren't the only one to suffer at his hands.' Mann turned to see her standing in the doorway, a genuine look of sadness and regret in her eyes. 'My marriage was a living hell. Every day of it was torture, physical and mental. I was glad for the fact that he liked to be away from home more than he liked spending time with me.'

'You knew about his business?'

'I knew about a lot of it. I followed him when he wasn't looking. I saw the people he did his business with. I never knew about the existence of his private club where he kept the girls hostage and used them in those films.'

'Snuff movies. That's what they were. That's how Helen died – in the process of pleasing sick perverts like Chan.'

'I am sorry for you. Sorry for all of us.'

'But you chose to stay with him. Why did you never leave him?'

She shook her head sadly. Her eyes drifted away as she thought. 'It is not the Chinese way, is it?' she smiled ruefully. 'I was educated in England. I was brought up to feel like I was just like every other young woman – that the world lay ahead for me; anything I wanted to achieve was possible.

417

But then I returned home. Suddenly I had to conform, put aside all my hopes and dreams. I wanted to be a lawyer. Instead of that I was married off to one. He was hand-picked by my father: ruthless, ambitious, an asset to the firm. I was his prize for coming into the Wo Shing Shing fold. I was his guarantee that he would someday be chosen to take over as the Dragon Head. I was his insurance. For years I did as I was told by my father and by my husband. I had no one to seek help from. I made up my own mind on how I would handle it. I shut my feelings away. I stayed out of his way. I planned for the day that I would be released. And then you came along and you did it for me. We have a lot in common, you and I.'

'No, we don't and I didn't do it for you.'

'No, but that was a happy coincidence for me that you were the other person who hated him as much as I did. You did me a favour. You knew you had at the time. Now let me do something for you. Let me help you become the man you are meant to be.'

Mann walked angrily away. 'I will die before I become a Triad.'

'You don't have to join the ranks. Just look on it as a business deal.'

'It's dirty money.'

'All money is dirty, Mann.'

He picked up the last of the piles of documents and took them into his bedroom. 'There's no way

I trust you not to pry into my business so I'll save you the trouble of trying whilst I go for a shower in peace.' He locked the bedroom door and came back into the lounge with a towel and shut the bathroom door behind him.

Mann was drying himself off when he heard music coming from the lounge. The telly had been switched off. He heard Victoria moving around and then he heard her come to stand outside the bathroom door.

'You know, Mann, I have never felt so much in common with anyone else as I do with you. I have never spoken to anyone before about my life with Chan. In some strange way I feel I can trust you more than anyone else.'

Mann stopped his towelling and listened. In some awful way he understood but it didn't make him happy. It scared him that she was right. In some ways they understood one another.

The door opened. She stood in the doorway with a drink in her hand. Her hair was down over her shoulders. Her blouse was open to the third button. 'Thought you might be thirsty?' She had a vodka in each hand.

CHAPTER 96

Ruby sat down against the white tiled wall a few feet away from Sheng and looked across at him. His chest was heaving up and down. All around him the dolls, their dresses and bonnets, their nylon hair, their painted rosy cheeks, were speckled with his blood. Ruby opened and closed her naked legs like windscreen wipers sliding the blood back and forth and along the floor, she watched delighted at the pattern they made. In her hands she held Sheng's small intestine. It slid through her hands as she pulled it and coiled it between her legs.

CHAPTER 97

'I want to show you my visions of the future. The future for both of us. But first let's eat.' She had the food out on the elephant table. Mann was stood in his jeans and t-shirt, towelling his hair dry as he watched her serve him. She knew he was watching. She was enjoying it. She kicked off her shoes.

After they'd eaten Mann took the debris into the kitchen. Victoria opened up her laptop and fired it up. The screen came alive with the image of the Leung Corporation. It was a tiny screen. Mann took it from her and sat on the floor to watch it. Victoria moved from the chair to kneel beside him. They watched the screen whilst a virtual tour of the new Mansions started.

'As you can see, we will keep the basic structure. We would demolish a block at a time – five blocks and the shopping mall beneath. We estimate it will take us six months to complete, working round the clock.'

Mann looked at it. 'Very impressive. What's supposed to happen to the residents whilst all the refurb is going on?'

'I can find alternative accommodation and we can ensure that only one block at a time is demolished. We will minimize disruption. That is, of course, one of the decisions I would expect us to make together.'

'What about CK? What's his involvement in all this?'

'He is, of course, being very supportive, but he has left it to me to make this project work.'

'You never wonder at CK's motives, Victoria? You never ask yourself if he isn't just giving you all the rope you need to hang yourself with?'

She flashed Mann a look and he could tell that the thought had definitely crossed her mind and it irritated her. 'I am the natural successor to my father's empire. Yes, he is making me prove myself, as you would expect but, ultimately, I am sure that he wants me to succeed in my ambitions. Why else would he bother?'

'Why else? Because he is CK Leung and he has got where he is by shafting everyone, including you. It wasn't so long ago you were forgotten, sold by him to the bright new star on the Triad ladder.'

'I would have done the same thing if I was him.'

Mann looked at her and realized she was telling the truth.

Victoria turned to face Mann and leaned towards him. Her lips were an inch from his. 'You like your women tough, don't you, Mann? You don't begrudge me getting my hands dirty once in a while?'

'I like my women dirty, Victoria, but only in the bedroom.'

'You have no idea how good I could be for you.' She opened her blouse further and took the tips of his fingers and ran them over her erect nipples.

'Oh, yes I do. I also know how bad you are.'

'We are the same type.'

'No.'

'Yes. You deny it but we are. I will never want to have your babies, Mann. I will never grow old gracefully. I will be a fighter till the day I die.' She leaned over him and her lips brushed his. Her cheek touched his as she whispered in his ear: 'I will keep you on your toes, never be boring. I will seduce you in ways that you didn't know possible.' She flicked her warm tongue deep into his ear . . . 'I will fulfil you completely.' . . . She moved her mouth to his. She kissed him tenderly at first and then she bit hard into his lower lip and pushed him backwards and straddled him. She undid her buttons and slipped her blouse off her shoulders.

Mann looked over her shoulder at the laptop as he ran his hands up her thighs to the tops of her silk hold-ups. The laptop was still showing its tour and it had now stopped outside the Delhi Grill. 'Have you made a deal with PJ?' He ran his hands up her thighs to rest on her hips. He traced the edge of her silk panties with his thumbs as he spoke.

'Yes,' she replied, distracted. She closed her eyes at the sensation of Mann's touch as he brushed her sex lightly with his thumbs. 'I told you, I will keep a flavour of what it is now. He will be opening up a bigger better restaurant.' She groaned. 'Fuck me, Mann.' She reached beneath her to undo his fly.

'Who else?' He held her hand, gently but firmly and went back to touching her. He would not be rushed. 'What about people like Michelle and the Filipino café? What have you got in mind for her?' His thumbs slipped beneath the lace.

'I have been in talks with her partner, Rizal . . . We have worked out a compromise . . . They will get a loan to start a restaurant in the new Mansions . . . Now, Mann . . . Please do it.'

'Really? And is Lilly involved in these negotiations?'

Victoria opened her eyes and looked at him curiously. 'She could be . . .' The minute she said it she froze. 'I mean . . .'

'You set me up.' Mann threw her off. 'You could never mean anything to me. Yes, we might both be hollow, damaged; we might be thrill seekers but that doesn't mean I want to share my life with someone like me. Now get out.'

CHAPTER 98

'Rizal?'

Michelle had been expecting the old woman down the hall, who was coming to pick up the twins whilst Nina got on with the cooking. She made the mistake of opening the door before she stopped to think. Rizal pushed her straight back into the flat.

'Get out,' she screamed at him.

'You changed the locks, you bitch. Did you think that was the last you'd see of me? Did you think you could just shut me out? I live here.'

'Not any more. Go and live with one of your other women.'

'You don't tell me what to do.' He jabbed her in the chest with his finger.

'You're drunk. I'm busy. I have to cook. I am expecting the kids back at any time now. Ring me. I'll meet you. We'll talk later.'

Rizal stood swaying. 'There's nothing to talk about. I am the man in this house. If anyone has to leave it's you. Where's Lilly?'

'You're not coming near her again. I'll kill you if you do, and believe me I can do it.'

Rizal picked up the ornaments from the dresser and hurled them at Michelle.

'Get out,' she screamed. She went to push Rizal out of the apartment. She felt the sting of his hand on her cheek and she lost her balance. Her head cracked against the side of the sofa. She wriggled backwards. She knew Rizal well enough to know that would not be the last blow and she tried to crawl to the bedroom as fast as she could. As drunk as he was he didn't have far to make it round the sofa. He stamped on her to stop her and knelt on her as he held her by the throat. She scratched at his face trying to find his eyes. He moved his head out of reach. She felt the world around her going dark.

She didn't know how long she was passed out for. She came to to a sensation of being shaken and the sound of screaming. Lilly was hysterical. She was knelt over her, shaking her, crying.

'I'm all right, Lilly, my love. I'm all right. Good girl. Where's Rizal?'

Lilly didn't answer. She started to sob. She held on to Michelle and sank onto the floor. 'I thought he'd killed you. I thought you were dead. You weren't breathing.'

'Lilly!' Rizal stood in the middle of the room. 'Come with me.'

Lilly stood and looked at him.

'No, Lilly, don't.' Michelle's voice came out broken, painful.

Lilly walked into the bedroom and came out seconds later carrying the urumi. She let its coils unfurl. Her hand was shaking violently.

Rizal watched it, terrified. 'Come with me, Lilly,' he repeated, still staring at the three strips of razor-sharp metal that Lilly had now lifted in her hand. Rizal looked incredulously at her. 'We can both get away now.'

'Get out,' Lilly screamed. She flipped the whip above her head and crashed it down on the top of the sofa, inches from where Rizal stood.

He jumped. 'Jesus. You're as mad as your mother.'

'Get out, Rizal. Leave my mother alone. Leave all of us alone. We don't want you here. We don't need you.'

'You will regret that decision, Lilly. You forget, little girl – I know a lot of your secrets. I know where you go at night. I know what you do.'

'Shut up . . .' Lilly gathered the whip back and lifted it again, ready to strike.

Rizal didn't need to be told again. He started backing out of the door. Michelle looked at Lilly, at the whip in her hand. Now she was shaking so violently that Michelle was frightened for her.

'Come here, my little girl.' Lilly dropped the urumi and Michelle hugged her as they wept in one another's arms. 'We are starting again, Lilly. Right here, right now. This is a new start for us. It won't be easy but we will do it. We don't need

427

anyone else. We're in this together. You ready for that?'

Lilly couldn't answer she was crying too hard. She was looking at the door at Mahmud who stood there waiting for her.

CHAPTER 99

Ng took the lift to the top floor of the Leung Corporation building and padded out onto the plush carpet, into the dark leather of the penthouse office suite. The PA greeted him with a low bow. Ng walked past him and into CK's office.

The room was icy. CK sat behind his desk. He looked up as Ng approached, placed his pen carefully down on the writing block and sat back in his chair. In the corner of the room a young Chinese girl sat motionless in a straight-backed chair. At first Ng thought she was not real. She sat like a wax works manikin. Her face was white except for rouged cheeks. But then he saw her eyes follow him across the floor.

'I am glad to see we remain old friends,' CK greeted him.

'I am no friend of yours. I have come to ask you what it is you want from Johnny Mann.'

CK lowered his chin, pressed his fingertips together. 'You have shown your cards too early, Sergeant. Friends are hard to come by in this world and they make you vulnerable. We were friends once.'

'I was doing my job. I made mistakes. I was young. I learnt that I was not strong enough to resist the lure of Triad money. I never took the promotion I earned through the undercover work. I always regretted it.'

'Yes, I was disappointed to see that you did not rise up the ranks as others have done. But, as you know the account is never closed, sometimes it is dormant, other times it is ticking along but it can be fully operational again immediately. Is that what you desire?'

Ng sat in the same chair that Mann had done days before but he did not feel as comfortable, nor cradled. He felt suffocated by it. 'I have come to ask for a favour.'

'What favour is that?'

'Let Johnny Mann be. Leave him alone. Give him time to decide his own fate.'

'Ah . . . I am afraid I cannot do that, not even for an old friend. Johnny Mann has things that I need. I feel my time running out. His father was clever; he invested in things that, at the time, seemed worthless. Now, they are worth millions and I feel the years creeping up on me. I want everything now.'

'Your daughter, Victoria. Is she the reason for all this?'

CK thought for a moment. 'My daughter is another piece in the jigsaw of my life. She has her place in it, as do others. She will never be all of it. I recognize her failings. They are the same ones

I had in my youth. She is greedy, she is hasty. She will learn a valuable lesson soon. She is also, unlike many other women of her type, ruled by the heart-beat between her legs. My daughter would make a good whore.'

CK leant back in his chair and touched his fingertips together in the air; they turned white at their tip. 'My daughter is impatient. She has been planning this for a long time. She sees that the time is right to strike. With her new army of young Outcasts she intends to teach the world a lesson. She is still learning. She is ambitious.'

'She is a murderer.'

CK looked momentarily astonished and then his eyes narrowed and a rare sound came out of his mouth, a peal of high-pitched laughter. 'Yes . . . yes . . . perhaps.' He placed his palms on the desk and leaned towards Ng. 'My daughter is capable of anything.' CK's eyes shone clear green and glassy. He turned back to Ng. 'I will grant you your request. But my deal is a favour in return for a favour.'

CHAPTER 100

Mann held his head in hands. He could still smell her scent on his fingers; feel her presence in the room. He was angry with himself. Despite knowing exactly what she was like he couldn't help but find her attractive.

He knew he had a self-destructive side but he hadn't known it was this bad. He knew he was lonely but he hadn't called it that before. At least he knew now that he didn't touch Lilly, that it had all been a set-up. He knew that he wasn't going mad. He knew he had reached rock bottom and he had had enough of swimming in the shit. He was ready to fight back. He stacked the dishes in the sink, picked up the crap lying around and put the vodka bottle away. He called Daniel Lu.

'Did you find anything that matched any DNA from the sheets to the head?'

'I shouldn't be talking to you. You're suspended.'

'Did you?'

'No. And I can also tell you there was no other form of DNA on your sheets.'

'Yes, thanks, Daniel. I worked that one out myself. I was set up.'

'But what I did find was bone fragments in your jacket pocket.'

'Bone? What kind of bone?'

'Human. I am analysing it to see if belongs to anyone we know. But it's only a tiny bit of dust. Any idea where you picked it up?'

'None.'

'I'll be back to you when I know more.'

'Thanks, Daniel.' Mann hung up and rang Shrimp straight after.

'Hello, Boss.'

'How's it going, Shrimp?'

'It's all right, Boss. You sound more like yourself.'

'I have nothing left to lose now, Shrimp. I'm going to have to start playing CK and Victoria at their own game. Did you release Mahmud?'

'Yes. He's back at the Mansions now. Sheng is still missing. Mia Chou has taken over the investigation for now. It's all been pretty shit for her, Boss. Things have come out about her and Sheng. Sheng's family are kicking off. Sheng's wife has accused her of running off with him. No one knows where he is.'

'What about Ng? I can't get hold of him.'

'I don't know. He's not answering his phone either. We need you back here, Boss.'

'Tell Mia, I'm un-suspending myself. I'll go straight round to Ng's. Keep me informed and you stay safe, Shrimp.' Mann was worried. He didn't much give a shit about Sheng but it wasn't like Ng to not answer his phone. He grabbed his jacket and went round to Ng's flat. He had been there many times before. They had played cards late into the night on many occasions and set the world to rights sat around Ng's kitchen table. He knocked and then let himself in with the key Ng gave him for emergencies. He stood in the doorway and called out. No answer. There was a scratching noise from the kitchen. The monkey greeted him by jumping out at him and hanging around his neck.

Mann called out again. He stepped inside. The place was old style, comfy sofas, carpet. It was a mess. The monkey had obviously been alone for a while; it was bored, hungry. It had been living on dried noodles and there was crap everywhere. Mann opened Ng's freezer, found some ice cream, opened the tub and gave it to the monkey.

He held his gun in his hand as he made his way through the flat. The place had a chilling quiet to it. Mann wasn't used to seeing it empty. He went into the bedroom, the bed was made, the old chintzy curtains drawn. He could hear the monkey moving the tub of ice cream around on top of the work surface as it devoured the contents. He went back into the lounge and switched on Ng's laptop which had been left on the dining room table. It took Mann three attempts to get the password right. Mann had told him so many times to choose something more original than his mobile number. He checked Ng's e-mails. The usual Viagra e-mails.

Enlarge your penis by three inches. Amongst the e-mails were ones from people Mann had never heard of. He opened them. They were from people Ng had worked with a long time ago when he was undercover. Mann skimmed through them. It looked like Ng still kept in touch with some of them. He wondered what hold CK could still have over him.

Mann shut the laptop. Now he was worried.

CHAPTER 101

My love is like a red, red rose, Ruby hummed quietly to herself.

Sheng was staring at her. She stopped humming and let go of his intestines, twenty feet of blue-grey tube spilled from her lap; she crawled over to him. She was naked, covered in his blood. She reached behind his head and undid the gag mask. His mouth was full of blood where he had broken his teeth biting into the rubber ball.

'Have you got something you want to say to me?' she said.

Sheng stared at her. Blood spat from his mouth as he tried to talk.

'I can't hear you,' said Ruby. 'Speak up.'

'Go to hell.'

Ruby picked up the saw and switched it on.

CHAPTER 102

Shrimp was back at the hotel, getting ready for the evening's undercover work, when his phone beeped – he had a message. It was from Nina.

Please Shrimp . . . I have to see you.

He knew he shouldn't go. He paced about the room. He tried the rest of his surveillance team; no one else was in situ yet. It was four o'clock. He had an hour. If he slipped in the side entrance to the Mansions, he could get away with it.

He didn't manage to escape the eye of the watchful Africans. David saw him arrive. He didn't stop him. David could see as Shrimp flew past him that Shrimp had other things on his mind.

When Shrimp reached her she was in her usual place on the landing. She was agitated, more than he'd ever seen her before.

'I am sorry about Hafiz.'

'It was so horrible, Shrimp. I can't forget it. Chief Inspector Sheng wants to meet with me and talk about it. I don't want to. He's a horrible man. Do I have to see him, Shrimp?'

'No. I'll talk to him. When I see him, I'll sort it out, don't worry.'

'Thank you.' She came towards him and wrapped her arms around him and held on to him tightly.

'Nina. I am sorry, I am working. I can only stay a few minutes.'

She drew back and looked at him panic stricken. 'Will you come back later?'

He shook his head. 'I am sorry, Nina, but I won't be able to see you for a bit after today.' She pulled away and looked up at him. His heart was breaking. 'I'll be back, I promise. I'll never stop thinking about you, not for one second. It's just for a few days.'

'Please don't leave me now. I need you so much. You have to help me, Shrimp. I feel so afraid.' Her eyes were fearful, starting to fill with tears. 'We don't have time to be apart. Shrimp, please . . .' She wiped her eyes. 'The wedding has been brought forward because of the problems with the Mansions, I'm going to be married next week. The man has money and my father thinks he can help us.' She clung tightly to Shrimp. 'You must help me, Shrimp. I need you to take me away.' The panic was etched in her face. 'Please. I love you.'

Shrimp pulled back and looked at her. He had never known love before and his heart was aching for her. He wanted to be with her every moment of the day. He couldn't bear the thought of another man touching her, of her belonging to someone else. He knew this was real because all he wanted to do was to hold on to her and not let go.

Shrimp breathed in the smell from her hair. It was a smell of jasmine or rose and patchouli.

He didn't want to let go. 'Will you run away with me, Shrimp?'

He looked down at her and felt himself completely lost in her beauty and whispered, 'Yes, I will but I can't leave yet, Nina.'

'No . . .' She started crying.

'Nina, please, don't cry. I don't have a choice. I'm sorry. So sorry. I would do anything for you but I can't go anywhere right now. As soon as I can I will be with you all the time, I promise. I can talk to your father. I can ask him to call the marriage off. I can tell him how we feel . . .'

Nina turned away from Shrimp and shook her head. Her shoulders slumped and she began to cry. He laid a hand on her arm.

'I am so sorry, Nina. I am sorry to let you down. It'll be the last time I ever do. I promise.'

'Have you got someone else?' she asked, her voice shaking.

'Of course not.' He smiled at her concern. He hugged her and kissed her head. 'I promise you, no one else.'

'Please just sit with me a little longer.' They moved to sit on the stairwell. 'I brought you some sweets.' She handed him two, wrapped in a napkin. 'Coconut sweets for lovers.'

He smiled, her face was so sad, trying to be brave, he couldn't say no. She watched him eat them.

'It's all over for me then, Shrimp.' She turned and smiled and in her eyes was more than sadness, it was desperation and something else that Shrimp hadn't seen before – desire. She kissed him, her mouth hard on his. Shrimp drew back. 'I don't want to give myself to an old man and never know what it is to feel the pleasure of someone's body who means something to me. I want us to lie together, Shrimp. Then we will never be apart again.' She leaned forward and kissed him lingeringly on the lips and then she held him tightly.

'Not like this, Nina.'

'I know. I shouldn't say it but I'm begging you, Shrimp. Just hold me. Come to my room, please.'

'Now?'

'Yes. My grandmother is asleep.' She took him by the hand.

'If I have to get married I'd rather get married knowing what it is to feel love.'

Shrimp followed her, feeling desire and despair at the same time.

CHAPTER 103

The Mansions were a flurry of activity. Hundreds of CK's employees slipped in unnoticed amongst the thousands of Mansion dwellers. They flooded the place with pieces of brightly coloured paper that seemed to appear from nowhere. They dropped leaflets in mail boxes, stacked them in the lifts, pasted them on all the walls, the stairs, the doors, landings – everywhere. They carried a simple message:

The Mansions are being demolished. You will all lose your homes. No one will be rehoused. No restaurants will be given new premises. It has all been a lie.

The leaflets littered the floors of the Mansions. Panic spread. By five o'clock everyone knew that Victoria Chan was their enemy.

Rizal had tried to warn her. He had not made it in time. His body was at the bottom of the maintenance shaft where it had been dropped. He had crossed Ruby too many times. He had not been worth the effort of kidnapping; anyway, Ruby did not have the room. She had another in mind for her bed. He was very close to it now.

It was six o'clock in the evening when Victoria

had her driver drop her around the corner from the Mansions. She had come to see PJ and the others. She wanted them to sign her deal. If they all signed then she could show Mann she had good intentions. She slipped in unnoticed, keeping her head down. She had dressed down for the occasion. But there was no hiding the fact that her jeans were designer, her sandals Gucci. There was no masking the smell of her expensive perfume. She felt watched. The Africans saw her coming. David and his friends sat on the steps whilst the world passed them by. Mahmud saw her pass. An Outcast pulled a whistle from his pocket and gave three small sharp bursts, gliding it beneath his hand as he did so. The Mansions echoed with the sound of answers.

She kept her sunglasses on as she walked towards the lift. She felt as though her heels were stuck in tar. She moved reluctantly forwards as she watched the people staring at her. She stopped at the lift on the left. She had decided to start in the Delhi Grill and pay her respects after the death of Hafiz. They would need reassurance now at this tricky time. She stood in the queue. The people turned to stare at her and the queue disappeared until there was just her in it. When the lift came she stepped in alone. Victoria's heart was hammering. It was a bad enough experience coming to the Mansions without feeling like everyone knew who she was. She pressed the button for the third floor and waited. She looked around the walls. They were covered in the leaflets. She gasped as she tore one down and read it.

She looked frantically all around. Everything was covered in the leaflets, the floor was littered with them. She knew she had been set up. Someone wanted to see her killed. She was never going to get out alive.

She pulled out her phone and phoned Mann's number. He didn't pick up. She was on her own.

CHAPTER 104

Mann was in Miriam's Cantina bar when he saw Victoria's number light up as his phone rattled on the bar top. He didn't answer it. The barman looked over at him.

'Is Miriam around?'

The barman shook his head. 'Do you want me to call her? She's just upstairs. She'll want to see you. She asked me to call her if you came in.'

Mann shook his head. 'That's okay.'

Mann heard the clash of a symbol from his message alert. He had voicemail. He picked it up and looked at the screen. He hated the fact that he wanted her, that when he listened to her voice his heart leapt. He had done nothing but try and not think about her and achieved the opposite. Now, he heard the frightened girl in her voice, whatever else she had lied about in her life, she wasn't lying now. He knew she was in big trouble.

CHAPTER 105

Victoria dreaded the lift door opening. She pulled a small handgun from her bag and loaded it. The lift came to a stop. She stepped onto the landing and looked across at the Delhi Grill. She saw PJ staring back at her; his face sad, angry; he was shaking his head. She tried the door, it was locked. It was then she heard the whistles and the feet running up the stairwell and she knew they were coming for her.

Victoria made a run for it. She pulled open the door to the next flight of stairs and listened. The shrill whistles had reached a deafening shriek, feet were like thunder on the stairs. There was nowhere else to go but upwards. Victoria sprinted up the twelve flights of stairs; her throat rasping and sore with the exertion. Her lungs screaming. She came to the end of the landings. She stood panting staring wide-eyed at the approaching mob. Only the stairwell to the roof remained. She had nowhere else to go.

CHAPTER 106

Mann hadn't even got a few paces inside the Mansions when he knew something major had kicked off. David came towards him. 'You need a hand, brother? You're Shrimp's colleague, right?'

'Have you seen a smartly dressed Chinese woman, mid-thirties come in?'

David nodded. 'Victoria Chan? They were waiting for her.'

'Where is she now?'

'You come to help her?'

'Yes. She needs a fair chance. She's been set up.'

'She is about to be killed. They've got her on the roof. Come on, I'll take you.' David shouted to his friends to come with them.

By the time Mann reached the lifts, the Africans were thirty strong, armed with sticks and batons. Some took the lifts, some the stairs. Mann came out onto the top landing and listened. He heard the whistles coming from the roof.

When Mann stepped onto the roof with David and the other Africans, it was dusk. In the half light he saw Lilly carrying the urumi. The eagles would soon be going back to roost, for now they cruised the evening sky and watched. Mann looked around him. He stepped cautiously out armed with only a baton. He had his weapons inside his jacket and his gun in his holster but he wasn't planning on using them. He looked at them now: they were a wild bunch of bloodthirsty kids, but they were still kids.

Lilly was in front. She had the urumi in her hand. She looked full of panic. Victoria was talking to her.

'We can work this out. Don't believe them, Lilly. I would never lie to you. I always intended to take you with me.' She looked at them: around seventy scrawny kids, frenzied with excitement. They were inching Victoria back towards the parapet.

'Kill her. Kill her,' they chanted.

Lilly drew the urumi up into the air but she couldn't do it. She brought it down either side of Victoria but was careful not to touch her. Victoria screamed and scrabbled to get away but she was pushed up onto the ledge. Below her the busy Nathan Road traffic hooted up.

'Please . . . I promise, I will take care of you,' she begged.

'This is our home. You're going to knock it down. You don't care about any of us,' Lilly said.

'Kill her. Kill her,' the Outcasts chanted, more insistently now than ever.

'Stop now.'

The Outcasts turned at the sound of Mann's voice.

'Stop now and come away from the edge.'

The children turned and drew back when they saw the Africans. So many together scared them. They looked to Lilly for guidance.

'Go away, Mann, otherwise I will kill her,' Lilly shouted.

'You're not going to kill her, Lilly, and you know it. She's your best friend. Haven't you told the others yet that you and her are in all this together?'

Lilly gave a nervous laugh and brought the urumi crashing down a whisker away from Victoria.

'No, you haven't. You don't care whether the Mansions get knocked down because you know you can just move into a luxury penthouse and be Victoria's little pet.'

Lilly tried to speak. The mob had turned their full attention to her. They were waiting. She shook her head, she spluttered. She didn't know what to say.

'It's true,' said Victoria. 'Lilly and I are a team. Lilly knew about everything.'

Mann advanced. 'It stops here on this roof. It stops before anyone else gets killed.' He lowered the stick. 'Come on Lilly, give that to me.'

'Kill him . . . use it,' they chanted as Lilly stood there shaking, panic written all over her face. She stared at Mann. 'Show us if you want us to believe you're with us. Show us . . . kill him.'

Mahmud appeared behind Mann. 'Don't do it, Lilly. We've had enough killing.'

Voices went up from the mob: 'Lilly has betrayed all of us. She's as bad as all the rest.'

Lilly raised the urumi and brought it down on Mann. He felt the bands of razors slice: one into the muscles on his arms, one across his chest and another cut his eyebrow open with its tip. The urumi wound its way around the stick and chopped it in half. The Africans surged forwards to help. They cut a path through the Outcasts.

Victoria looked at Mann and saw how badly he was hurt, her eyes were wide with terror, her hair streaming out behind her. She was a she-wolf trapped on the ledge. She looked behind her nervously. One slip and she would be gone. She looked to her right. She watched as the attention shifted on Lilly. She saw a gap appearing to her left. She hesitated, they sensed she was about to run and they surged back towards her.

'Lilly . . .' Mann called, drawing their attention away again he clutched his bleeding arm to his side and wiped the blood from his eyes. Lilly raised the urumi again. It caught Mann across his face, his chest and his legs. It had cut him to the bone. In the pause when the three strands left his body and wheeled back into the air to join together and become one again he gritted his teeth and caught the ends of the weapon around his fist and held on to it tightly. Victoria seized her opportunity to run along the ledge and out of reach. The Outcasts stared frightened at the approaching Africans, they retreated towards the parapet, pushing Lilly ever closer to the edge. She held on to the handle of the urumi and Mann held on to the other end as he beat the kids back with what he had left of his baton.

Lilly screamed as she was driven over the edge by the mob. Mann wound the ends of the urumi round his hand and Lilly dangled at the other end. Its razor-sharp edges bit into his hand. He clenched his teeth against the pain. Blood dripped onto Lilly's upturned face. She looked at it, horrified. David and the Africans forced the Outcasts to the other side of the roof, away from Mann.

'Don't drop me, please, please.'

'Hold on, Lilly.' Mann tried to pull against her weight. 'Reach with your other hand.' Lilly looked at him, terror and panic in her eyes. 'Come on, Lilly, try . . . reach for me . . . do it.'

Lilly was terrified. She was dangling off the roof of a skyscraper and she was crying. He could see the whites of her knuckles around the hilt of the urumi. Her hand was slipping. Mann reached down with his other hand and tried to grab her, but she was too far away. He wrapped another coil around his wrist. He was so far over the side of the parapet now that he was struggling to stop from toppling over. He pulled with all his might and the urumi bit further into his hand; it was now cut so deep it had became stuck. He looked at her face and saw the splashes of blood, his blood, as the razor blades bit deep.

He heard Victoria screaming in his ear. She was

holding on to him. 'No, Mann, you're bleeding. You're losing your hand.'

He pulled harder as he saw Lilly's hand weakening. She looked at him, terror in her eyes. 'Hold on . . . hold on . . .' He shouted down to her and with one almighty pull he lifted Lilly two feet upwards. Mahmud reached down and grabbed her other arm and pulled her up onto the ledge. The urumi snaked in the air as its coils unravelled. The only thing still attached to it were three of Mann's fingers. The Outcasts scattered from the rooftop like scalded ants as they ran back down the stairs and through the Mansions.

Mann lay on the roof. His wounds were deep. He was losing blood fast. He felt the cold of the concrete under his back. He shivered. He closed his eyes. He heard Victoria talking to him and he heard the whoop-whoop of a machine overhead and then the world went dark.

CHAPTER 107

Shrimp lay in the absolute darkness trying to work out where he was and how he had got there. It was so dark he didn't know whether his eyes were open or not. He tried to move his legs and arms and couldn't. He was aware that he was naked. The last recollection he had was of being with Nina and now he was here in a place that smelt of death. There was an odour in the room of guts, faeces, carnage. He was lying on plastic. There was only darkness around. Next to him Sheng's body lay. Shrimp felt its presence but he couldn't see it. He could hear someone in the room with him.

'Nina?' he called. He could hear the sound of someone moving closer. 'Nina?' he said again.

The heat in the room was unbearable.

'Nina?' He was beginning to feel fear now. Then soft hands reached out to touch him in the darkness. 'Nina, is that you?' Someone ran their hand over his body lightly and then he felt the sting as a knife dragged across his thighs. Just once. Shrimp heard movement again, she was gone.

Ruby left Shrimp with a taster of what was to

come later. For now she was busy. She went into the other room. She had to get her nurse's outfit on, ready for the hospital. She took her spare urumi out from the cupboard, She had unfinished business with Mann. She knew which hospital they would take him to. There weren't many capable of reconstructing a hand. Ruby slipped on her mac over her uniform and left.

CHAPTER 108

Mann lay in the hospital bed. His dreams took him flying on the back of the eagle. His eyes were on the horizon. He soared on the air currents, turned and faced the wind and then swooped. The wind was in his face, feathers beneath his hands, the sun on his back. Then he was falling through the air, hearing Lilly scream, seeing the terror in her face and hearing Helen calling him. 'Wake up wake up sleepy head.'

Mann tossed and turned. He felt the stitches throb in his hand. Three hours of surgery had reconnected two of his fingers, but the third one, the forefinger, the eagle had recovered from the gardens below the Mansions and eaten it; it had developed a taste for fingers. The wounds from the urumi had cost him two hundred and forty stitches. Thirty of them were across his face; one more scar to add to his collection. He touched his face as he came out of the anaesthetic, prodding it with his numb bandaged hand. The fingers weren't going to be working for a while.

He looked around the room. He heard Mia's voice. He felt panic. He didn't know why.

He heard the footsteps in the corridor. He lay there listening, hearing his heart hammer as he fought to come out from the anaesthetic. Mann heard the swish of a uniform, starch, shoes, leather soles slapping on linoleum. Mann stirred in his drugged stupor. Helen was talking to him again now. 'Get up! Move. Run . . . run . . . she's coming for you, darling.' Click, clack down the corridor . . . He stumbled out of bed and doubled over with the pain. He pulled his clothes from the locker and rested against the bed as he got dressed.

CHAPTER 109

Run, Johnny, run. He staggered as he bounced off the walls of the hospital. He felt the adrenalin in his body as it met drug sedation head on and had nowhere to go. In the middle line they fought for ground. He ran down the corridor, his legs buckling. *Click, clack.*

He heard Mia's voice. 'Where's Mann? He's not in his room. Find him, quick.'

Mann didn't know why but he knew he had to get away. *Turn left at the end of the corridor, first right, now stay, stay, stay . . . breathe . . . wait, listen. Shush . . .* He slid down the wall and stayed there. *Click, clack . . . click, clack . . .*

He crawled along on his hands and knees, his eyes struggling to keep focused, he was seeing double on double. His bandaged hand was bloody now.

He turned a corner and looked down the empty corridor – he could see the empty reception. He stood, found his balance, lurched on his feet and very carefully inched forward.

Now Ruby came click-clacking down the corridor, the urumi coiled in her hand. She would finish him off. She would flail him to death whilst he was lying in his hospital bed. Ruby could be anyone; nurse, patient, saviour, murderer. Ruby was Ruby.

He felt a hand on his arm, guiding, supporting. A young police officer looked at him. 'You all right, Inspector?'

'Yes. Where's your car? I'm borrowing it.' He took the keys from the flustered young officer. He staggered outside and unlocked the car door. He slipped into the driver's seat and managed to manoeuvre his body into a position where he could drive. He switched on the engine, slammed it into reverse and then sped forward and away from the hospital.

He got halfway back to his flat when he got a call. It was CK.

'Hello, Inspector. I heard about your unfortunate accident this evening. I do hope you will feel recovered enough to accept an invitation from me.'

'I'm busy right now.'

'Nursing your wounds? I have a friend here who wishes to talk to you.'

Mann heard Ng's voice. 'Genghis . . . don't do it. They will kill me anyway.'

CK took back the phone. 'That's enough talk from Sergeant Ng. What he meant to say was that we have rekindled an old acquaintance, him and I, and now we have made a deal. You sign your father's estate over to me and I will give you his life in exchange. Friendship is a dreadful thing, just like the love one feels for a woman, a daughter even. It weakens a man. It makes him vulnerable. But, your friend's fate depends on you. How much is his life worth to you? I have the document ready. You just have to sign it. It means I take everything out of your hands. You no longer need to worry about your conscience. It will be as if you never knew. How does that sound?'

Mann heard an awful sound of Ng screaming and choking.

'Meet me on the top floor of the Piccadilly Club in Central.' CK hung up.

CHAPTER 110

Mann went home to pick up the one weapon he would be able to conceal beneath his bandages: Delilah. This time she was modified, made special. He re-strapped himself to keep her pressed flat against his chest. He drank a large vodka to take away the pain.

He got back in the car and phoned Victoria en route.

'Thanks for asking. I'm okay.'

'I went with you in the helicopter, don't you remember? I left you when you went in for your operation. I'm glad you're okay. Thank you, Mann. They would have killed me on that roof if you hadn't come. Someone set me up. I thought it was you at first. But then I realized you wouldn't do that kind of thing. You feel something for me, don't you, Mann?'

'No. I can't and I won't. I am going to see CK. He has my friend, Sergeant Ng. He wants to exchange his life for my father's estate. He wants me to sign it all over to him.'

'Don't do it, Mann. It's a trick.'

'I know but I am going to kill CK, Victoria. Don't come near me as I may have to kill you too.'

He drove back into town and parked outside the Piccadilly Club. The street was being watched. He saw CK's men everywhere. He would have a hard job getting out alive but then he wasn't thinking that far ahead. He hoped his body would last long enough to do the job he came to do and to rescue his friend. He realized now that nothing meant more than that to him. He had weathered so many storms with Ng's help. He would lay down his life for him now if he had to.

The bodyguards on the street nodded to him. They frisked him. They checked his boots and up his sleeves. Mann had known they would. He had hidden Delilah along the gap between two ribs. They were rough enough to open up some stitches. He knew they would. He had purposely left his bandage bloody across his chest.

The bodyguard looked at the blood on his hands and stepped back in disgust. 'Jesus Christ, let him through. He isn't carrying anything.'

Mann took the lift up to the top; eighty floors in a high-speed elevator.

'No Mann, please . . .' Victoria had raced straight there. She met him as he got out of the lift, she tried to make him turn around. 'You're sick. You're bleeding. Leave it now. Look at your face.' Victoria went to touch his swollen, stitched cheek. He pulled away. 'I'm sorry for what has happened. It's all gone wrong.'

'Get out of my way, Victoria. You play around with people's lives all for your own gain. You leave a trail of destruction everywhere you go. You're a fucking tornado destroying everything in your path. You're just like him.'

CK's bodyguard was waiting at the door for him. He held a gun to Mann's back. Mann put his hands in the air and walked slowly into the Red Salon. As he entered he saw Ng on his knees. His head was bowed. CK stood over him with a gun at his head.

'Ng? You all right?'

Ng lifted his head and Mann could see his mouth was pouring blood. He looked at Mann with the hopelessness of one in the world between life and death where there was only pain and fear and sad regret.

'You bastards.' Mann lunged at CK, the bodyguards held him back and punched him in the mouth. 'I should have killed you a long time ago, CK.' Mann wiped the blood from his split lip.

The bodyguards pinned Mann's arms back. CK smiled. In the gloom of the office Mann saw it was a strange sight like a grinning dog that should not be able to grin.

'Then why didn't you? You were not able to then and you are not able to now.'

CK looked Mann up and down. Mann's wounds were breaking open on his legs. Blood seeped in dark patches through his jeans. Victoria looked anxiously at Mann.

'Show him.' CK turned to his bodyguard. 'We saved it for you.' The bodyguard came forward, opened his palm and showed Mann Ng's tongue. 'You can have it sewn back on if you hurry. Now sign it.' CK pointed to a table where the contract was waiting for him with a pen.

Ng shook his head at Mann. The front of his shirt was saturated with blood. CK swiped Ng's head with the butt of his revolver. 'Sign it. You are wasting precious minutes.'

Mann went over to the writing desk. Its hand-made parchment paper contract, a gold Duofold Parker pen waiting for Mann to use. He picked up the document. He glanced over it. He picked up the pen, held it tightly as he pressed, there was the faintest sound of a snap. He signed and leant over the desk, resting as he wiped the blood from his mouth. He recovered, stood back up. His body stopped hurting. His head cleared. His pulse slowed. His bleeding stopped. Mann's body was turning to icy hatred. A bodyguard stood behind him, a gun at his back.

CK turned to Victoria. 'This is the time you have waited for. You see me as old now, you think it is your time. You think that I must have grown tired of the business world and I want to retire.' He paused. 'Of course that is what you think, my darling daughter. You think you are being so clever: you would play us all. Ensnare Mann with your beauty and your sex, get your greedy hands on his father's estate and then have me killed. I have no doubt that you would kill me yourself if you had to. But, it seems your ample feminine charms were not enough to turn him and I must do it myself. You will never be strong enough to be my successor. You have failed, my darling daughter.'

CK called and the door opened. Four more bodyguards entered the room. 'Mann, before I kill you I want you to know that I watched Helen die. I went to that club often. I enjoyed the company of many women there but I had my favourites. They were friends of yours. Some of them you knew intimately. Helen was one. She was my favourite. She took a long time to die. But you saw that didn't you? You watched the recording. You weren't thinking dispassionately when you listened to the voices in the background. You failed to recognize mine. I've always suspected you would have in time.' Mann didn't speak, he bowed his head. Now he knew why Helen hadn't wanted to let him go. He knew why every time he closed his eyes he saw her face, he heard her pain. 'Thanks for this,' CK waved the contract in the air, 'I waited a long time for this. Your father beat me to some of the best deals. He was a very clever man. He turned moral in the end, tried to save the world. See, you are the same type after all? Such a waste but I am too old to keep playing games; now it's just about the money.' He turned to his bodyguards. 'Take my daughter and the inspector and kill them.'

Victoria screamed. 'No, Father, please.' She tried

to run but the bodyguard held her back. He stared coldly at her.

'You were never my favourite. Take her . . .'

Two of the bodyguards came forward and dragged her away from her father. Another walked towards Mann. Mann's pulse slowed right down. He felt the adrenalin turn his blood to ice. In his mouth he moved the arrow that he had snapped from the Parker pen out of his cheek and into the centre of his tongue and he waited until he was within range, he eased himself to his left slightly and felt the gun in his back travel two inches to his right and then he shot it straight into the body-guard's eye. It pierced his retina and exploded his eyeball. At the same time Mann twisted his body away from the gun in his back. The shot missed Mann and hit the bodyguard who keeled clutching his eye. Mann back flicked his fist into the man's face and he broke his nose, cheek and cracked his eye socket. He dived forward towards Ng and caught him around the shoulders and rolled with him to protect him, laying his body across his, but it was too late. CK had already shot Ng through the head. His skull shattered. His body lifeless beneath Mann's. Mann gave a cry of pain, a roar of anger as he turned, rolled away from Ng and reached inside his shirt with his left hand. There, between the cloth and the bandages, pressed around his chest, was Delilah. And on her hilt she bore something precious. The bodyguards reached for their weapons at the same time as Mann dropped to one knee, rolled and fired Delilah over their heads. She turned direction in the air, almost hovered and then dropped blade first as CK looked up to see what it was. A flash of steel, a plume of black. It sunk deep into his left eye, so far that Delilah was pushing to come out the other side of his skull. CK was driven back by the force and smashed against the mahogany book shelf and slid down to the floor.

Victoria screamed. There was a pause as if the room stood still and then she laughed. Mann thought at first it was shock but it gathered momentum and the bodyguards joined in. She went over to her father and stared down at him and giggled at the kite eagle's long black tail feathers that were a perfect manoeuvring tool in the air. They were still vibrating as they protruded from his eye socket. She went over to CK, put her foot on his face, her Jimmy Choo heel dug into his chin and she pulled on the eagle feathers, wiggled them to dislodge them and then slid Delilah out, brain matter and eye attached.

'You know, Father, you disappointed me too.'

She came over to Mann, who was knelt beside Ng, feeling no triumph now, only a bitter loss. She put Delilah in his lap. It was as if Mann had stuck to the script when he hadn't realized there was a whole different play going on.

She leant over to kiss his lips softly. 'I intend leaving the country for a while. I will be going to the Philippines. But, don't think it's the end for us, Mann, think of it as the beginning.' She stood up, picked up her bag. 'And, by the way,' she tore up the contract and handed it back to Mann, 'you don't get out of it that easily. I prefer to be partners, lovers even, who knows, Mann? I never wanted my shares in the Mansions. You own it all, baby.' Then, she moved towards the door. 'We have a plane to catch. Don't hurt him. Drop him back at the Mansions,' she said to her hovering bodyguards who were still waiting for the satisfaction of kicking the shit out of Mann.

By the time the bodyguards had thrown Mann's body out of the car and it had rolled to a stop in front of David, he had only three of the hundred and thirty stitches remaining. And three of the four bodyguards would never make it on the plane. Victoria had already left.

CHAPTER 111

Shrimp floated in and out of the dark world of pain. He heard someone singing, a haunting wailing song like he had heard on the stairs in the Mansions. He heard the soft giggles of a child and felt something cold and plastic brush his face. He heard the cries of a baby and a mother soothing it. His pain came in searing stabs, in long excruciating waves that felt as if someone was twisting his gut inside out. Sometimes it was accompanied by crying, sometimes laughter. He felt his tongue swelling. He tried to keep his pulse slow and stem the loss of blood. He tried to talk but as if in a dream the words went unheard. *Help me. Help me.* The woman muttered to him, he couldn't make it out. She sat beside him in the dark. She held his hand and sometimes she stroked him tenderly. Shrimp felt her body on his. He felt the sting of a knife. The deep pain that was working its way into his heart.

CHAPTER 112

'**F**uck. Am I dead?' Mann awoke to find himself being sewn up by Kin Tak. In the background he could hear an angel singing. He tried to sit up but he couldn't; he was restrained.

'We couldn't stop you moving. Very hard to sew neatly when you keep moving. I am not used to that.' Kin Tak was sewing him up and Lilly was hovering over him.

Mann grabbed at her wrist as she hovered over his face with a wad of cotton wool. She shrieked in fright. 'Where am I?'

'In my bedroom.'

'Oh God . . .' Mann moaned as he pulled against the strap.

'No, it's all right. The Africans brought you up here.'

Mann stared at Kin Tak not understanding. 'What are you doing here?'

'Lilly asked me to sew you up.'

'Yeah . . . that reassures me.'

'I had no idea men bleed so much. No one usually bleeds when I stitch them up.'

'You didn't want to go back to hospital,' said Lilly.

The singing stopped. Michelle came to stand and watch. 'You were really beaten up. Blood everywhere,' she said.

'Yeah, I wonder why that was.' Mann touched the swellings on his face. The stitches were back.

'Very clean. The wound was very clean. Made by the same instrument that took that young girl's hands off. I recognized it.' Kin Tak beamed proudly as he carried on sewing up the gash across Mann's stomach.

'Yeah. Sorry about that. I got scared. I didn't know what to do,' said Lilly.

'Save it, Lilly. I could see it was just a lucky hit.'

'Thanks. You never touched me, you know.'

'Yeah. I know.'

'I put Rohypnol in your drink. Victoria Chan gave it to me.'

'And, you know one another?' Mann asked Kin Tak.

Kin Tak nodded, and looked away guiltily.

'He's been teaching me to read and write Mandarin,' said Lilly whilst dabbing at Mann's wounds.

'She's an excellent student.' Kin Tak covered his mouth and giggled into his hand. 'There you are – finished.' Kin Tak stood back to admire his handiwork.

There was a knock at the door. Michelle went to answer it.

'I need to speak to Mann. Is he here?' Daniel Lu stood in the doorway.

'I haven't seen him,' Michelle lied.

'He was seen being helped in here.'

'He doesn't want to talk to you.'

'I'll speak to him. Come in, Daniel,' Mann shouted from the bedroom. Daniel walked in and stood next to the bed. They were left alone to talk.

'Mia is mad with you. She says there's a warrant out for your arrest for the murder of CK Leung. I went there to clean up. I'm sorry about Ng. Now, I have to tell you something, I know you'd want to know but looking at you, I'm not sure how much help you can be Shrimp's missing.'

CHAPTER 113

*R*oses *are red. Rubies are too. My heart was broken. Now yours is too.*

Shrimp heard how far the echo of the woman's voice went to the wall and then stopped. He realized it was a voice he knew. 'Nina?'

'You betrayed me, Shrimp. I gave you my heart and you betrayed me.'

'Nina . . . please, where am I? What's happened? Put a light on; let me see you.'

'You were going to be different. I gave you the chance to be the one. I saw you at that bar. I saw you playing with your wedding ring. You didn't notice me. I was tucked behind you, out of sight. I had a long caramel-coloured wig. For a second I thought you had recognized me but you didn't. That evening I watched you taking girls to your room, one after the other. You make me sick. You're no better than all the rest. I thought you were the love of my life. But you lied, cheated on me. You are just like he was . . . how could you, Shrimp? I loved you.'

'I was working undercover. If you saw me pick up girls it was because I've been working on a

471

case, that's all. I never touched them, Nina, I wouldn't, I promise. Please, Nina, let me go. I love you.'

'You're just like him. He used to come to Hong Kong once a month. He came for five days. He came to eat in our restaurant every night. He made me feel special. He took me out and he bought me things, clothes, shoes. We had to sneak in and out of here. He bought me wigs to wear, so no one would know it was me. He took me to bed. He promised we'd elope. He promised to take me away. I didn't know I was pregnant until it was too late. Then he told me he was married. He never came back for me. He left me to face it alone.

'The girls started to make fun of me in school. I couldn't hide it any more. I didn't know what to do. I was so frightened. The girls shouted names at me. The girls just like Rajini, just like that officer, Tammy. Just like her. They thought they were better than me then. I couldn't hide it any more. I had to tell my parents. They were so ashamed. I was six and a half months pregnant when my grandmother held me down and my mother gave me an abortion with a skewer, on this bed. The same skewer we use on the tandoori. The same one I use to pierce a man's heart. I was not allowed to see the baby, a baby girl. They threw her in the rubbish. I found her in there. Someone had thrown some old flowers in on top of her. She was covered in rose petals. I dried her body on the roof where its spirit could be free. I called her Rose.

'I killed my mother in the kitchen. I held her head in the deep fryer. I have killed my grand-mother. She deserved to die for her part and she has no one to look after her now. She hasn't got me any more.

'"Nina do this. Nina do that. Nina fetch the lobsters to marinate for the tandoori grill, speciality of the house." I loved watching them eat those lobsters: crack open the claw and know that they were fed with human flesh, handpicked by me. All those men deserved to die.' She stopped. She gave a sob in the darkness. 'I think about him sometimes and wonder if he ever thinks about me.

'He called me Ruby. "Hey Ruby," he would joke. He talked like Michael Caine. "My Ruby Murray."'

CHAPTER 114

'How long since he's been seen?' asked Mann.

'He never made it to the bar yesterday evening. He didn't wear his wire and he hasn't made contact. He was seen by one of the Africans, David, coming in here at four yesterday. I just talked to him. He hasn't seen Shrimp since. He didn't see him leave.'

'That's an hour before Victoria came here. What's been done about it?'

'You know the hair ornament you had in your pocket? I sent off the hair for analysis.'

Mann had to think what Daniel meant. His mind flipped back to that day in the corridor with Ali and the plaited hair ornament. 'I was given that by Flo, Nina's grandmother.'

'Well, someone's keeping the old woman sedated. She's got Haloperidol in the hair. And that's not all. The pin that secures that hair ornament is part of what was left of Ishmael.'

474

CHAPTER 115

Shrimp saw the light from the door when Ruby went into the other room. He turned and saw Sheng staring back at him, slumped, disembowelled, his intestines splayed out around him.

Shrimp pulled frantically on his arms to try and free them. He twisted his head to look up. He was chained to the wall behind. He pulled on the chains but couldn't budge them. He looked down at his injuries. His body was being sliced open bit by bit. He heard the Indian music playing from the other room; haunting, a woman wailing. It was the same music he had heard on the stairs. He saw his clothes in the corner of the room. His gun was there, his microphone. He couldn't reach any of it.

Nina returned. He could see her properly now. She was naked. Her long glossy black hair fell all around her shoulders to her waist. Even now he loved her. Even though it made no sense. 'Please Nina, let me go . . .' She came towards him with her hands holding a small object.

'Kiss Rose, Shrimp.' She held the dried parchment

face of the mummified baby next to his mouth. 'This was going to be your baby. You were going to be special. You were going to want to live with us forever, me and Rose. But, maybe this was the only way for us.'

'No, Nina, we can still make it work. We can still get away from here. Please, Nina, let me go. I will help you. I love you. I will do anything it takes to help you. Don't kill me, Nina.'

'It's too late for both of us, Shrimp. Don't worry, I won't let you die alone. I will come with you.'

Beside the bed she laid the scalpel and the skewer.

Ruby went quiet for a few moments and Shrimp watched her moving around the room. She lit a candle in the corner. She placed her dolls around the bed.

CHAPTER 116

'Which flat does she live in?'

'She lives with her grandmother on the fourth floor, flat B. No one is invited in there. She says she's ashamed of the place. She always comes here when Kin Tak teaches us Mandarin,' Lilly said.

'He was teaching her too?'

Lilly nodded. Mahmud stood in the doorway. 'I'm sorry.' He had a key in his hand. 'She does anything Victoria Chan wants her to. And more, much more. I didn't realize she was killing men until now. Can I come with you?' Mahmud handed a key to Mann. 'Here is the key to the apartment. I can help. She will listen to me.' Mann eased on his clothes over his bandages.

'No Mahmud. You stay here. I promise we will do all we can to help her. Lilly, you and Michelle stay here too.'

Mann and Daniel left Michelle's apartment and walked down the flights of stairs to the fifth floor. David was waiting for them. Mann looked at him and nodded. 'You know who it is?' David nodded. 'I saw them in the shadows of the stairs, kissing when they thought no one saw. If she is the woman who murdered my brother I have to come with you.'

'No, David, you stay here and guard this entrance with Daniel. I need to go in alone. I don't want any mistakes in there. This is my one chance to get my friend out alive. If we make a noise, if we frighten her, it could be the end. I will call you if I need help. Just be here and be ready.'

'Here, Mann, have my gun?' Daniel took it out of his holster to give to Mann. Mann shook his head.

'I trust Delilah now more than ever. I can't afford to make mistakes.' Mann had taken the feathers out of her hilt; she was clean, sharp. She was in his hand as he placed the key in the apartment door. 'Which is Flo's room?' he asked Mahmud.

'First one on the right.'

Mann turned the key and pushed the door. The place was dark. Inside was the fuse box, he tripped the main switch. He took out his phone, he found the light setting. A tiny bright beam shone out from the back of the phone. He shone it straight ahead into a small kitchen at the end of the hall. The smell of ham cooking hit him. His light glanced over a patella as it shone glossy from the top of the pot, the place was still steaming, the walls wet. He walked inside. The door closed behind him; he let it go.

He opened Flo's door and flicked the light around the room. The room smelt of old, it smelt of neglect. He scanned it, it was full of human bones, bleached white, stacked in the corners, laid across the floor at the edges of the room. The bone dust covered everything. Flo was slumped in her chair. Mann inched closer to her. He shone his torch into her face. Her eyes stared back, bulging from her head. Her mouth gaped open. Around her neck was a ligature.

He heard the sound of wailing music coming from the next room. This was one of his nightmares: a corridor with no doors, no beginning and no end. Somewhere along it he could hear the sound of crying. He felt his way along in the total blackness. He could not see his feet. He did not know how high the ceiling was above him. The heat bounced off the walls. It ran down his face; it stuck his shirt to his back. He ran his finger along the wall and touched something wet and sticky. He smelt blood. He smelt panic. Mann stopped. His heart raced, the blood pumped in his ears as he strained to listen.

Nina was crying.

'Nina . . .' Shrimp could barely speak. 'I can help you, Nina. I will do anything for you. Please, don't do this to us.'

Mann moved along the corridor in the dark. He didn't want to alert anyone to his presence. He felt his way in the darkness. His shirt stuck to his wounds, stinging now from the sweat in them.

But he didn't notice. He had one purpose left for his body, one more thing he asked it to do. His fingers tingled with adrenalin as he gripped Delilah tightly in his hand and called out.

The candle flickered a ghostly sheen up the white tiles and over the faces of the dolls.

Nina sat on top of Shrimp and felt along his ribcage.

She picked up the scalpel and cut along the bottom of his rib.

'All right, Nina.' Shrimp struggled to talk through the pain. 'You kill me now but understand one thing, Nina . . .' Nina cut him again twice more. She lifted the section of skin and exposed his ribs '. . . I will love you forever.'

He couldn't talk any more. Nina picked up the skewer. The pain shook his body and he gave one deep cry; all the pain and all the love found a harmony in the last few seconds of his life. Nina slashed through the artery in her left wrist. There was a pause and then blood shot out and covered the wall behind and extinguished the candle and, in pitch darkness, Nina pressed the point of the skewer into Shrimp's heart.

'Shrimp?' Mann's heart pounded in his ears as he waited for an answer. There was none. He felt along in the pitch darkness. He came to the second door and he turned the handle, pushed, and stepped into the room. In the darkness he called out again.

From the far end of the room he thought he heard what sounded like Shrimp's voice. Mann inched forwards. At the far end of the room he felt a curtain beneath his fingers and behind it the solid feel of a door. He felt for a handle and turned it.

The door opened and the heat from the room stuck in Mann's lungs along with the smell of atomized blood as thick as a cloud. He heard the sound of dripping. His fingers tingled with adrenalin as he gripped Delilah tightly in his hand. He took another step and his foot touched something on the floor. He shone his light into the room. Hundreds of pairs of eyes stared back at him. In the middle of the room were bodies. Nina slumped forward, naked, her long hair hiding whoever was underneath. Mann knelt down beside them. Mann saw Sheng, what was left of him. He pushed Nina over. She rolled to one side on top of Sheng.

Mann's heart broke when he saw Shrimp. His chest was opened. His ribs showing. He was covered in blood. He wasn't moving and a skewer was deeply imbedded in his heart. Nina's weight had driven it in. Mann looked closely; there was the faintest sign of movement; the heart was still beating. Shrimp was hanging on.

'I'm here, Shrimp. Stay with me. Hold on. You're going to be all right.'

Mann turned and shouted out for Daniel Lu. He looked back at Shrimp. The heart was barely beating now, growing fainter every beat. He knew he shouldn't remove the skewer but it's all he wanted to do. It was killing Shrimp and he couldn't stop it.

'Shrimp, stay with me. For fuck sake listen to me and stay alive.'

He looked around for something to pack inside the chest cavity to try and stem the bleeding that was filling the cavity with blood. The nearest thing he could find was Shrimp's shirt. He grabbed it, pulled it to him and gently folded it around the knife. He cursed his useless hand. He needed more. He reached for Shrimp's jacket, to tear out the silk lining. He turned back. The heart had stopped beating. Mann tried to tear more of the lining free. Something hard in the pocket stopped him. In the inside pocket he found a syringe pouch. He tore the pouch open with his teeth and bit off the top of the packet. He pulled off the cap and then he plunged the epinephrine syringe straight into Shrimp's heart.

CHAPTER 117

Mann ran at the dummy and let fly his shuriken. Six gleaming stars spun through the air, and missed.

'Fuck. I'm going to have to practise. It's not so easy when you've only got four and a half fingers and you can't feel three of them.'

Mia, Daniel Lu and Shrimp were standing on the rooftop with him at sunrise. They scattered Ng's ashes to the morning breeze. Tom Sheng's body was buried in a family plot. Mia hadn't been allowed to attend the funeral; she was just the mistress.

'What are we going to do with the monkey?' asked Mia. 'It's not meant to live on ice cream and takeaways. Ng liked things to be what they were meant to be.'

The mention of Ng's name sat heavily in the air.

'You two are going to have to take some time off. Shrimp, we have to count ourselves lucky you're still here.' Mia smiled at Shrimp.

He nodded his head but he didn't smile or answer. Mann looked at him and he understood that this would change Shrimp forever. The pink flush of dawn was on his pale face. He would carry with him scars on his heart that would cut deeper than any knife could.

'We can't get to Victoria Chan now,' said Mia.

'She'll be back. She'll be wanting to take over as the Dragon Head of the Wo Shing Shing,' Mann answered. He went to stand by the edge. He looked out at the morning blossom-coloured sky.

'What about your father's affairs? What about the Mansions?' asked Daniel.

'I am giving it to the people who deserve it. I am turning it over to the people who live there. They can own a part of it. They can also be responsible for it. They will have their own community police inside it, made up of all the nationalities. They can meet regularly, sort out differences. The refurb can go ahead but just floor by floor. Michelle will have a restaurant. PJ can have a secure tenancy with the Delhi Grill. I am giving everything else away. It might take me a while but I intend to do it somehow. It will never bring me happiness. Then I am taking Shrimp away somewhere to heal his soul and mine.'

Mann could hear the black-eared eagle kite calling. It flew near the edge now. It watched them as it always did.

When they'd all left him, Mann stayed on the roof. He took out his phone.

'Alfie? Tell Jake I'm coming. Tell him his brother wants to see him. Tell him I miss him.'

He stood on the parapet. Mann looked back at the horizon. He looked down on the eagle, the blush of the first rays of sun touching its back. He looked out on the Hong Kong he loved. He picked up the last handful of Ng's ashes and let them seep through his fist like powder. They flew off in a swirl.

'Goodbye, my friend. See you on the other side. The way is not in the sky. The way is in your heart.'

CHAPTER 118

Across town in the Mansions, Lilly was serving customers and helping her mother out with the stall. The Mansions had a new calm about them. Without their figurehead or their *Red Poles* the Outcasts had collapsed. The kids wandered the streets in search of a new gang.

A young backpacker couple from England stopped by Michelle's stall to buy dinner. It was their first time in Asia. They were on a gap year. They were young and excited and it was lovely to see. Michelle gave them an extra helping. They took it to the Mansion steps on Nathan Road to eat it. It was their first taste of Filipino food. Crackling pork with fried rice. As he used his fingers to pick up the pieces of meat, the lad paused and smiled and showed his girlfriend.

'Look at this on my crackling. It must be a pig brand. How funny. Look what it says . . . *MUM.*'

Back at the stall Michelle looked at Lilly.

'We'll have to get pork from somewhere else now that Nina's gone.'

486